A SCROOGE MYSTERY

Before writing her first novel, Andreina Cordani was a senior editor and writer for women's magazines including Good Housekeeping and Cosmopolitan. Her assignments included interviewing gun-toting moms on the school run, ordering illegal DIY Botox online and learning to do the splits in eight weeks.

She lives on the Dorset coast with her family where she reads voraciously, occasionally makes TikTok videos and swims in the sea.

Also by Andreina Cordani
The Twelve Days of Murder
Murder at the Christmas Emporium

Ā SCRŌOGE MYSTERY

ANDREINA CORDANI

ZAFFRE

First published in the UK in 2025 by
ZAFFRE
An imprint of Bonnier Books UK
5th Floor, HYLO, 105 Bunhill Row,
London, EC1Y 8LZ

This is a work of fiction. Names, places, events and
incidents are either the products of the author's
imagination or used fictitiously. Any resemblance to
actual persons, living or dead, or actual
events is purely coincidental.

A CIP catalogue record for this book is
available from the British Library.

Hardback ISBN: 978-1-78512-632-1

Also available as an ebook and an audiobook

1 3 5 7 9 10 8 6 4 2

Typeset by IDSUK (Data Connection) Ltd
Printed and bound in Great Britain by Clays Ltd, Elcograf S.p.A.

MIX
Paper | Supporting
responsible forestry
FSC
www.fsc.org   FSC® C018072

The authorised representative in the EEA is
Bonnier Books UK (Ireland) Limited.
Registered office address: Floor 3, Block 3, Miesian Plaza,
Dublin 2, D02 Y754, Ireland
compliance@bonnierbooks.ie
www.bonnierbooks.co.uk

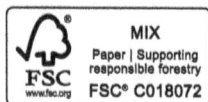

'He had no further intercourse with spirits . . .'
Charles Dickens, *A Christmas Carol*

. . . As far as he would admit, at least . . .

THE GHOST

THE PAIN IS SUDDEN AND SEARING. I FEEL A BLOW TO THE BACK of my head, then a slice at my throat. It is at once cold and on fire with agony. My hands clasp at my neck as if my fingers can keep the blood inside, but there is no time. I am already on my knees, and then I am pulled from my body like a child being jerked away from a beloved toy. I barely have time to think I am dead before a tide of fear swallows me, sucking me under, deep into the darkness, whirling me around, engulfing me in a sensation that is new and strange. A feeling of nothing.

No. It is too soon. I want to live.

I flail frantically with limbs I no longer have, claw with fingers which do not exist, as if I have tumbled into the freezing Thames but without the pull, the buoyancy of being in water. There's no chance of struggling to the surface. I am trapped in terror and blackness, fighting against nothing.

I feel it now, the temptation to relax into slumber, to admit I no longer have arms or legs or a voice or any power at all and simply allow myself to drift. But I cannot. I will not. I fight, like I always have.

1

I feel eternity passing, and no time at all.

And then I hear the voice. The only part of me which is not frenzied with fear wonders if it is an angel calling me to the afterlife, but this is not a heavenly sound. It is creaking, dry and crabby, and it says: 'This is a good proposition. We could make a lot of money.'

The voice acts as an anchor, pulling me towards it, back to the living. There is a whirl of colours and light and then the familiar scents of Christmas draw me in – spiced, mulled wine and a warm coal fire. Then, the complacent sound of male laughter. My surroundings are a blur but amid it all I can see one face. It is a miser's face, hard and craggy, brow lined from years of frowning, lips thin from a lifetime of being pressed tight together in disapproval, skin pale from hour after hour spent inside hunched over ledgers, counting coins. I know him. I have seen him before.

It is Ebenezer Scrooge.

1

MARLEY WAS STILL UNDOUBTEDLY AND UNDENIABLY DEAD. ONCE a week, his former business partner Ebenezer Scrooge visited his graveside to confirm that he remained so. And also, if he was honest with himself, to talk.

Time was he would have thought it foolish to sit at a deceased man's graveside and chit-chat as if Marley could hear – the man was dead as a doornail, after all. Even deader, since doornails had never even lived. But that was before last Christmas Eve, before the terrible visitations which had changed the way he saw the world for ever.

Scrooge shivered, pulling his weathered greatcoat more tightly around him as he picked his way through the frozen church-yard. It was an uncommonly cold day, even for the middle of December. The feeble half-light of the sun had done nothing to melt the frost which lingered on the tombstones, sprinkled like sugar on the fat cheeks of each carved cherub. However, Scrooge had never been susceptible to the cold. It was not the temperature which made his skin chill.

A churchyard is a place for ghosts, and Scrooge never wanted to see another spirit in his life. And so he kept his gaze fixed on the uneven ground before him and continued.

Marley had been buried with minimal pomp. Of course he had, because his business partner had been the one to bury him. Scrooge had chosen a burial plot in the cheapest, meanest corner of the churchyard. Not for him the grand statuary which was becoming the fashion. No weeping angel or veiled urn to signify the passing of such a solid man of business as Mr Marley. No, his gravestone was the smallest and plainest Scrooge could get away with while remaining respectable. Why waste money when it benefits no one living? Which meant that as he picked his way carefully across the rough, weed-tangled ground, nearly tripping over the tumbled tombstones, he had only himself to blame.

He rested for a moment, leaning on Marley's grave, his breath puffing steam into the cold air while he recovered and noticed, to his consternation, that there was another mourner hunched in the tangled weeds nearby. The figure of a woman, kneeling on the patchy frosted ground, grey skirts billowed out around her. There was something familiar about her shabby attire – the faded, worn quality of the skirt. There was a grubby, reddish heart-shaped stain on the sleeve and Scrooge was sure that he had seen it before but could not recall when. He had no intention of asking the woman herself. She was slumped forward, arms outstretched as if prostrating herself on the grave of her loved one. Scrooge turned away. The sight of someone else's grief disturbed him, making him feel that his own deep-buried and less intense ache for Marley, and all the others he had lost, was somehow not good enough. In the past, he would have masked his own unease by scoffing at the woman's mawkishness, but he knew better now. He was a changed man. He truly was.

'Good morning, old friend,' Scrooge spoke softly. He might be a changed man, but he did not want the woman nearby to hear him do something as foolish as talking to the dead. He still had a reputation to protect, one which had been damaged somewhat by last year's singing and dancing and throwing coins in the street. He had kept the supernatural part of the story to himself, as few men of business wished to deal with a fellow who swore he had seen the past, the future and the dead carrying chains through his own bedchamber. But without this added colour, his joyful display of festive feeling was regarded by some as quite improper.

He crouched low next to the grave, close enough to see the lichens forming on Jacob Marley's name, and talked on, telling his partner of the progress of their business.

He had imagined that profits would be damaged by his new softer-hearted approach to affairs, not least by all those extra lumps of coal expended on keeping Mr Bob Cratchit from freezing to his clerk's stool. But there had been surprising benefits to the expenditure.

'It turns out, my friend, that warmer hands make for swifter writing, and when a mind is not focused on fear and hunger it becomes sharper and more efficient,' Scrooge told the lump of granite. 'He is completing six days' worth of work in the space of five. Would you believe it?'

As a result, Scrooge had begun to allow him a few extra hours to himself on Saturdays and he returned to work on Monday morning replete with energy and eager to continue. Scrooge did not share this fact with Marley, though. He knew what his old partner would have said in life. *If a man completes his work early, you are clearly not giving him enough to do!*

Scrooge still found it difficult to tread the path between being a good, fair man and being a naive milksop, disrespected by all, and was never quite sure on which side he currently stood. But it was strangely satisfying to see Cratchit scuttling off early, weaving his threadbare white comforter around his neck and bidding his master a good day.

'I know,' Scrooge admitted. 'I have grown soft-hearted towards my clerk and his family. I even have his young lad in my employ! In between his schooling Tiny Tim is my office boy. Of course, he is not precisely fleet of foot when I send him on errands, but his strength has revived somewhat this last year. The boy is eager and willing, and nobody could question his trustworthiness. Oh, my friend, how you would mock me now! But . . .'

He gave a sigh. His knees ached from crouching to hide from the nearby mourner, and he eased himself down onto the frozen turf at Marley's graveside. Scrooge could not remember the last time he had sat upon the ground in this way. It was freezing and uncomfortable.

'Goodness is not an easy path, Marley. Last year, it was simpler. I was so full to the brim with the joy of living, the sight of my own grave still fresh in my memory. I danced and sang carols and played parlour games through sheer relief that I had survived. But as the season approaches I find . . . merriment is not in my nature.'

He hesitated, the admission hanging in the air as he struggled to find the words to explain himself. Changing one's ways was not as straightforward as changing one's socks. Each morning when he rose from his still-meagre bed, dozens of decisions lay before him. Was it miserly or saintly to keep the grate in his own room cold, to breakfast on the thinnest of gruels? Was it generous or foolish to lend that street-boy Jem money to buy boot polish to start his own enterprise? Was it kind or madness to allow the Scrapley family extra time to pay their debt to him, even though he knew they would never be able to afford to pay, no matter how much time he gave? His reputation as a changed man had spread as the new year had begun and since then he had been subject to hordes of chancers and tricksters thinking him a soft touch, trying to wring money out of him. Those he had not trusted, he had sent packing. Had that been wrong?

The compassionate choice might prove disastrous for his business now, but the tight-fisted, hand-at-the-grindstone choice could provide another link in the heavy chain of sins he would have to bear in the afterlife.

That chain.

He dreamed of it. It clattered, link by link, through his mind every night, and by day he fancied he could still hear it clinking in the background of his thoughts with every choice he made. He could still remember Marley's own burden from last Christmas – the sins of his lifetime weighing him down, preventing his soul from taking flight. And Scrooge had been far, far worse.

'Better, I know, to suffer now than in eternity,' Scrooge said with a sigh. 'But maybe a small extra link would be preferable to another meeting with the widow Tassell and her charity committee.'

Scrooge laughed a dry little *hah* and began the difficult prospect of struggling to his feet. It was no easy matter and was not conducted with dignity involving, as it did, pivoting onto his knees, then enduring their creaking protests as he dragged himself upright using Marley's tombstone as a support. Conscious that the woman nearby might have noticed him, he pulled himself up to his full height and brushed away the crust of ice which had formed on top of the stone.

'Farewell, old friend, until Christmas Eve.' Those words hung in the air and Scrooge realised what he had said. He flushed hot, his breathing became rapid with panic. 'That is to say I will return here, to your graveside six days from now. Please . . . do not feel obliged to visit me on Christmas Eve night once again. I would not put you to the trouble.'

The thought of another visitation ripped away the shreds of Scrooge's dignity, the pride he still foolishly clung to, and once again he was the begging wretch he had been on Christmas morning almost one year ago, clinging to his own bedpost in fear. He backed away from the grave, bowing obsequiously to his old friend's memorial, stuttering his excuses and fleeing across the crunchy, frosted grass.

In his haste, he stumbled into the part of the yard he hated the most. A corner even more tangled and neglected than Marley's grave site, where a few narrow spaces remained, awaiting new tenants. Just there, in a space currently occupied by a clump of withered weeds, was where his grave had been in the vision he'd seen of Christmas future. Where he would be buried some day, if he did not change his ways. The late, unlamented Ebenezer Scrooge.

Scrooge struggled to control the creeping, clawing fear inside him. Of all the spirits that had visited him, the . . . the *creature* . . . which represented the future had been the most terrifying, the most merciless. Faceless, voiceless, wrapped in grey robes – its bony finger pointing the way. And it had brought him here. He hurried back towards the path, and in doing so nearly tripped over his fellow mourner.

'I do beg your pardon!' He righted himself, lifting his hat and adding an overly cheery 'good morning to you, madam' to compensate for his previous odd behaviour.

She didn't respond. She was still slumped in front of the grave-stone – quite unnaturally now Scrooge came to think of it, her pale white hands clawed into the frozen dirt. They looked like they were carved out of marble. She was still, too still.

Scrooge leaned closer, a sickening feeling creeping over him. 'Madam, are you quite all right?'

That was when he saw the blood.

2

THE OLD MAN WAS LATE FOR WORK. BOB CRATCHIT FELT A
prickle of unease down his already chilly spine. The old man
was never late. Even now, after his strange festive transformation
last year, Scrooge loved his business more than anything and was
always the first in the office in the morning and the last to leave
at night. He glanced up towards the door, then over to the clock
on the wall, then back to the meagre fireplace.

He shivered. Here was a dilemma. The office was cold, so icy
he could see his breath as he bent over his ledger, and he needed
to start a fire. The old man had been very clear when he reset the
rules last year. Whenever Bob needed fresh coal for his fire he
should not hesitate or be in the slightest bit afraid to come into
his employer's office with the shovel and request it. It had not
occurred to Bob to ask Scrooge what he should do in his absence
because, apart from the occasional visit to the Royal Exchange,
he was always there.

Bob slid hesitantly off his stool and picked up the shovel.

Surely the old man wouldn't mind if he just went in and helped himself . . .

He took a couple of steps across the office floor, his heart beating faster at the excitement of his own daring. Scrooge was different now, he told himself. He rewarded industriousness, he gave him time off. Last Christmas he had dandled Tiny Tim on his knee and laughed – actually laughed. He was compassionate and warm-hearted now. He was good.

And yet still Bob hesitated in the middle of the room, his hand trembling as he gripped the shovel. Yes, the old man had changed, but he still knew, down to the last lump, exactly how much coal was in the scuttle. And if he came in to find a merry fire already blazing, would he say that Bob had overstepped?

Bob did not fear losing his job, at least not as much as he had last year, but he had more to lose now. Scrooge & Marley had become a good place to work. He had decent pay; he had Saturday afternoons off; his employer had even taken Bob's sickly youngest son under his wing, paying his doctor's bills and employing him when no other person would. Scrooge was kind to him now, but if he ceased to trust him, would that kindness disappear?

He is a good man now. Bob stepped towards the office.

But what if I disappoint him . . .? Bob stepped back again.

The door flew open with a crash and Bob flinched, instinctively trying to hide the shovel under his desk. It slithered from his cold-fingered grip, streaking his waistcoat with soot before it fell to the floor with a clang loud enough to wake old Marley from his resting place.

'Sir, I was j-just . . .' he stammered, whirling around.

And then he stopped. It wasn't Scrooge. It was worse than that. It was the widow Tassell bearing down on him, a vision in black bombazine.

Mrs Lucretia Jane Tassell always seemed to be in motion, performing at least three tasks at once. Currently she was striding across the office floor towards him, while also rummaging for something in her reticule and simultaneously casting her eye towards Scrooge's office door.

'Is he at home?' the widow asked. 'Stupid question, of course he is. Come now, Mr Scrooge, you know that hiding under your desk doesn't work, I will find you out!'

Bob experienced a rare moment of pity for his master. 'He is not . . . I swear it!'

Mrs Tassell produced a large handkerchief from her bag, too large to be fit for a lady, and handed it distractedly to Bob. 'Here, to brush off the soot. What do you mean, he's not in? He's always in.'

'Not today.'

Her eyes narrowed thoughtfully. 'Is he ill?'

Bob looked aghast; the thought hadn't occurred to him. Scrooge had never had a day's illness in his life beyond his happy episode of madness last Christmas. He felt a pang of concern, and wondered if he should send someone over to Scrooge's house to check on him.

'No, it can't be that.' Mrs Tassell dismissed the idea almost immediately, shaking her head, causing her numerous veils to flail about. She was around forty-five years old, but the air of energy about her made her seem younger. She had a neat waist (not that

Bob noticed such things), sparkling eyes and hair which, while threaded with silver, was still several shades darker than the norm. There were whispers that she was not a native to these shores, although nothing in her demeanour ever gave that impression. Widowed some two years ago, her only outward signs of mourning was her black attire and the occasional reference to her 'dearly departed Hubert'. Beyond that she seemed happily engaged in offloading her husband's entire hard-earned fortune trying to, as she put it, 'repair the world'.

'I need to talk to him about the Benevolent Christmas Feast. I can wait.' She produced another large handkerchief from somewhere and flicked it over the chair in the corner of the room which, to Bob's embarrassment, sent up quite a cloud of dust. She settled there, pulling a notebook and pencil from her reticule. 'Goodness me, it's freezing in here. Couldn't you start that fire?'

Bob was halfway across the office with his meagre shovel of coal when the door opened again. He jumped and, although this time he managed to keep hold of the shovel, several lumps of coal slid across the floor.

Again, it was not Scrooge, though this man seemed to be cut of similar cloth. He was thin and grey, with vertical lines carved into his face, giving it a permanent expression of disapproval. Bob wondered if there was a manufactory somewhere up north which turned out these gentlemen by the hundred, complete with their meticulously tied neckcloths, tall, well-worn hats and contemptuous sneers. He recognised this particular specimen, though.

13

'Mr Scabble, how wonderful to see you and may I offer you the compliments of the season?'

'You may not. Christmas is still another week away. Gracious, the build-up seems to get earlier every year.' He sighed. 'Bah. I think your master spoke right when he said that Christmas is nothing but humbug.'

Over the years Bob had perfected a technique of bobbing his head low and muttering something which sounded a little like 'yes, sir, quite right, sir,' which kept his betters appeased without him having to agree outright. The widow, though, let out a peal of mocking laughter.

'Oh,' Scabble said in tones chillier than the room. '*You're* here.'

'It's not too late to donate to the Benevolent Feast!' Mrs Tassell's tone tinkled, her smile glinted.

Scabble looked at her with the expression of a man who wished to bring back the good old days of the ducking stool. Mrs Tassell ignored him, going back to her notebook where she seemed to be ticking items off a list, which only seemed to infuriate him more.

'I don't know what it is you think you are achieving with this Benevolent Feast for the Poor, madam,' Scabble said at last. 'Exposure to rich food will only spoil their stomachs and give them a taste for things above their station in life.'

Mrs Tassell peered at him curiously. 'Do you experience any joy in your life, Aldous?'

'What a pointless question. Joy does not make money. Joy does not build industry, which helps this country grow mighty. It does not—'

Just as Scabble was building up to full flow the door flew open again and there stood, to Bob's absolute horror, a police constable. He was in his early twenties, brown-skinned, which was most unusual in a policeman, and somewhat out of breath – he had clearly been running. There was a dapple of pimples on his cheek and his smart blue uniform jacket seemed too large for him, as though he was a child playing at dressing-up.

'Constable Baldock,' he panted. 'I need to speak to Mr Scrooge about the murder.'

Murder. Bob's heart thudded at the word. His mind flew, irrationally, to his own home, his wife and children. He knew they were safe, he knew that this was unlikely to involve them, but still the fear reared up inside him. *Love is weakness*, Scrooge had once said to him, and in moments like this, it was.

'What is the meaning of this? Ebenezer Scrooge is a respectable man of business . . .'

Scabble's contemptuous outburst gave Bob a few moments to collect himself. He realised he was still holding the coal shovel and set it down, brushing his hands clean on the widow's handkerchief. A policeman in the office was not a good thing. Scrooge traded on his reputation and, despite the fact that this was obviously some kind of mistake, Scabble would no doubt tell everyone at the Royal Exchange, who would then enjoy a raucous laugh about this fresh scandal at Scrooge & Marley. The widow might also tattle, although she seemed to be ignoring the officer and remained intently focused on her to-do list.

The policeman, evidently assuming Scabble was the man he sought, was babbling about churchyards and bodies when Mr Scrooge himself appeared in the doorway.

'Cratchit, what is the meaning of this commotion? I . . .'

Scrooge's voice trailed off as he looked around the office, which seemed much smaller now it contained Scabble, the policeman and Mrs Tassell's not-insignificant skirts. For a moment Bob could swear his master's gaze rested on the discarded coal shovel, and he gulped. But Scrooge was distracted, though not by the police officer. Instead, he was looking at Scabble with a curious expression: a mixture of respect, dislike and . . . was that *fear*?

'Sir . . .' Scrooge said. His face, always pale, grew whiter. His fingers appeared to tremble as he unbuttoned his greatcoat. 'Well, well, well, what a p-pleasure to see you!'

Scabble was quick to see that he had the advantage. 'Mr Scrooge, I stopped by as I had a proposition for you. However, if there is any chance of a scandal, I may need to take my opportunity elsewhere.'

'Oh no.' Scrooge shook his head, waving the policeman away with one hand. 'This was purely a matter of doing my civic duty. I stumbled upon a poor wretch in the churchyard this morning. Quite dead, poor thing. I reported the death and had thought my duty in that direction was already done.' He gave the policeman a stern glare.

Constable Baldock shifted uncomfortably. Policemen were commonly much more at home breaking up pub fights than they were interrogating respectable business persons about murder.

'You left in rather a hurry, sir, and my inspector sent me after you.' The constable was still panting although trying to cling to his dignity. 'I must have run right past you! I need to know if you lost anything at the scene of the crime. Anything of value.'

'Well, I did not,' Scrooge snapped.

'Cratchit, give this man a guin— no, a shilling, and send him on his way. Mr Scabble, please make yourself comfortable in my office. I shall join you shortly. Mrs Tassell, I suppose there is no point in my asking you to go away?'

'None whatsoever,' the widow said happily.

'Then you must wait. Business comes first.' A shadow seemed to pass over him at those words. He hesitated for a moment then nodded to himself and repeated: 'Yes, business comes first.'

He ushered Mr Scabble into his office, away from the departing police officer and the tenacious widow, sighing with relief as he shut the door. But momentarily he opened it again, poking his head out to add: 'For goodness' sake start a fire, Cratchit. You will freeze to death out there.'

Scrooge's own office was also cold, but as he shut the door once again his body was generating a wave of panicked heat all of its own.

Already shaken up by his graveyard chat with Marley, the sight of the dead woman had frightened him more than he would care to admit. Scrooge had reached out and touched her cold hand, brushed back a lock of her dark hair to check if she was still breathing, and so he had seen her pale face, eyes open in an expression somewhere between horror and wonder.

She had been young, possibly in her twenties. The police officer at the station had implied she was likely a prostitute and that this kind of thing happened 'all too often' to young persons of her ilk, but that had not been Scrooge's impression at all. She had been shabbily but respectably dressed. In fact, her clothing had looked oddly familiar. He was no expert on women's fashion, but he had definitely seen that heart-shaped stain before. Her hair had been tied up neatly in the same practical but elegant style affected by Mrs Cratchit. She had been wearing a bonnet but no gloves. Her fingers had been holding something which looked like it was made of gold, although Scrooge had not had the stomach to inspect it, for fear of touching that cold hand. Perhaps this was the valuable item of which Constable Baldock had spoken. There had been a wide, evil-looking gash at her throat. And those eyes, those pale blue eyes staring blankly back at him . . .

Scrooge was no stranger to death; he had sat with Marley's corpse after his passing. But this woman was different. She was young. She had been afraid.

He needed time alone in his office to recover. An hour with his balance books, the comforting smell of ink on his fingers would be enough to restore his calm. But instead, Mrs Tassell had been waiting in ambush, and there was a policeman. And, worst of all, Aldous Scabble was now here in his office.

The society of London commerce was every bit as stratified as the *haut ton* – a mighty pyramid of moneymakers – and in this scheme of things Mr Scabble was at least the equivalent of a minor duke. Scrooge had always admired his uncanny knack for spotting a good opportunity to make money and his reputation was such that if Scabble invested in something, the rest of the Royal Exchange would follow. In his former days, Scrooge had looked upon the man as a pattern card, a role model to be admired and imitated, and he had treasured the few conversations they had, fancying that they had much in common, that they both respected each other as men of business. Even now there was a part of him that skittered with excitement at the thought that the great man desired his attention.

But it was not Scabble's reputation which caused Scrooge's heart to pound or his body to sweat under his winter layers.

The truth was, he had avoided the man, and several other stalwart pillars of the business community, since his visitation from the spirits last year. When the terrifying shrouded Spirit of Christmas Yet to Come had transported him forward in time, he had seen them, gathered in their habitual spot at the Royal Exchange, clinking money in their pockets, checking their gold watches and idly gossiping about Scrooge's own death.

'I thought he'd never die . . .'

'It's likely to be a very cheap funeral . . .'

'What has he done with his money?'

'He hasn't left it to me, that's all I know.'

Scabble had been there, laughing with the rest of them, lip curled in an urbane sneer. That was his future, the butt of a joke among his former cronies, nicknamed Old Scratch after the devil himself.

He played for time, rearranging the papers on his desk – tucking some discreetly away from Scabble's gaze and arranging others so that he might show off his proudest investments. The papers ruffled, sliding to the floor as if blown by some chill draught. Scrooge felt a prickle of goosebumps on his neck and checked to see if a window had been left open. They were all firmly shut.

'I must say this is not what I expected,' Scabble said, surveying Scrooge's shabby office. His contemptuous glare took in the dusty panelling, the cold empty grate with the battered scuttle next to it, the scratched surface of a desk which had probably been an antique during the Napoleonic Wars and the single miserly lamp which shed a small splash of extra light on Scrooge's work.

'I was under the impression that you had become a festive sort of chap recently.'

Scrooge fought to maintain his businesslike mask, despite the panic seething inside him. Scabble was a predator, he sensed weaknesses and used them to his advantage.

'I plan to keep Christmas as well as the next man this year,' he elected to say. 'It's my duty to do so.'

'I rather preferred "humbug",' said Scabble with a sigh. 'But it seems you are in the rising majority. The common people cannot get enough of this . . .' he paused, and his lip curled, 'this *Christmas*. And it's not just commoners. The Prince Consort, I hear, is also partial to it and the malaise has spread to the rest of the Royal family. Tell me, Scrooge, do you know what this is?'

He produced a rectangle of card, about five by three inches, from his pocket and slid it across the desk. Scrooge rummaged for his spectacles and slid them onto his nose, peering closely.

It was a quaint engraving, an image of a merry family gathered around a table, each raising a glass of dark red wine – even the children. On each side of the picture were small vignettes of food and clothing being handed beneficently to the poor and beneath it was a banner which read: *A MERRY CHRISTMAS AND A HAPPY NEW YEAR TO YOU.*

'Apparently it's called a "Christmas card",' Scabble said, his voice heavy with contempt. 'The idea, I am told, is to send it via penny post to one's friends and family to wish them compliments of the season.'

'And then afterwards, what is done with them?' asked Scrooge.

'The family displays them for the festive period,' Scabble replied. 'What happens to them after that I do not know, but the next year one sends them again. And again, the following year. This fellow Cole printed one thousand of them last year and they sold out. It is quite absurd, but could be rather lucrative. If we work quickly enough we can print a series of superior designs and have them all sold by Christmas morning.'

'*We . . .?*' Scrooge stood up straighter, felt the stirrings of excitement.

'I am putting together a group of investors and thought you might be interested. You are, of course, Christmas personified.'

Scrooge felt a flush of embarrassment at this. Several newspaper reports had appeared after his dancing and singing and Merry-Christmasing the year before and although, thankfully, none had heard his talk of spirits, he had still been subject to some ribbing from his contemporaries. But Scabble had clearly not come here to mock, and as the man outlined the costs and projected profits involved, Scrooge began to understand the cleverness of the idea.

This could change everything. It could move him from mid-level moneylender into the upper echelons of the commercial *haut ton*. It could make him rich.

As part of his transformation, Scrooge had worked on his smile. According to Jem, the street-boy turned boot-boy, it still looked 'a bit like you're a crocodile about to eat someone', but it was better than it had been. And now it spread slowly across his face, sharp-toothed and eager. This was how it used to feel before, when life had been simply a case of adding extra figures to his balance book and not worrying about the reckoning which would come after.

21

'Mr Scabble,' he said, 'I believe we can come to an arrangement.'

Deep in his consciousness, a voice which sounded much like the ghost of Marley asked: *How does this fit in with your fresh start? Will it bring you profit in this life, or add a heavy link to your chain in the next?*

Scrooge shook the thought away. This endeavour was all about celebrating Christmas, the cards a delightful addition to the merriment of the festive season. Besides, in order to do good he needed money, which meant that he needed to make money. And he was about to make an awful lot of it.

'You must meet my associate, Merrypaw,' Scabble said. He reached into his waistcoat pocket, rummaging around for his watch in a rare lapse of dignity, until Scrooge drew out his own and showed Scabble the time.

'Ah! He will be at his place of business now. Are you available to meet him?'

Scrooge looked through window pane into the office, surveyed the waiting lady. If he left now on urgent business, she would surely be forced to give up and go home.

'Yes, I am perfectly available.'

As Scrooge left his office, crocodile-like grin firmly in place for Scabble's benefit, he thought he caught a glimpse of something in the room behind him. A flicker of movement, the flutter of a piece of fabric. But this time there was nothing in his office, no tattered skirt hem blowing in the breeze.

Perhaps it was simply grey dust blowing along the floor in the draught.

Or . . . a thud of dread sounded in his chest.

Or it could be the shroud of that terrifying final spirit.

3

TINY TIM LOVED THE WAY THE STREETS OF LONDON CHANGED
as Christmastime approached. The shop windows aglow, full
of toys and treats that he would stare at and imagine touching.
The link-boys dashing around with sprigs of holly in their caps,
lighting the way for women and men laden down with parcels
as the sound of carols filled the air. But there was an extra hum
of excitement on the streets this afternoon as he made his way
slowly from his schoolroom to Scrooge's office.

It was a long, steep route, but a year of decent food and medicine had made him stronger. And even if he was tired after his
day's schooling he was determined not to take a rest. His hand
ached as the handle of the crutch wore into his palm; his foot
throbbed inside its iron support. His father had fashioned him a
special crutch for winter weather, with a sharp tip which bit into
the ice. It helped as he struggled along.

A knot of people stood on a street corner and at first he thought they were huddled around a hot-chestnut vendor, but in fact it was a man selling broadsides – the large, single-sheet news-papers which appeared on the streets when something exciting or important had happened. As he passed he caught snatches of conversation.

'So young.'

'Such a shame.'

'Did she have a sweetheart? It's usually the sweetheart . . .'

So this was not about Christmas then. It sounded sad, and serious. Tim dismissed the matter as irrelevant grown-up stuff, and continued to move along the darkening street, heading for the offices of Scrooge & Marley.

His mother had thought he was too weak and sickly to do this job, but he had been determined to prove himself.

When his older brother and sister had started working he had watched them bring their wages home to Mother each Saturday and drop the coins into the broken custard cup which stood on the kitchen mantelpiece. Peter and Martha would beam with pride at each satisfying clink and Mother would ruffle their hair and tell them what wonderful hard workers they were, a special smile of pride on her lips. Tim wanted that too. He didn't want to be poor Tiny Tim anymore. He wanted to be Mother's hard worker.

And there was the other reason too. The secret one that weighed down his mind constantly. He had to stay as close to Scrooge as he could.

As it turned out, his work for Scrooge was not difficult, consisting mainly of reading aloud to his new master and 'checking that your silly father has added up his balance book right'.

'If I didn't know better, I'd say he was just giving the lad extra schooling in reading and arithmetic,' Tim had overheard his father say. But that couldn't be right. Mr Scrooge had told Tim that the work was vitally important and that the whole company would crumble without his help.

As he approached the office building, his shoulders tensed. There was a small group of boys standing in the shadows between him and the battered door. For the most part people were kind to him – adults seemed naturally inclined to cosset him and offer help. Boys his own age, though, were another matter and he read trouble in the way they held themselves, in their sneering smiles. He had no choice but to draw closer, though, hoping he could creep past as they talked.

'Slit from ear to ear she was,' said the biggest of them, a gangly boy of about twelve whose nose was streaming with a winter cold.

'Dawson said her whole head was cut off.'

'I heard she was just a torso and when they came to move her skirts they discovered that her legs had been sliced clean away.'

The assembled boys made a sound of awed delight and Tim crept closer, suddenly curious to know what they were talking about. That was when he heard the word, whispered between the three boys with a thrill of delight. *Murder.*

Tim shivered and drew back – the movement attracted the attention of Drippy-nose, who whirled round.

'What have we here? It's Limpy, Old Scratch's boy.' He moved towards Tim, who stood frozen to the spot, clinging tightly to his crutch. Drippy-nose took his time, circling around Tim, wiping said leaking appendage on his sleeve.

'I suppose you want to go inside, Limpy?'

Tim did not answer. He knew his role in this particular scene; he had played it many times before and knew that whatever he said only made things worse.

Another boy, a redhead, leaned in close, until Tim flinched from his foul breath. And as he recoiled, Drippy kicked his crutch hard and it whirled out from under him. He crashed to the icy cobbles – agony shot up his wrists, his good ankle twisted. Tim bit back a sob. He couldn't get to his feet, not with his ankle hurting like this and with the boys ready to punch him back down. The only solution was to curl up and take his punishment.

'Oh whoopsie, Limpy seems to have taken a tumble,' Drippy -nose said, jeering.

A different boy might have fought. Ideas shot through his head that he could lash out with the pointed end of his crutch, cause damage with the metal frame on his foot. But what was the point? He was weak, he was small. *He was Tiny.*

A third assailant's boot thudded hard into his side, but he did not cry out. This wasn't real pain anyway; this was a mere shadow of what he had been through and he would not give them the satisfaction of seeing him cry.

The blows came hard and fast, then one of them suggested they check his pocket for pennies, their fingers jabbing at him as they rummaged through. There was nothing there – just a few interesting stones and a piece of string he'd found – but they took it all nonetheless.

Not much longer.

'Still not crying,' the redhead said, admiring his newly acquired string. 'Let's see how much he can take.'

Tim curled up once again. *He would not cry. He would not cry.*

'Oi!' A voice rang out and as it did, a stone hit Drippy, pinging off his temple. Two more followed, hitting the others like well-aimed bullets. Spitting curses, they turned and ran, jeering back over their shoulders, but it was several moments before Tim could bring himself to uncurl.

'Here.' A hand reached down, grubby and clad in the remains of a grey fingerless glove. Tim took it gratefully and managed to pivot into a sitting position.

'Give yourself a couple of minutes,' his rescuer advised. 'You've had the wind knocked out of you.'

Through the poor light, Tim could see a boy a few years older than him. He was brown-skinned and wearing an oversized top hat not dissimilar to Mr Scrooge's, but this one looked like it had been stolen from a snowman and then stuffed with paper to fit this boy's much smaller head. Over his shoulder hung a satchel overflowing with brushes and tins of boot blacking. That's when Tim recognised him as the local boot-boy.

'Jem?'

'You're Scrooge's lad, ain't you?' Jem said.

Tim felt his cheeks redden. What a sorry state he must look – bruised, his new coat torn and the sleeves covered in slush. Hardly someone of whom Mr Scrooge could be proud. But he could not tell a lie.

'Yes, that's right.'

The boy laughed. 'Ain't you fancy! Surely you know that if you come around here every day you'll need to learn to stick up for yourself. Why didn't you hit them with this?' He pointed at Tim's crutch.

Tim did not want to admit weakness.

'It's the Christian thing to turn the other cheek,' he said.

The boy let out another peal of laughter as he helped Tim to his feet. 'Turn the other cheek and you're just giving them something else to hit. I'm amazed you're still alive.'

He picked up Tim's lost piece of string, which the redhead had dropped, and gave it back to him. 'Listen, why don't you come with me down to St Gideon's churchyard after the old man's gone home? Me and some of the boys are going to take a look.'

'A look at what?'

'Haven't you heard? Some poor soul had her throat cut there. They took her away, but Simeon Katz says there's still a huge bloodstain by one of the gravestones.'

Tim hesitated. He didn't really want to see a huge bloodstain, and he had a feeling Jem was one of those ruffians his father had warned him about, possibly even a scoundrel. And besides, his father always walked home with him so he would have to dodge away from him somehow. But still, he didn't have many friends, and wasn't this what hard-working boys did?

'I'd like that,' he said.

'Knew you had a bit of pluck in you.' Jem nodded approvingly. 'Meet you here after six.' He hefted his shoe-shining equipment onto his shoulder and waved as he disappeared around the nearest corner.

Tim was about to enter the office when the door opened and his master appeared, accompanied by another tall, stern man of business. Scrooge looked uneasy somehow, and Tim felt a prickle of anxiety.

'Ah, boy,' Scrooge said. 'I am going to visit Mr Scabble's business associate.' He leaned in closer, white brows knit with concern. His gaze flickered up towards the nasty-looking man, then he spoke quietly to Tim. 'You look unwell. Perhaps you should remain here with your father.'

Tim was tired, parts of his clothing were soaked with slush and he was still trembling from the attack, but he was also fine-tuned to Scrooge's moods, his facial expressions, and he sensed danger. He could not allow his master to go alone. With some effort, he pulled himself up to his full, regrettably short, height and tilted his chin bravely upwards.

'I will come with you, Mr Scrooge, if I may.'

It took a while to arrive at Merrypaw Printworks. The walk there, easy for a full-grown man, was long and difficult for Tim, and Scrooge repeatedly feigned a backache as an excuse to rest and allow the boy to catch up. This only added to his irksome reputation as 'the old man'. Scrooge was not vain about his appearance, but he had not yet reached his mid fifties and could not understand why people spoke of him as if he were seventy.

At last they arrived at a large warehouse built of blackened bricks. Scabble led them into a noisy, airy space filled with clattering machinery and whirling activity. Workers bustled back and forth – men heaving bales of paper, women hunched over workbenches, boys and girls darting between them, running errands.

At the centre of it all was a merry, rotund gentleman, directing activities. He looked up and beamed at Scrooge.

'Oho, and here he is! I am Felix Merrypaw, sir. It is a pleasure to meet you!'

Almost everything about Merrypaw was cherry red. His waist-coat, which was embroidered with a swirled pattern of ivy and mistletoe; his button nose; his ruddy cheeks – although his hair was a shock of white. He held out his hand and Scrooge could see that even the tips of his fingers were stained with red ink.

'Welcome!' He chuckled. 'Do excuse the noise, we are having an exceptionally busy morning – but that's a sign of a healthy business! Come to my office, and I will show you our plans.'

As they made their way across the printworks, passing employees greeted him with a smile or a cheerful 'Morning, Mr Merrypaw!'

'Your staff seem very content,' Scrooge observed.

Scabble scoffed.

'Oh, my friend Scabble does not approve at all,' Merrypaw said with another bubbling chuckle. 'He enjoys disparaging things, but he does have a lighter side! He's very much one for the ladies on the sly, aren't you, old boy? If you ask me, that's where your watch chain went, into the purse of a fair Cyprian!'

'It is merely lost,' Scabble snapped, directing a withering glare at Merrypaw, who seemed completely unaffected. Scrooge briefly tried to picture Scabble as a romantic figure and shuddered.

Merrypaw led them up a flight of stairs and into a warm, spacious office lit by, in Scrooge's opinion, far too many lamps. An internal window looked out over the printworks below and a hearty fire blazed in the grate. There was a high desk not dissimilar to Scrooge's own, but in the middle of the room stood a large table, scattered all over with piles of paper. In the centre of it all someone had laid down a handkerchief-sized piece of red silk.

There were a few moments of activity. Merrypaw summoned drinks for them all, lifted Tiny Tim onto a high stool in the corner so he could 'rest that poor leg of his', all the while show-ering Scrooge with compliments about both his business acumen and charity work.

'You are the perfect man to be part of this endeavour,' he said, before looking at Scabble. 'Well, shall we show him?'

'Without further delay,' Scabble said drily.

Merrypaw went over to the table and pulled away the red silk.

Beneath, mounted on a piece of card, was a design that caught Scrooge's breath. It was not so much the image itself, a deli-cately drawn robin redbreast sitting on a sprig of holly; it was the colour. The red of the robin's breast, the deep green of the leaves seemed to leap off the page in a way he had never seen before.

Scrooge leaned in closer, fighting not to gasp in surprise.

'Ooh, it's lovely,' said Tiny Tim from his perch, before clap-ping his hand self-consciously over his mouth.

'It is indeed,' Merrypaw agreed. 'Mr Scrooge, you are looking at the world's first chemically synthesised ink. This is made not by using the Chinese or Indian methods, not by crushing substances found in nature, but by creating something using "chemical reac-tion". It is the result of many years' painstaking research by the talented Alastair Bailey, nephew of our respected associate here.' He made a comically elaborate bow to Scabble. 'Young Dr Bailey is one of the finest, most serious minds of his generation . . . Unfortunately, he is not able to join us today, being indisposed, but you shall meet him soon enough, is that not right, my friend?'

Scabble inclined his head and spoke. 'My nephew has devel-oped a workable red and green, which will do very well for the designs Mr Merrypaw has in mind – one of which you will find particularly amusing, Scrooge.'

Merrypaw handed the robin redbreast image to him and Scrooge leaned in to examine it, brushing his bitten thumbnail over the card. The colour seemed imbued in the paper somehow.

'Remarkable,' he murmured.

'At this time of year, we are starved of colour,' Merrypaw said. 'It is why our hearts leap when we see a sprig of holly peeking out from beneath the frost, or the flash of a robin's red breast. It reminds us that life endures and that, come springtime, colour will return. That is why people will buy these "Christmas cards", and the brighter they are, the better.'

He reached into a drawer beneath the table and pulled out an ordinary-looking ink bottle, removing the cork and tipping it onto a blank piece of paper before him. A red stain slowly spread across it.

'It does not fade. It does not smudge,' Merrypaw said.

But Scrooge was not listening; he was staring at the tide of crimson ink, his vision blurring so that the paper transformed into the frosted churchyard, the red fluid became the young woman's blood, creeping slowly through the grass. And then he heard the heavy metallic clanking of chains. Scrooge whirled around, looking over his shoulder. There was nothing there.

'I say, dear chap, are you quite all right?' Merrypaw asked.

Scrooge gave him what he hoped was a reassuring smile and asked whether they really could complete the endeavour in time for Christmas.

'Of course,' Merrypaw assured him. 'My workers will have no problem producing the cards in time. At present they are all working doubly hard. Do you know why that is? Because Christmas is coming, and if we stay on schedule I plan to close the press for three whole days!'

'Good God!' Scabble cried.

'I find that a happy workforce is a productive workforce,' Merrypaw said. 'With this incentive in place, they will do the work on time and do it with joy in their hearts.'

Just then a clerk came in with a stack of papers for his employer to inspect. It looked like a broadside newspaper, and Scrooge caught sight of the headline:

FOUL MURDER IN ST GIDEON'S CHURCHYARD

He wrinkled his nose in revulsion. Every time a major crime occurred, these broadsides sprang up like weeds. They were not respectable newspapers, just unofficial printed sheets sold en masse, often emphasising the more lurid aspects of the case. He checked his watch – it had only been a few hours since he had found that poor wretch's body and yet somehow the broadside writers had sniffed out the story, written it and sent it to press.

Merrypaw must have seen Scrooge's distaste, for he shook his head sadly. 'I know, it is a tragedy, is it not? We print so many terrible, sad things. I think that is why I am so excited about Christmas cards – not only will we make a profit, we will bring pleasure to our customers.'

Scabble rolled his eyes, but Scrooge felt a dart of hope. The idea that he could do business while doing good was intoxicating.

'This is a good proposition,' he said. 'We could make a lot of money.'

And as the words left his lips, Scrooge imagined he saw the poor dead woman's face again. He rubbed his eyes. He was tired. It had been a busy morning.

But when he looked up again, she was still there. Truly there. She was standing on the opposite side of the table between Merrypaw and Scabble. Still deathly pale, her eyes wide with fright. On the cuff of her grey dress, he could see the same distinct heart-shaped stain, but her presence was filmy as if he was looking at her through a rain-blurred window or a sheet of clear ice.

Scrooge staggered back, a strangled cry in his throat. *Please no. Please, spirits, not again . . .*

Merrypaw laughed nervously and as he did his hand swooped clean through the apparition, leaving a trail of smoky mist, but the figure remained.

'Are you quite all right, sir?'

Scabble muttered something Scrooge could not catch, but it contained the word 'asylum'.

He knew he must cover his tracks, think of some excuse for his cry, before the two men wrote him off as insane and found someone else to invest, but though he tried to speak, his dry lips could not produce a word. His flesh was cold as ice, his hands trembling. The phantom screamed silently, one blueish-white hand clasping her throat, scarlet blood gushing out between her fingers before she slumped forward, as though re-enacting her death. Scrooge fought not to look at her, to pretend she was not there. *Speak, Ebenezer*, he urged himself. *Don't just stand there gawping like a surprised codfish . . .*

There was a loud clatter from the corner of the room – Tiny Tim had fallen from his stool.

'Oh, poor child!' Merrypaw exclaimed, rushing around the table to aid him, pushing entirely through the apparition.

It disintegrated, and the icy feeling vanished.

'I'm ever so sorry, sir,' Tim said as Merrypaw helped him up. 'The stool was awfully high, and I couldn't get down. No . . . no, I'm not hurt. I've been taking notes for you, look!'

He held up a slate upon which he had written: *New ink. Kemical prosess. Pretty red. Smol financial outlay.*

Scrooge's gratitude at the interruption was immense, and when his voice returned he praised Tim's spelling of 'financial outlay', nodded as Scabble talked about drawing up a contract to sign tomorrow. The world felt normal again. The office was warm and bright, his new associates were excited and his first merry Christmas in years was just around the corner. But his stomach heaved with dread. He had seen another ghost.

Lord have mercy, it seemed the spirit world was not done with him, after all.

THE GHOST

I AM UNRAVELLING.

Nothing makes sense. My mind is caught at the point of my death, experiencing it again and again. A player on stage at a penny gaff, acting the same short tragedy, speaking the same lines. I cannot free myself. Terror overrules my every thought, panic repeating in my mind. And the only certainty:

I am dead. I am dead. I am dead.

I can remember being somewhere . . . outdoors, among standing stones. A place other people feared but one which made me feel safe. Someone grabs me from behind, holding my jaw with a strong, gloved hand. I try to cry out, but nothing passes through my lips — no air, no voice. I squirm and thrash backwards with my fists but they lose strength before they even make contact. My killer releases me and I crumple forward onto the frozen ground. The last thing I feel is the cold earth under my fingers and a sudden terrible weakness. I have felt weak before, and I have always pushed through, kept going, stumbling forward one footstep after another, but death defeats me. I claw my fingertips into the ground, my last breath in the world is a desperate, wet gurgle that fills me with sadness and shame.

And back I tumble, yet again.

Is this my punishment? All my life I had been told that retribution awaits all sinners in the afterlife. And yet still I sinned and now I re-enact my death over and over, and in between I see flashes of the old miser's harsh, pinched face.

Am I haunting Ebenezer Scrooge? Why would I do that? I do not know him. I only saw him twice in my life.

But still, I sinned against him.

As I think those words, a thin sliver of metal appears out of the darkness, twisting and turning and glinting although there is no light. It coils before me and comes to rest around my insubstantial waist, closing with a sharp, cold clink. Aside from the pain of the blade at my throat and the cold of the ground I have not felt a single sensation since I died. But now this strip of silver is here, locked around me. It is harsh and heavy, and I instinctively know it is my burden to bear for my sins in life.

I see Scrooge again, his lips pulled back from his teeth in a twisted parody of a smile. I try to pull away, but it is as if I am bound to him. Why him? I have hurt many people in my life – people I love – but he is the one I am doomed to be with.

I begin to wonder, is it because I sinned against him – or because he found out what I did?

A new outpouring of terror floods my mind as I work it out.

He must have been the one who killed me.

4

TIM DID NOT LIE TO HIS FATHER. IT WAS AN IMPORTANT, IF SMALL, distinction. Had he told Father that he was going to play with a friend of his? Yes, he had, and Father had seemed happy about this, ruffling his hair and telling him that he was glad that he was finally making some friends of his own age rather than hanging around with old Mr Scrooge all the time.

Had he told him he was meeting a gang of street children to break into a churchyard after dark in order to inspect a giant blood stain? No, he had decided not to do that. It wasn't precisely a lie, Tim told himself, just more of a *not telling*. Still, his fierce little conscience whispered away in his mind that what he was doing was naughty and wrong.

But then he saw Jem smile at him and his conscience shrivelled.

'Tim, I knew you could make it! Lads and lasses, this is my new pal, Tim. Tim, this is Simeon, Winnie and Mags.'

The assembled group of grubby children looked at Tim doubtfully.

'He's a bit clean, ain't he?'

'Why's he dressed like a clerk?'

'What is he, four years old?'

'I'm eight!' Tim spoke up for himself before he had time to think. 'I'm just a bit small for my age. I've been ill.'

'Haven't we all, *Tiny* Tim?'

Tim felt a flare of irritation. 'Don't call me that.' Then he added, because he was still a good boy, 'Please.'

'Right ho, Titchy,' the boy, Simeon, said. 'Come with us!'

The streets were dark, and their way was lit only by Winnie's small lantern. Tim soon fell behind, but luckily he knew the way and when he arrived at the churchyard fence, the other children were still assembled by the wall. Tim was surprised when they looked pleased to see him.

'There he is!'

'Just what we need!'

'Chuck him over, Jem!'

Tim stared at his new friend, panicked. Jem's smile was probably meant to be reassuring but it wasn't.

'It seems the vicar has not been informed of our arrival,' he said, affecting upper-class tones. 'Which means one is going to lob you over the wall, and you can pertain to undo the latch for us from within.'

'You're the smallest, Titchy,' Mags added, not without satisfaction as she was the second-smallest. 'There's a tree on the other side. You'll climb down easy.'

Tim's limbs, already tired from the visit to Merrypaw's and then the further trek with Jem's gang, were shaking with fatigue. His fingers and the tip of his nose were numb with cold and the idea of trespassing, into a place of worship too, filled him with horror. But hadn't his brothers got up to worse high-jinks when they were his age – scaling walls, climbing trees? And besides, he could not back down now.

There was a momentary feeling of flight as Jem launched him up into the air, and he landed on his belly on the crumbling top of the wall. With incredible effort, he swung his legs over and from there he could just about reach the branches of a nearby yew tree. Tim's legs were weak, but his arms and shoulders were strong from using the crutch and he dangled himself from the branch, then dropped quietly onto a soft, frosted tuft of grass.

'Ow.'

Which was growing over a fallen tombstone. The iron frame on his foot took the worst of the impact, and shortly after his crutch sailed over the wall too, clattering onto the ground nearby. As he crawled for it, he could hear the children on the other side of the wall talking about him.

'I'm not sure about him, Jem.' Simeon's voice. 'He seems like a bit of a goody-goody.'

'Yeah, are you sure he won't just tell on us?'

'He's solid,' Jem replied, and Tim's chest puffed up a little. 'Besides, he works for Ebenezer Scrooge, he deserves a bit of fun.'

Fortunately the churchyard was unlocked and unguarded. Tim simply pulled aside the bolt on the wooden gate for his new friends. The five children crept on through the dark. He scored extra points with them when he stopped them wandering randomly and directed them towards Mr Marley's resting place. If Scrooge had found her, it was likely she'd been near his friend's grave.

It was not until they came upon Marley's tombstone that Tim began to think about the significance of where he was. Last Christmas, while the rest of his family had been celebrating, exclaiming over the giant turkey and playing games, Mr Scrooge had taken Tim onto his knee and told him a story of ghosts and spirits, of the true meaning of Christmas and an old miser who was forced to change his ways. He had told Tim it was just a fairy tale, but Tim had seen through that lie. He believed every word. So he knew that ghosts were real, and that spirits could be dangerous. And now here he was in a churchyard at night.

He gravitated towards Jem, who had just scooped something up off the ground – something that seemed bright and pale – and was inspecting it furtively.

'What have you got there?' Tim asked.

Jem looked uneasy, his hand slipped protectively into his pocket

'I found a sixpence,' he whispered. 'One of the sightseers must have dropped it. Don't tell the others, they'll only start asking for their cut, and I really need the money.'

Tim was not sure – the thing he'd glimpsed in Jem's hand had been pale, and too big to be a coin, but he did not begrudge his new friend a windfall, so he nodded.

'Here it is!' Simeon called nearby, and they quickly ran to join him. There, close to Marley's stone, lay the scene of the crime. The ground about it had been churned into slush, first by busy police boots and then by local sightseers keen to see the location for themselves.

And there, soaked into the snowy ground, was the bloodstain. It had turned brown over the past hours, and crystallised with the first frost, glittering in the lantern light. Tim had never seen so much blood, did not know that this much could come from one person.

The children all shivered theatrically.

'Whose grave is it?' Mags asked.

Winnie held up her lantern, the flame flickering against the mottled stone. She gave a little gasp and drew back quickly, nearly losing her grip on the lantern. Tim expected the children to mock her, but instead Jem kneeled next to her, leaning forward in concern.

'What is it, Wins?'

'It's Butch Parley's grave! We'd better get out of here and don't tell anyone we came.'

The other children scrambled across the scrubland and if it hadn't been for Jem still holding his hand, Tim would have been left behind again. Once they were safely in the shadows outside the gate they leaned back against the wall, panting. Tim looked at them – these brave, daring children who moments before had been ready to tackle anything. Mags was white as one of his mother's fresh-laundered sheets. Jem and Winnie were clearly shaking. Simeon's eyes were downcast, unwilling to meet the others, as if still ashamed of running like a coward.

The name Parley rang a bell with Tim, but he couldn't place it. 'Who's Butch Parley?' he finally asked. 'Why's he so scary?'

'We're not scared,' Simeon snapped. 'We're just realistic. Parley was the leader of the Sharps, the biggest gang around Camden Town. His son Edgar took over after he died – surely you've heard of the Gentleman? If that girl was something to do with Parley we don't want to be involved. Not ever.'

Tim thought perhaps he had heard his parents mention the name once or twice. He had certainly heard of the Sharps and knew enough to avoid them. At the thought that this dangerous gang might be involved and that their trespass might have provoked them somehow, the last of the strength went out of Tim's legs. He wanted to go home.

Ebenezer Scrooge had not enjoyed a restful night. Shaken from his vision at Merrypaw's printworks, he had returned home the evening before with the intention of hiding under his bedclothes with a brandy and convincing himself he had imagined it all.

Instead, he had arrived home to find that Mrs Tassell, after being thwarted at his office earlier, had decided to ambush him at home. She had forced him to listen to a brutal litany of all the things that were going wrong with the Feast for the Poor. The butchers supplying the food were trying to fob them off with cheap, second-rate cuts of meat; the ladies who had volunteered to serve the meal were now throwing their hands up in horror at the thought of actually encountering the poor; worst of all, the local Friendly Society was trying to go back on its promise to offer them a venue as they had received a better offer from another party. He had listened to this with half an ear, his mind racing through what he had seen. Had it been real or was he simply overworked? Was it, as he had told Marley's ghost the year before, simply a case of indigestion?

And was it his imagination, now, that he could feel the cold touch of a finger on the back of his neck – chilly and sticky with blood?

'I suppose you want more money,' he had snapped eventually.

As his curt voice rang out, he thought he heard another clink of that hideous, ghostly chain that awaited him in the next life and shuddered once more. Fear drove him to soften his sharpness with one of his smiles.

'It's not just your money I need, Mr Scrooge, it is your influence,' the widow had said. 'You are in a position of privilege; your name is respected. If you write a strongly worded letter to the Friendly Society holding them to their contract with us I am sure they will relent.'

Eventually he had got rid of her by suggesting that she write the letter herself, and he sign it. He had closed the door with some relief, consumed some cold cuts for his supper and retired. There followed many hours huddled under the bedclothes, his hands clawed into the shabby counterpane, frightened that this new haunting would herald another visit from those three terrifying spirits.

'I have been good this year,' he had repeated. 'Spirits, I have been good!' When sleep finally claimed him, he had plunged into dreams of blood-chested robins, pale, terrified women in grey, strangely familiar dresses and heavy, clinking chains wrapping around his body like iron snakes.

He woke with a dry mouth, an ache in his back and relief that the Spirit of Christmas Yet to Come had not returned to drag him back into his hellish future.

He had also remembered where he had seen that grey gown with the distinctive heart-shaped stain before. It was last Christmas, and at the time Mrs Cratchit had been wearing it. She had been upset when she spilled mulled wine on her sleeve, although the children had been charmed by the shape it had left.

That was the gown, that was the stain he had seen on the young woman's cuff in the churchyard. But how had the gown passed from Mrs Cratchit to this poor unfortunate person? An uneasy feeling crept over him.

Did the Cratchits know her? And might they know why she was following Scrooge now? Because this was different from the hauntings of last year. Marley had spoken to him, had warned him to change his ways. This creature just seemed frightened.

Scrooge left his bedchamber cautiously, looking around him for the ghost. The day was bright and cold, and a shaft of dusty sunlight cut through his hallway as he made his way to breakfast. There was no sign of the ghost, but he could not escape the feeling that it was still there, just outside his field of vision. Waiting.

Another determined woman – this one living – waited for him at his breakfast table.

In his miserly days, Scrooge had employed a housemaid to take care of the basics of the house, the emptying of chamber pots, the acquisition and basic preparation of food. In the wake of his transformation, knowing that he needed to show what an affable sociable fellow he was by entertaining, he had promoted said housemaid to full-time housekeeper. Thus, Sarah had been transformed into Mrs Miller, as was the tradition despite her unmarried state, with several employees working under her. The title had given her new confidence to dominate every aspect of Scrooge's home life.

It had been Mrs Miller's idea to rent the vacant rooms beneath Scrooge's own meagre residence, to add a space for dining and entertaining this Christmas. Mrs Miller had done the best she could, but the rooms, which had previously been offices, were large and cavernous and did not have the cosy effect that Scrooge had been hoping for. He longed to show his nephew Fred and his lovely wife Petunia how well he could keep Christmas, but as his voice echoed off the bare boards he was not sure these rooms, for all their generous proportions, would ever be as merry as Fred's.

Mrs Miller had her own ideas for transforming the house, and they all seemed to involve vast expense. 'The florist is selling ready-made holly wreaths,' she told him as he sipped his morning gruel. 'We shall hang one on the door to show that it is the season of goodwill.'

'Nothing says goodwill like a prickly bush which bears poisonous berries,' Scrooge observed. He had never quite understood that particular custom.

'It is the done thing. Mr Fred will greatly admire it, sir.'

Scrooge gave a sigh. Well, if his nephew thought it was the done thing then it would be done.

'And shall you be doing your own Christmas shopping, sir? Or shall I pick some suitable items up for Mr Fred and his family?'

He felt a stab of horror at the thought of giving Sarah Miller an open purse. 'I shall do it,' he said hastily. Although he had no idea where to start with that. What did one buy a nephew? And should he buy something for Bob Cratchit too? Would he really expect a gift on top of his bonus and extra day off? Surely not. But then what if Bob bought something for him – he would not put anything past that man – and he had nothing to give in return? Scrooge cringed inwardly at the thought.

Christmas was a complicated business. There had to be yule logs and gifts and boughs of evergreen and such a ridiculous amount of wax candles that he would be using a twelve-month supply in the space of a week.

Scrooge could almost feel penny after penny draining away from him. Perhaps he would have gruel for supper as well today.

The office was even colder today than it had been the day before, frost lining the windows and filtering out the light. Even Scrooge felt the need for a fire in the grate before he settled in to work. He wondered if warmth warded off spirits, and threw on an extra lump of coal. Bob arrived, precisely on time as usual, shuffling off that comforter of his and creeping into the office to ask for coal. Scrooge still heard the residue of fear in Bob's voice as he made his request and felt an ache of guilt.

I am a good man now.

And then, in the darkest, dustiest corner of the room, he heard the rattle of a chain. Not his imagination. Not an undigested bit of beef. Fear writhed in his belly and he tightened his grip on his quill pen, as if the feel of it between his fingertips could keep him rooted in the real world.

The chill in the room crept up his spine. He did not look up, fixing his attention on his ledger, on the sound of his pen as it scratched the page. Life was complicated, but money made calm, wonderful sense. He chanted the figures he wrote, as if they were a litany, a spell to ward away the dead, or to drown out the faint clinking of his waiting chain.

'Finch, seventeen and six. Watson, five shillings . . .'

He did not look up.

He felt a closeness, a movement of air upon his neck as if someone were standing there, reading over his shoulder. He tugged at his collar but still, he did not look up.

'Scrapley, two shillings ninepence . . .'

The ghost appeared at the edge of his vision, a flicker, a presence. Its hand held to its throat once more, as if it was trying to hold the jagged tear closed. The ghostly fingers were dirty, with some black substance under the nails, and red with blood. He tried to look away again, but it was as if the apparition held his head in a vice, forcing him to see her.

He wanted to roar, to banish it, but he was afraid of what would happen if he acknowledged her so he stood, transfixed, helpless as a rabbit in the jaws of a fox.

And then the apparition's mouth parted in a silent scream. Scrooge quaked, flinching away and spilling his ink bottle. The ghost held out one bloody hand, pointing at him.

No, not him, at the door.

He turned around and saw Constable Baldock had come back, with another policeman in tow. Scrooge slid to his feet, heart thumping wildly, and charged through to the main office.

'As I have already said, I have nothing more to tell you about this . . .' he began. But the officers weren't paying attention to him. They approached Bob, and his clerk whirled to meet them, politely confused.

'Search his desk,' the other officer ordered and Baldock pulled out the drawers where Bob had been sitting, rummaging through papers, knocking ink bottles together so they clanked.

'This is an outrage—' Scrooge began, but Baldock had found something, drawing a small, unfamiliar leather-bound case from the drawer.

'Is this yours?'

'It's a gift . . .' Bob began. His mouth opened and closed a couple of times, he could not meet the policeman's eye – Scrooge recognised the panicked expression of his honest clerk trying to lie. 'It's . . . ah . . . for my son Peter.'

The officer glared at him darkly and flipped the case open, Then his stern look contorted into one of horror and disgust. He held up the case, displaying a shiny wooden-handled cut-throat razor. One which had dark brown stains at the edges – marks which looked like dried blood.

'That's not the razor I bought!' Bob cried. 'This one is old, and the handle is wood, not bone. Someone must have put it there!'

The officer did not seem to hear him. He held the stained blade up to the light. 'That's the murder weapon all right. Robert Cratchit, I am arresting you for the murder of Christina Ann Parley.'

5

THE NEWS FLEW THROUGH THE STREETS, SPREADING FASTER AND wider than even the broadsides could keep up with. From his office window, Scrooge could hear snatches of gossip.

'Haven't you heard?'

'Who would have thought it of old Bob?'

'Well, it's always the quiet ones.'

He walked over to Bob's desk, the man's papers scattered all around, the fire dying in the grate and, worst of all, the white comforter which had fallen to the floor, trampled by the policemen's grimy boots. Scrooge sank to his knees, a tremendous sense of loss wrenching inside as he gathered the long, wide scarf up in his arms.

'I didn't do it!' Bob's urgent cries still rang in his ears. 'It wasn't me! Officers! Mr Scrooge! I swear. Oh, oh poor Christina, how could this have happened to you?'

It had not even occurred to Scrooge to question Bob's word. Bob Cratchit was a pattern of goodness. He had led a faultless, if somewhat dull, life. He was incapable of violence; he could no more cut a woman's throat than he could compose a symphony.

But he had known the woman who died.

And Scrooge was certain he had lied to the officers outright.

Scrooge busied himself tidying Bob's papers into a pile, as if that mattered. As if Bob would be back in five minutes with a smile and a 'Merry Christmas!'. As he pulled them together the ink on the pages began to move by itself. It seemed to liquefy into a million tiny dots of Stephens' blue-black writing fluid. The pigment oozed across the page, reforming into big, jagged letters.

Scrooge. Betrayer. Liar. Murderer.

'No!' He sprang to his feet, whirling around in search of the spirit. 'No! You have it wrong! Ghost, you have it wrong!'

The last embers of Bob's fire died out and the room filled with an icy fog which scratched at him with cold claws, chilling him to his core. Scrooge let out a breath, a puff of steam twisting out into the cold air. And then she was there, her face inches from his own, tears flowing silently over grey, lifeless skin.

'Please,' he whispered. 'Mercy.'

The ghost's response was a silent snarl of fury. She opened her mouth to scream—

'Mr Scrooge?' It was Jem the boot-boy, trying not to look shocked. 'Sir, I just heard . . .'

The ravening mist was gone; the ghost – vanished. Scrooge took a ragged breath. Another one. He was Ebenezer Scrooge, respectable businessman, reformed miser. A good man, but a man who got things done. He picked up Bob's comforter, folded it neatly and tucked it under his arm.

'I don't know what you heard, but it's wrong,' he snapped, sweeping past Jem out into the street and locking the office door behind him.

'Oh, that's obvious enough! Bob Cratchit wouldn't hurt a mouse!' Jem was trotting to keep up with him. 'The coppers have no idea what they're doing. They probably just read that stupid broadside and felt like they had to do something.'

Scrooge stopped so suddenly that he very nearly lost his balance on the icy paving stones. 'What broadside?'

Jem removed his top hat and rummaged inside it, bringing out a ball of grubby newsprint and opening it out.

THE MURDER OF CHRISTINA PARLEY

The broadside ran on for several paragraphs of detail about the cutting of Miss Parley's throat, the macabre location at which she was found. It informed him that she had been a housemaid working for a respectable family but was believed to have had *an illicit sweetheart*. She had been seen arguing with him near the churchyard on the day before her murder.

The man in question was wearing a large white comforter, evidently too poor to afford an overcoat . . .

Scrooge looked down at the comforter in his arms and came to a decision. He held it out to Jem.

'I need you to run another errand for me. First, give this to Mrs Cratchit, and apologise for the boot prints on it. Then go to Tiny Tim's school and tell him I will not be requiring his services this afternoon. His mother needs him more than I do. Now go.'

Jem hesitated, probably waiting for the coin that should surely come his way given how far he was going to have to run. Scrooge looked hard at him, waiting for the boy to remember how expensive the brushes and blacking had been, and how he was already two payments behind on what he owed.

'Right, will do,' Jem said, and took flight.

Christina Parley. The name did not ring a bell for Scrooge. *But then if she was his fancy piece, he would not have talked about her with me! And if he has the time and money to court a woman other than his wife, I'm definitely paying him too much.*

But then Scrooge chided himself. He was a student of human nature – which was partly what made him so cantankerous – and he would lay money that Bob was not the sort of man who kept secrets, let alone ones involving women.

No, he was certain of that. The spirits had taught him that the world was divided into good men and bad men, and Bob Cratchit was one of the best. He had to be – for who else could Scrooge use as a pattern card for his own redemption?

Scrooge had always maintained that money solved most of life's problems, and his plan was to use it to gain admittance to Bob's cell, but when he presented his bribe, the police sergeant at the desk – a pugnaceous-looking man with ruddy cheeks which spoke of too much liquor – shifted uncomfortably.

'Is it not enough?' Scrooge said irritably. 'This seems like a perfectly reasonable amount.'

'It's not that, sir, it's just that Cratchit currently h-has . . .' Again that awkward look. 'Has another visitor.'

Oho, it must be Mrs Cratchit, reading him the riot act about giving her gown away to a woman such as her.

As he said it, he looked guiltily around the small room. Was the ghost here? Could it read his thoughts? There was a flash in his head, a brief vision of a bloody, screaming face that made him flinch away from the officer's gaze – was it the ghost, or his own mind playing tricks? When he opened his eyes, there was nobody there, just a small, battered-looking side door but it seemed to pulse strangely in his vision, as if he had a fever. He turned back to find the sergeant surveying him curiously.

'I must say, sir, we never expected to be back at your office so soon. It's a coincidence, is it not, that you found the body and the culprit turned out to be your clerk!'

The ghostly writing flashed through Scrooge's mind again. *Betrayer. Liar. Murderer.*

He schooled his features into an expression of outrage.

'I do not know what you are implying, but if you continue to be so rude, I shall report you to your superiors.' He put his hand on the side door and opened it. 'I shall wait in here until my clerk is available.'

'You can't go in there, sir!' the sergeant's voice rang out, but the impulse which had led Scrooge to go through the door was strong, and so was his stubbornness.

The sergeant hung back, strangely reluctant to follow. 'Hope you've got a strong stomach,' he said in a sneering voice.

Scrooge found himself in a cool, dark chamber full of strange and unfamiliar smells with an undercurrent of butcher's shop. Before him stood a heavy table on which lay the shape of a human body, covered by a sheet. He caught his breath. This must be Christina Parley's remains.

'Sir, you intrude!' A small, rodent-like man, stood on the opposite side of the table, a sheaf of papers in his hand. A coroner perhaps.

'I really must ask you to leave,' the man continued, but again, Scrooge's stubbornness kicked in. This man clearly did not know to whom he was speaking.

'As the one who found her I have every right to be here,' he said, and then sweetened the rebuke with a lie: 'I would be interested to hear your expert opinion. I understand you are well versed in all the latest scientific research.'

The man softened a little, and a little more once Scrooge slipped a coin into his palm.

'Victim is female, thought to be in her mid-twenties – although she looks much younger, doesn't she, sir? It goes to show that sin does not stamp itself upon the features! I would place her time of death at between four and six in the evening, the cause of death is severance of the carotid artery, caused by a slash to the throat.'

The man lifted the sheet, pointing to the slash that Scrooge had already seen, that bled still on the ghost's gory neck. Scrooge looked away from the injury and studied her features, suddenly swamped with a deep sorrow that he had never seen her alive.

'Poor child.'

'Hussy more like. She was meeting a lover, and she had definitely been, shall we say . . .' his tongue darted out and moistened his lips, '. . . *sexually active*. Some women are destined to be hit over the head in churchyards, let me tell you.'

As he spoke, the gas lamps in the room flickered and died. Scrooge froze with fear.

'Good lord,' the man said, rummaging for matches. 'What on earth could have done that? He could not see the strange whitish glow which resolved itself into the form of Christina Parley. She stood before him, hand raised as if to strike.

Scrooge tried to cry out, but terror had dried out his throat, and the scream crawled out of his mouth as a half-hearted croak. The ghost's hand pushed into the man's body and a wave of cold radiated out. His body dropped onto the chair behind him where he sat, staring fixedly ahead, seemingly unable to move.

She had touched him. She had put him in some kind of catatonic state. This was no insubstantial phantom, but one with very real power.

The two figures stayed like that for a moment, spectre and victim frozen in a grisly tableau, and then the ghost flickered and vanished. The gas lamps began to glow again but still the man stood gazing glassily ahead.

It took Scrooge a few moments to regain the power of movement in his feet. When he could finally tear his gaze from the frozen coroner, he turned to look at Christina's body.

She had been lovely. Her eyes were peacefully closed, fringed with light brown lashes. A curl of brown hair stuck to her smooth, pale forehead and staring at it, Scrooge felt overcome by the wrongness of it all. She was too young. It was too soon.

He remembered the flash of gold that he had seen in her hand in the churchyard, and – very carefully without lifting the sheet from her body, found her left hand and checked it. Her hand was empty, but there was a dainty ring on her third finger. He reached out and touched the cold flesh, shivering as he twisted the metal. His miserly instincts assessed it − the enamelling was weathered and scratched, but it was a respectable piece of jewellery for one such as her. So she *had* had a sweetheart − and it was unlikely to be Bob, who spent all his money on his growing brood and medicine for the boy.

It's always the sweetheart. That's what people said when an unmarried woman like Christina was killed. What the French called a *crime passionnel.* To Scrooge this was nonsense, a cliche made popular by cheap fiction and tacky plays. In the real world, there was always a true motive underneath, and it was usually financial.

He peered down at Christina's features, studying them as if trying to know her more.

'Who were you?' he murmured. 'And what did you have to do with my Bob?'

There was a sudden sound from the corner of the room, a guttural groan. The snivelling coroner had been restored to life, struggling to understand what had happened to him. He stirred in his chair, eyes bulging and swivelling. His jaw worked, trying to form words, and then he evidently decided to forget it had happened at all.

'Sir,' he said, 'I really must insist you leave!'

Scrooge felt a surge of relief that the man was unharmed and seemingly unaware of what had happened to him. He did not even take him to task for his disrespect as another thought had seized him.

'Hit on the head, you said.'

The man looked mystified.

'You said women like her get hit on the head in churchyards. What did you mean? I thought her throat was cut?'

'Indeed it was, but she was struck on the head first by a blunt instrument, perhaps a cudgel or stick, to allow the killer to do his work.'

'And the piece of gold in her hand? What became of that?'

'What gold? There was no such thing in her hand when she came to me.'

Scrooge looked thoughtful. It would not be the first valuable piece of evidence to vanish at a police station. As Scrooge doffed his hat in polite farewell he felt something shift within him. He was no longer an innocent bystander and accidental haunting victim. He was making an active inquiry into the murder.

The ruddy-cheeked sergeant surveyed him with a half-smile as he emerged, as if hoping to see Scrooge flustered by the sight of the body. Beside him stood the constable who had been at Scrooge's office.

'You, Baldock,' Scrooge said curtly. 'You attended the scene after I found Miss Parley's body. Was there not something gold, a watch chain perhaps, in her hand when you found her?'

Baldock opened his mouth to reply but the senior officer spoke over him.

'Nothing like that was found on the body, sir. Perhaps you were confused, finding a corpse like that. It's enough to shake a man up.'

Next to him, Baldock shifted uncomfortably, his eye sliding to his superior officer. He was the honest one, the weaker link in this situation.

Scrooge crossed his arms, surveying the officers coldly. 'I have a certain reputation, and although I have changed in my approach to life, I can still recognise gold when I see it.'

'I'm afraid we cannot help, sir,' said the sergeant.

Scrooge continued to regard them unflinchingly. Baldock sweated and squirmed.

'I would hate to think it had found its way into the pocket of any of our boys in blue,' Scrooge mused.

That was enough for Baldock. 'Of course not,' he burst out. 'The watch chain was stolen property and has been reunited with its owner.'

The sergeant spat a slur at his colleague and elbowed him aside.

'As I was about to inform you, sir,' he said, 'it is thought that Christina Parley stole the watch chain from a respectable gentleman earlier that day.'

'I see,' Scrooge said. He glanced about him, looking for any sign of the ghost. When she was close he had begun to notice a tension within himself, like a knot of piano wire strung inside his ribcage. He could not feel it now but still he proceeded with caution.

'So, the woman in question was a thief?'

'Well,' the sergeant said with a crooked grin. 'Once a Parley, always a Parley . . .'

'What was that?' a cheerful voice called from the corridor opposite.

The police officer stiffened with fear. 'Just saying how I was glad we found the culprit, sir!'

A tall, young man with an impressive set of side-whiskers stepped from the shadows. He was dressed as a gentleman with a smart watch chain and fob, an elaborate waistcoat and a dark tailored coat of quality fabric. But although he had the trappings of a gentleman, he was clearly not one. It was evident from the cut of his coat that it had not been made for him, and this shirt and collar were not as clean nor as starched as they should be. He still held himself haughtily, his chin tilted, pale eyes gazing disdainfully at the officers. He was using a quality silk handkerchief to wipe his right hand. The knuckles looked red and swollen and . . . was that blood?

'Good, glad we cleared that up,' the man said briskly. He was a little out of breath, his eyes glinting with pleasure. 'I wouldn't want to have to set my friend on you.'

It was then Scrooge noticed another man, at one with the shadows behind him. He was tall, with broad shoulders and was dressed similarly to his companion but lacked the other man's swagger. He carried a black walking cane with a broken handle but didn't seem to need it. He surveyed Scrooge with the blankly hostile expression of a street ruffian, and his hands were also smeared with blood.

'Officer, have these men been attacking a prisoner?' Scrooge asked. 'Have they hurt Bob Cratchit?'

'I have no idea which men you are talking about, sir,' said the sergeant, gazing with interest at a pile of papers on the desk.

Baldock leaned forward, gripping Scrooge's elbow and whispering, 'Hush. That is the victim's brother, Edgar Parley, the Gentleman, and his man Amos Buddle. You know them, don't you?'

Scrooge had indeed heard the names in street gossip, had seen them in broadsides. Names associated with violence and organised crime. So, Christina was one of those Parleys?

His perception of her was slowly shifting from innocent victim to . . . something else. A thief, a member of a criminal family and a spectre who was capable of doing harm. He shivered.

'And who is this pale streak of nothing?' Edgar Parley was not much taller than him, but he seemed to loom over Scrooge, giving him an almost overpowering urge to shrink away. Parley leaned closer. He smelled of gin and tobacco and too much eau de cologne. There was a fleck of blood on one sideburn. Scrooge felt like the air was being crushed out of him.

But Ebenezer Scrooge, respected man of business, would not give in to a petty criminal. He stared back at him, summoning all the complacent confidence of a man who had never had to deal directly with the criminal classes before.

'That is Ebenezer Scrooge, sir, the culprit's employer.'

Parley gave a dry laugh. 'Oh yes, I have heard of you. The former miser, the new-minted lover of Christmas – running through the streets in your nightgown throwing money. Don't you know that Christmas is for children and sentimental fools?'

'I was *not* in my nightgown, I was fully dressed,' Scrooge snapped. He did not know where this exaggeration had come from, but an uncommon number of people seemed to believe it. It had woven itself into his story, taken on a life of its own no matter how many times he denied it.

Parley tucked the bloodied handkerchief into his pocket and leaned in even closer. 'Either way, I will make Bob Cratchit pay for what he did. He isn't just a murderer. He defiled my sister. *My* flesh and blood.'

Scrooge pulled himself up to his full height, forced himself to look Edgar in the eye. 'I can assure you, Parley, that Bob Cratchit is an honest man of good character. He would never think of committing violence on another person.'

Edgar's laugh was loud and unexpected. He looked over his shoulder at his henchman, who joined in – a dry, humourless wheeze.

'Did you hear that, Amos? Not violent – that's rich! Here, look at this.' He pushed back his hair to show a thin white scar on his forehead. 'Bob did that to me when we was eleven years old. He was one of Pa's finest recruits. Maybe you don't know as much about your precious clerk as you think. I hope you're not thinking of buying him out of this somehow, you old fool. Nobody harms a Parley and lives. If the judge don't give him his just desserts, I will. And if you try to stop me, I'll come for you too.'

'Officers, this man has threatened me!' Scrooge cried, but the two policemen had returned to whatever had been so fascinating on their desk. It was not until Parley and Amos had left the police station, their harsh laughter echoing behind them, that the officers looked up, surveying the Gentleman's retreating back with awe.

'I've never seen him in the flesh before,' Baldock said, as if he had caught sight of Father Christmas himself. 'Edgar controls the Sharps and all the other gangs north of here, and Amos is his attack dog. Did you see that walking cane? I've heard about that, it's a sword stick Amos took off some swell. Cut a fellow's fingers off with it once, just because Parley told him to.'

'If you know what he did, why on earth don't you arrest him?' Scrooge said.

'Bloody hell, what part of "fingers cut off" didn't you understand?' the sergeant said. 'We're not paid enough to mess around with the likes of Edgar Parley.'

THE GHOST

I DO NOT MEAN TO STRIKE OUT, I DID NOT EVEN KNOW I WAS capable, but the strange man's words cut through me and I reach forward, as I would in life, to give him a good shove. Just like I once did to the workhouse boys who got too cheeky and once even Amos when he stepped over the line. So I push and my hand sinks into his body. Warmth floods in. I have no body, but the sensation is almost physical, like the feel of my hands around a hot cup of tea on a cold winter's morning.

The man is frozen, stock-still. He can feel this. It is frightening and hurting him, and I am flushed with power and strength. Perhaps this is what I am here to do, to suck the life out of those who did me wrong and have my revenge. The cold metal around my waist writhes against my belly, telling me that I am wrong. I am no avenging angel, just a sinner on her way to hell.

Scrooge whimpers, a fearful cry, and I pull my hand away in shock and tumble back, away from this cold room, from my murderer and my butcher. Back into the darkness again I fall, seeking somewhere to feel safe.

And I land. I am running through the street. I am small and nimble, my hair whipping around me, the cold air filling my lungs. I am alive again, I have a body – I am seven years old.

Just in front of me Edgar and Bob are running.

'Keep up, Tina,' my brother yells. 'Or he'll get you!'

I realise there is an apple in my hand, shiny and juicy and blushed with red, and on my heels, Mr Bunclatter, the fruiterer, descending on me, purple-faced from running and rage.

I let out a joyous laugh as I know where I am now, and nobody knows these alleyways like we do. I veer left into a narrow gap between backyards and slide through a hole in a fence, under a neat row of laundry then round the back of a tumbledown outhouse. Bunclatter's growl of frustration rings in my ears as I put on an extra burst of speed and get away.

'Those Parleys have been stealing since they could crawl.'

I would shove anyone who said that, but it is true. It's how we were raised. We have no apples, and no money. Bunclatter has lots of apples and lots of money. To our young minds, the solution is obvious. As I bite into my sweet, crunchy prize I hear the sliding of metal on metal, and feel a new link close around the first. It drags me down, forcing me to slow to a walk and turns the piece of apple in my mouth to powder.

I weave through the streets without thinking, back to the alleyway behind our house, to Midden Mansion.

I built the mansion myself from old pieces of wood and discarded bits of cloth in the back alley behind Minnie's kitchen. I decorated the walls with my drawings and made a table by turning over a rusty old tin bath. At first Edgar, Amos and Bob laughed at me – the little girl playing house when they were thirteen and almost men. But they soon recognised how good it was to have a place away from Minnie's gin-soaked rants and Pa's changing moods. Hidden from his business partners, who rinse blood off their hands in Minnie's washing-up bowl. We need a place that's ours.

The boys are already lolling on the old blankets I've piled up, enjoying their apples. Their breath, plus the heat of the nearby midden, makes our mansion cosy.

And it is there that we celebrate our Christmas the following day – just like the one Bob and his family have, with feasting and goodwill and gifts.

True, our feast is smaller but it is only partly imaginary. Bob has brought some delicious scraps of potato and even some shreds of goose. Amos has found a bit of pork rind somewhere and I have raisins stolen from Minnie on stir-up Sunday. I have decorated our mansion too. I scavenged a piece of charcoal and drew a jolly image of Father Christmas, the lord of misrule – an old man with a wicked grin, a crown of holly and a flask of ale.

'You know he looks exactly like Pa,' Edgar says. 'What's the point hiding from him if he's staring down at us the whole time?'

'Well, I think it's wonderful.' Bob's voice is heavy with admiration. 'The way you've captured every curl of his beard, it's astonishing.'

Edgar laughs – and because Edgar is laughing Amos laughs too. He hasn't had his growth spurt yet. He's a thin scribble of a boy – so skinny we call him Scrag, and Edgar often has to stand up for him in fights. Even then Amos followed him in everything.

'She needs to practise with those nimble fingers of hers,' Edgar says. 'She's to go to Wantage in the New Year to learn the trade.'

'That old crook?' Bob looks horrified. 'But that means you're to become a . . . a . . .'

'Why are you surprised?' Edgar asks. 'You know what we are, what this family is. You've even joined in when it suited you. She could be a lot worse off – it's less risky than pickpocketing. Or the workhouse. She's got to make use of the gifts God gave her, ain't she?'

A shadow crosses Bob's face. He is different to us: his father has a respectable job; his mother is a God-fearing woman who doesn't like him hanging around with us one little bit. If they find out we'd taken him stealing with us, or that he has liberated some leftover goose to share with the disgraceful Parleys, he'll catch a beating.

But now I wonder if it's even worse than that, if his stealing will form a link in his own chain when he dies.

He only did it because we asked him to.

I feel it again, the solid metallic clink of another link adding to my chain, the solid dead weight of sin.

'Do you truly want to go to Wantage?' Bob asks me. 'What we've done up until now, that's just been larks. Stealing the odd bruised apple, swiping shirts from a washing line. Wantage is a bad lot, you know he is, and you don't have to do it. You don't have to follow your pa. You're good and honest and kind . . .'

'Hark at his preaching, Scrag!' Edgar nudges Amos. 'But how else are we to get rich and get out of Midden Mansion? By the honest labour of our hands? Don't make me laugh.'

Amos laughs on cue, and Bob shifts uncomfortably. I feel a rush of fear that he will go, that our precious hard-won Christmas will be over. But then he smiles.

'Look at us,' he says. 'We're sitting in a homemade hovel which, sorry Tina, stinks worse than a privy. We're using a rusty bathtub as a dinner table, and we're dining on scraps. But we're together. And our hearts are full, aren't they? We don't need to be rich to be happy. We just need each other.'

Amos stares at Bob with hostile eyes, as if he is speaking a strange and disturbing language, but I can see Edgar wavering, mulling over his words. That is the joy of Bob, he can always convince you to do anything.

'Think about it,' Bob says, and then he rummages through his pocket, drawing out a greasy-looking package. 'In the meantime, I brought plum pudding!'

Edgar's expression transforms immediately. 'Bob Cratchit, you're a prince!'

Laughing, we pick the sweet fruity scraps Bob has brought until the paper wrapper is clean.

'This Christmas ain't so bad after all.' Edgar smiles, clapping Bob on the shoulder.

After that, gifts are exchanged. Amos has stolen some sweets from Edmunds' Emporium. He gives Edgar the biggest chunk of hard candy I have ever seen. There is a smaller piece for me and some crushed leftover shards for Bob. Bob gives me a ring he has made out of a plaited piece of ribbon, slipping it onto my finger as if I am a princess in a fairy tale. Then he gives Edgar a battered box which, when opened, reveals a tatty shaving brush with sparse, broken bristles. Obviously a hand-me-down from Bob's father.

'What should I use it for?' Edgar asks. 'I haven't got a single whisker!'

'You have to start shaving to make the whiskers come,' Bob says. 'Everyone knows that.'

We laugh and lie back, our bellies full, our hearts spilling over with this tiny snatched moment of joy, and I wish that Christmas could last for ever.

I think childhood-me senses that everything is about to change.

After that Christmas Edgar will soap his jaw and cheeks with the brush every day, scraping at them with Pa's razor, peering into a shard of mirror, talking about how a gentleman must never be seen with stubble. Like I say, he can talk you into anything, that Bob.

Within a few months Midden Mansion will be gone, ripped apart by a heavy storm. Father will be dead, Minnie will have taken off with all our valuables and I will be huddled in my cot at Wantage's with Bob's words repeating over and over in my head. 'You're good and honest and kind . . .'

And Edgar? He will be treading a path straight to hell.

6

BOB CRATCHIT SHIFTED UNDER THE THIN, STINKING BLANKET, and even that slight movement caused a fresh wave of pain to burst over him. He had never felt such agony, not after the beatings his father had given him, not even after the time that he and Edgar had . . . no, best not think of that now.

His face felt stiff, swollen, more like a mask than something that was a part of him. One of his teeth was loose and wobbled when he pushed at it with his tongue. Breathing hurt – he wondered if Edgar had cracked a rib.

He closed his eyes, dots of bright light flashing behind his eyelids. His old friend had been so vicious, his eyes blank and determined, biting his lip as he dealt that last kick. As if Bob were a stranger or a rat to be exterminated. But then, how would he feel if one of his family had been killed? Grief can do terrible things to a man, and Edgar had been on the edge of madness for many years.

The cell door opened, and Bob braced himself for more blows, turning his head to the wall. But then he heard a quiet gasp of shock, a familiar, curt voice call for warm water and clean bandages. It was Scrooge.

'You, sir? Here?' he cried out, ignoring the pain in his split lip. 'Oh no! Oh no, no, not with the ledgers looking the way they are, and the end-of-month accounts to be wound up – there is too much to do in the office! I suppose you have come to dismiss me. I know you might not trust what I have to say now but may I recommend Nathaniel Jones as an excellent clerk and a willing hard worker? I know he will not steer you wrong. Not like me.'

Scrooge was peering at him, his brow furrowed as if he did not understand Bob's words. Then he shook his head and pulled himself up to his full height.

'What is this nonsense? Of course I would not cast you off at a time like this!'

It hurt to smile, but Bob did so anyway, pouring out his thanks until his master shifted uncomfortably.

'I-I mean I cannot allow this kind of slur against the business to stand,' Scrooge added. 'The very idea that I would suffer such a lapse of judgement as to employ a dishonest man!'

Bob wondered then if he should tell all – about Christina, the trouble he was in, the truth about his past. But his employer had always been quick to judge, to condemn, and Bob had brought the company to the brink of disaster. Scrooge would never forgive that.

His master held a cup of water to Bob's broken lips, waited patiently while he took a sip, and Bob wanted to curl up with shame at the wrongness of it – of Ebenezer Scrooge caring for him. After he had drunk his fill, though, Scrooge's countenance hardened into its familiar old shape, his mouth became a thin line.

'I have heard a few things about you these past hours which do not please me. I have heard from Edgar Parley's own lips that you were once an associate of his. That you . . . ah . . . enjoyed a friendship with his sister. Of course he is a criminal and wont to lie, but why would he lie about this?'

Bob twisted the blanket in his fingers, gazed down at the rough-woven wool.

'I knew him many years ago, sir. I was foolish, I learned from my mistakes, and we have not seen each other for many a long year, not until this day. It's all behind me now, I swear it.'

'And . . . and Christina Parley?' Scrooge looked nervously around the room as he said her name and Bob felt a stab of fear. Maybe the old man knew all, and just wanted Bob to confess it? But he could not, for that would send him to the gallows for sure.

'I did meet Christina on the day that she died,' he said. 'I know, I told you I was leaving the office to get medicine for Tim. It was the worst kind of lie and for that I beg your forgiveness. I met her at four o'clock outside the churchyard to talk about a private matter, but I swear she was alive and well when I left her!'

'And what of this razor blade, found in your drawer?'

'I have never seen it before in my life. I had bought a new one, in a leather case, for . . . for my eldest son . . . but it had a bone handle, not a wooden one. And it was shiny and new, not stained with blood.' Bob's voice cracked as he said it.

Ebenezer Scrooge surveyed his clerk. One white-bristled brow lifted sceptically.

'For your son Peter, eh?'

How did the old man do it? How did he find the lie in everything? Bob shrunk down miserably in his blanket.

'Yes, sir.'

'Peter, who is not fifteen and is yet to sprout a single whisker?'

'Yes, sir. You know that the sooner you start to shave, the sooner the whiskers come in. Please, sir, I beg you to trust me. I did not do this.'

He had never asked anything of his master before, beyond extra lumps of coal and time off for Christmas, and he half expected Scrooge to sneer, but instead his gaze continued to dart around in that peculiar, wary manner. Eventually he nodded slowly, thoughtfully, still staring at the cold, empty air beside him.

Bob felt a strange wave of nostalgia for Scrooge & Marley, for the wobbly desk and chilly office he had left only hours ago. Would he ever see them again? He looked at Scrooge and felt a flush of hope. Scrooge was a man of influence; his word was respected at the Royal Exchange. He could make this unpleasant business all go away.

'You will speak for me, sir?'

Scrooge nodded. 'I will try.'

Just then the cell door opened, and the red-faced officer blustered in with a bowl of water and a half-clean-looking cloth.

'Get yourself cleaned up,' he said. 'You're off to the magistrate to be committed for trial. First step on the road to seeing you hanged. Don't look like that – you're a damn sight better off with a gibbet than with Edgar Parley. Because if you don't swing for his sister's murder he's going to take you apart piece by piece and send your body around Britain by penny post.'

It did not feel like a courtroom, it felt like a circus. The chamber was packed, and Scrooge was forced to cover his nose and mouth with his gloved hand as he encountered the stink of the general populace, a miasma of sweat and gin and perfume and damp and carbolic soap. He had never enjoyed forced proximity to his fellow man but still he felt relief as he edged onto a bench because at least he could not see the ghost.

He was still confused after his interview with Bob in his cell. Scrooge had worked with Bob for years. He knew him – the names and habits of his children, his quirks, the way he chewed the end of his quill pen when he was thinking and exactly how many pieces of coal it took per week to keep him comfortably warm. It had never occurred to him that Bob had secrets, that he had had a different life before clerking. *It is all behind me now*, Bob had said, but Scrooge knew all too well that the past is never truly behind you, that it weaves you into the person you are today. Scrooge felt adrift. How could he become a good man without Bob as his model?

He pushed through the crush of people and found himself a place next to a woman with unwashed blonde hair tucked carelessly under an ill-fitting bonnet. She gave him a gap-toothed smile as she made room for him on the bench. Across the courtroom he could see gentry gathered – *ladies*, even. Good grief, there was Mrs Tassell herself, gaze flickering around the room, her brows pinched together in concern. Behind her was another charity do-gooder Lady Crick, wife of Sir Crispin Crick who was doing terribly well in shipping. A resourceful lady, she had thought to bring opera glasses to improve her view. She was talking to a young fashionably whiskered gentleman who was also no doubt here for the spectacle.

He searched the crowd for Mrs Cratchit and found her towards the front, with her eldest daughter Martha at her side, whispering urgently into her ear. Her jaw was set, her clothing neat as a pin as she stared straight ahead. The picture of virtue and dignity. He thought about going to her side and trying to comfort her, but although she was always polite to him, he sensed her mistrust. *And who could blame her*, he thought with a stab of shame. If he had not been so tight-fisted Tiny Tim might never have been so ill.

Bob Cratchit was dragged into the courtroom, not because he was fighting against his police captors but because he could barely walk. Mrs Cratchit gasped as he clung to Constable Baldock for support. He was hunched, his clothing was stained with blood, one eye blackened and there was a swelling around his mouth which made his face look curiously simian. This was not the gentle, merry Bob Cratchit that Scrooge knew so well. To someone who did not know him, he looked like a brawling ruffian.

'There he is!' A ripple of excitement ran through the assembled crowd.

'Murderer!' someone shouted.

Bob looked at the floor, broken, and Scrooge felt a surge of guilt that it had come to this. After Bob had been dragged off, he had sought out the station's superintendent and petitioned for his release, but the man had refused to listen. Scrooge, with all his influence, could not make the charges go away. This was a travesty, a gross miscarriage of justice.

When the magistrate entered, Scrooge recognised one Mr George Frome, an associate of Scabble's with whom he shared a nodding acquaintance. To Scrooge's mild surprise, Scabble himself was there too. It was true that half of London seemed to be in attendance, but Scrooge had not imagined Scabble to be interested in the latest crime sensation. So, why had he come?

With sickening certainty, Scrooge understood. Scabble was there to make sure that scandal did not attach itself to Scrooge & Marley, that their joint venture would not be dragged into this sordid affair.

Scrooge raised his hand nervously, beckoning Scabble to come over, but the man merely inclined his head and continued to stand aloof by the door.

He is afraid to be seen with me, Scrooge thought.

Out of the corner of his eye, he saw Edgar Parley take a seat towards the back of the courtroom, near to where Scabble was standing. His shadow, Amos, stood behind him, as though on guard. Other members of the public scattered before him, eager to offer him their place. His man Amos sat down beside him, the flimsy bench straining under his bulk. Edgar whispered something to his henchman as a well-to-do-looking clergyman with a size-able belly and a double chin straining against his collar ascended to the stand, was duly sworn in and pronounced to be the curate of St Gideon's Church.

'I witnessed the deceased in the churchyard, with the accused,' he said, pointing at Bob to make himself completely clear. 'They were having what looked to me like a lover's tiff.'

'Do you mean to say a disagreement of some kind?'

The curate nodded. 'The young person was clutching at the man's arm and appeared to be imploring him about something.'

'Could you hear what they were saying?'

He shook his head. 'No, I was too far away, and besides, eavesdropping is a sin. But the chap looked furious and pulled himself away from her. Then I clearly saw him grab her shoulder and shake it.'

Someone seated near Lady Crick murmured 'the brute!'.

It was Scrooge's turn to shake his head. The Bob he knew did not tell lies. He did not meet young women of dubious family. And he would never, ever shake a woman by the shoulders. *But clearly he did lie, clearly he did meet this young woman . . . Have I been mistaken in him all along?*

No, this curate must be lying. As he stepped down, he cast another glance towards the back of the courtroom. Towards Parley.

Next, the red-faced sergeant Scrooge had encountered at the police station, whose name was Dumberley, took the stand.

'The corpse was discovered by the defendant's employer, Mr Ebenezer Scrooge,' he said.

Frome raised his eyebrows, and across the room Lady Crick turned her opera glasses upon him. Scrooge fought to keep his demeanour as still and dignified as Mrs Cratchit's.

'We do not suspect Mr Scrooge to have any connection with the crime,' Dumberley added hastily.

'I should think not!' Frome said. 'Mr Scrooge has his – ah – eccentricities but his name is still good upon 'Change and should be respected.'

Scrooge's cheeks burned, but thankfully the audience lost interest in him as Dumberley described the situation of the poor wretch's body, the dress which police enquiries had confirmed had formerly belonged to Mrs Cratchit. Dumberley notably failed to mention the gold watch chain that had been found in her hand.

His assessment of Miss Parley's character was also very different when there was a judge present.

'It's true she's not from a reputable family, but Christina Parley and her brother have been estranged for many years. She left his care as a child and willingly entered the workhouse, where she remained until she left to go into service with a respectable family. We have reason to believe she did not see her brother for that whole time.'

Scrooge glanced surreptitiously over his shoulder at Edgar Parley, who sat, face neutral as stone as his reputation was discussed. He wondered what the quarrel had been between them. Had it been bad enough to kill over – and then frame his former friend Bob?

'It is clear to us,' Dumberley continued, 'that Miss Parley was a naive innocent who was led astray by a married man, who no doubt charmed her with the gift of a dress and false promises he had no intention of keeping.'

There was a murmur of outrage from the assembled crowd. Women whispered *'poor angel'*. Men proved themselves right-thinking by murmuring threats. The woman next to Scrooge wept into a grubby handkerchief.

Dumberley then held up the razor blade that had been found in Bob's desk and pointed out the dried brown bloodstains. The public craned forward as one to gain a closer look. Bob gave a desperate kind of half-sob. Scrooge could see it as panic, but to the rest of the room, it clearly looked like guilt.

'Watch out, Cratchit, the Gentleman's gonna skin you alive!' a female voice in the crowd shouted, causing a ripple of agreement from the people around her.

Scrooge glanced towards Edgar, whose lip twitched into a superior smile.

'If there is any further disruption I shall be forced to clear the court,' Frome said sternly. 'Now we must hear from the prisoner himself.'

Bob was helped to his feet. The prosecuting solicitor told him that he was not obliged to answer any of the questions put to him unless he chose, and that he was not at all bound to incriminate himself.

'Did you know Christina Parley?'

'I did.'

'And did you know her well?'

'I did.' Bob's voice wavered. 'She was a dear friend. But there was no impropriety between us.'

There were murmurs of 'tommyrot' and 'that's what they all say', but Mrs Cratchit's tightly controlled neutral expression did not waver for a second.

'None at all?' the prosecuting solicitor asked. 'Then your wife knew about this dear friendship? She knew that you had given this young woman her second-best dress?'

Bob's gaze sank lower. 'No, she did not.'

There were wry chuckles from some of the men in the room. Mrs Cratchit reddened, but she remained motionless.

'And she knew you were meeting Miss Parley outside the church?'

'She did not.'

'And your employer, Mr Scrooge? Did you tell him where you were going?'

'No. I told him I needed to fetch medicine for my boy.'

'Mr Scrooge is a good man of business and known to pay you well . . . at least he does now.' A small titter ran around the court and Scrooge flushed. 'Why would you lie to him?'

'It . . . it's private. But I am innocent! I would never hurt anyone, least of all a woman.'

There was a flurry of voices and activity. Mrs Cratchit got to her feet and tried to speak in defence of her husband, but the judge's voice overruled her.

'A wife's testimony has no value,' the judge said. 'Is there nobody else who will speak for you here today? Someone who will bear witness to your supposed strength of character?'

This was his chance. Time to stand up, to declare his own sworn testimony that Bob Cratchit would never commit violence upon a woman, that he would trust the clerk with his life. He took a breath to do so, but then he heard something: the polite clearing of a throat.

He looked over his shoulder to see Edgar Parley's gaze boring into him. His words echoed in Scrooge's ear: *I'll come for you too.*

He was trembling now, but still ready to stand, to speak. But then another figure caught his eye. Aldous Scabble surveyed him with heavy disdain and then, ever so slightly, he shook his head.

What would he think if Scrooge became part of this public spectacle? He would cancel their bargain but, still worse, a man of his stature could ruin Scrooge's reputation. He would never be able to do business in this city again.

But . . . *Bob* . . .

Scrooge remained frozen to his bench, gaze fixed to the floor, shame washing over him until it was too late to stand. The prosecutor was talking at length now about brown smudges which had been found on the defendant's shirt, which could possibly be blood.

'It's not blood. I don't know where those marks came from. The night before I was playing with my children, my shirtsleeve was probably dirtied then and I just did not notice it the next morning. I would never hurt Miss Parley, I swear.'

The jeers of disbelief were open now, as Frome called the court to order. 'Robert Cratchit, it is my intention to remand you until Wednesday next for the production of further evidence and witnesses.'

There was a murmur about the court, and a clerk approached Frome, whispered in his ear.

'Ah yes, I am informed that Wednesday next is in fact the twenty-fifth of December. So we shall instead convene upon the twenty-seventh of the month, in order that we may celebrate the season.'

There was a scoff of contempt from the back of the room. Scrooge glanced back and saw Edgar sneering at the mention of Christmas.

With the court adjourned again, the assembled masses flocked to the door and Scrooge remained on his bench for a few moments longer, hoping to avoid the press.

'How anyone could hurt that poor young thing I do not know,' the woman next to him said, genuine sorrow in her voice. 'She was the sweetest soul and did so much to help the poor!'

Scrooge was perplexed by this statement. He had been under the impression that Miss Parley *was* the poor.

'You knew her?' he asked.

'I did. She was a dear friend of mine from our workhouse days. She was always different, she was. The rest of us had been dragged kicking and screaming in there. She turned up one morning and asked to be let in to get away from that brother of hers. She was sweet and kind and honest – and there's nobody I'd rather have had beside me in a fight!'

Scrooge knitted his brows, struggling to align the two qualities of *kind* and *good in a fight* and to apply them both to the spectre which currently stalked him with such relentless determination.

He leaned in closer, gritting his teeth at the proximity.

'Listen to me, madam, this is very important. Is there anyone else who might have wished the poor girl harm? Anyone other than Bob Cratchit?'

The woman gave a slow smile. 'Oh, there were so many. Like that toff she worked for. Led him a merry old dance, she did! What was his name again? Scratchit? No . . . Scribble? That's it. Mr Scribble.'

After the main attraction was dragged out of court into a waiting Hackney carriage, the last of the crowd quickly dispersed, leaving Scrooge alone feeling drained and disorientated and most of all shamed that he had not spoken out, not once, to defend his trusted clerk.

As if sensing weakness, the ghost flickered into life, inches from him, her neck still bleeding scarlet, soaking into the faded grey of Mrs Cratchit's dress. There was a smell, too – lavender and blood. She gazed at him, accusing.

His breath grew short, tiny puffs of steam; his shoulders tightened, rigid with fear. If she took him now, froze him like she had the man in the mortuary, he would deserve it.

'I'm sorry,' he whispered. The spirit screamed silently, her mouth a gaping red chasm. It warped and grew, bigger and bigger as if to swallow him. Scrooge cried out, throwing up his arm in defence. But the pain and cold were relentless, he felt his very soul being dragged from his body and—

A polite cough caused him to look up into the piercing grey eyes of Aldous Scabble.

'I thought I would find you here in this circus,' he said, his every word dripping with implied contempt. He drew out a fine gold pocket watch and inspected it. 'We are late already. The paperwork is ready and waiting at Merrypaw's for you to sign. To business, Mr Scrooge.'

The apparition had gone, and with it the sense of cold, of being swallowed whole. Scrooge's heartbeat began to return to normal. He clenched his gloved hands tight, urging himself to stay calm, professional. He was a sober man of business, reliable and solid. Not weird, not haunted and definitely not the sort of man who would abandon his work merely because his clerk had been arrested for murder.

'Very well,' was all he said, in clipped tones. As he followed his business colleague out of the courtroom, the blonde woman's words sprang back into his mind. She'd said Christina had worked for a Mr Scribble. And it seemed that Scabble had recovered his watch and chain after losing it the day before. And Merrypaw had mentioned that he was one for the ladies . . .

Scrooge shook his head. It was impossible. Scabble was a grandee, a leader of the business community, well known to be of upstanding moral probity, not to mention Scrooge's new business partner in an exciting and profitable new venture. The idea that he could be a vicious killer was unthinkable.

Absolutely unthinkable.

7

TIM HAD NOT REALLY TAKEN IN THE NEWS THAT JEM HAD BROUGHT.
Yes, he had heard the words 'your pa's been arrested for murder'
but they didn't make sense.

As he and Jem moved through the streets he could hear the
gossip buzzing around them, the broadside sellers screaming head-
lines of FOUL BLOODY MURDER and CAMDEN TOWN MAN ARRESTED
YOU WON'T BELIEVE WHO IT IS. He could not comprehend that
they were talking about his father. This was not his reality, this
was not his life.

But then he arrived at the family's cramped two-storey terraced
house to find Mother was not there.

Mother was *always* there. She rose before him each morning,
so that by the time he stumbled sleepily downstairs the stove
was already on and the air was warm and full of her voice. At
night she would stay up late, talking with Father or bent over
the sewing that had kept the family afloat for years. Other family

members came and went, but Mother's presence was constant, as solid and reliable as their worn oak kitchen table.

Instead, his eldest brother, Peter, sat there, holding court over a concerned huddle of friends and neighbours and assuming the role of man of the house as if he had been rehearsing it for years. His thirteen-year-old sister Belinda was in Mother's place at the stove, heating a large and delicious-smelling pot of soup.

Unease seethed in Tim's stomach. This was all wrong.

'Mother's at court,' Peter explained, ruffling his brother's hair the way Father often did. 'That's a big room where a judge sits. He will hear Father's case and hopefully release him. Have courage, Tiny Tim. Not a soul on our street believes these lies and the judge will see through them soon.'

There was a murmur of agreement from the surrounding neighbours.

'He's a good man.'

'He helped us so much when we had that trouble last year!'

'Salt of the earth! And as for the girl, she comes from a family of ne'er-do-wells . . .'

But Tim was not reassured. Peter had spoken with that gentle, soothing tone that his parents used when they lied to him, and the feeling in the pit of Tim's stomach got worse – a curdling mix of anger and panic and sheer helplessness.

Then he remembered the one saving grace: his father was not without powerful friends.

'Mr Scrooge will speak for him,' he said.

Belinda, who was spooning out a bowl of soup for her brother, scoffed. 'That old skinflint? Only if there's money in it for him.'

She dropped the ladle back into the pan at the sound of hooves outside. The Cratchit children, plus assorted hangers-on, crowded outside to see a Hackney carriage standing in the street, the horse stamping. Tim's heart leaped. A cab – only Mr Scrooge could afford one of those! He must have intervened, secured Father's release and was bringing him home in style. Beastly Belinda would have to eat her words.

But instead Mrs Tassell descended, followed by Mother. There was a bleakness, a mechanical nature to the way she moved. His eldest sister Martha supported her – she had been crying too.

'They have committed your father for trial,' Mother said quietly. 'It will take place next Friday and he will be held in prison until then. I'm afraid your father won't be with us for Christmas this year.'

The entire company fell silent with shock. Everyone knew how important Christmas was to Bob, how joyful and playful it made him.

'But . . . Mr Scrooge, did he not speak up?' Tim's voice cut through the silence. He felt the reactions of the people as they looked at him, their emotions shifting to one he had experienced all his life – pity.

'Mr Scrooge was there,' Mother said, her tone tight and clipped. 'But he did not speak. Not a word.'

A strange, sickly feeling curdled inside him. Belinda poked out her tongue, but he ignored her. This was his fault. He should have been there. If he had been at his master's side things would have been different.

Back in the kitchen, he drank his soup as Mother sat Mrs Tassell down at the table and bade Belinda make tea for their guest, 'and mind you use the good teacup.' The widow laid her little notebook out on the table, and they began to discuss the wording of a letter to the superintendent.

'The detective department is newly established,' Mrs Tassell said. 'They are still trying to prove themselves useful and they won't want to admit they are wrong, so they are unlikely to go looking for another suspect now they have one. But they do not always have public opinion on their side.'

Mrs Cratchit's red, work-worn fingers curled into fists.

'Have you seen what those broadsides have been saying, ma'am?' She thrust a crumpled piece of paper towards the widow. 'Of course not, a lady such as you probably doesn't read such things but this is what sealed his fate. See, here? *The man in question was wearing a large white comforter, evidently too poor to afford an overcoat . . .*

'That's what started it all! Everyone around here knows about my Robert and his white wrap. He could quite easily have bought himself a coat this past year but there's always something better to spend his hard-earned money on – coal, clothing for the children, a bit of beef to build up Tiny Tim's strength . . .'

Tim felt the familiar warm flush of guilt combined with love for his parents. He ducked his head down and took another spoonful of soup.

'As soon as that broadside came out, the whole street knew the man it described must be Robert . . .' Mother's voice cracked.

A shadow seemed to cross Mrs Tassell's face, and she fiddled with her pencil. 'And Mr Cratchit never told you he knew this young lady?'

Mother glanced at Tim and Belinda, who both pretended they weren't listening, and then shook her head. 'No. They were acquainted in childhood, but Robert had put all that in the past. I had no idea that he had given my second-best dress to her until the police came asking about it . . .'

She bit back a sob, pressed her lips together. 'But we will keep Christmas, all the same,' she said. 'It will not be a merry one without him, but it is what my Robert would want.'

The brave tremor in her voice was too much for Tim to take – he pushed his bowl away and slipped from the table.

The air was cooler out in the narrow hallway, less full of noise and steam and his mother's hot, feverish desperation. He sat on the cramped staircase, trying to think of what to do and was overwhelmed with a sense of uselessness, of his own tininess. He looked down at his thin, white bony hands and bit back a sob.

'Right, what's the plan?'

Jem was there, wiping soup from his mouth and sitting next to him. When Tim did not answer, Jem continued. 'I know you want to do something. You're not the sort to just sit around when your pa's mouldering around in jail. So come on, let's get on with it.'

Tim hesitated.

'Don't tell me you're still thinking that old Ebenezer will solve everything!'

Perhaps it was his belly full of soup, or perhaps he was just tired of feeling so useless and small, but Tim suddenly felt a flush of strength and determination. Jem was right, he couldn't just sit there waiting.

His mind flailed about as he remembered his father slipping out of the office on the day of the murder. He'd said he was going to get Tim's strengthening medicine, even though he knew full well there was plenty left in the bottle they kept on the mantel.

'He came back with a small brown package,' Tim told his friend. 'I saw it in his pocket and asked what it was, and he said it was boring grown-up stuff. I thought it might be a Christmas gift for me so I didn't ask any more questions, but what if it wasn't?'

There was only one place in the house where the boring grown-up stuff was kept. 'I think I know where he put it,' Tim said. 'The problem is I'm not allowed to touch it.'

'That sounds like the best place to start then.' Jem's smile was crooked, infectious. *Ruffian.* But right then, Tim could not think of a single other thing he could do.

Just off the cramped hallway at the front of the Cratchits' house lay a tiny parlour which was used only on the rare occasion that the family had extremely respectable visitors, but even then was often forgotten. Even Mr Scrooge sat in the kitchen on his occasional visits and Mrs Tassell had walked straight past it to establish herself in the kitchen. His mother cleaned the parlour assiduously twice a week, dusting off the unused chairs and rubbing beeswax into the dark wooden cabinet in the corner which, she had told him proudly, had been in her family for two generations. In the bottom of this cupboard, beneath a stack of unused good linen, lay the family strongbox.

When he was very small, Tim had thought it might be a treasure chest, but Father had laughed and explained it simply contained important but very dull things essential to the family. And he must never, ever touch it. Ever.

Jem closed the door and positioned himself just inside, keeping guard as Tim retrieved the box. His fingers trembled as he got the key out of a drawer and slid it into the lock. At school once his teacher had read them the tale of a boy who told a single 'white lie' which had spun into bigger and bigger sins until the boy ended up on the hangman's gibbet. Would this happen to him? Was this his path to badness? He froze. *If I turn bad, then all is lost.*

'Come on, Tim,' Jem whispered. 'It'll be all right. We're doing it to help your pa.' His voice was gentle, patient even, and Tim wondered how a ruffian could be so kind. It occurred to him that, as a ruffian, Jem might return later and steal the strongbox, but his instincts told him that was more of a scoundrel thing to do.

He felt a rush of guilt and excitement as he opened the box with a click but as he did so he heard a bashing at the door, a harsh masculine cry.

'Open up! Police! We have orders to search this property!' Tim made to shut the box, but Jem whispered at him to keep going.

'Be quick, we've got to see what's in there before the coppers come in.'

Trembling, Tim scrabbled through the grubby, dull-looking papers. He found one brown paper package which looked promising, but it turned out to be full of several locks of baby hair tied with ribbon and neatly labelled, one for each Cratchit child. His heart beat faster as he kept searching.

In the hallway voices rose as the neighbours who had been gathered in the kitchen barred the policemen's way, jeering at them.

'Get out of here! You should be ashamed! Raw lobsters, harassing an innocent family like this! Go knock some drunks on the head, you're not wanted here!'

'Please, friends!' Mother's voice was strained and desperate. 'Do not make a scene. We have nothing to hide, officers.'

'Come on, search faster,' Jem urged.

Birth certificates. Keepsakes. Newspaper cuttings referring to Mr Scrooge's transformation but underneath it all . . . there it was. Tim's hand closed around it, and he stuffed it into his shirt, slammed the strongbox lid closed. He fumbled for the key.

In the hallway, Mrs Cratchit was speaking soothingly to the neighbours and the police officers. Smoothing things over.

'Let me,' Jem shoved him aside and turned the key smoothly in the lock, sliding the box back into place in the cupboard, pushing it shut with his booted foot and slipping the key under the cabinet, out of sight.

When the police looked in on them, the two boys were pouring out a set of spillikins onto the floor. A pair of innocent non-ruffians engaged in a wholesome parlour game. Tim was painfully conscious of the paper rustling between his shirt and vest, and was astounded the police didn't hear it too.

'Go and play outside, boys,' the officer said. 'We could do without you two underfoot.'

Jem protested that he had always wanted to be a police officer and wanted to see how they worked, but he was too cheeky-looking to carry this off and within moments they were ejected onto the pavement, along with the other outraged occupants of the house, with the exception of Mrs Tassell who insisted on staying to 'ensure the officers performed their duty without overstepping'. Tim lingered guiltily near his mother for a while, feeling it was his job to comfort her, but then Jem grabbed his arm and dragged him into the nearby alley.

'Come on, I'm desperate to see what this is!'

Safely hidden, Tim reached under his shirt and pulled out the package, unfolding it carefully.

Jem whistled slowly and swore. Tim gaped. He had never seen anything like it before in his life. It was treasure.

It was a bundle of fresh five-pound notes.

They counted it together and it came to fifty pounds. How could his father have something this valuable just lying around in his strongbox? And then say there was not enough money for Tim to have a toy sailboat for Christmas?

Attached to it was a note. The writing was neat, looping and perfect, the kind the hardest-working children often produced at school and then he would be forced to copy.

Last one. Until Christmas and Midding Mansion! Your dearest friend, C.

THE GHOST

I PULL AS HARD AS I CAN AWAY FROM EBENEZER SCROOGE. HE disgusts me. I see him surveying my corpse. I see him looking down at Bob Cratchit, frightened and bleeding. I hear his dry, rasping tone as he talks about making money. Bob told me that he has changed since Christmas last, but I cannot see it. He is everything I hate, and he killed me. I want to plunge my hand into his feeble, skinny chest and wrap my cold fingers around his heart. But instead, I run from him for the sake of my own soul, rather than his.

My chain is heavy enough already. It moves and clinks against my waist as if it is alive. It shows that however hard I tried I could not escape being a Parley. A liar, a thief and worse.

I realise my fingers are clutching a rough piece of charcoal and I look up. I am back in the past again. I remember this. I am drawing Father Christmas, the master of revels, on the greasy grey surface of Pa's old wall . . . why? Ah, the memory comes back. It is Christmas Eve, two years after our celebrations at Midden Mansion. Pa is dead,

92

our stepmother Minnie is who knows where and this is my brother's kingdom now.

It looks different to when Pa was running the place. The table is a jumble of oddments – stolen wallets, purses and reticules, weapons, empty gin bottles. But on the grubby plastered wall is something which doesn't quite fit: a large gilt-framed mirror carved with cherubs, leaves and fruit.

It reflects Edgar, who sits at the head of the table, talking to Amos. My brother's friend has grown tall and strong this past year – nobody dares call him Scrag now except me, occasionally, when I am foolish enough to bait him.

Edgar is admiring his new prize, a high-crown beaver hat with a lustrous shine.

'Fogo Finn took it off a toff just last week,' Edgar tells his friend, setting the hat on his head, adjusting it until it sits at a jaunty angle. The fit is a little small, but Edgar wears it with style – his hair is much more well kept than his kitchen, and at last some whiskers seem to be coming in.

'Do you know what this makes me?' he asks, but expects no answer. 'It makes me a gentleman. Not just because this hat is fine quality, as befits a man of means such as myself, but because I'm not the one who stole it. Finn took it, and because he's my man, he gave it to me.' Edgar flashes a grin. 'I grow fat off the labour of others. And if that don't make me a gentleman, I don't know what will.'

I concentrate on Father Christmas's crown, drawing a berry on the mistletoe.

'That's not to say I'm afraid to get my hands dirty, on occasion,' he adds. 'Generals still go into battle, after all, don't they?'

'So, tonight. What's the plan?' Amos asks. That's all he ever says these days. Years ago, the four of us had slipped out to the travelling fair

93

and seen an automaton — a creature of wood and metal, nuts and bolts that only performed limited movements. That is all Amos is now; he does not move unless Edgar winds his key and sets him off. I remember wishing I had someone to love me that much.

'In through the larder window,' Edgar says. 'Old lady Tatterbrook is soft-hearted, she's sent all her other servants home for Christmas. It's just her and the foreign maid that ain't got family. You see to her, I'll go upstairs, tie up the old witch and search for the jewels. They'll be hidden in a box under the bed — they're always hidden in a box under the bed.'

Dry laughter from both — it makes them feel like they know everything, like they're Pa.

I think about this woman somewhere across town, who spends every Christmas alone so her servants can see their families. I imagine her tied up and cowering in the cold while joyful bells peal out over the city. Is this what my brother has become?

'Do you have to do this?' I do not think I've spoken aloud until I see Edgar is staring at me, his lip curling. 'What are you even doing here? Don't Wantage have work for you?'

I picture Wantage, with his bulbous, putrescent nose, his stinking breath and the stick he keeps propped up by the fireside and I shudder. I hate him and I hate the work he makes me do.

'Even he lets his workers go home for Christmas,' I say. 'I thought you'd be pleased to see me.'

'And why are you scribbling that picture of Pa on my wall?'

'It's Father Christmas! Just like at Midden Mansion, remember?'

Edgar gets up, grabs the bucket of water that rests by the sink and dashes it against my drawing. The old man's features blur and drip, his cheery smile twists into something monstrous.

Edgar points at the ornate mirror. 'This is the sort of decoration I want in my place. No hand-drawn rubbish but high art, stolen from the very finest people!

'We don't need Father Christmas. We don't need Christmas at all. Christmas is for sluggish folk with no ambition, office boys like Bob Cratchit in his stiff white collar, toadying to rich men in the hope they'll give him a copper or two. And he thought I'd better myself by joining him! He even took me to meet his master!'

Here, the necessary pause for Amos's scorned laughter.

'Well, we're not like him,' Edgar continues. 'We don't have masters. We're free. If we make enough money, we'll have Christmas every day of the year and that bony old bird and her jewels will help me get there. Then you can come back from Wantage and rule my empire with me. Won't that be grand?'

I sink down onto Pa's old rocking chair, the horror of my life stretched out before me. Years as a slave and a tool for Wantage, then a life of crime and cruelty with Edgar — that is if we did not all end up on the hangman's gibbet.

'I'd rather starve,' I say.

Edgar and Amos laugh together, long after the joke has ceased to be funny. They slap their thighs, wipe away imaginary tears. 'She'd rather starve!' my brother laughs. 'Then off to the workhouse with you — a few months there and you'll soon come crying back to me.'

Edgar and Amos fall asleep just before dusk. They need their rest if they are to be up in the night robbing. I sit there in the darkened kitchen thinking about Mrs Tatterbrook and the fate that awaits her, until an idea springs into my mind.

I could warn her. I could stop this happening.

I light a lamp and find a stray piece of paper in a stolen satchel. With the last stub of my charcoal I write a note warning the old lady that robbers will come to her house that night. I sign it 'A Well-Wisher', fold it in my hand and creep from the house.

The night is cold but bright as I move silently through the streets, weaving past laughing revellers and the thieves who prey on them. I wonder if I will be safe. But I am Butch Parley's daughter, Edgar Parley's sister. I may not be proud of that, but it does offer some protection.

The house Edgar mentioned is on the edge of a serene crescent with neat black railings and smart brass door fittings. A lamp burns in an upper-floor window, but the rest of the house is in darkness. So, she truly has sent her servants away.

The note is hot and damp in my palm as I creep closer to the front door. My plan is to push the paper under it, knock on the door and run, but as I start to push the paper, I hesitate.

Mrs Tatterbrook is the mother of Colonel Tatterbrook, a famous military man. If she is warned, he might set a guard upon the house. What if the guards are armed with guns?

Indecision curdles in my stomach. Edgar could get hurt, killed even. If he is caught, he could go to the gallows.

I have been to hangings. I have seen them all – long drop, short drop, ones where the rope snapped and the condemned broke his leg, but was dragged straight up again for another try. Ones where the hangman made a mistake and the poor wretch danced for what felt like hours, struggling to survive. Everyone loses control of their water, everyone dies with piss dripping from their feet and their faces contorted with fear. I cannot see Edgar dance the Newgate jig. I cannot be the one who makes it happen.

I pull back into the shadows, push the note into my bodice, and flee.

The next morning the Christmas church bells ring, and Edgar and Amos celebrate. They have bags of jewels, a strongbox full of coins, and some pieces belonging to the Colonel, who is away with his regiment. A new gold fob to add to Edgar's gentlemanly ensemble, a sword stick topped with a carved ivory elephant for Amos. And they have stories. How she whimpered! How she wept! How she begged them to leave the silver locket, it had sentimental value.

It tears at my heart, makes me dizzy and weak. I could have saved her and yet, I chose to protect Edgar instead. I fall back onto Pa's old chair, and that's when I feel it. Another ice-cold link added to the chain at my waist.

Clink.

Edgar is steaming drunk when he finds the note. It must have slipped out of my bodice while I was clearing up after the feast that was, he insisted, definitely not Christmas dinner.

For a while he cannot speak, simply shows the paper to Amos and then hurls it into the fire. He does not beat me as Pa or Wantage would. Instead, he snatches me up by the hair, pushes me to the door and throws me into the slush outside.

'Get out. I never want to see your traitorous snitching rat face again. I no longer have a sister.' He steps outside, stands in the middle of the

street, *holding out his arms like a showman introducing an exciting new act. 'Let everyone know this, from this day forth I no longer have a sister!'*

I do not go back to Wantage on the twenty-sixth of December that year. Instead, I present myself at the gate of Clack Street workhouse.

I tell myself that if I am no longer Edgar Parley's sister, then I will be someone else. Someone good and honest and kind.

As the door opens, I feel the pull again of the chain at my waist as another link adds itself. It seems lying to myself is also a sin, a burden to bear in the next life. Because in the end I did not change my ways. I stayed a sinner, and my sins would get me killed.

8

THE MAKING OF DEALS AND THE MAKING OF MONEY HAD ALWAYS been a great comfort to Scrooge and yet as they arrived at Merrypaw's printworks the noise and bustle added to his sense of unease and disorientation. Why had he not spoken out in court? Why had he betrayed Bob Cratchit when he needed him most?

For a few moments the noise around him became muffled, and he thought he could hear the soft clink-clink of a chain being dragged across the floor. He hadn't just let Bob down, he had given in to his old, baser instincts of profit and self-preservation. Now an extra link awaited him in the afterlife – one he fully deserved. Out of the corner of his eye he caught sight of her again, the ghost, flitting in between the noisy printing presses. Scrooge tensed, bit the inside of his cheek to keep from crying out at her to let him be.

He and Scabble started up the stairs towards Merrypaw's office, but a clerk intercepted them and directed the gentlemen to the factory floor.

Scrooge passed the mighty presses, watching as a fresh new batch of robin cards were printed out and taken aside for cutting. A row of women added extra colours by hand, bringing the design to life.

Merrypaw himself was standing near a large, long table leaning over a set of Christmas cards with his foreman. Today's waistcoat was embroidered with a pattern of red-breasted robins. Workers sat around him, clearly taking a break from their labour, nibbling hunks of bread and cheese, talking, cleaning the ink off their hands with grubby rags.

'Ah, Mr Scabble, Mr Scrooge, welcome!' Merrypaw threw out his arms in a welcoming gesture, then shook Scabble's hand before moving onto Scrooge's, pumping it up and down with a good deal of energy. His hand was warm, the palms smooth, his grip like iron. 'You have found my little mess area. As you can see I have all this extra space, which is not, as yet, full of printing presses. So I created this small place for my workers to eat, to talk through the problems they may be encountering with their work, or simply to take a break.'

'And they do not sit here all day, slacking?' Scrooge asked.

'Oh lord, no! They take short breaks and return swiftly to work.' Merrypaw raised his voice so it could be heard by his workers. 'And if we get everything done in time, we shall be feasting at this table on Christmas Eve – and then this whole building will be empty on Christmas Day, because my people will be at home with their families!'

There were some small cheers from the assembled workers. Scabble muttered something sceptical under his breath but Scrooge wondered what it would feel like to be beloved in this way. Like his own former employer, Fezziwig, who had been a father figure to all his young employees and . . . oh, he had thrown such Christmas parties!

Scabble drew out his watch again, and Scrooge recognised the habit for what it was. A tactic, a way to say *your chit-chat bores me*. He used it to set people off balance and hurry them along. But it also gave Scrooge the chance to look at the chain more closely. It was indeed similar to the one he had seen in Christina Parley's hand, if not exactly the same.

But that does not mean Mr Scabble is involved, he reminded himself. The police themselves had said the chain was stolen property and had been returned.

A flicker. A chill. And the ghost was at his side. Scrooge determined to ignore her, to block her out. He would not behave like a frightened child in front of his business associates.

'Well then, gentlemen,' he said with only the slightest tremor in his voice. 'Let us get down to business.'

Merrypaw led them both up to his office, which was as overheated as before, but in the corner upon the stool previously occupied by Tiny Tim sat a gentleman with a sketchpad on his knees. He looked up as Scrooge entered the room, but his eyes shot straight back down to the page and he began sketching.

'Ignore him,' Merrypaw said. 'He is one of our finest engravers and we are running behind at the moment – even I have staffing problems sometimes! He is working very hard to catch up.'

Paperwork was brought forth, and Scrooge parsed the dry, legal words with his usual vigilance, feeling sad that Bob was not at his side to read it too. He had an eye for detail, a talent which Tiny Tim shared. The contract seemed standard enough – there were the terms of his investment, his portion of the business. His gaze flew naturally down to the small scrawl on the final pages. Funny how clerks' handwriting became more cramped and illegible when the finer, less appealing details of a deal were being laid out. He found nothing too amiss there, though. The agreement stated that Merrypaw retained something called *creative control* over the images on the proposed Christmas cards and Scrooge did not have a problem with that, he was no artist. There was also a clause which stipulated Scrooge would be publicly involved with the venture. He had expected this, after all Merrypaw had said his association with Christmas was partially what drew them to him, but it felt strange to see it in black and white. To put his name and his reputation out in public for all to see.

But then, would this not please the spirits? To have Scrooge famous across the land as a caring, warm-hearted, festive man? It would be known by all that Ebenezer Scrooge was a man who knew how to keep Christmas well.

'Our other associate, Dr Bailey, is not here again? Is he still unwell?'

'Tied up with matters of research,' Scabble said. 'He has already signed, and I shall speak for him if you have any questions about the scientific process.'

'I'm sorry to see your young assistant is not here this time,' Merrypaw said as Scrooge's pen hovered over the line where he was to sign next to the other parties. 'A bright young lad, that.'

Scabble gave one of his laughs, dry and brittle as straw. 'I expect he is needed at home, given his father's current situation. I trust there will be no scandal upon our venture, Scrooge? The man will be dismissed forthwith? I am all sympathy. It is all too easy to be deceived as to the character of one's staff.'

Scrooge immediately signed the contract with impressive speed, splotching the paper with ink in his haste. It was done now; they could not take it back. And now he was free to speak. He could not betray Bob again, the way he had in court.

'It is most unfortunate, I am sure, but I am convinced of Cratchit's innocence. And did you not also know the victim, Mr Scabble?'

Scabble flared his nostrils in disgust.

'The girl worked for us for a time, but I was forced to dismiss her, and she has not been part of my household for almost a year now. You would do well to follow my lead, Scrooge. This is a nasty business.'

There was a pause, an impasse between them, the silence only broken by the increasingly frenzied strokes of the artist in the corner. The man looked intently at Scrooge, then bent down and continued his work.

'Well then, let no more be said about it!' Merrypaw cried, breaking the silence and tipping some rich golden liquid into three glasses. 'I insist you both join me in a toast to our success, and to the merriest Christmas we have all ever had.'

Scrooge delivered another of his particular smiles, but it was a facade. Because as the glasses clinked together, they sounded like the clinking of chains. As if the sound had summoned her, the spirit appeared behind Merrypaw's desk, grisly and baleful, fixing him with her heavy, serious stare as if to say: *You will never be happy, sinner. Not while I am here.*

The pressure of being near the spectre was like an itch under the skin, a compression behind the eyes. Worry about Bob and guilt at his own behaviour weighed him down. Scrooge would steady his nerves in the only way he knew how. He hailed a cab – a decadent expense but a worthy investment as it enabled him to collect some ledgers from the office and bear them home, to work on after he had dined. He longed for the familiar smell of ink, the certainty of his rows and columns. If he kept gazing at the page, he could ignore the ghost at his side, the unruly chaos of his life.

His house looked different when he arrived. There was Mrs Miller's precious holly wreath tied to the door, its twisted, pointed leaves hanging close to the door knocker which had once transformed into Jacob Marley's face. *Maybe that will stop it happening again*, he thought. *A good prickling would serve the old fool right.* But that was not the only difference. The house was suspiciously well illuminated with candlelight twinkling through the hallway windows.

'Mrs Miller!' he called as he walked into the door. 'What is the meaning of this extravag—?'

He trailed off. On a chair next to the door sat an unknown serving woman of middle years, engaged in knitting. She looked up from her work, then stood to bob a curtsy and cleared her throat.

'I am Mary-Ann, sir. I am Mrs Tassell's maid. She has instructed me to remind you that there is an emergency meeting this evening to discuss the Benevolent Feast for the Poor.'

Scrooge groaned. He had written enough banker's drafts for this, couldn't Mrs Tassell and her team of ladies just sort the rest of it out themselves? No, he could not deal with this right now. Not with the ghost flitting about him, and Bob in prison and his work falling shockingly behind . . .

The maid sighed.

'My mistress did say as how you would try to cry off, but that I was not to take no for an answer and that I was to stay here until you agreed to accompany me.' She made another small curtsy, as if to soften the blow. 'Begging your pardon, sir.'

Planning to ignore Mary-Ann until she went away, Scrooge turned to go into the new downstairs parlour, meaning to bellow again for his housekeeper, but as he opened the door he ran smack into a wall of pine needles.

Scrooge dropped his ledgers in shock.

It was a tree. A whole fir tree, taller than him, *inside his house.* What insanity was this?

'Oh, thank heavens you're here, sir,' said a voice from among the boughs which he recognised as Mrs Miller. 'I thought I could do this by myself, but this thing really is rather tricky. I have set up a pot by the window, but I cannot seem to move it there by myself. Mary-Ann did help a bit, but we could only get it this far.'

'It's . . . a tree . . .' he repeated. 'A whole, entire tree. It's wet and . . . good God, is that a bird's nest?'

Scrooge knew that the royal family went in for this kind of thing, that it was some tradition brought over from Germany but really, if one lived in a castle one did all sorts of odd things which weren't suitable for respectable folk like himself.

'I just thought Mr Fred would love to see it, sir,' Mrs Miller said. 'But if I could prevail upon you to take the trunk end, while I handle the top?'

At those words, Scrooge surrendered. He longed to show his nephew just how well he could keep Christmas.

As it turned out, Mrs Miller was an absolute stickler for the straightness of a Christmas tree. It took almost an hour of heaving, propping, shoring up on one side and then another to get it standing to her satisfaction. Scrooge was tired and even crankier than usual, his hands sticky with tree sap. Even the tolerant Mary-Ann was beginning to look weary.

'There.' Mrs Miller smiled, brushing pine needles off her apron. 'That's perfect. Now all we have to do is decorate it. I have a very precise plan of how to do it and will instruct you both.'

Scrooge and Mary-Ann exchanged aghast glances. This could take hours.

'I'm sorry, Mrs Miller, I must return to Mrs Tassell to help with her meeting.' Mary-Ann stood, brushing the pine needles from her skirts.

'And I must go with her,' Scrooge added, trying to ignore Mary-Ann's triumphant smile.

With a pang of regret, Scrooge left his ledgers behind on the hall table, noticing as he did so a rectangle of paper on the doormat which looked as though it didn't belong.

As he bent to pick it up, he felt a chill behind him and knew that the ghost was near again. Gooseflesh prickles crept up the back of his neck she leaned in close to him. If she had been alive, he would have felt her breath. Instead, there was only a sharp chill, like snowflakes on his cheek.

He focused on the folded scrap – it was not as good as the kind he used in the office, and there was a smudge of odd-looking brownish ink upon it. He unfolded it, and there, scrawled on it in the same low-grade ink, were eight words.

Rot in hell, miser. You killed that girl.

9

THE WIDOW'S DRAWING ROOM WAS A SPACIOUS, ELEGANT PLACE, simply decorated and brightly lit by a positively shocking number of wax candles. A fire burned merrily in the grate, but Scrooge was chilled to the bone.

Rot in hell, miser. You killed that girl. The sensible part of him knew the note, which now sat crumpled in his pocket, was arrant nonsense. His name had been mentioned in court, and years of penny-pinching and ruthless business practice meant he was not without enemies. No doubt some low-bred individual had seen his involvement and decided to stir up trouble. But the words blended and curdled in his mind, mixing with the spectral words which had appeared on the papers in his office. *Betrayer. Liar. Murderer.*

That was what people thought of him, even now. That he was so cold-hearted, so lost to all virtue, that he was capable of taking a human life.

The ghost seemed to be getting stronger, bolder and would not let him alone. Her filmy form darted around him from place to place, droplets of blood spattering about her, making him flinch with horror every time, feel a tinge of clammy wetness on his skin before the stain vanished. It was if he was holding her, like a dog on a leash, and she was frantically pulling, pulling to get away. With every tug Scrooge felt colder and more weary.

She does not know who killed her, he thought. *And if even she does not know, how am I supposed to find out?*

Scrooge flinched as the spirit thrashed and fought against him, looking for a dark corner in which to hide. The steering committee for the Benevolent Feast for the Poor was full of sharp-eyed ladies ready to pounce eagerly on the slightest social faux-pas.

There was Mrs Tassell, sitting at a small occasional table writing yet another list in that notebook of hers. Around her fluttered a number of vivacious young wives who seemed to look to her.

Scrooge was reluctantly impressed by the widow's drive and influence. Her darker looks made her an outsider and yet she forced them to accept her not just as one of their numbers, but as some sort of leader. She chose not to blend in, to be sweet and pliant, but to speak her mind – always a dangerous path for a woman.

Nearby, her greatest rival, Lady Crick, held court over a more sizeable group of hangers-on, particularly older matrons who were drawn to her social superiority. They wore dull, muted shades and sat poised upon the chairs around her like scrawny birds perched in a bare oak tree. Sir Crispin Crick himself was absent, and there were but two or three other gentlemen in the room apart from Scrooge himself. The business of aiding the poor seemed to be a largely feminine pursuit.

Scrooge hovered between the two groups, unsure of what to do. In his experience meetings were held to deal with a specific point of business. They took place quickly and at the end a decision was made, hands were shaken or papers were signed. But meetings of the Benevolent Feast for the Poor were rarely like that. Lady Crick's group was currently talking about . . . he strained his ears . . . bonnets, it seemed. And Mrs Tassell was saying something about giving a man a fish, which hardly seemed relevant.

Mrs Tassell looked up and seeing him waiting there, cleared her throat.

'Ladies and gentlemen,' she announced, and after a few moments the buzz of chatter settled down. Mrs Tassell beamed with self-importance. 'Welcome to our final planning meeting! The Christmas feast is nearly upon us, and I am so proud of what we've all achieved so far. But sadly, we do still lack a venue. I extend my thanks to Mr Scrooge for so generously addressing a letter to the Friendly Society requesting that they change their minds, but in the event that it is unsuccessful we need to think of an alternative place to hold our feast. I would dearly love to host it here, but there is insufficient space. Unfortunately my dear departed husband did not feel we needed a ballroom. Does anyone else have space available?'

The room, which had been full of whispered chatter before, fell silent with shock.

Scrooge toyed with the idea of dropping a pin to see if the saying was true, but then Lady Crick broke the impasse with a snort.

'Our own homes? Are you mad?'

Scrooge did not disagree. He was happy to donate to the Feast for the Poor but the idea of them in his home, pocketing his silverware and putting their grubby fingers upon his curtains – it was unthinkable.

'I don't think we are that desperate, my dear,' Lady Crick continued. 'I shall send a message to Mr Teale at Clack Street workhouse. He was formerly in my husband's employ and should be happy to accommodate the feast.' There was a relieved murmur of assent from the room – even Mrs Tassell's faithful group looked amenable to the idea.

Mrs Tassell's mouth gaped in the most unladylike fashion.

'Do you seriously believe the poor of London would willingly enter a workhouse on Christmas Day? I recommend that you all read more widely and educate yourself on the realities of London life.'

'Oh, come now, I'm sure they would do anything for a good meal.' Lady Crick waved her hand dismissively. 'Heaven knows, maybe some of them will be persuaded to stay there, rather than cluttering up the streets, living in squalor.'

There was a gasp of horror from Mrs Tassell's end of the room, a murmur of agreement from the Crick followers.

Scrooge shifted uncomfortably as he was reminded of the charity collectors' words less than a year ago, that many would rather die than enter a workhouse. And his own callous response: *If they would rather die, they had better do it and decrease the surplus population.*

He had been pleased with the line at the time. It was sharp, succinct and had put the pushy charity collector in his place. But thinking of it now left him hot with shame and . . . yes, he could definitely hear the clanking of a chain now.

Mrs Tassell had gone a shade of puce Scrooge had never seen before. He saw her bite back a retort and understood that the alliance between her cadre and Lady Crick's was a delicate balance, and without it the feast would not happen. He had not known being female was so complicated.

'I am sure it will not come to that.' Mrs Tassell changed tack briskly. 'Moving on, I would like to make a plan for how to proceed in the new year. Once our feast is successful we need to build on it, to create a bridge between rich and poor and see how we can help them further improve their lot.'

'Oh,' exclaimed a jowly woman sitting on the Crick side of the room. 'But surely once the Feast is over, we have done our Christian duty . . .?'

'Yes, quite,' the lady herself spoke with a nod. 'There are limits.'

Mrs Tassell put down her notebook – always a danger sign – and placed her hands on her hips.

'That's it? You think that one feast is going to solve the dreadful poverty of this city?' Her voice was assertive, a little too strident for the confines of a drawing room. Scrooge's fleeting moment of admiration for her was crushed by bone-deep embarrassment on her behalf.

Lady Crick rose to her feet, clawed hand leaning heavily on a silver-topped cane but keeping her back ramrod straight, her piercing glare fixed on the widow.

'It is our duty to help ease the burden of the poor,' she enunciated. 'But it is not our place to interfere with the Lord's plan. His

111

guiding hand put them in their lowly station just as he granted us our high estate. That is simply the way things are.'

It was a view Scrooge had heard time and again, from the pulpit, at the Royal Exchange, in the newspapers. He had never thought deeply about it before, but now he felt there was something awry with Lady Crick's words and it added to the deep quagmire of turmoil in his soul. That uneasy suspicion that he had got something wrong again, that goodness was a lively, living creature which constantly squirmed out of his grasp.

Just then, he noticed that the spectre's fluttering had ceased. She was beside him, stock-still, gazing at the group ahead of her. For the first time she had removed her hand from her throat, and Scrooge caught sight of what was beneath. He fought not to cry out. The wound was scarlet, gleaming. He could see layers of tendon and muscle, sliced clean open like a surgeon's diagram but bright as Mr Bailey's ink.

He gradually became aware of Mrs Tassell's voice in the background. And then slowly, to his horror, discovered that everyone in the room was looking at him.

'Mr Scrooge, you are by far our most generous benefactor,' the widow was saying. 'What do you think? Should we continue the movement into 1845?'

The widow's words made Scrooge even more uneasy. He was the Feast's greatest patron? Truly? Did this mean he was giving more than was appropriate?

Lady Crick's needle-sharp gaze fixed on him. Mrs Tassell folded her arms, the corner of her mouth tugged slightly upwards in amusement. Damned woman, she was enjoying this! The thought of being carried further along by her wild schemes filled him with dread.

The ghost chose that moment to move forward, silently gliding across the room towards the Crick group. Scrooge twitched in panic.

'Well . . . I think the Feast is quite enough to handle at the moment.' His voice came out as an unmanly squeak, causing him to flush with shame. Mrs Tassell made a sound akin to disgust.

'Search your hearts, ladies and gentlemen,' she said. 'We shall discuss it again at Lady Crick's festive fundraising party. I will not let this matter drop.'

Scrooge did not have time to respond. He followed the ghost across the room, to where it had approached a quiet, colourless young lady sitting at the edge of Lady Crick's camp and had begun to raise her hand again, just as she had done in the mortuary that morning.

'Mr Scrooge, will you kindly stop gaping at Miss Frome?' Lady Crick's tones were chilly and Scrooge flushed. He *had* been staring, although it had been at the apparition in front of her. Now all the ladies in the room were looking at him – even Mrs Tassell had looked up and raised an elegant, dark eyebrow. With a surge of shame he thought he was in danger of becoming one of those strange older bachelors Mrs Cratchit warned her daughters about.

'Miss – ah – Miss Frome, is it?' he stammered wondering whether to venture another of his smiles but settling for a polite bow. 'George Frome's daughter? Ah, I saw your father in court today.'

The ghost glared at him translucently and his heart thudded. There was nothing he could do to stop her attacking the poor young lady in front of him.

'Of course, a most disreputable business,' Lady Crick said. 'You must be so disappointed in your clerk. One must be so careful who one employs . . . Goodness me, man, kindly stop staring at my niece, she is to be married on Christmas Day.'

Scrooge jumped, flustered, unsure of where to put his eyes.

'That is very fortunate!' he said. 'What a lucky, lucky, lucky young man!' It dawned upon Scrooge that he sounded *exactly* like one of the bachelors Mrs Cratchit warned her daughters about. The spectre gazed at him thoughtfully, blood still pumping from the glistening gape at her throat.

'Her betrothed, Dr Bailey, is here. Have you met him? I believe you two are about to do business together.' Lady Crick raised her gloved hand and beckoned. 'Alastair, come here.'

A slim, carelessly dressed fellow with light reddish-blond hair and side whiskers detached himself from the Tassell group and sped across the room. Scrooge recognised the gentleman he had seen with Lady Crick in court. He was carrying a half-full wine glass – Scrooge was not sure where it had come from since everyone else was drinking tea. He was smiling in an overfriendly, almost maniacal fashion. Scrooge drew back instinctively. *This* was Aldous Scabble's nephew?

'Why, Mr Scrooge! It is so, so, sooo wonderful to meet you!' Bailey grabbed Scrooge's hand with his free one and shook it vigorously, spilling a little of his wine on Scrooge's sleeve. His accent was Scottish, and his words slightly slurred. 'It is my ink you are using for your cards! We are part of a wonderful joint venture! I with my chemical formulations and you with your . . . own singular qualities!'

Scrooge leaned away from the alcohol fumes on his breath and as he did, he stumbled back into the ghost, which had been lurking behind him. Instantly, it was as if freezing water flooded the marrow of his bones.

'We must celebrate!' cried the oblivious scientist. 'You must join me in a toast! And you too, Maribel! And Lady Crick! To Blood Scarlet and Foliage Green! May many people enjoy them this Christmas!'

Scrooge felt his mouth settle into that familiar line of disapproval. The man was drunk. And he seemed to speak almost entirely in exclamations. Was this truly the serious-minded individual Merrypaw had talked about, the one who had been unable to attend the meeting earlier because he was 'tied up with matters of research'? His presence was agitating the ghost, who had shot to the ceiling and was weaving in and out of the chandeliers, darkening and growing in size like a blood-tinged storm cloud. He shuddered.

Lady Crick flared her nostrils in distaste and Miss Frome reached out and touched Bailey's sleeve.

'Alastair, perhaps this isn't the best time?'

'Oh, dear heart, you're right, you're right as ever, my pumpkin of joy! We must meet again, Scrooge, and then we can celebrate!' He drew out a card. 'Come and visit my laboratory! I have so, so much exciting work in progress!'

Miss Frome coloured deeply as Bailey tossed back the remains of his wine, his throat moving as he swallowed the red liquid. A tiny drop escaped and ran down his cheek, but he did not seem to care. Scrooge saw it now, the brittle edge to Bailey's smile, his bloodshot and red-rimmed eyes. When Scrooge looked into them he did not see merriment and joy, but a well of desperate sadness.

It was then that the room seemed to darken. The ghost-cloud above had grown thicker and blacker. A wisp of shadow began to move slowly downwards, one tendril reaching towards where Lady Crick and Miss Frome were standing.

The background noise of the room fell away as Scrooge's heart thudded in panic. A scream caught in the back of his throat as the dark, tangled cloud reached closer to the two ladies. And there was that smell again – lavender and butchery.

'I must go,' he panted, and fled as quickly as he could to the door, hoping for the first time that the phantom really was tied to him, that in leaving them behind he would pull the ghost away too. It worked – the invisible string between them snapped so tight he could feel it, a ripping pain in his belly as if it was knotted there in his viscera. The creature seemed to claw the air, to fight it, and as he reached Mrs Tassell's front door she was still pulling, fighting to get back inside.

'I'm surprised you lasted as long as you did.' Mrs Tassell's amused voice rang out through the hallway as Scrooge struggled into his shabby coat. Curse this woman and her habit of popping up when he was at his most flustered, his most disarrayed.

He mouthed a few polite words of thanks, which she waved away.

'I need your help. I will pick you up in my carriage at nine o'clock prompt tomorrow morning. Please do not try to hide again.'

Scrooge fought to stay upright, the tearing feeling in his stomach growing in severity until he feared that she might be able to see his flesh distend from his belly. He wrapped his arms around his middle.

'Uh . . .' was all he could manage to say. He tried to flee, but her voice summoned him, and politeness made him turn to look at her once more.

'I meant it when I said you should read more widely,' she said, handing him a small booklet. Scrooge took it, wondering what deathly dull religious tract she was attempting to foist onto him, but it turned out to be a flimsy-looking booklet which bore the title *Virtue and Vice: a Tale of London* by LJ Pettigrew. A cheap penny blood, dreadful sensational fiction that rotted the brain and – he had definitely read this somewhere – encouraged moral decay.

'Why would you give me this?' he asked, the shock jerking his attention away from the pull in his stomach. 'It's just rubbish produced to entertain the masses!'

Mrs Tassell smiled. 'Exactly. And because the masses read it, it's the only place you're likely to find a convincing representation of the problems of our city. I'm not saying the plots are realistic, but they are often rooted in true crimes, and they are an excellent place to start if you wish to learn a little about your fellow man.'

The air outside was cold and a fog was starting to weave itself through the streets of London, so thick that Scrooge could barely see the gas lamp on the corner. The ghost's pull on him slackened to a dull, hopeless tugging, and he slumped against the widow's iron railings for a moment to catch his breath.

He pushed the penny blood into his pocket alongside the mysterious note. He felt the corner of Alastair Bailey's card in there too. His pockets were filling with scrap paper, it seemed.

Drawing the card out, he sighed at the thought of meeting the young chemist again, as politeness decreed he must. Scrooge had disliked him on sight. He was too merry, too much.

It was then he looked at the address on the card. He had half expected it to direct him to a laboratory at one of London's new colleges, but instead it gave a location in the city that Scrooge already knew. It was Aldous Scabble's residence. So Bailey's laboratory was in his uncle's own house.

Which meant it was likely that he too had known Christina Parley. The ghost had been drawn to Miss Frome at first but became extremely agitated when she saw Dr Bailey.

Could he be the one who gave Christina Parley the ring?

The ghost was dancing circles around him, occasionally pulling, trying to get back into the house, to get back to the young betrothed couple. Her movements were becoming smaller, sadder, and Scrooge could feel heartbreak and grief thrumming across the connection between them. He understood then, without a shadow of a doubt, that Alastair Bailey had been her sweetheart.

THE GHOST

I SINK BACK INTO THE DARKNESS WITH A TEARING, AGONISING GRIEF.
I recognised his too-bright eyes, the too-wide smile on his lips, I have seen
them before when he has dipped too deeply into the bottle. I feel guilty.
This is my fault, I have driven him to this.

And yet I saw her too, at his side, meek and pink-cheeked, innocent
and unknowing. His betrothed. So, he has not told her. His uncle, too,
has kept the secret, shielding her from my existence in the same way the
slaughtermen don't show cattle the knife. No need to spook the merchan-
dise, it spoils the taste of the meat.

I have no body, I do not sicken, but the chain writhes around my waist
as I think of it, of him going through with this marriage, with my corpse
not even in the ground yet. His uncle and her family must be thrilled that
I'm out of the way. I wonder how he feels about it, when not two days
ago he made outlandish gestures to prove his love, swore we would run
away together and make a new life, tucked away in the country where
nobody would know us. I almost believed him, but Minnie's words came

back to me unbidden. 'All men are liars,' she always said. 'All men will take what they want and think only of themselves.'

Remembering those words pulls me back again into the darkness. This new afterlife seems to give me two choices: Either stay in the present by my murderer's side or relive my life and confront my own sins. And now I am in the past again, kneeling down, a grubby cloth in my hand. My fingers are stained black, but that is no clue to where in my life I have landed – my fingers are always stained black one way or another. I look up to see I am kneeling in front of an ornate cast-iron fireplace, in the process of blacking the hearth. I shudder because I know what is about to happen. I am eighteen and everything is about to change.

The master of the house comes in, kneels behind me, his body close as he leans into me, a gentle pressure on my back. I breathe faster, my chest pushing against the stays I fastened too tight this morning, as if they were some kind of armour. His hand closes over my black-stained fingers.

'Those poor hands,' he said. 'So hard-working. So dirty.'

A shudder runs through me, and I start to tremble. Minnie once told me that this moment would come, that it came to all young women whether they are fair of face or not. 'It's the youngness they like,' Minnie had said. 'New flesh. Innocence what they can bend and break. You won't be able to scream for help – they know how to get you in places where that won't work. You've got three choices. Firstly you can knee 'em in the balls. It's satisfying but you need to have somewhere to run to where you won't never see them again. Or you can close your eyes and put up with it, get it over with. Most of us prefer that.'

I had been young then, but even so I'd connected her words with the muffled sighs she made in Pa's bed late at night. The sounds I blocked out with a blanket around my head.

Still, her advice rings in my head as his body presses closer. I play for time, pretending it isn't happening, polishing the plump limbs of a cast-iron cherub with my cloth.

'Why so shy?' he says. 'You are a member of my household. It is my right to inspect your work. Very fine attention to detail. Excellent.'

For a mad moment I believe him, that he is merely being a conscientious master and I a servant who needs proper instruction. Then he leans in closer, so I can feel hot breath on my earlobe.

'Let me see those dirty hands.'

I put down my blacking and cloth and stand. He removes his gloves and takes my cold hands in his warm ones. I resent the relief this gives me as he rubs at the black stains with his fingertips murmuring. 'Oh no, no, no, we cannot have this.'

A strange sensation prickles up my spine. A combination of revulsion and longing. He has a way of talking that makes me feel small and less than human, but pushing against this is another feeling. Not since those times in Midden Mansion has anyone been so tender with me. I can almost believe he cares. Maybe he does, in his way. Maybe he thinks he will Improve me and Raise Me Up.

He puts my hand to his lips and kisses it. A little blacking smudges onto his mouth and I fight an instinct to brush the mark away for him. If I do that, I am no longer the victim, the put-upon housemaid. That gesture would make us co-conspirators, and my sin would be a hundred times more disgraceful than his.

The way I choose to react now will set my future on a different path, and my options are narrowing.

As wise Minnie said, there is no point in screaming. If my cries reach the ears of my mistress I'll simply be accused of hysteria or deliberately tempting my poor employer, and turned out onto the street. The knee to the groin would give me a moment's satisfaction, but again, it would be cobbles for me. I'd have to go crawling to Edgar, or to Wantage if he'd have me back. I fled that life years ago to be good. To be virtuous. I can almost hear Edgar's mocking laughter because look where I ended up – covered in hearth blacking and a rich man's plaything.

'Most of us prefer to endure it,' Minnie had said. But to submit, to just let him, as if my body doesn't matter, as if I am just a part of the furniture designed for his comfort and relief? No. A fire of rebellion pushes up inside me and I remember Minnie's third choice.

'Make them think you enjoy it – then take them for everything they've got.'

A decision hardens inside me. I take out my handkerchief and fold it over my dirty hand, then gently brush the smudge from his upper lip. He looks surprised, intrigued, as if I have suddenly become more interesting. This is a dangerous game, but I shall play it anyway.

'I may be dirty, Mr Scabble, but it's not proper for you to be so.' I cast my eyes down modestly, let a smile touch my lips and leave the room without being dismissed.

I feel it then, another link in the chain closes around my wrist, connecting my hand loosely to my waist, like a shackle. Tempting a rich man. Using him. Committing sin with him. And not even for love, but for simple self-preservation. More heavy links to bear.

I cannot stay here and see myself fall again. And so I pull myself back towards the present day. Towards the light, and Ebenezer Scrooge.

10

SCROOGE WAS IN THE HALLWAY THE NEXT MORNING WHEN HIS letterbox rattled and another small slip of paper fell to the floor. He rushed to pick it up, lest Mrs Miller see it – although why he cared what his housekeeper thought of him he could not begin to explain.

It was the same as the previous letter – cheap paper, curious brownish ink.

You are a <u>coward</u> to let your poor clerk hang for your crimes.

Scrooge scratched his thumb on the paper – one spot was slightly crinkled, and the ink was blurred where it had been wet and then dried out. A tear stain. Could this be from a friend of Christina's? Perhaps even the woman who had sat beside him in court the day before? But why would the letter writer suspect him?

Then again, the ghost had screamed and raged at him as well. *She thinks I did it too.* When she first appeared to him, the ghost

123

had seemed like she was made of pure fear, beyond reason, beyond sanity. But since last night he had noticed a shift in her behaviour, signs that she was becoming capable of seeing the outside world, able to think. And if she suspected him of killing her she must think he had a motive, even though he'd had no idea of her existence until he found her body.

He did not feel the chill, smell the stink of lavender and death which told him the ghost was near, but still he checked warily over his shoulder before cracking the door open and thrusting his head out. The morning was foggy, and he could just about make out the figure of an urchin fleeing into the blur of white – he had obviously been paid to deliver the note and run away as fast as he could. Scrooge did not have the bones or the energy to pursue him.

The dark bulk of a carriage emerged from the gloom, halting outside his door, and his heart sank. Mrs Tassell had held true to her threat of picking him up first thing in the morning. Could she not understand how precious his working hours were to him, with Bob gone and Christmas looming? He stepped out, intent on telling the widow that he would not go with her. But the fog seemed to crawl towards him, wrapping itself close like a damp, chill blanket. It was the ghost – larger somehow. Looming. The blurred edges of her form blended with the cold vapour, filling the very air around him with that sickening smell. Was he . . . *breathing her in*? His lungs convulsed with coughs, and he threw himself into the waiting vehicle.

'You're not ill, are you?' Mrs Tassell asked. 'You look ghastly.'

The carriage moved off through the dim morning light, and Scrooge could swear that the spectre had wrapped herself around it, making the fog thicker and colder.

'Where are we going?' he asked the widow.

'Why, to Clack Street Workhouse of course,' came the reply.

He fidgeted in his seat, frustrated. His work was falling behind, poor Bob Cratchit was mouldering in jail – he should be doing something, not taking a pleasurable jaunt with a pushy busybody. But then, Christina Parley had lived at this workhouse; perhaps he could find out more about her while he and Mrs Tassell were there. Something, he hoped, which would take suspicion away from the Scabble household as well as Bob.

Scrooge would rather have lost himself in thought, but the widow turned the conversation to the murder case, asking a series of ever more perplexing questions. How long had Bob been absent from the office on the day of the murder? Was there a chance that the razor blade had been planted in Bob's drawer? How did Bob know Christina? Until finally he had snapped at her.

'Please cease talking as if my clerk is guilty of murder! It is a slight upon my judge of character even to imply it!'

Mrs Tassell looked up at him, and appeared genuinely hurt.

'You wrong me,' she said, voice heavy with sadness. 'I know beyond doubt that Bob could not do such a thing.'

'I do not know why they have even imprisoned him, when the victim's brother is a hardened criminal,' Scrooge said. He glanced cautiously around him, but the ghost did not seem to react.

'So you suspect Edgar Parley?' Mrs Tassell looked at him, one eyebrow raised.

'He is clearly a violent man, perhaps there was some enmity between them.' The theory became more solid as Scrooge spoke, as if saying it aloud made it more real. He had certainly seen it over the years – twisted, angry men who would beat a woman over a burned supper or a disrespectful look, and Edgar Parley certainly seemed like the type. The widow looked thoughtful.

'So you are not of the theory that the lover did it?'

'I do not subscribe to the idea of a crime of passion. People kill because they feel threatened by something or stand to gain something, perhaps financially, not for love. It could be that she had information about his crimes that could finally send him to the gallows.'

'Oh yes, it's all about money with you, isn't it, Mr Scrooge?'

Scrooge felt a flush of irritation. The idea that Edgar was involved had taken a foothold in his mind and the more he thought about it, the more sense it made – especially when compared to the more outlandish Scabble theory. And what would a rich, sheltered widow know about it?

'I feel we have gone beyond the bounds of propriety,' he said, attempting to shut the conversation down. 'I fail to see how gossiping about it will achieve anything,'

Mrs Tassell looked away, her gloved hand smoothing her skirts. 'The world runs on gossip,' she said. 'Even your precious Royal Exchange fluctuates according to rumours and innuendo. And somewhere out there is a piece of gossip which will free Bob Cratchit.'

Before he had a chance to reply, the carriage drew to a halt outside the unwelcoming facade of Clack Street Workhouse.

'Is it really necessary to come here?'

'Entirely so,' Mrs Tassell answered. 'Lady Crick feels that this is an appropriate location for the Feast, and you did not disagree. Therefore, we must inspect it.'

As he handed the widow from the carriage, the ghost seemed to ooze into shape next to him, and resume her original form. Scrooge fought to tear his eyes away from that terrible, cavernous slash in her flesh. So red, so bloody, when the rest of her was pale as a daguerreotype.

Don't look, he urged himself. *If I don't pay her attention, perhaps she will leave me be.*

The workhouse had been constructed many years ago, the building adapted and adjusted as the needs of the poor – or more accurately, the needs of the rich to keep the poor out of sight – had changed. The wall surrounding it was made of pale yellow brick, but years of coal smoke, London particulars and damp weather had darkened them until they were only a few shades lighter than the black-painted gate. When they knocked, a small hatch in the gate snapped open to reveal a porter with a large purplish nose and very few teeth.

'Mr Teale is expecting us,' Mrs Tassell said.

They found themselves in a cramped courtyard. A few sad-looking men wearing ill-fitting blue uniform jackets stood huddled together on the far side, gazing suspiciously at them as they passed. Mrs Tassell stood tall, her shoulders back, her ebony skirts brushing the grimy, slushy cobbles as she walked. She did not bother to lift her hem out of the mire. Scrooge cast a longing glance back at the gate – a sudden fear overtaking him that he would be trapped here for ever. He understood now what the charity collector had explained to him last year. He would rather die than live here, too. He felt angry, sickened with remorse and overwhelming helplessness. What use were any of his philanthropic dabblings when people were forced to live like this?

Mr Teale, the workhouse master, was strangely unavailable to meet Mrs Tassell – Scrooge assumed he had met her before and was hiding. So their guided tour was undertaken by the portress, Jenny, a small, wan woman with a grubby apron and a painful-looking boil on her left cheek. She swept them through room after room of tired, skeletal men, women and children, making little comment. There was the filthy receiving room, where vagrants were put up for the night. Then they inspected a miserable row of workshops where poor folk were engaged in grinding gypsum for plaster or something called oakum picking, which looked completely pointless. Then there was the infirmary, which Scrooge could not bear to enter, such were the foul smells and sounds of misery emanating from it. Throughout it all, the ghost clung to Scrooge, winding round him like Bob's white comforter. Wisps of her presence touched his skin so that he was chilled to the bone and could barely stop his teeth from chattering.

'I need to see the dining hall,' Mrs Tassell said and, keeping her tone even, added: 'My associate Lady Crick feels it is an appropriate location for a Christmas feast. What is your opinion, Jenny?'

Jenny snorted before remembering herself and, putting on a straight face, said that Lady Crick clearly had better judgement than the likes of her.

A new stench wafted into his nostrils as the dining hall door opened. The smell of watery vegetable soup, damp and despair. Rows of long, well-scrubbed wooden trestle tables lined the room. The ceiling was high, but the result was that the light from the lamps barely made it to the tables below and the entire room was cold, even without the presence of the ghost.

'Well now, this would be just right, don't you think, Scrooge?' Mrs Tassell said facetiously. 'A sprig of holly here, a candelabra there and the place becomes a festive paradise. Of course, our guests would take some convincing. Many people believe once they have entered the workhouse they will never be free. But clearly they have nothing to fear. This place is delightful.'

Jenny, who clearly didn't encounter much sarcasm in her day-to-day life, wrinkled her brow and stared.

'I . . . I had not comprehended it was quite this bad,' Scrooge admitted. His legs gave way, and he sagged onto one of the rickety benches.

The widow insisted on getting the full tour, inspecting room after squalid, dingy room as this ghost cleaved to him, choking him. Scrooge hung back, its presence leeching his energy to the point of exhaustion.

Just then Mrs Tassell, who had been walking with Jenny, swayed slightly. Scrooge felt a stab of panic; was the ghost affecting her too?

'I'm afraid I feel a little faint.' Her voice was heavy with fatigue, most out of character for her. Scrooge swept forward and offered his arm.

'Madam, allow me to support you back to your carriage.'

She shook her head, leaning heavily on him. 'Oh no, I wouldn't think of it, you need to take the full tour!'

'I'm sure I don't!'

The widow looked up, her gaze boring into him, her voice gaining a thread of steel. 'I insist. Jenny, may I wait in the guardian's office until Mr Scrooge is finished here?'

'Of course, madam!'

Was it his imagination, or did he see a tiny, triumphant twitch at the corner of the widow's lips? But never mind, it suited him too, as it would give him a chance to ask the portress some questions.

Jenny was silent, matter of fact, as she guided him through the last stops of the tour.

'Men's dormitory.'

'Workroom.'

'Women's wing.'

Scrooge arranged his features into a smile. He had not much experience in putting people at their ease, but he knew that smiling was part of it.

'So, Miss Jenny, I hear Christina Parley used to live here, before going into service.'

Jenny surveyed him suspiciously. 'Is that why you're here? Are you press? Or just one of those souvenir-hunting ghouls? Is this the next stop on the tour after you've seen the bloodstain?'

'I am no such thing!' Scrooge snapped which was enough to make Jenny remember her station and bob an apologetic curtsy.

'I only seek to help,' he added. 'I am a respectable businessman, not without influence.'

Jenny looked unconvinced. 'That's what they all say, all those broadside scumbags. But then they go off and blacken her name, saying she was carrying on with that Cratchit fellow, saying she's a bad 'un, like her brother. Tina was different to everyone else. She walked through these doors willingly to get away from that brother of hers. And when she left, she didn't forget us. There's blankets on the beds in the children's wing thanks to her. And medicine in the infirmary too.'

Jenny had gone red, a tear sparkled at the corner of her eye.

'But how did she do this? Where did the money come from? Was it stolen?' The accusation left his lips before he remembered the ghost. He felt it quiver, tighten around him like a violin string.

The portress glared at him. 'Never. She was good and kind. A modern-day saint, but one of them fighting ones. Like George and the dragon.'

The violin string loosened slightly at those words.

'And did that anger her brother?'

'He couldn't stand it,' she said. 'The Gentleman doesn't like his folk doing as they please. And when he gets angry, people get hurt.'

Mrs Tassell seemed quite rejuvenated by her short stay in the empty office and it was with great relief that Scrooge climbed into the carriage next to her. The stink of the workhouse lifted; the ghost relaxed its anxious hold over him.

'Now tell me, have you had a chance to read *Virtue and Vice* yet?'

As it happened, Scrooge had resorted to reading it the night before when he had been unable to sleep. It had been surprisingly compelling, although he was reluctant to concede that to Mrs Tassell.

'It merits further study,' he said. 'I don't suppose you have the next instalment?' He was more eager to get his hands on the second volume than he would care to admit.

She inclined her head and, with a chuckle, drew a bundle of papers out of her pocket. She began to parse through.

'Do all ladies have such enormous pockets in their skirts?' Scrooge asked.

'No, it is most peculiar,' she answered. 'All this space in our gowns and nobody thinks to make use of it! Some say it ruins the fit, but it's worth it. I have my dressmaker sew them in especially. Ah, here it is.'

She produced the next booklet with a flourish, and as she did so another scrap of paper fluttered out of her pocket and fell unnoticed to the carriage floor. He was about to say something about it, but then a brilliant thought struck him.

'Merrypaw!' he exclaimed. 'Mr Felix Merrypaw, the printer – he has space in his printing house and his workers will all be on holiday on Christmas day so the place will be empty. He is a charitable fellow who loves the festive season, I am sure he will welcome the chance to host the Feast.'

The widow smiled, a wide, shining beam of happiness, and Scrooge felt his heart leap at the idea that, finally, he had solved one of his numerous problems and done some good.

He did not see the scrap of paper stuck to his foot until after he had got out of the carriage. Snatching it from his shoe, he held it up, but Mrs Tassell's driver had already urged the horses into a trot.

The paper looked like it had been ripped from a ledger similar to his own, but instead of incomings and outgoings, this one bore a neatly written list of people's names. *Pandle, Parrish . . . Parley*. Christina Parley's workhouse records. The entry laid out the date of her admission, noted that she had presented herself of her own free will. Other notes were added too. *Troublemaker.*

Argumentative. Does not display sufficient gratitude or know her place. Scrawls pictures on walls and paper meant for schooling.

Scrooge stood for a while staring at the page. Mrs Tassell had stolen Christina's workhouse records. Her fainting fit must have been a ruse, a pretext to search the master's office. But why would a respectable widow do such a thing?

11

FOG WAS THE WRONG SORT OF WEATHER FOR CHRISTMAS, THOUGHT Tim. Especially this fog. It was the kind of pea-souper that had a personality of its own. It curled around corners, lingered in alleyways and clogged up his delicate lungs. He wound his scarf tighter round his neck as he watched the passers-by emerge from the thick, almost tangible whiteness, and then vanish back into it again.

No, this was not the right weather for Christmas, but then it didn't feel like Christmas right now anyway. Not without Father, and with his mother declaring that Christmas must go on, and bustling from task to task, finishing none of them.

He was supposed to be at school today and still felt a sting of guilt whenever he thought about it, but when he had arrived that morning a crowd of boys had been waiting for him jeering, shoving. *'Your pa's a murderer.'*

He had turned and left, hiding from the boys in the murky gloom. He couldn't go home; it would only add to his mother's worry. At first, he started out towards Scrooge & Marley, but then he ran into Jem coming the other way.

'Just the fellow!' Jem said cheerily. 'I've got an idea to do some spying, want to come?'

It turned out that Simeon – he of the graveyard and the giant bloodstain – had set up a shoe-shining pitch opposite the scene of the crime and needed an extra pair of hands. 'Half of London's trampling in there to see where the body was found and coming out with their boots all scuffed up,' Jem explained. 'So I'm plan-ning to make some money and see if I can find something out while I'm at it.'

Simeon did not look pleased to see the 'titchy kid' in tow, but Tim offered to act as a barker for the two boot-boys and proved highly effective at calling in passing trade, until Simeon grudg-ingly admitted he was an asset. 'That angelic face, that crutch, that sweet little voice – people can't resist, can they?'

There were certainly plenty of potential customers, with a steady trickle of people going into and out of the churchyard, including many gentlefolk.

The customers talked of nothing but the murder, and the latest details released in the broadsides.

'They've arrested the culprit already.'

'A married man! A respectable clerk too!'

'My aunt Gertrude's housemaid's sister does for his neighbour's family, and she said he was a quiet chap, kept himself to himself.'

'It is the quiet ones you have to watch . . .'

As he took money from another customer, Jem laid a gentle hand on Tim's shoulder. 'Keep your trap shut,' he murmured. 'I know it's hard to hear this stuff but let 'em talk. If people keep talking eventually someone will say something useful.'

Even the church's curate stopped to have his old-fashioned buckled shoes buffed, telling the boys what a shocking business it was, and how glad he was that the police had arrested the killer.

'I'm sure you know all about it,' Jem said, buttering him up.

The curate was a portly, comfortable-looking man who developed additional chins when he smiled. The beam he bestowed on them produced at least three. 'Oh, indeed my testimony was vital to the case! I saw the poor creature talking to that . . . that *blaggard* in his white comforter at four o'clock that day and if only I had known, I could have intervened and saved her life!'

Tim felt his heart crash. So it was true. This man of God really had seen his father with that poor lady.

'Did you see the crime happen?' Jem asked.

'Oh no, of course not, otherwise I would have raised the alarm! Maybe taken the man on myself!' The curate smiled again and puffed out his chest – the combination made another chin materialise.

'So you didn't see anyone else meet her after then?'

The chins vanished; his guard went up. 'No, of course not. The poor child was dead, wasn't she? Hurry up and finish, I need to get back to my duties.'

136

After the man had gone, without leaving a tip, Jem nudged Tim and muttered: 'I wouldn't trust a word that bloke says. He's a proper crook, that one. Got arrested last year and only got off because he's related to a duke or something.'

Tim looked at the curate's retreating back. How could a man of God be a rascal? But then how could a rascal-looking boy like Jem be so clever and kind?

And so Tim continued his barking job, reeling in the customers through the freezing fog, in the shadow of the churchyard. The shouting kept his body warm, but his fingers and toes were feeling the cold now, and in a quiet moment he found himself huddling into a shop doorway. Suddenly the door opened, and an enraged shopkeeper appeared – all shaking fists and grey whiskers.

'Move along there, you young ruffia—oh!' At the sight of Tim's sweet, big-eyed self the shopkeeper's irritation vanished. 'Are you all right, son? You look poorly.'

'Just c-cold.'

'Come inside and rest a while,' the man said gently. Simeon rolled his eyes, but Jem urged Tim on. 'Ask him what he saw,' he whispered.

The shop was cramped but warm, with bolts of fabric stacked up on high shelves in a multitude of colours. The shopkeeper had wound ivy around his front window and through the steps of his ladder.

'It makes all the difference, you know,' the shopkeeper explained, seeing Tim's awed look. 'Men pass the shop, and the ivy catches their attention, makes them think of Christmas. Then they might think their wives would like a bolt of cloth to make up a new dress, and they come inside. It works. We've been extremely busy this year – although we have also had plenty of passing trade after that unfortunate business with that poor wretch in the churchyard.'

The shopkeeper nodded across the street and Tim could see there was a clear view of the gate from the window.

'Did you see her that day?' he asked.

The man shook his head playfully. 'You're not one of those pesky broadside writers, are you?'

Tim giggled obligingly. 'No, sir! I heard she was a pretty lady, like an angel.'

'That she was. But she was crying mightily when I saw her. She had a fight with the white-comforter feller, then ran off into the graveyard in floods of tears.'

Tim froze. Had he heard that right? 'She ran away from my ... I mean, the man in the comforter? So she was still alive when he left?'

The man's expression changed. He looked shocked, stricken. 'I—no, you heard me wrongly. I . . .'

Recalling Simeon's words earlier, Tim looked up at the shop-keeper, his eyes wide, shining with innocence. Nobody could lie to this angel.

'I won't tell anyone,' he said.

The man broke into a smile. 'Of course you won't, you're just a little thing, aren't you? Well, it won't do no harm to tell you, but yes. After that man left, there was another gentleman, a mighty fine-looking one he was too. Top hat, fob seals, gold watch – the lot.'

Tim felt a surge of excitement. 'But that means the police have got the wrong man! You have to tell them!'

The man shook his head, a flicker of real fear in his eyes. 'I can't. It's more than my life's worth.'

Outside, Tim told Jem what he had heard and his new friend's brow creased in thought.

'Did he say a gentleman?'

Tim nodded.

'But people ain't *scared* of gentlemen. Not in that way. A gentleman can ruin your business or your reputation, but they don't normally take your life. Unless . . .' Jem stopped talking, his jaw clamped shut.

'Unless?' Tim prompted.

'Nothing.' Jem's gaze slid away from Tim's clear-eyed gaze. 'It's just there's a bloke in this town who calls himself a gentleman and who tries to dress like a gentleman, but who ain't remotely gentle. And we want to avoid him at all costs. If it's him behind all this, your Pa's doomed.'

As time dragged on, the fog closed itself more tightly around the boys, and although it was not yet midday, it already felt like night. Soon it became too cold even for the bloodstain sightseers and custom petered out. Then, just as they were beginning to pack their gear, Tim saw a figure in a shabby maid's dress and shawl slip out of the churchyard and cross the road. There was something oddly familiar about the woman's gait that caught his eye, and as she walked past in the gloom, he snatched a glimpse of her face beneath the poke of her bonnet.

It couldn't be . . . could it?

'Jem, that's Mrs Tassell! The lady who's organising the feast with Mr Scrooge!'

'What, in that tatty dress? Don't be daft!'

'It is, I swear. She's in some kind of disguise. Let's follow her!'

Jem scooped up his brushes, muttered an excuse to Simeon and they set off. It was hard to keep sight of her as she rounded a corner and wove through Christmas market stalls with a singular sense of purpose. It had to be her – no other lady strode about like that.

Somehow they managed to keep her in sight as the streets around them began to change, becoming narrower, more cramped until they came to a part of town Tim had never set foot in before. This was a place of twisted alleyways and fouled cobbles, where ragged beggars hunched in corners, cold and trembling. A mixture of fear and pity and shame curdled in Tim's stomach. His foot was throbbing now, but there was no way he could rest, not here.

Mrs Tassell kept moving through the mist with surprising confidence, until she turned into an alleyway so narrow that there was barely any room for the fog to curl into it. They followed her, positioning themselves behind a broken barrel and watching as she approached what looked like a dilapidated shop.

It was more of a doorway, really, and the ground in front of it was laid out with oddments gleaned from other people's lives. There were cracked chamber pots, bottles of assorted sizes, grimy, patched fabrics. Tim noticed a single shoe, the sole coming away from the toe. No doubt someone would still buy it. There was a use for everything, no matter how old and worn. An attendant sat in the doorway, wrapped in rags. She was red-eyed and squinting, her fingers curled around knitting needles. She didn't stop working stitches as Mrs Tassell leaned forward and spoke to her quietly. The attendant gave a gap-toothed smile.

'Amos,' she called. 'Her Ladyship's here to see Him.'

A tall man stepped from the shadows with a thick brow and a blank, impassive face.

Jem pressed himself further into the shadow of the barrel and Tim did likewise, painfully aware that he couldn't run, couldn't fight. *What good am I to Jem? Or to Mr Scrooge – or Father for that matter?*

'That's Amos Buddle,' Jem whispered. 'If Amos is here, Edgar Parley won't be far away. Simeon's people have this legend, a creature called a golem who only obeys one person. Amos is kind of like that, with the Gentleman in charge. Which means this must be Parley's flash house!'

A flash house – Tim had read about those thieves' dens in the penny bloods Belinda and Martha read in secret.

His heart beat hard under his layers, and he became painfully conscious of the bundle of five-pound notes, which he had tucked inside his vest. He still didn't know what to do with it. If he gave it to Mother she'd think he'd stolen it. If he hid it again the police might come back and find it, use it against his father somehow. He had resisted the childish temptation to run to the nearest toymaker, knowing that a shabby, unaccompanied boy with a five-pound note would invite immediate suspicion. And so the notes were still here, tucked into his vest. He shivered, wondering if the flash house thieves could smell money.

Jem nudged him with a sharp elbow. 'Look at that, she's going in! Cool as you please!'

Sure enough, the respectable widow, renowned for her charitable works, stepped calmly into the robbers' den.

Scrooge's hands gripped the edge of his desk, clawing tightly as he resisted the urge to strike at that impertinent boot-boy. He gritted his teeth tightly as he spoke.

'You took Tiny Tim into the darkest part of town.'

'He didn't slow me down any,' Jem interjected. 'And he was brave. Why when we were hiding outside the Gentleman's flash house . . .'

Parley's flash house. Jem had taken meek and helpless Tiny Tim to a criminal's lair. Scrooge felt a rush of rage. He took a deep, ragged breath in, biting on the inside of his cheek to keep himself from cursing.

The sickly boy stood next to Jem, clearly tired from his exertions but trying to look brave. It wrenched at his heart. Tim had almost died last year because Scrooge had not paid his father enough to give him food or medicine, because Bob had been so terrorised he was afraid to ask for more. Scrooge owed this boy a debt which could never be repaid. He had sworn an oath that he would never let harm come to him again.

And now this impertinent urchin had led him straight into danger.

He was so blind with rage, it took him a while to comprehend what Jem was saying, but slowly the information sank in. Mrs *Tassell* had been walking around disguised as a maid? And – worst of all – she was associating with Edgar Parley somehow. A decision snapped in his mind. He would end his dealings with that woman as soon as the feast was done.

'Sir, don't you see,' Jem continued. 'We know now that Miss Parley was talking to a smartly dressed gentleman-type after Mr Cratchit left her, and that the shopkeeper was scared into keeping it secret. And we know where the Gentleman's flash house is now. We could spy on him, wait for him to make a false move and—'

'Silence!' Scrooge snapped. 'I will hear no more of this nonsense. You are not to take my office boy on any more jaunts. And remember, I am still waiting for those outstanding payments on your loan. Now get out of my sight.'

'Sir . . .' Tiny Tim stepped forward. He was pale, his eyes filled with unshed tears. Scrooge felt a pang. *Was Tim frightened of him?*

But then, if he had heard how Scrooge had failed his father in court, who could blame him?

'Please, sir,' Tim said. 'It was not Jem's fault, I insisted on coming. It was my idea to follow Mrs Tassell.'

'Enough,' Scrooge snapped. 'You should be at school, Timothy Cratchit. But seeing as you are here, make yourself useful with the accounts. There will be no more investigating. Is that clear?'

Tim hung his head, uttered something which sounded like 'yes, sir'.

'And Jem, get out.'

The boy scuttled off, shaken. Scrooge knew he had been too hard on the lad, but the guilt just made him angrier. Leaving Tim at his father's desk, he slammed his office door hard enough to make the interior wall tremble, and ground out a curse between gritted teeth.

Bob Cratchit had been in prison little more than a day and already Scrooge's carefully constructed new life had fallen apart. He had spent two sleepless, haunted nights. His business – aside from the Christmas card project – had fallen to the wayside. Tim had been put in danger. The woman he trusted with his charity money was a liar who associated with criminals. He had had enough of this nonsense.

There was a flicker, and the ghost stood in the corner of the room, wordless, accusing. Exhaustion, fury and fright mixed in him, and he roared with frustration. He grabbed his inkwell and threw it at her as hard as he could.

'Go!' he shouted. 'For the love of Heaven leave me be!'

The inkwell passed through the spectre and dashed against the wall, leaving a splash of blue-black on the grubby white surface. The ghost flickered and vanished.

Scrooge did not feel any better.

THE GHOST

SO IT IS TRUE. EBENEZER SCROOGE HAS NOT TRULY CHANGED, NOT *since the night I first set eyes on him, last Christmastide. I feel it now, the deep cold of the windowpane beneath my sore, reddened fingers as I stood outside his office window. I am bone-tired from work, but it is worse than that. My soul is worn out.*

I am supposed to be working now, helping Mrs Paddlewick lay out the obscene amount of food the Scabbles will eat tomorrow, but I cannot. I am pulled and torn between the master – who sends for me whenever the need takes him and then sends me away when he is done – and his nephew who says he wishes to drown in my eyes.

I had been at Scabble's for seven long years when Alastair arrived. The other servants loathed him – he had taken over one room in our quarters with his stinking laboratory, meaning several of the men now had to share, and his manners were odd and informal. He chatted to us. He did not dress for dinner. But his presence had brought life and humour to the house and a few times, when we were in the same room, I found myself smiling at some ridiculous thing he had said. He noticed. He started catching my eye and all of a sudden I was smiling even more. After years without love, Alastair makes me feel strong and valued and respected, but he will not understand why I can't refuse his uncle.

'I have a plan,' he tells me. 'I have a place you can go, where you can work until we have enough money to run away.'

But it's a place that will draw me even deeper into sin, and so I resist.

This is the path I have chosen, I tell myself. A path of goodness, virtue, suffering and service. Of knowing my place. Of snatched and secret moments of pleasure. 'You've made your bed,' Pa would have said. 'Now lie in it.'

Still, at this time of year I need to experience that Christmas feeling. And even though I am long past twenty years of age and no longer a child, Christmas still means Bob – with his silly smiles, foolish games and talk of hearts being full.

I have not seen him for many years, but I heard a rumour that he was clerking at a business called Scrooge & Marley. And so here I am, peering through Scrooge's window, hungry for a glimpse of Bob, like a beggar scrabbling for scraps. He is there, hunched over his desk pretending to work, while a bitter old wreck of a man glares across the room. Ebenezer Scrooge.

He is talking to two portly gentlemen holding collecting boxes. Both men look well-fed, smartly clothed, their cheeks flushed with festive cheer. They are respectable, God-fearing gentlemen upon the path of righteousness . . . but also fond of brandy and pudding. The window is cracked – Scrooge is clearly too much of a skinflint to repair it – and their merry voices drift through the hole. I press my ear close when I hear talk of Christmas.

'A few of us are endeavouring to raise a fund to buy the poor some meat, drink and means of warmth,' one of them explains, shaking his collecting box so it makes a cheery jingling sound.

Scrooge scoffs, his lip curled with disgust. 'Are there no prisons? And the union workhouses, are they still in operation?'

There is a moment of silence, of shock as these men who are so used to politeness and good manners struggle to respond. The second, larger gentleman recovers first.

'Many can't go there, and many would rather die,' he says. I nod, unseen, on the other side of the frosty windowpane. I may have entered the workhouse willingly, but I loathed every brick of that place and would appease a hundred Scabbles to stay out of it now. I would smash it to pieces if I could, then grind the rubble to dust.

Scrooge's lips become a hard, stubborn line.

'If they would rather die, they had better do it and decrease the surplus population.'

I stagger back, away from the window, my mouth hanging open at the sheer ignorance, the nastiness of what I have just heard. And just like that, it lights a flame in me. Those words change everything.

The rich are never going to rescue us. No matter how kind they think they are, no matter how many coins gentlefolk drop in those collection boxes, they will always see us as something less than human. A problem to be dealt with. A Social Issue. Even those stout, virtuous men in their brightly coloured coats with their brightly coloured beaming faces. They would only go so far to salve their own consciences.

No. The only way to change things is to do something myself, even if I have to break the law to do it.

I am yet young, I have passion and I have skills. Alastair's plan will work for me after all.

Suddenly I am pulled away and out of the past, into the black space which seems to lurk behind everything. I whirl and struggle like a fish on a hook as new chain links come towards me. Living metal, shining and writhing like an armoured snake. They bind themselves about my waist, my hips, my shoulders, pulling me down and down into the depths where punishment awaits. My chain grows longer and longer with a link for every single wrongdoing I have committed. And there are many.

12

THE GHOST WAS GONE. HE WAS FREE – AT LEAST FOR NOW. Scrooge ignored Tim's shocked stare through the office window, hunched over his desk and opened his ledgers, waiting for the wave of comfort and security to wash over him. He checked his donations to the Benevolent Feast for the Poor – something had niggled when Mrs Tassell had called him 'our most generous benefactor'. But the amounts in his book, laid out in Bob's neat handwriting, were solid, respectable sums. Lady Crick and the others must truly be short-changing the charity if his own contributions stood out.

Soon he was settled into his old pattern of tallying and double-checking, but it did not bring him the relief it usually did. Instead, his mind kept drifting back to the mystery, the puzzle. From the moment he had first thought of the theory that Edgar Parley had something to do with his sister's murder it had taken hold of him and dug its claws into his mind – and Jem's news had only added to it.

But the police were too frightened of Parley to take him in for questioning. He needed evidence. He needed to talk to Bob at the police station again. He slid down from his stool and threw on his coat.

He almost forgot Tim sitting there, concentrating hard on his sums and chewing his pen in exactly the same way that poor Bob always had. A tight feeling formed in his chest at the thought of the poor lad without his father at Christmas. He thought briefly about taking him along to the cells, but he knew Bob would never want his son to see him imprisoned and humiliated.

'When your work is done, lock the door and take the keys to Cruttle next door. He has agreed to take you home while your father is . . . absent.'

Tim looked up at him, his gaze flying to the ink stain on the wall and back to his master. He did not dare ask what had happened, and Scrooge could not begin to explain, so he put on his hat and left. He started towards the police station, finding his way through the gathering darkness and lingering fog and taking care as he moved over the uneven cobbles. The people around him were mere shadows – errand boys flitting back and forth, busy housemaids bustling past – but he could still hear cheerful talk of Christmas, and joy and 'only four days to go!' through the whitened shadows.

And then a strident voice rose above them all.

'Most horrible murder! Further particulars!'

A broadside seller on the corner. Scrooge stopped to buy the latest edition and scanned the text. Most of it was filler – a poorly constructed poem about 'the Angel of St Gideon's', more pointless colour from alleged friends of Bob. But there were a few fresh scraps of detail, including a description of the razor found in Bob's desk observing that it was unusual to find a second-hand blade in a new case. The report also mentioned that a watch chain had been found in Christina's hand, which surprised Scrooge as the police officers had clearly been paid to keep quiet about it – the journalist must have an alternative source. None of it helped though, none of it connected Parley to his sister's death. And he didn't like the sullying of Christina's name, he was starting to feel strangely protective towards her.

As Scrooge was about to ascend the police station steps, he almost ran straight into a woman wrapped up tight in a familiar white comforter, hat pulled low to hide her features.

'Mrs Cratchit!'

'Oh! Sir!' Bob's wife eyed him with her usual mixture of curiosity and suspicion.

'Good day to you,' he said politely. 'I hope our prisoner is faring better today.'

Mrs Cratchit shook her head and to his horror, a tear trickled down her cheek. 'I'm afraid not, sir. He has taken a fever after his beating and has lost his senses. When I think of what that brutal man did I could . . .'

She trailed off, afraid to vent her rage in front of her husband's employer.

'I quite agree, Mrs Cratchit,' Scrooge said. 'Edgar Parley will pay for what he did, I shall make sure of it.'

He saw her bite back her response. *You should have spoken up in court. You should have moved heaven and earth to get him out,* and guilt writhed in his belly. No words, no assurances could win her over now, only the safe return of her husband. Preferably in time for Christmas.

'Will I be able to see him?' Scrooge asked.

'He's sleeping now. I dosed him with laudanum for the pain – we had a tiny bit left over from the bottle you gave us when Tim was sick. He is quite lost to the world. It's a healing sleep though . . . I hope.'

'And you too must rest, madam. But before you go, may I ask you – did you notice anything unusual about Bob recently? Anything strange about the way he acted?'

Mrs Cratchit's mouth became a thin line, she drew herself up to her full height. 'If you are suggesting my Robert was in any way unfaithful . . .'

'Not at all, madam. But he did creep out of my office, giving me an excuse about Tim's medicine. That is not usual behaviour for our Mr Cratchit.'

'Indeed not.' She wrinkled her brow. 'There is one thing. He told me that he needed to leave the family for a few hours on Christmas Day, to perform an errand. At the time I did not enquire too much, I thought he was planning some Christmas surprise for us, but now I wonder if it was something else. It would have to be something important for him to miss even a few moments of Christmas with us.'

Scrooge nodded. Nothing would usually separate Bob from his family on Christmas Day. Whatever it was must have been vital.

Scrooge escorted Mrs Cratchit to the nearest pharmacy and purchased some more laudanum, then she left, going back to her needy brood. He waited a while for her to disappear around the corner, guilt still churning in his stomach, and then headed off in the same direction himself.

Bob spent his life shuttling back and forth between the office and his home, and if he had bought the razor blade brand-new from a shop, then it would be from one of the stores which lined his route to and from work. It should be a simple matter to visit each one and make enquiries. However, Scrooge had not bargained for the marketplace which had sprung up for the festive season. The streets were lined with stalls, populated by merry-faced individuals calling about their wares. The fog only added to the prettiness of the lanterns the stallholders had strung up, and nearby, a group of carol singers urged all gentlemen to rest merry. Then a fine-knitted scarf caught his eye which he knew his nephew, Fred, would find useful. At the next stall, a brightly painted comb caught his eye, something that would look very nice in his niece-in-law's curls. By the time he had made it one hundred yards down the street he had four parcels in his hands, and was several shillings the poorer. He called in to the poulterers and ordered an even fatter turkey than last year for the Cratchit family, hoping that Bob would be home in time to enjoy it.

It was then he decided that he *would* give his clerk a gift, if only as an act of faith that Bob would be free in time for Christmas. But what should it be? What did one get for a man who is already so happy with his lot in life?

Just then, he ran into a portly gentleman in a blue coat – it was one of the charity collectors from last year.

'Ah, Mr Scrooge! A pleasure to see you again!' He held up a slotted tin and rattled it. 'As you can see, I am still collecting alms for the surplus population.'

He knew that it was his duty to give money to good causes, but handing over the coins still gave him pain – a pain which was shortly followed by guilt that he still felt that way and fear that the Spirit of Christmas Yet to Come was still watching, waiting to drag him to his miser's grave. He was certain then that he could hear the clink-clink of his waiting chain. So it was a very uncomfortable Scrooge that slipped into the cutler's shop ten minutes later. The owner popped up from behind the counter like an eager jack-in-the-box.

Scrooge drew out some of his remaining coin, which helped a little, and said he required information.

'Oh, not you as well. Time was people dropped in here for things, not words.'

'Why, who else has been in here asking questions?'

'Oh, the boys in blue to start with. That Baldock feller. Then some housemaid who was no better than she ought to be. Right bossy she was.'

Scrooge sighed. 'Did she have dark hair and a high-handed tone?'

The man's expression hardened. 'She don't work for you, does she?'

'Thankfully, no.'

'Well, I'll tell you what I told them. If . . .' He eyed the money meaningfully, until Scrooge handed it over. 'Right. So yes, I did sell a razor to that Cratchit bloke. One of my finest, better than he

154

could afford or so I thought. You see, I have a range of the very latest developments in whisker-removal technology including razors and a range of shaving accessories . . .'

Scrooge wondered what on earth a shaving accessory was but feared that if asked the man would tell him at length. So he urged him back onto the subject of the razor blade.

'Did he tell you who it was for?'

'A friend, he said.'

'And the handle was made of wood?'

'Not at all, sir. The handle was bone, and very well carved I might add. They come in these fine presentation cases and make the perfect gift for the gentleman about town.'

The man held up a neat leather case, exactly like the one which had been found in Bob's desk, and sure enough, inside was a shining blade with a bone handle – nothing like the blood-stained and rusted one which the police had seized.

So the razors definitely had been switched. It would have been no easy feat – Scrooge and Bob were in the office all day, every day – which meant someone must have broken in overnight, without being detected. An experienced housebreaker.

Again, the clues pointed to Edgar Parley.

Scrooge left the shop with a brand-new bone-handled razor and a gadget called a Self-Cleaning Shaver's Friend, both of which he planned to offload onto his nephew as soon as possible. He also left with growing certainty that the Gentleman was mired in this mess, right up to his elaborate whiskers.

How to proceed? If he were a police officer, he would haul Parley in for questioning, and his natural instinct was to march to Parley's flash house, now the boys had told him where it was, and confront him. But such an act would be incredibly foolish. The man was ruthless, and far more savage than the gentleman he clearly aspired to be.

Scrooge stopped still, so suddenly that the urchin who had been about to pick his pocket yelped in surprise.

That was the answer.

Scrooge presented himself at the shabby shopfront as if he were making a morning call, giving the young woman his calling card with elegant courtesy. She was so taken aback she dropped her knitting and withdrew inside. Beneath his calm demeanour, though, his heart thudded, sweat prickled the back of his neck. Here he was, an old fool with a pocket full of change and arms full of expensive Christmas gifts, standing on the doorstep of a thieves' den. But then all that had been said about him flooded into his head now. *He was a squeezing, wrenching, grasping covetous old sinner. Hard and sharp as flint.* There was power in that.

The woman reappeared.

'He says come in.'

The broadsides and newspapers liked to terrorise their readers with lurid tales of criminal flash houses – the idea that London was teeming with secret thieves' dens gave honest readers a pleasant thrill of fear and so Scrooge had read a few descriptions of these miserable places. He braced himself for squalor, for hopelessness, for danger.

He found himself in a small room which was dingy but clean, full of people engaged in quite ordinary pastimes. There was a grubby man feeding coal into a fire. There were two other men, playing dice in the corner and talking. A tired-looking woman in slovenly attire sat by a small broken window, engaged in mending, a cup of gin at her side. Children darted about – some playing with rudimentary toys, some on secret errands for their elders and definitely-not-betters.

A shadow in the corner grunted and moved. It was Edgar's man, Amos, leaning on his cane. He beckoned Scrooge to follow and led him down a panelled corridor to a room beyond. Scrooge wondered if he was about to get beaten as badly as Bob had been – or worse. His fingers tightened around his Christmas shopping, and he tried not to think of them being cut off.

But when the door opened he heard . . . was that really music?

Parley's chamber was brightly lit and spacious. In one corner there was indeed a violinist, scraping busily away at his instrument. This must be what Edgar Parley thought gentlemen did when at home. Parley himself was seated at a writing-table near the fireplace engaged in a pastime Scrooge knew well: counting money. It struck Scrooge how similar the clinking of coins was to the clinking of a spectral chain. He looked warily about but saw nothing supernatural.

Upon seeing him, Edgar rose and made a bow.

'Well, if it ain't Mr Christmas.'

Scrooge greeted him politely, as he would any business associate, any gentleman. Edgar sat back and removed a gold pocket watch from his waistcoat, spinning it lazily on its chain, around in one direction, then another. He did not ask Scrooge to sit down, but nevertheless, Scrooge sat, spreading his parcels out before him. *This is just a negotiation,* he told himself. *And now it begins in earnest.*

'Sir, I am here with a proposition. Along with a number of ladies and gentlemen in town, I am organising a Benevolent Feast for the Poor this Christmas Day, and I wondered if, as a prominent figure in your field, you would be inclined to make a contribution.'

Parley's brows lifted ever so slightly – the only outward sign of his surprise.

'I am aware, of course, of your feelings about the festive season,' Scrooge continued smoothly. 'Indeed, as you know, I felt similarly until quite recently, but whether or not you celebrate the season yourself, it is certainly the duty of a gentleman to help the poor during the depths of winter.'

He was tempted to go on, to tell him about the joy of letting go, of making a difference to someone's life and joining in the celebrations, but that argument was unlikely to appeal to Parley, so he let his words hang there for a few moments, waited for the man to respond.

Parley's expression was a strange mixture of thoughtfulness, wariness, perhaps a worry that he was being mocked or patronised. And then he threw back his head and laughed.

'You want *me* to give to the poor this Christmas? As a gentleman?'

Scrooge swallowed. Here was the difficult part. 'Yes, and in memory of your poor sister.'

Keeping his own countenance calm, he studied Edgar's reaction. Not that he was expecting any outright admission of guilt, but just some flash of human weakness. A hint of remorse or a flash of rage.

Instead – sorrow.

'She *was* uncommonly fond of the season,' he murmured, as if to himself. He felt it then, Parley's sadness, his grief, as strongly as he would have done if the man had burst into tears.

The moment of weakness lasted less than a couple of ticks on Parley's watch. The Gentleman glanced at Amos, who stood by the door, and they shared a look of amused scorn.

'Christmas is a nonsense. It is a conspiracy by the rich to part complacent fools from their money. That's what I told her back when we were children, and I have not changed my mind.'

The words brought Scrooge up short. Had he himself not thought something similar in the past? And was he not proving it himself, by making money from the Christmas cards?

He shook the thought away and tried to focus upon Edgar, who was studying him closely in return, eyes narrowed.

'That's not why you're here though, is it?' he said eventually. 'You want me to leave your murdering clerk alone.'

Scrooge shivered. Parley's fixation on becoming a gentleman might make him absurd, but he was sharp-witted and perceptive, alive to any form of doubt or disrespect. Still, he kept his voice steady as he laid out his argument.

'You and I both know Bob is not capable of such a thing. You must have sensed it, back there in the prison cell as you were beating him. I cannot speak for the boy you knew years ago, but my clerk is the gentlest, kindest man of my acquaintance and would never raise his hand to anyone – let alone to a woman whose friendship he clearly cherished.'

He thought, with a flush of shame, that this was what he should have said in court. If the opportunity came up, he would not stay silent again.

'Hah! What do you know about good men? The men you deal with have even less conscience than old Amos there.' He nodded towards Amos, who stood in the doorway, grinning at the compliment.

'They are men of business. That's different.'

'How is it different? I'm in the business of making money, and if people get hurt while I'm doing it then that's their problem. Your business mates are the same. Kids get hurt in factories, men cough their lungs up down mines, but that's fine as long as the money's coming in. They're the same. They just wear better clothes and don't get their hands dirty.'

The thought wound its way inside Scrooge, constricting his insides, making him dizzy and disorientated. *Now is not the time to think about this*, he told himself. But then, it was nearly Christmas, which was the perfect time.

Parley peered at him, fascinated now. 'Besides, didn't I tell you to keep your beaky nose out of this? First that interfering old bat, then that light-fingered mooncalf swell, and now you. None of you want to believe that virtuous Bob Cratchit could kill.'

Scrooge's mind crowded with questions: what old bat, what mooncalf swell? But he had to concentrate on the task at hand. This was a business negotiation, even if he was seeking truth rather than profit.

'Bob Cratchit is innocent,' he said. 'Do you not want to know who truly killed your sister?'

Edgar shrugged. 'Bob was always sweet on her, and I know she was meeting him in secret. Love makes men do terrible things.'

Love. Scrooge resisted the urge to retort with '*humbug.*' He drew himself up in his seat, allowed his features to harden.

'I spoke of a bargain, Parley, and this is what I am offering you. Leave the Cratchits alone and I will show you that Bob did not do this. I can do it. I am cunning, every bit as ruthless as you, and I have connections, ones you may not have.'

Edgar looked at him curiously. 'And you'd do all this for Bob?'

'All this and more.'

Edgar snapped the watch shut, levelled his gaze at Scrooge. His eyes were like his sister's, Scrooge thought. He pressed on:

'I know that it pains you to speak of her, but please share with me any information that you can. Why did she leave her position in the Scabble household? Do you know where she lived or where she was working?'

'I have not spoken to my sister since we were children,' he says. 'She betrayed me. She was untrustworthy. It was easier for a time to pretend she was dead, but now . . .'

His voice cracked and the words hung in the air unspoken. *Now she is.*

Scrooge studied him, understanding now that Edgar Parley's anger had been a mask for deep, agonising grief. This was not the face of a man who had murdered his sister.

'She always did love Christmas,' he said with a sigh. 'Every nonsensical detail of it, though we could ill afford it in our family. At the beginning of December she sent me a note, wanted to make amends. I burned it.'

A lesser negotiator would have leaped in here to try and put Parley at his ease, to comfort him. But Scrooge let the silence stand for five heartbeats, six, seven . . .

Finally, the Gentleman spoke.

161

'You do what you can, old man, with your old business friends, and I will share with you anything I hear. I will send Amos here to check up on you, make sure you're keeping your promise. And remember, whoever killed my sister deserves to suffer in the longest, most painful way possible. So mind when you find who it is, you come to me, not the coppers.'

Scrooge nodded his head in assent. He would cross that moral bridge when he came to it.

The two of them shook hands, and Amos ushered him to the door, surveying Scrooge in a flat, unemotional way.

At that moment Scrooge caught a whiff of that familiar smell of flowers and butchery. He whirled round, searching for the spectre – but the room was only occupied by the living.

Parley was looking at him expectantly, wondering why he had turned. And at that moment one final question burst into his mind.

'What business do you have with Lucretia Tassell?'

The Gentleman gave a wry chuckle.

'Ah, the delightful Black Widow. Steer clear of that limb of Satan if you know what's good for you.'

13

For a while after his master departed, Tim sat there like a good boy, trying to work his way through his arithmetic, but he was still shaking from fright at Scrooge's outbursts. His rage at Jem had been wild, vicious, and Tim had seen him dash his ink bottle against the wall, breaking it and wasting valuable ink. Tim shuddered. Ebenezer Scrooge did not waste ink. Not when he was in his right mind, at least.

He's slipping back into darkness, and it's all my fault.

But mixed in with the feeling of guilt was another, newer feeling. Anger. Tim did not usually get angry. Other people lost their tempers, and it was his job to calm them down, to speak softly, to act sweetly until everyone was happy again. But now there was a small but furious spark in him. *I'm just little, weak Tiny Tim to him. Mother thinks so too. Even Jem does. But none of them understands that I'm the only one who can save Mr Scrooge.* Last Christmas had taught him that and he had lived with the secret burden ever since. So he had to do something, but what?

Reaching into his vest, he drew out the folded papers he'd concealed there. The sheaf of five-pound notes. He stared at them again, wondering at the intricate lettering that transformed it from being just a plain old piece of paper into money. Into something that people kill for.

After they had tracked Mrs Tassell to the flash house, he'd told Jem he was still carrying the notes and he'd been horrified, urged him to find a good hiding place. And where better to hide money than in a former miser's place of business?

The most secure spot would be among all the other notes and coins in his master's strongbox, but since nobody in London knew where it was kept besides Scrooge, that was out of the question.

Sliding from his father's stool, he went over to a chest of long, narrow drawers where Scrooge kept his documents and maps, thinking to conceal the notes among the papers.

The wide drawer was designed for longer arms than his and it took some effort to pull it out, but in Scrooge's absence he could take it as slowly as he wanted. It was full of large, flat papers and Tim lifted them, slipping the money underneath. It was then he noticed the map of London.

Tim loved maps, he could look at them for hours, tracing his finger down the streets on the paper, comparing those etched lines to the streets in his memory. On this one, the locations of Scrooge's properties were marked out, each with its own number which corresponded with a ledger kept by his father's desk. Father had once said Scrooge owned a great deal of property but none of it was a nice place to live – definitely no mansions there. There was, however, a Midding Street. Tim ran his grubby fingertip along it and there it was, property number eleven. Could this be the Midding Mansion to which the note with the money referred? Father sometimes called their house Cratchit Castle; perhaps Midding Mansion was more of a jokey title than a real one.

Clutching on to this weak straw of a discovery, Tim went back across the room to his father's ledger and located the number eleven. It gave an address for a small room in Midding Street, a rent which seemed to Tim to be an astronomical sum, but in truth was a pittance. In the column marked *occupant*, Father had written *Currently Unoccupied. Not for rental.*

This was odd. Scrooge did not like unoccupied property. And London was a crowded place; he would have had no trouble finding a tenant, even if the chimney had been smoking and the roof was falling down.

Of course, Tim could wait until his master came back and ask him why the property was unoccupied, but he hesitated. For years, Scrooge had checked and double-checked everything his father had done, but over the past year he had trusted him and let him run much of the business himself. If Father had made a mistake or abused that trust . . . Tim shuddered at the thought of how Scrooge would react.

Another idea formed in his mind – a way of showing both Scrooge and Jem that he was more than just tiny. Midding Street was not far from here. He could go there himself and investigate.

Without giving himself time to hesitate, he shrugged into his winter jacket, locked up and left the key with Mr Cruttle as instructed.

'There is no need to take me home, Mother is meeting me on the corner.' The lie tasted strange on his tongue but it was like medicine – bitter but necessary. He set off into the cold, foggy darkness.

🕯

Tim had an excellent memory for detail, and despite the fog, only got lost once. By the time he arrived, though, full darkness had fallen and most of the lamps had been lit. There was a tavern on the corner of Midding Street – not a raucous, disreputable one, but still lively and filled with the buzz of early Christmas revellers.

Tim did not consciously think about such things, but still the freshly swept cobbles and scrubbed front steps told him that Midding Street was poor, but respectable-poor. The door to Scrooge's property was the shabbiest one on the street, the paint peeling from weathered wood. He pushed it quietly and it opened a crack, looking into what was evidently a shared hallway. It was dark and deserted and smelled of fried fish. He could hear the creaks and mutterings of people at home on the other sides of the doors. A chair scraped on a bare floor. Somewhere, a baby cried.

Tim's heart thudded. Nobody knew where he was – not his parents, not his master, not even Jem.

I don't need them, he told himself. *I've got to show them how big I am, I've got to do it myself.*

He went inside.

From his father's ledger, Tim knew the room was on the top floor, which meant ascending a steep, narrow stairway which would be difficult with his crutch. He began to climb it on his hands and knees, dragging the crutch alongside. He wondered what he would do if he found someone was home and decided he would give them the innocent angel face, pretend he was collecting alms for the poor and try to gather information somehow. He smiled inwardly; he was getting more rascally by the day – Jem would be proud.

But as he approached the top of the stairs, he found the door was ajar.

Cautiously, he pushed it open a little wider with the tip of his crutch. The room was in darkness, there was just enough lamp-light leaking in from the street for Tim to see a small shelf by the door with a box of matches and a small lamp upon it. When he lit it, a warm glow filled the room. It was tiny. Most of the space was taken up by a neatly made truckle bed by the window, a table and three chairs. The room was chilly and there was an unlived-in smell to it which made Tim think nobody had been here for at least a few days. But someone had gone to a lot of effort to make it homely. The grate was cold, but a meagre fire had been laid out, with kindling and scraps of paper set aside to light it. And although there were still days to go until Christmas, someone had placed sprigs of holly on the mantel and had drawn a picture of Father Christmas in charcoal directly onto the wall of the chimney piece. There was a cunning look to him, a narrowing of the eyes Tim did not usually see in pictures of the jolly master of revels. Underneath, written in a fine, flourishing script, were the words: *From Midden Mansion to Midding Mansion, God bless us, every one!*

The words gave Tim a pang of sadness, as did the three stockings hung beneath the drawing, awaiting gifts.

Was this where that poor murdered lady had lived? That would make sense; the note had said that Father was to come here. But Tim's instincts told him this wasn't her home.

It took him a while to determine why. Despite the Christmas decorations, the clean linen on the table and neatly arranged crockery, it didn't feel real. Tim's mother was neat and tidy to a fault, but even so their house was still full of a jumble of things – drying laundry, too many hats and scarves on the coat hooks, a jar of bent nails that might come in handy for something, the bathtub which hung on the back door and got in everyone's way when it wasn't being used.

Tim thought about the time his father had taken him to the theatre. The stage had been set to look like a lady's parlour. There was a real chair for the actress playing the lady to sit upon, a table next to it for her gloves, but everything else had been painted on a backdrop – the fireplace, the windows, an elegant clock. That's what this room reminded him of. Someone had been setting the stage for a perfect Christmas, without really living it.

He rested for a moment on the chair by the fire and, out of curiosity, picked up the paper scraps. There was a bit of an old playbill, some neatly torn broadside and some strangely thick scraps of paper. She had been working on a letter, writing and rewriting the opening lines, crossing them out, screwing the papers up, not seeming to care about waste.

I am not your enemy . . . Forgive me . . . Will you intervene on my behalf? I am writing to implore you . . .

Each draft was scored through, the pen scratched into the paper with frustration. It was then that he caught sight of another letter, a sheet of cheap writing paper scrawled in a different, far uglier hand with brownish-coloured ink.

STAY AWAY FROM BOB CRATCHIT OR I WILL MAKE YOU PAY

14

NEXT MORNING, SCROOGE TOOK HIS BREAKFAST IN WHAT Mrs Miller insisted on calling the Christmas tree parlour. Somehow, his housekeeper had managed to find ribbons and bright red berries to decorate the branches and had added nuts and little parcels of dried fruit. Candles had been fastened to the end of each bough, but were thankfully unlit. Scrooge shuddered – how could this be safe? One lopsided flame and the whole thing would light up like a . . . like something. He couldn't think what.

Despite Mrs Miller's best efforts though, and the scrubbed-clean floor and fresh coat of paint on the walls, the place still felt cold, echoey and unlived-in. He could not picture it full of laughter. Last year Fred and his wife, Petunia, had hosted a merry band in their tiny home and blind man's buff had been a particularly high moment. The whole point of it was to play in a cramped, cosy little drawing room with obstacles to stumble around. He remembered how Fred's friend Topper had cheated wildly, chasing Petunia's youngest sister into a corner. The two of them were engaged now – he could not imagine such a love story sparking in this cavernous room. But he wanted it so desperately, the feeling of hosting Christmas, of making people happy with good food, good wine and song. He wanted to be that person.

'Don't worry, sir, it'll work,' Mrs Miller said, as if she had read his mind. 'The things we're doing – the wreath, the tree – will help guests relax, but it's the people that will make it feel homey.'

Scrooge held back the retort that sprang to his lips. His house-keeper was overstepping, but it was not her fault he was out of sorts this morning. Once again he had not slept well, but this time it was the ghost's absence, rather than her presence, which had bothered him. She had been murdered in the most dreadful, violent fashion. She was lost, alone and clearly terrified of him, and instead of comforting her he had tried to ignore her, then shouted at her, then thrown an ink bottle at her. And now she had vanished he did not feel free of her, he felt twice as haunted and was wondering, *how does one apologise to a ghost?*

'Note for you, sir,' Mrs Miller said. Scrooge felt a wave of dread, wondering if it was yet another poisonous, anonymous letter. But the writing paper was thick and high quality, the ink was dark and clear rather than that strange brownish colour.

You are a treasure, Mr Scrooge. I could kiss you! Mr Merrypaw has generously agreed to open his printworks to us for the Benevolent Feast. Thank you, once again, for your clever suggestion. I shall see you this evening at Lady Crick's fundraising gala.
  Lucretia Jane Tassell

Scrooge's face went hot. He slid his gaze over to Mrs Miller, who was making herself look flamboyantly busy by straightening all the candles on the tree. She had clearly read the note. Blast that Tassell woman – he would almost prefer the poison pen.

The note did confirm one thing, though. The bold, impatient strokes of Mrs Tassell's handwriting were nothing like the scratchings of the anonymous writer. Still, he would do well not to trust her and to cut all contact with her as soon as the Feast was done.

Stray tatters of fog still clung to the morning as he left the house. As he paused to adjust his hat, a figure loomed at him through the shadows. Scrooge cried out; his hand flew protectively to his pocket watch.

Amos gave a slow, lazy grin.

'Not today, old man.'

'Why are you here?' Scrooge snapped, clawing back some shreds of dignity. 'I don't need you.'

'Not your choice,' Amos said. His voice was rough and croaky, as if it had atrophied from disuse. 'I'm to stick to you like gum arabic, that's what the Gentleman says.'

'I suppose it would be pointless to offer you money to go away?'

'Yes.'

'Well, try not to get in the way.'

Scrooge's office was a strange silent place with this criminal slouched at Bob's desk instead of his loyal clerk. It was difficult to work with the man watching him as he filled in his rows and columns.

'Make yourself useful,' Scrooge said. 'Someone broke into my office a few days ago to put something in my clerk's desk drawer. I cannot see how it was done. Your expert eye might see something I did not.'

The corner of Amos's mouth tugged into a half-smile. 'I don't work for you.'

Scrooge opened his mouth to rebuke the man but thought better of it. He had evidently grown bored watching Scrooge, though, because after a couple of moments, Amos put his hands into his pockets and circled the room, inspecting the windows. Scrooge could not return to his work with him pacing about and began to think instead of Christina Parley's death. Her brother had shown true grief at her loss and Scrooge's instinct had told him it was genuine, but if Parley was not guilty, who was the 'gentleman' she had been seen arguing with after Bob's departure?

He was certain of one thing: no matter how this looked, Mr Scabble was not involved. He was a respected pillar of the community. Yes, he was prim and unfeeling – a little humbug-ish – but Scrooge of all people knew that an upright demeanour did not make one into a cold-hearted killer. Yes, Miss Parley had known him, and yes, there was the troubling matter of the watch chain, but that could have been a coincidence.

And no, he was most certainly not ruling Scabble out because of their business association. He knew this because, worryingly, he was beginning to suspect the fourth partner in their endeavour: Dr Alastair Bailey, ink innovator. He had only met the man once, but he was clearly unstable, mercurial and given to flights of fancy. Perhaps she had been killed for love after all.

No. Nonsense. More likely that Miss Parley had threatened to reveal their affair, or was with child, and Bailey had acted to preserve his status and financial interests.

If only he could ask Christina Parley herself.

He closed his eyes and reached out with his senses, searching the room for signs of her haunting. The flutter of her skirts, the chill of gooseflesh or that floral-gore stench. For a moment he felt a whisper of it on the air, as if the ghost were not truly gone. He took in a deep sniff, tried to reach out with his senses, to summon her here . . .

Amos cleared his throat.

Scrooge jumped, a flush of heat prickling through his skin – all sense of the ghost was gone and he was instead looking into the henchman's weathered face. Amos stood before him, pointed at a tiny leaded window which faced onto the street outside.

'That one there. They lifted the pane out of that cracked window. Stuck their hand in and opened the latch. Someone sent a young 'un in to do the job for them then slid the pane back in place after.'

Scrooge stared at the window, which he had been meaning to repair for over a year now. The opening was too small for any adult to fit through, and a feeling of helplessness washed over him. One could hire an urchin to do almost anything in this city. Just as one could hire a poor and desperate man to commit murder. Money made all one's problems go away and made the true culprit a little less traceable.

How would he ever find the killer?

But then, he would never do so just sitting here scratching figures into his ledger. He slid down from his stool, took up his hat and coat and set out to call upon Scabble and Bailey.

The Scabbles lived in a smart, well-maintained townhouse and, despite the head of the household's contempt for the festive period, his wife clearly knew what was proper as a prickly holly garland had been hung from the door, dressed with a sumptuous red bow.

A manservant opened the door, looking Scrooge up and down with scepticism.

'Mr Scabble is not at home,' he informed him.

Scrooge felt relief at that. He was not sure how to begin interrogating his haughty business partner. Better to start with the odd nephew instead.

'I understand Dr Bailey's laboratory is here?'

The servant gave the ghost of a sneer. '*Master* Bailey is at home. You may come in. Your manservant may not.'

Scrooge turned around, realising that Amos was standing behind him, leaning on his cane.

'Perhaps you could make yourself useful again,' Scrooge told him quietly. 'Go round to the servants' quarters and ask what they know of Christina Parley.'

A normal man would have nodded, or shaken his head, or at least acknowledged that Scrooge had spoken, but Amos stayed there, impassive as a wall as Scrooge went inside.

Scabble's house was, as one could predict, a very picture of respectability. The hallway was furnished modestly, with exactly the right number of family portraits, some of which were hung with green festive garlands. The room was not fashionable or lavish, because showiness would not do at all, but one would have no doubt that one was entering the home of one of the City of London's leading lights.

The decor became plainer as Scrooge ascended. Bailey's laboratory was at the top of the house, up in the eaves in a converted servants' bedroom, and by the time Scrooge reached it he was wheezing. The manservant opened the door, and a terrible stench filled Scrooge's nose and lungs, provoking a coughing fit that almost doubled him over. The servant, keeping his expression blank, announced him as if he were attending a ball.

'Mister Ebenezer Scrooge!'

Scrooge covered his nose and mouth with his handkerchief. The smell was quite overpowering, a strange mix of chemical odours, foetid sweat, a wisp of opium smoke and a dash of rot and decay. Was there a trace of the same scent he detected from the ghost? It was so powerful it was hard for him to tell. He swallowed back bile.

The room was dark and cluttered. There was a heap of clothing on a truckle bed in the corner, but the rest of the room was filled with benches and shelves bearing row upon row of earthenware bottles and stacks of paper debris. The curtains were sloppily drawn, and most of the light inside came from a lamp on the workbench, which had been adapted into some kind of miniature stove, gently heating a flask of some substance suspended above it. Vapour curled from it, across the room towards a row of jars which contained . . .

He froze in horror. They could not be real. *Dear God, I hope they're not real.*

'Oh, Mr Scrooge.' A flat voice came from the pile of discarded clothes, which turned out to be Dr Bailey, lying in a tangle of blankets and wearing a florid, patterned dressing gown. 'I know I asked you to call but I did not expect you this morning.'

Scrooge, who was still staring at the jars, bit back a reply that it was past midday. Bailey got to his feet with some effort and Scrooge could see the after-effects of drink on him – his eyes were bloodshot and heavy, his skin waxy and his jaw stubbled. This was a very different man to the sprightly, effervescent Dr Bailey of the night before. Did Scabble know how unstable his nephew was? He wondered if the modern inks were really all that necessary to the Christmas card project after all. Was it too late to use conventional pigments instead?

'You asked me here to inspect your work,' Scrooge said, still not taking his eyes from the jars.

'Oh . . . oh yes, give me a moment,' Bailey said colourlessly, taking a silver flask from his pocket and downing the contents. 'Here, I am working on a particular shade of greenish-blue which I'm calling kyanos after the Greek for . . . Ah.' He stopped, finally noticing that Scrooge's attention was fixed on the jars. 'I see you have noticed my hands. Well, obviously they're not *my* hands in the strictest sense of the word, but . . .'

'They are real human hands, then?'

Scrooge took a wary step towards the closest jar and peered at it. The severed hand within looked bloated and distorted through the glass. Flakes of pale loose skin were pulling away from it, and it was dotted with tiny bubbles. Curious how the dead flesh was repulsive, and yet he could not stop looking.

'Of course.' Bailey shrugged as if it were the most natural thing in the world. 'I'm researching the effects of prolonged acid exposure upon human skin and this is the only humane way to do it. You don't want me dipping a live subject into a corrosive substance now, do you?'

Scrooge pressed the handkerchief to his mouth again, suppressing a gag. Bailey warmed to the subject, his former bleak mood lifted by the stimulus of talking about his work.

'They really have deteriorated faster than I expected. The whorls on the fingertips were the first thing to degrade. Did you know there are studies which show each human being has a finger pattern unique to them? And we leave little imprints of ourselves on everything we touch.'

Scrooge had no time for such a whimsical idea; he needed hard evidence to tie a suspect to a crime. He forced his gaze away from the jars to look at Bailey, who had slumped back onto the truckle bed. Confronting Edgar had been easy, a matter of negotiation, of finding and exploiting his weaknesses. But this subject was all weakness and didn't seem to care.

Then an idea popped into his head – one to divert the subject and put Bailey at his ease. He reached into his pocket for the screwed-up poison-pen letters.

'I wonder if you could tell me about this ink?'

He found an uncluttered area of the workbench and laid out the first letter, folding the paper so that only the phrase *rot in hell, miser* was visible. The curiously coloured brown ink had already begun to fade. Bailey surveyed it with a flicker of interest.

'Did you never make acorn ink as a child? Perhaps that was just me – I have always been fascinated with ink and chemical processes. A simple mixture of acorn pieces and iron vinegar, it produces a most satisfying colour.'

'So the ink is homemade?' That was a clue, of sorts. A rich person might use poor-quality paper to disguise the origin of the note, but they would not go to the trouble of making their own ink.

Now, time to ask some more awkward questions. 'You do not look like a man on the verge of matrimony, Dr Bailey.'

Bailey's shoulders sagged again. Scrooge leaned into his subject.

'In fact, you look like a man who has suffered a terrible loss.'

Bailey just looked up at him miserably, and when Scrooge broke the silence he did it gently, almost kindly.

'Dr Bailey, I know what Christina Parley was to you.'

Bailey sat up, defensive. 'I am fairly sure you do not!' he snapped. 'I am sure you have put two and two together in your sordid little mind. Perhaps you think I am the sort of gentleman who fools with his serving maid. Or maybe you imagine her as the temptress, seducing me in the hope of jewels and gifts. Neither of those things are true. I am not a gentleman; I am a scientist. And she is not a serving maid; she is an artist. *Was* an artist.'

He reached for a nearby pile of papers and thrust them at him. They were sketches – remarkable, detailed sketches of Alastair Bailey, of Aldous Scabble and one of a bearded gentleman who looked alarmingly like the Spirit of Christmas Present. Scrooge did not have the soul of an artist, but even he could see the young woman had had a gift.

Scrooge turned away, overcome with emotion, as Bailey began to speak, to describe how remarkable Christina was and how strong – to walk away from a life of crime into the workhouse, and then into service.

'She deserved far more.'

'So you continued to see her, after she had left the household. Where was she living? Did she find a new place elsewhere?'

Bailey's eyes slid away from contact with Scrooge's, suddenly cautious. 'I cannot say.'

'Why not? Had she returned to thievery? Is that why she had your uncle's watch chain?'

'And what if she had?' Bailey asked. 'What business is it of yours, old man?'

Frustration bit hard into Scrooge's patience. 'My clerk is in prison, falsely accused of killing her. It is very much my business.'

Bailey gave a shout of laughter. 'Oh, you want your clerk back! Poor Mr Scrooge, cheap labour must be so hard to find these days! Well, you should make enough money from my ink and your festive foolishness to replace him. And when *I* get him released, he will be free to find another job. I think we are finished here. Good day.'

Chest puffed out with indignation, Scrooge descended the stairs taking grateful gasps of clean air and ignoring the man-servant's barely concealed amusement as he passed him on the stairs. His head began to clear, and he thought of what he had seen – a man clearly deranged, perhaps from working with so many dangerous substances for so long or perhaps from guilt at committing a terrible crime. He had loved Christina Parley, that much was true, but that did not make him incapable of killing her. Any man who kept human hands in a jar was capable of anything.

Scrooge thought of the cluttered, filthy workbench with its grisly experiments and shuddered. And then he froze on the staircase as he remembered catching sight of something else lying there. Amid the mess of papers, grubby flasks and unspeakable jars there had been a small leather razor case, exactly the same as the one the police had found in Bob Cratchit's desk drawer.

THE GHOST

THE NEW PLACE IS NOT SO BAD. CLEANER THAN WANTAGE'S. No beatings yet. No wandering hands – and I certainly don't miss my former master. There is just work here, and lots of it, until my back aches, my limbs are sore and I feel like I can barely stand. And although treated fairly, I am constantly watched. I am a valuable asset to be guarded.

Still, I am permitted to leave, sometimes, to creep back to Alastair's foul-smelling loft. Oh, my bonny Alastair. We spend hours in bed, laughing, playing. He tells me fantastical scientific tales, shows me his latest experiments. As a scientist he keeps an open mind, which is why I like him. But he will never fully understand or know where I have come from, and perhaps that is why I can never trust him.

He believes all the nonsense he has read in books and seen in plays. The romantic, noble version of villainy. He thinks of Edgar as Dick Turpin, living the high life, slipping through the fingers of the police and wreaking vengeance on the rich. He is full of his own foolish plans, too.

'Perhaps we don't have to wait for the ink money,' he says. 'Uncle has enough valuables in this house for us to start over again. I could just fill up a few sacks and leave in the night. Even if he found out, he'd never come for me.'

I answer silently: No, you fool. He'd come for me.

There is another thing which unnerves me, which makes my skin creep with unease when I think about it. He has still not broken off his betrothal. There is always a reason. The lady is delicate and sensitive; he needs his uncle to seal the deal on his new inks, so we'll have the money to flee. But I wonder if he will ever tell them or if he is leading me on. If I will be quietly got rid of. It would be easy for him to cut me out of his life. I would arrive one day to find the back door barred against me. The staff who usually turn a blind eye to letting me in will pretend not to know me. And then I will be reduced to chasing him down the street begging him why. He holds all the power in this love affair . . . except for one tiny detail. One word from me could bring scandal down upon him. It is the only power I have, and I only once threatened to use it.

Then, in a blink, I am there – in his laboratory, holding what I have just found. A bundle of newspaper cuttings about Edgar's 'exploits' that Alastair has hoarded in one of his desk drawers.

'I cannot help but admire him,' he admits. 'He is a man of enterprise, and I think if you let us meet, we would be friends.'

I shake my head in exasperation. 'This is not make-believe, Alastair. He is not Robin Hood. Promise me you will never contact him.'

Then I see it, a little spark in his eye and I understand. 'That's what you plan to do, isn't it? You want to approach Edgar and try to make things right between us.'

His sheepish silence is all I need to know I've guessed correctly.

'Edgar is dangerous, Alastair. I don't want him to know where I am. I don't want him to know who I love. He would only use it to hurt me.'

Alastair looks away from me, a sulky child.

'But he's your brother, surely you want to see him again?'

I feel a wrench inside my belly at that, because yes, I do want that – one day. But it is not for Alastair to decide.

'Promise me you will not speak to him while I live,' I say. And then I use the only leverage I have. 'If you do, I shall tell Miss Frome about us.'

I see a flash of fear in him. He knows I'll do it if I have to. And then, his jaw clenched resentfully, he agrees.

And I turn away, burning with hurt. Because his reaction has showed me the truth. Despite everything he has said, he will never walk away from this life to be with me. He will never break his engagement. At that point the last shreds of my trust in him fade away.

Minnie was right: all men lie and all women pay the price.

And look, here comes another heavy link for my chain, punishing me for knowing the truth and for loving him anyway.

15

SCROOGE'S BEST COLLAR WAS TOO HIGH, TOO STARCHED, AND IT was already irritating him. He had not worn his formal get-up for some time, and he was surprised to learn that not only was it about fifteen years out of fashion, but it also hung loosely from his shoulders where once it had been tailored to perfection. Decades of miserly dining had caused him to shrink, to take up less space in the world as his money took up more.

He ran his hands over the fine wool of his best winter coat – he had bought it years ago when he had thought appearances mattered but had never worn it because there had been plenty of wear left in his shabby old greatcoat. It was warm, it was sturdy and, he thought suddenly, it would fit Bob Cratchit like a glove. He knew exactly what to give his clerk for Christmas now. Something practical that he would never buy for himself. He just had to get him out of prison first.

He slowed his pace a little for Tim to catch up. He too was looking a little uncomfortable in his Sunday best coat and hat, which he had clearly outgrown over this past year, and perhaps it was a little eccentric to bring an office boy to Lady Crick's fundraising party, but it kept him out from under Mrs Cratchit's feet so she and Martha could busy themselves caring for Bob. Besides, Tim would definitely appreciate the food and decorations far more than any of the lady's other guests.

He felt fortunate that he did not have another shadow this evening. Amos had been waiting for him outside Scabble's house and had interviewed the staff as he had requested.

'For the Gentleman, not for you.'

When pressed he had revealed, in words of not more than one syllable, that Bailey had been agitated the day Christina had died. He had had a quarrel with his uncle and left the house in the late afternoon, returning home in some kind of stupor in the early hours of the morning. Mr Scabble had also left the house in a high temper and remained out past supper. The cook assumed he had dined at his club, a most unusual occurrence for a Wednesday night, but not unheard of.

So both men had been unaccounted for at the time of Christina's murder and for some hours afterwards. Amos had refused to share any more information than that, and shortly afterwards disappeared to report to his master. Scrooge hoped that would be the last help he would get from the Gentleman.

Tiny Tim curled his hand around the skirts of Scrooge's coat, something he seemed to do without realising, for comfort. The gesture brought Scrooge back to the present – they were here, at the well-appointed Crick residence. He smiled and patted the boy's shoulder.

'Ready?' he asked, as they reached the doorstep of a large, brightly lit house. A servant opened the door, gestured for them to enter and the two of them walked into the welcoming warmth of Lady Crick's hallway. Several thoughts struck Scrooge at once.

This place was huge.

This place was beautifully lit and sumptuously decorated.

Lady Crick must be wealthy beyond anything he had anticipated.

He must seek her approval.

Only to further the cause of fundraising, of course.

He hovered in the doorway to the lady's reception room. Never a sociable man, he had always found this moment hard, the transition from being alone with his thoughts to being on display for all of society to see.

Beside him, Tim had no such inhibition. His angelic jaw dropped as he gazed around the room. It was decorated in the latest style and draped all around with holly and ivy. He noticed one of those Christmas trees in the corner, larger than his, and lit perilously with tiny candles. Next to it, a group of musicians played merry carols, and the room was thronged with elegant people, talking and laughing, and dressed in their finest.

'It's beautiful,' the boy said.

I want to go home, Scrooge thought.

He was still relatively new to charitable work, and could not understand why it involved so many social events, or why other people seemed to enjoy them. But still, he would stay, to merit the lady's approval at least.

'Still lurking on the sidelines, Mr Scrooge?' It was, inevitably, Mrs Tassell. The woman was dressed in a black silk evening gown with long black gloves. A diamond necklace sparkled at her throat, but she had left off her veil, sporting instead a black feather in her dark, silver-threaded hair.

The widow broke into a charming smile, laughing softly. 'Oh, Scrooge, cheer up. I am only funning. Oh, and young Master Cratchit, how delightful to see you here too!'

Scrooge surveyed her with suspicion. She was involved in Christina's murder somehow; he was certain of it – if only he could work out how.

Mrs Tassell continued talking, quite unaware of his suspicious thoughts. 'Well, young man, there is a large plate of mince pies over there with your name on it. I say go and get them before Sir Crispin eats them all and ruptures his corset.'

The boy giggled and Scrooge's irritation grew. Why was she ingratiating herself with Tim? Was this part of her plan somehow?

Tim looked up at Scrooge, all hungry excitement. 'May I?'

'Indeed, you may,' he confirmed, and the lad rushed off, leaving him alone with the widow. His mind seethed with questions he longed to throw at her – why do you consort with criminals? What is the purpose of sneaking around a workhouse, stealing their property? What do you know about Christina Parley's death? But this was a party, he could not cause a scene, so eventually he simply said: 'It is a fine gathering, is it not?'

Mrs Tassell made a *pfft* sound. 'Well, if Lady Crick is determined to spend a fortune on a glamorous gala instead of using it to feed and clothe the poor, we might as well enjoy it. And maybe she's right, perhaps we will raise even more funds this way. Your friend Mr Merrypaw has already donated a considerable sum to the cause.'

She indicated Merrypaw, who was standing with Lady Crick, his head thrown back in laughter. He was wearing another flamboyant waistcoat – this one looked like it was embroidered with holly leaves.

'I cannot thank you enough for suggesting him,' Mrs Tassell added. 'He seems to understand what we are trying to achieve and . . .' She paused, peering at Scrooge. 'Why are you looking at me like that? Usually you have some kind of riposte for me, a cheerful put-down or a provoking opinion to share.'

At this, Scrooge's patience snapped.

'Madam, why do you insist on speaking to me like this? As if we are friends or allies in something? You know nothing of me, and I am certain I know nothing of you.'

Mrs Tassell gave a little gasp of shock and hurt, her jaw dropping open, but Scrooge could not hold back now.

'You eavesdrop, you steal, you walk the streets in improper dress, you associate with criminals and yet you treat *me* as someone who needs moral improvement and lecture me on charity!' he snapped – and by God this felt good.

'Mr Scrooge, I . . .' The widow began, but Scrooge barely noticed.

'I am beginning to think that you have no idea of propriety,' he said. 'I should inform Lady Crick of your pernicious nature!'

'Well!' Mrs Tassell's shocked expression turned into one of outrage. 'I was about to explain myself, but as you are determined to share your knowledge with that hatchet-faced viper I shall remain quiet! Good evening, Mr Scrooge.'

She swept away, dashing something out of her eye with her gloved hand as she went. For a moment Scrooge stared after her, heart pounding, blood singing through his veins. The joy, the satisfaction of speaking his mind lasted only a few moments before the guilt crashed in. He stared downward in shame.

A drop of something red landed on his shirt cuff. The redness bloomed and spread across the white, growing faster, spreading further than was natural for such a small drop of liquid until the whole of his cuff was red, and the stain was spreading up onto his coat. Blood. It was blood. He looked up, into the angry, cadaverous eyes of the ghost.

His heart thudded. She was back – just in time to witness him berating someone again. Fear warred with a strange kind of relief at seeing her. He opened his mouth to speak, to try and explain himself, to apologise, when his nephew Fred appeared, walking straight through the apparition. She broke apart like a puff of cigar smoke.

'There you are, Uncle Scrooge!' Fred's smile, his infectious laugh had an immediate calming effect. He clasped his uncle's hand, pumping it with violent enthusiasm. The lovely Petunia appeared next to him, snaking one shapely arm through her husband's, and beside her was the pale blonde lady he knew to be Miss Frome, evidently a friend of theirs. Her hair had been styled into pretty ringlets but she looked distracted somehow.

'Well, this is quite a squeeze, isn't it?' Fred said. 'So wonderful to see the great and the good doing something for the poor this Christmas!'

Scrooge glanced at a nearby gentleman, who had crammed a whole mince pie in his mouth and was washing it down messily with a glass of mulled wine.

'Indeed,' he said, with a note of scepticism. 'But the key is to keep the charity going beyond Christmas, to provide lasting aid. Build a bridge between rich and poor, so to speak.'

Fred raised an eyebrow at the words, and then smiled.

'I knew you had changed, Uncle Scrooge, but I did not appreciate just how much until now!'

Scrooge was even more surprised than Fred that he had parroted Mrs Tassell's words. But it made sense. You couldn't just let the poor starve all year then feed them up on Christmas Day. There was something almost grotesque about the thought, now he looked closely at it. No, you had to build something bigger, something lasting. Then an idea struck him with such force that it made him gasp: you needed to work with the poor themselves, to ask them what they needed to make their lives better. That was not just Mrs Tassell's influence, it was Christina Parley's. She had been poor, but somehow she had found a way to help her fellow man.

'We are very much looking forward to spending Christmas at your house, Uncle,' Fred continued. 'I hear there is to be a tree like this one!'

'Indeed, there is, and the word "humbug" will be completely forbidden!' Scrooge attempted what he hoped was a playful smile, and Petunia drew back a little.

'You must join us on Christmas Eve, though, Uncle! That is when we tell stories around the fire, it is one of our favourite traditions! Miss Frome was with us last year, weren't you, ma'am, but this year she will be preparing for her . . . Ah, are you quite all right?'

Miss Frome had turned pale and seemed unsteady on her feet. Scrooge saw the shade of Christina behind her – her bloodied, black-tipped fingers were at Miss Frome's neck hovering less than inch from the lady's pulse.

'No!' he cried out before he had a chance to think.

'It's so cold in here . . .' Miss Frome's voice was a whisper. 'So very . . .'

Christina's fingers brushed against Miss Frome's ringlets, the spectre stared at them in sad fascination. There was no jealousy or spite in her expression, but the contact was too much for Miss Frome – Scrooge just had enough time to hold out his arms to catch her swoon.

Fred found a seat nearby and together they lowered the young lady onto it.

'Uncle, could you fetch Dr Bailey?' Petunia asked.

'He is not here,' Miss Frome said faintly. 'He said he would be here, he promised, but he is not. Please do not disturb yourself, I will be fine after a sip of lemonade.'

Tiny Tim was under a table. It seemed like the safest refuge in a room full of such strange people. The women wore outlandish, glittery clothes and their hair was twisted into funny shapes. The men had funny, too-happy smiles and smelled of mulled wine and smoke. One of them thought he was a pickpocket who had crept into the party. Several more had tried to pinch his cheeks. So he had become a thief indeed, piling up an armful of mince pies and other assorted sweets and hiding under the elegant damask table-cloth. It was a comfortable little world here, beneath the table, although it was a little dusty. Mother would definitely not have approved.

Snatches of conversation drifted down at him as he worked his way through his haul. There was talk about a horse that was going to win a lot of races, some discussion of an opera dancer who was apparently very pretty and had a lot of 'charms', whatever they were. Tim soaked up the words like a sponge, planning to figure out what it all meant later. Then a familiar voice drifted towards him.

'. . . I suppose the Parley situation is resolved now?' Tim almost choked on his pie crumbs. It was that nice Mr Merrypaw – his voice as jolly and friendly as ever, but lowered, as if he did not want the other partygoers to hear.

'Indeed, the watch chain was removed and my name kept out of it, as much as it could be.' That was Mr Scabble's brittle, crabby voice. He'd know it anywhere. 'A small payment to that crooked curate was sufficient for him to lose his memory. The shopkeeper required slightly more physical persuasion though – my footman was equal to that task.' Scabble gave a sigh. 'That foolish boy does not know the expense he has caused. He had damned well better get married now and move his awful laboratory out from under my roof.'

As with the other conversations, Tim did not fully understand what he was hearing, but he knew enough. So Mr Scabble had threatened the shopkeeper Tim had spoken to – had he also been the smartly dressed gentleman Christina Parley had met? Scabble and Merrypaw had seemed like an odd partnership to Tim, but now they seemed in perfect harmony. He thought back to when he had first met Merrypaw, the way he had swept him up onto a high stool without asking, left him trapped there and unable to get down. He had sensed then that a man who needs to wear Christmas on his waistcoats rather than his face did not have such a generous spirit as he pretended.

'It is fortunate indeed that the police pursued the Cratchit route, rather than looking too closely into her other associations,' Merrypaw said.

In his hiding place, Tim froze.

Scabble gave a thoughtful grunt. 'I would have preferred a different culprit. Mr Scrooge is too closely associated with our enterprise.'

Merrypaw gave a low chuckle. 'Don't worry, after tonight, Scrooge's name will be on everyone's lips for an entirely different reason.'

Mr Scabble replied with an odd, dry-sounding noise which Tim realised must be a laugh. He felt a stab of panic – they meant to harm his master somehow! He must warn him! Dropping his remaining mince pies, he crawled out the other side of the table and crept away, concealing himself in the press of people. He could see Mr Scrooge across the room, giving lemonade to a young lady who looked a little dazed.

Tim squirmed through the crowd towards him. He called out, but his tiny voice was drowned out by the hubbub of happy fundraisers. And before he could reach Scrooge a deep voice boomed out over the assembled crowd.

'Ladies and gentlemen, pray be silent for Lady Crick!'

Scrooge did not see his young apprentice, instead he was searching the room for the ghost as Lady Crick rose from her seat.

'It is my pleasure to welcome you here for Christmas, and for such a good cause.' Lady Crick shone a beneficent smile around the room. 'Every farthing you donate tonight will go towards the Benevolent Feast for the Poor. And it is my great pleasure to announce that we have a new venue for the unfortunates this festive season, courtesy of our new friends, Mr Felix Merrypaw and Mr Aldous Scabble. Please, sirs, come and take a bow.'

There was much applause again. Scabble stood and took an austere bow, and Merrypaw danced a happy jig of excitement, smiling at the assembled party.

Scrooge felt a tremor next to him, a chill as the ghost drew closer to him, almost as if she was doing so for comfort. Her form flickered like a guttering candle, so rapidly he could not make out her expression. He wanted to watch her, study her for clues, but his own name was being called out across the room.

'I must thank Mrs Lucretia Jane Tassell and Mr Ebenezer Scrooge, for alerting me to the problem at hand and allowing me to help!' Merrypaw said. 'Step up, Scrooge old fellow, will you?'

Beaming with pride, Fred nodded eagerly, pushing his uncle forward to a fresh – although slightly more sceptical – round of applause. Scrooge took his place alongside his business associates, painfully aware that once again he was the centre of attention. Should he attempt another smile? It seemed to be expected. He prayed that they would not ask him to speak; luckily, Merrypaw took the lead.

'Mr Scrooge is one of the chief benefactors behind this year's Benevolent Feast for the Poor. Yes, that is correct, Ebenezer

Scrooge, once known – forgive me, dear friend – as the greatest miser of this parish! If you remember he underwent a remarkable revelation last year, discovering the joy of Christmas spirit, which transformed him from a renowned pinch-penny to a generous and friendly fellow. And now he has joined with me and my associate in finding a new way to celebrate the festive season!'

Scrooge felt a flutter of unease in his stomach as he looked out at the sea of gawping faces. His mind raced, searching for a way he could escape, but there was none. In the corner of the room, Mrs Tassell eyed him and smirked.

'He is far too modest to tell you about our latest Christmas venture so I shall do so. In the spirit of Sir Henry Cole's famous Christmas card of last year, we have produced a whole new selection of greetings cards to give to your friends and family for Christmas, including one inspired by the story of our own dear Ebenezer Scrooge.'

A servant approached bearing an easel covered in a cloth, which he propped up next to Merrypaw. Once it was secure, the businessman pulled the cloth off with a flourish, to reveal a large board displaying all the new Christmas card designs.

Scrooge, who had not seen them all before, turned to look. At first, all that registered was the vivid red and green colours that leaped off the page, the more delicate shades which had been added by hand. The gathered gentry crowded forward, blocking his view as they cried out about the brightness of the colour, the innovation of the design.

The tittering began slowly, and at first Scrooge did not notice, but then a moustachioed gentleman cast a sidelong glance at him, looked back at the board and laughed out loud.

'Why, it's the old man in his nightgown!'

The laughter spread, along with exclamations of 'so it is!' and 'look at his scrawny legs!'

Scrooge grew hot, prickling with sweat. His heart hammered. The false smile slid away and his mouth dropped open. He pushed his way to the front of the crowd until finally he could see what everyone else was looking at.

There, between the image of the robin and one of a cherub bearing a bouquet of flowers, was a design he had not seen before. It was divided into three sections – the first featured a thin, grumpy-looking man pushing a pauper into a midden. The second featured the same familiar-looking man asleep in a shabby-looking nightcap with a cloud over his head, which Scrooge assumed indicated a dream. Inside the cloud were angels and stars and sprigs of holly. In the third box, the man was dancing through the streets in his nightgown, throwing coins with one hand and gifts with the other, displaying a terrifying rictus of a smile and, yes, a pair of skinny hairy legs. The title of the card was emblazoned across the top in beautiful lettering:

EBENEZER SCROOGE: A MISER REFORMED

Anger and humiliation whirled inside him and Scrooge could not move from the shock. The people around him were still laughing uproariously. Everywhere he looked he could see gaping mouths, ladies and gentlemen wiping tears from their eyes. He whirled to confront his business partners. Scabble's countenance was impassive, dignified; Merrypaw's was wreathed in smiles as if he had not just humiliated a respectable business partner.

'Sorry for the surprise, dear chap, but you must agree that this will set tongues wagging, and when tongues wag, money changes hands! After all, everything is a business opportunity, even Christmas. No, *especially* Christmas.'

It was true, the moustachioed gentleman was already placing an order for a dozen, the men and women around him were laughing and clamouring, offering to buy them all.

Since their first meeting, he had been astounded by Merrypaw's gift for commerce, for selling, and only now could he fully understand the man's talent. A tiny part of him was in awe of his abilities. He could see now it was all part of the plan: Scabble's sly references to Scrooge's 'fame', the artist sketching in the corner at their meeting, Bailey's reference to Scrooge bringing his 'singular qualities' to the deal. Scrooge felt an urge to rip the board down, stamp on it and storm out of the room, but he knew that would only make things worse. And he was using every atom of his strength to focus on holding the last scraps of his dignity together.

Smile, Ebenezer. Smile.

He widened his lips into what he hoped was a convivial, relaxed grin, and forced himself to take a bow.

The assembled party let out a resounding cheer.

Someone thrust a full glass of mulled wine into his hand. Someone else slapped him on the back, knocking the wine down the front of his good waistcoat. His collar dug uncomfortably into his chin again and he loosened it, struggling to breathe.

He caught sight of Fred in the crowd, hands thundering together in applause. And Tiny Tim, who clapped, but had a look of deep concern as he studied his master's face.

And then amid the tumult Scrooge saw something strange, something which did not belong there. The figure of a man, crouching on the patterned carpet next to the Christmas tree. His shoulders hunched, he seemed to be trembling. Scrooge felt a pull towards him which jerked him out of his shock and shame. He started forward towards the man.

'What's he staring at?' he heard a voice say.

'Who knows, he's a strange old buzzard. Good sport though. I'll buy one of those card things for Great Aunt Gertrude . . .'

Scrooge ignored them, reaching out towards the man. Just as his fingertips connected with the man's shoulder, he saw the figure had a transparency about it which had become all too familiar. When he touched him, his form dissipated like vapour.

Scrooge found his voice. 'Sir . . .'

The figure turned and looked up. His features were young and painfully familiar. He was pale, terrified just like Christina's ghost had been when she had first appeared. Dr Alastair Bailey gaped, trying to cry out, but no sound came. His neckcloth was stained scarlet. His throat a jagged, open wound.

Ebenezer Scrooge screamed.

THE GHOST

MY LOVE IS CURLED ON THE FLOOR, HUNCHED AND WEEPING AS HE clasps his throat with gloved hands. I remember how invulnerable he used to feel, how he walked the streets of London full of curiosity and confidence that a young, vigorous gentleman such as himself could come to no harm. He flickers and fades, he screams a silent scream. I too was like this when I first arrived, the shock of my death still fresh in me. I reach out to reassure him, but he is like smoke under my hands. He flickers in and out and I let out a silent sob, knowing what he is going through, that he is being forced to relive his death, and dragged back through his life, weighed down with his own chain. And then I tumble back again, away from his ghost and into our past and find myself tangled in his sheets, still warm from his body. I remember this happening, only three weeks ago.

'When will you tell her?' I say.

'Soon.'

'Christmas is coming.' And by Christmas I mean the wedding. He must see the doubt in my eyes, because he kisses my cheek and smiles.

199

'Christmas will be our saving grace, my love! The Merrypaw deal is nearly done. Once those cards are printed and money starts coming in, that's when I can call off the wedding.'

I stiffen, wrapping the sheet around me. This feels like a lie. It's not as if I believed in the dream all along. When he first spun me this ridiculous plan of a cottage in the country with a studio and a laboratory I had even laughed. But then he had kissed me and shut down the doubts in my mind, as if reality no longer mattered.

'And besides, one has to consider Miss Frome,' he says. 'I've known her since she was in the cradle. This will destroy her reputation.'

He is squirming on a hook, watching, waiting for me to say something which lets him off it, which allows him to go easily through his life as he has up until now. I feel a flare of fury, but when I open my mouth, it's laughter that comes out.

'You're afraid,' I say. 'You like to talk about how you will leave this comfortable life, how you don't care about reputation and respectability, how you admire people like Edgar who live free of it. But you'll never give it up. You're a coward.'

I get up, allowing him one last glimpse of my legs, before pulling on my skirt and re-tying it around my waist. I had not expected a fairy story, I had never asked for him to whisk me away and make a home for me in a castle, but now it is as if some spell had been broken and I can no longer bear to be in his bed. Not for a second more.

Instead of the servant's back stairs, I take the main way down. Jobbs, the footman, tries to stop me but hesitates. He sees steel in my gaze. His cries draw the attention of the master of the house, who appears at his study door.

Scabble sees me – my hair ruffled, my clothing hastily put on, and his jaw falls open in a most satisfying way. He looks like a trout.

An irresistible idea pops into my head, and I smile.

'I am here to announce my betrothal to your nephew,' I tell him. 'Kindly adjust the wedding arrangements accordingly. I shall see you on Christmas Day.' It is exactly what Alastair promised me, after all, and it feels good to hear Mr Scabble's strange clucking noises of outrage as I sail past him and into the hallway. It is not until I reach the door that he finds his voice.

'Harlot!'

'Don't stand in my way, old man,' I call back. 'I can destroy your reputation as well as his.'

'Jobbs,' Scabble orders. 'Stop her!'

'But, sir, she's a Parley . . .' he protests. It's good to know that protection still holds true.

Scabble's roar of rage and frustration is the last thing I hear as I leave.

I add blackmail to my list of sins, and I accept a further link in my chain as something I fully deserve.

16

SOMETHING WAS WRONG. SOMETHING WAS VERY, VERY WRONG.

A cold, jabbing fear closed around Tim's heart as he struggled along in the wake of his master. The colour had returned to Scrooge's cheeks a little, but he was still clearly trembling as he strode away from the Crick house and into the night.

An icy wind blew away the cursed fog and Tim held the collar of his smart coat closed, but the wind bit through the thin weave of the mittens his mother had knitted for him. He shivered. He felt colder than he had done in a long time, even more so than when he had stood outside the churchyard for those long hours. This chill was bone-deep, and out of the corner of his eye he thought he saw something, wisps of filmy matter blowing in the gusts like discarded broadsides.

'Dear God have mercy,' Scrooge muttered to himself, his voice catching in a sob. 'There are two of them. *Two.*'

Tim was afraid. For the past few days he had been trying desperately to gather clues, to figure out who had killed that poor lady and to exonerate his father, but he had not honestly expected himself to succeed. He was, as everyone kept telling him, but a tiny child. It was beyond him. It wasn't his job. His true job was the care and betterment of Ebenezer Scrooge, and now he had failed at that too.

Some memories lived in Tim's mind for ever, and one of those was from last Christmas. When everyone else was laughing and joking and exclaiming over the fat turkey and hamper of food that Mr Scrooge had brought, Scrooge himself had gathered Tim onto his knee.

Tim had been weak then, coughing and ill, and he remembered Scrooge's lap being a warm, if uncomfortably bony, place. Still nervous of his father's terrifying employer, Tim had felt uneasy at first, but then Scrooge had said, *let me tell you a story.*

The old man had laid it all out before him, how he had been visited by three spirits who had taught him the true meaning of Christmas, and of humanity. The visions of Christmas past, present and future. Tim had listened, entranced.

'It's a wonderful fairy story, is it not?' Mr Scrooge had said, but Tim always knew when adults were lying and when they were telling the truth.

Since then, Tim had appointed himself the guardian of Mr Scrooge's goodness, the conscience who sat upon his shoulder and guided him towards the right thing to do. Away from sadness and troubled waters, towards happiness. It was why he felt afraid every time his master's brow furrowed, why he sought to conceal unpleasant facts from him, like Father letting Christina Parley stay in Midding Mansion. Saving Scrooge's soul had become Tim's life's work.

Now, his master stalked further and further ahead of him, muttering curses and clearly in turmoil. He rounded the next corner without even looking back. How could Tim have ever believed he was strong enough to do this task? Last year he had been barely clinging on to life by a thread and even now his cursed body was holding him back.

Tim stopped in his tracks, suddenly unable to go on. He was out of breath, a sob welling up inside. But then the sob became something else – a tightness, a tickle in his chest.

He coughed.

Scrooge strode ahead, the ghosts keeping pace with him. Christina drifted at his side, holding her bloodied hand out in entreaty. The other, newer spirit loomed ahead, screaming silently at him mouth agape like a red chasm of fear.

'Go away,' he muttered, flailing his arms at them as if they were pestering flies. 'For goodness' sake, leave me be!'

His was mind a boiling mass of confusion, frustration and rage. In the space of one night, he had been haunted and humiliated. He had quarrelled with Mrs Tassell, frightened that young lady Miss Frome and made a cake of himself before his nephew, his business associates and all the guests. Worst of all was the underlying fear that he was slipping, that goodness was evading his grasp again. The spirits had told him that this was the season of merriment and good cheer, but how could he keep Christmas well when all this was going on?

And then he heard the cough – a thin, tired sound he had heard many times in the past. It pulled him back into the real world and froze him with terror. *Not Tim. Not again.*

He found the boy quite far behind him, tearful and tired.

'Come on, boy, what is this?' he said gently. 'No, no, we cannot have this. Come.'

He swept the boy up onto his back, the way Bob Cratchit often did when he carried Tim home. Tim gave a weak murmur of protest, then clung on tightly with his slender arms and legs, burying his head in Scrooge's scarf. Scrooge could feel him trembling as if racked with sobs, heard the faint hint of a sniffle.

He kept his head down, staring at the grimy cobbles for the rest of the walk home, afraid to look up lest he saw either the screaming, writhing ghosts or, possibly worse, some member of the public ready to laugh at him over his Christmas card humiliation.

As he reached his door, the holly wreath hanging there seemed to mock him. How could he celebrate Christmas, feel warm and merry and bright when there was death all around him, and this innocent boy was ill again? He grabbed it, ripping the string which held it in place and tossing it aside as he entered his home.

'Humbug,' he growled, and slammed the door behind him.

He ordered Mrs Miller to make up a bed for the boy in his study, lay a nice warm fire and send word to Mrs Cratchit that Tim would be staying with him tonight. Ignoring the ghosts screaming around him, he himself eased off Tim's boots, laid a blanket over his knees and pressed a warm drink into his hand. He held a chilly palm to the child's warm forehead. Yes, there was a fever coming. He fixed his attention on Tim, only Tim. He must not flinch from the spirits around him. He must not frighten the child.

It was only after Tim was fast asleep on the sofa in his study that Scrooge retired to bed. But the ghosts would not let him rest. For a while he cringed under his thin, shabby counterpane, but the new spectre thrust his head through the bed covers and dripped that strange, vanishing gore upon his sheets. The two phantoms gestured at each other, gestured at him, trapped in a cycle of agitation he could not interpret.

He tried to focus on his ledgers, but the figures swam around on the page. At last, in desperation, he turned to the latest edition of *Virtue and Vice: A Tale of London,* as provided by Mrs Tassell.

He drew his covers up around him and began to read aloud. The spirits, possibly out of mystification, stopped their whirling and hovered just at the edge of his field of vision. He felt like a father reading a bedtime story, but if it kept them still, then so be it.

The hero of the tale, brave Adam Sparrow, was in dire straits, reduced to poverty and torn from his beloved by the villain, Baron Odioso. Moved by the plight of his virtuous poor neighbours, Adam pronounced: *I dream of creating a bridge between rich and poor, how much we could learn from each other!*

Scrooge grunted. So that was where Mrs Tassell got her ideas from.

Then he froze, a thought snagging in his mind. He rummaged on his nightstand for a previous volume, flicked through it and saw another phrase: *Finding a reticule too small for her needs, the lady had asked her dressmakers to sew hidden pockets in her voluminous skirts . . .*

And then further on: *'Give a man a fish,'* cried Adam, *'And you feed him for a day. But teach him to fish and you will feed him for a lifetime.'*

He looked once again at the title page:

Virtue and Vice: A Tale of London
By LJ Pettigrew

LJ – Lucretia Jane. Mrs Tassell was the author of this cheap, tawdry tale.

Which meant . . .

Scrooge leaped out of bed, and stalked across the room, searching through the scrap paper he used to light fires until he found it, the screwed-up remains of the broadside Jem had given him.

THE MURDER OF CHRISTINA PARLEY by LJ Pettigrew

She was also the one who had written the broadside about Christina meeting and arguing with a man in a white comforter. Lucretia Tassell was the one who had brought Bob to public attention. Her words had got him arrested.

Ebenezer Scrooge cursed long and low. He was not a man given to foul language, but 'humbug' did not seem strong enough for the situation.

Fuelled by pure anger, Scrooge dragged his clothes on and set out again into the street. Staring at the cobbled road ahead, he did not look to see if the ghosts accompanied him.

It was late. The old church clock chimed a quarter past one and all respectable folk were in their beds. And although Lucretia Tassell was by no means respectable, she would no doubt be sleeping too. Scrooge stood before her door, fist held up as if to knock on it, but held back. He had already made a spectacle of himself at the party; he had no desire to do so again in the darkened street. No, he would have it out with that hypocritical termagant during daylight hours and relish every moment of it.

Scrooge walked on, past the wreath-decked houses and through the deserted Christmas market where he had squandered all that money on festive fripperies. He remembered the last time he had been abroad this late, on Christmas Eve last year, flying through the air by the side of the Spirit of Christmas Present, and he shuddered. After his last visitation he had vowed that he would be good, in part so he would never have to see another spectre again. And yet now there were two, tormenting him, following him.

Well, so be it. If he was to be haunted, he would visit the only ghost he knew who talked any sense.

Like Tiny Tim before him, Scrooge arrived to find the church-yard locked, but the bolt was rusted and after a heavy shove, it gave way. He promised himself, and any spirits who might be watching, that he would make a donation to the church in the morning.

He began to regret his decision as soon as he entered the churchyard. Away from the gaslit street, it was pitch-dark, unlit by even the smallest lantern. He could not see more than three feet in front of him. He took out his tinderbox and struck it experimentally, but the wind which had cleared out the fog would not allow it to light. It was no good, he would never find what he was looking for in the dark.

Just then he became aware of a soft glow at his side. Christina Parley stood by him, somehow emitting just enough light that he could see the path ahead.

The other ghost, that of Bailey, had vanished but Christina was steadier now, seemed more in control of her faculties, even though the sight of her lover's spectre must have been terrifying to behold.

'Please take me to Jacob Marley's grave,' he said quietly. 'It is close to where I found you.' He worried that this would cause distress, make her vanish again, but she nodded and glided forward slowly, taking care to go around the graves. Scrooge struggled after her across the frozen ground, the hardened snow crunching under his boots. He knew this path. He had trodden it so many times over the last eight years since his friend's death. His fingertips brushed the tombstones as he passed, until he arrived at Marley's sparse monument. Feeling it appropriate, he knelt.

'Greetings, old friend,' he said.

As ever, Marley did not reply, but this time Scrooge wanted him to.

'I need advice,' he continued. 'I need you to tell me what it was like to die.'

Scrooge waited. The cold set into his bones and he began to shiver. Perhaps he was a fool to come here every week and talk to a gravestone. Perhaps Marley had better things to do than lurk in churchyards listening to the witterings of his partner. After a few moments he struggled, huffing, to his feet – but then a thought occurred to him. Rifling in his pocket, he found a coin and pulled it out.

Damn, a shilling. A sixpence would have served, but still, it was all he had. He reached out and placed the coin on Marley's gravestone.

'Here's a shilling for some Christmas cheer,' he said. He turned and made to leave, when he heard it. The laugh.

Marley had not laughed often. And when he and Scrooge had laughed at something it had usually been cruel – chuckling over the inventive sob stories of their debtors or the misfortunes of one of their business associates. It was this laugh which rippled through the air now, with an added dry, dusty quality as if the laugh had not been used for some time.

'A whole shilling, you old blaggard.' Marley's tone was amused. 'You must be desperate!'

Slowly the man's face rose out of the surface of his tombstone, like the very rock itself was bending and transforming into his features. It was lit with an eerie blue-green light.

And there was Marley before him, spectral spectacles pushed up on his forehead, still wearing the kerchief he had died in, tied around his head and chin. Scrooge still found it hard to think that his closest friend had been carried off by a toothache. He could not see his former business partner's body, but he could hear the faint clanking of Marley's chain – the heavy burden of links and locks he had to carry after a lifetime of caring far too much about money.

'You filthy hornswaggler,' Scrooge said, as pleasantly as if he were saying good evening.

Marley chuckled again and Scrooge felt a genuine smile touch his lips. He had missed the old pinch-penny. Strange how he had never wanted to see the ghost of Marley before, but now, after Christina and her lover, the fear of good old Jacob had left him.

He cast a look over his shoulder to see Christina standing there, keeping her distance, while Bailey was still nowhere to be seen. The wind played with the edges of the apparition, blowing her this way and that like a flag.

'Why do you call upon me? You haven't run the business into the ground, have you?'

'No, nothing as bad as that, I am simply being haunted.' He indicated the spectre nearby. '*Again.*'

Marley cackled with glee. 'Oh, you must be livid,' he said. 'Please tell me, does she plague you day and night? Does she follow you everywhere?'

'Yes.' Scrooge did not bother to mince his words. 'Although there are two of them now. I'm not sure where the other one is but he is not someone I much liked in life, so I would very much like to be rid of him immediately.'

Just then, as if summoned, the spectre of Bailey roared into being, rushing at him, ghastly mouth agape, his blood- and ink-stained fingers tearing at his scarlet neckcloth. Scrooge started back, tumbling onto the grave behind him.

'Oh yes, I can see how that would be a little wearing,' Marley said. He looked pityingly at his partner, shaking his head. 'But don't you see, you old mountebank? The more you try to rid yourself of them, the closer they will stay to you. The more evil you do, the more haunted you will be. Keep going along this path and you'll be inundated by ghosts by next Christmas. You may even receive another visit from my friends, the spirits of Past, Present and Future.'

No. This could not be allowed to happen, he could not face that terrifying spectre of Christmas Yet to Come. Not again.

'Why me?' he wailed. 'I learned my lesson. I am trying to be a better man. Surely there are worse men out there that deserve to be haunted more.'

And yet . . . he thought about how he had rejected Mrs Tassell's suggestions about the Feast and about the charity. He thought about how he had gleefully looked forward to making money from the Christmas cards. And how he had stayed silent in court, not speaking out for Bob Cratchit for fear of what Scabble would think, what Edgar Parley would do.

He had been falling back into bad habits. And he knew it.

'Once you have had dealings with the spirit world you are more . . . shall we say . . . attractive to them,' Marley said. 'Like moths to a flame. And in deepest midwinter the wall which divides the living and the dead grows thinner; it becomes easier to pass through. Beware, too, because that border works both ways.'

A shiver passed through Scrooge's body at the thought that he could tumble through some unseen wall into the spirit world.

'But why can you speak, where they cannot? Is it because their throats have been cut? I cannot imagine it would stop them. Living people need breath and vocal chords to give voice. You are not breathing at all, and yet you have no trouble reading me lengthy lists of my flaws.'

That dry chuckle again.

'The manner of one's death affects one,' Marley said. 'I died in unspeakable pain, and for what seemed like an inordinately long time afterwards I felt as though my belly was on fire. I do not like to admit it, but I felt fear and confusion too. There is a strange kind of blackness after one dies. It is all-consuming and terrifying and like nothing we experience in life. And just when we are at our darkest, that's when our chain begins to form. I cannot describe how harrowing that can be.

'Perhaps those two young things don't speak because they *think* they cannot speak. In time they might become aware that their bodies are gone now and that spirits are made of stronger stuff. But some ghosts never recover from the trauma of losing their earthly body.'

'Tell me what I must do, old friend.'

'You already know,' Marley said. 'Tread the path of goodness. *Help* them, you rascally old knave. Just help them.'

17

TIM WAS DRIFTING, TWISTING AND TURNING IN HIS UNFAMILIAR blankets, his woollen underthings tangling around his legs and itching uncomfortably.

He opened his eyes enough to see he was in Scrooge's study. There was a desk scattered with his master's papers and ledgers, a meagre bookshelf containing nothing but a few treatises on economics. His head hurt, his lungs hurt. His mother had said this would happen – that he was recovered but he had to take care, to keep warm in winter, not to over exert himself. And over the last few days he'd been outside almost constantly, trailing after Jem in adventure after adventure. He'd climbed trees, helped shine shoes, followed Mrs Tassell, been beaten by bullies. All this he had survived, but then he had fallen ill after a party crowded with beautiful people, heavenly carols and delicious food.

He was weak. Useless. He had failed.

'He is waking.' His master's voice, tinged with relief.

A hand was laid gently on his forehead. Not Scrooge's, it was too young and soft for that. His sleepy gaze focused on his sister Belinda.

He tried to sit up, but Belinda shoved him down with the no-nonsense roughness that only a loving sister could wield. 'You. No rushing about. Mother sent me here to look after you. She's got enough to worry about with Father in prison and falling ill without you doing something stupid to make yourself more sick.'

Father was ill? Another secret that has been kept from him to protect him. The thought made Tim want to cry, but that would only make Belinda cosset him more. He looked around the room for his master and saw he was over by the window, gazing out and avoiding Tim's eye. *He's so angry he can't even look at me.*

A memory came back to him of last night. Of Scrooge carrying him through the door, grunting and groaning from the effort. He had ripped the holly from his door with a low, furious *humbug.* Tim felt another wrench of fear. He was losing him again. And if Mr Scrooge was lost . . .

Now the tears came.

'Don't cry, Tiny Tim,' Belinda said gently, stroking his head. 'Don't be afraid. I'm here. You're not just stuck here with him.'

Tim opened his mouth to say he wasn't afraid of Mr Scrooge, but a cough came out instead. It turned into two coughs, then half a dozen, then he stopped counting. Tim knew better than to fight it and sank down against the soft pillows beneath him as his chest ached and convulsed.

For a moment he thought he saw . . . It wasn't possible, the fever must be worse than he thought, but there seemed to be two greyish shapes whirling around his master. Like tissue paper they were, filmy and light but human-shaped. He blinked, stared. They were definitely there.

'He's exhausted,' Belinda said to Scrooge, her voice full of barely contained fury. She placed her hands on her hips, adopting the brave, protective stance of his mother. 'You've been working him too hard, wearing him out. Father would never say it, he trusts you and look where that has got him! But I'm not afraid.'

But Scrooge didn't seem to be listening, his nose was pressed close to the frosted glass. He rubbed at the window with his sleeve and muttered something that sounded like, *I cannot believe it. The cheek of that woman.*

And then he sprang from the room.

Scrooge stormed down the stairs into the hallway, his blood hot with rage. How dare that Tassell creature show herself here after last night, after what he now knew? The ghosts travelled in his wake, becoming more frantic as his wrath reached fever pitch.

He almost missed the letter waiting for him on the mat. The familiar cheap paper, the scratchy disguised handwriting in brown ink. Ripping it open, he read: *I will see to it that you will pay for what you did.*

Another poison-pen letter. Just as Mrs Tassell arrived. It was all the evidence he needed. She must have disguised her handwriting, used homemade ink to throw him off the scent. It had to be her.

He pulled the door open to find the widow on the door-step, one hand raised ready to knock, the other holding the holly wreath he had discarded the night before. Her widow's veil whipped around in the wind, making her look dramatic, like a heroine in one of her own ridiculous stories.

'Oh, Mr Scrooge! Here, your wreath fell off.'

'I have nothing to say to you, madam.'

'From your words last night, it seems that you have a lot to say,' she replied, keeping her voice infuriatingly light and airy. 'And it would probably be best to say it inside, rather than in front of all your neighbours.'

Scrooge cast an eye around his street. After last night's humiliation, he did not want a further public spectacle. Reluctantly he stepped aside and waved her in, taking the wreath and casting it irritably out of the door again. His skin crawled with loathing as her skirts brushed past him. What was it about her that made him so furious?

She started upstairs towards his study, but this was not a conversation he wanted to have in front of Tiny Tim, so he directed her instead into the Christmas tree parlour.

Mrs Miller had been busy over the last twenty-four hours. The tree was bedecked from top to bottom – candles still mercifully unlit – and she had garlanded the walls with ivy, cleverly weaving each strand with sprigs of holly. The bright berries seemed to pop out of the rich green background and, in the corner of his brain which was not furious, Scrooge had to admit his housekeeper had some talent.

'This is a very large, festive space,' Mrs Tassell said, looking around her. 'It would have been just right for the Feast, don't you think?'

'Oh, you would love that, wouldn't you?' Scrooge snapped. 'My house full of paupers on Christmas Day. I sometimes think

217

that I'm some kind of hobby of yours, that you torment me for sport. I can't think of any other reason that you behave this way in front of me. You drag me to workhouses, lecture me on poverty, badger me, make me read tawdry penny bloods which you yourself have written. How much money have you made out of exploiting the poor yourself, *Mrs LJ Pettigrew?*'

The widow sank down onto a chair, let out a long sigh.

'Well, if anyone was to work it out, it would be you.'

'You were the one who incriminated Bob Cratchit! You're nothing but a cheap journalist trawling the gutters of London for lies.'

The ghosts were no more than white, filmy blurs now, a whirlwind with his anger at its centre. Scrooge ranted on – she was a termagant, a harpy trampling on the good name of her late husband. She wrote poison in the broadsides and pushed poison through his letterbox.

The widow, who had been sitting with infuriating poise through the entire tirade, suddenly sat forward.

'What poison in your letterbox?'

'This.' Scrooge threw the screwed-up letter at her. She bent to the floor and picked it up, studying the handwriting thoughtfully.

'Well, I am guilty of all else, but this is not my work. Contrary to your belief, Mr Scrooge, I actually like you. Or at least I did until recently. It takes courage to change your ways so thoroughly, so publicly, especially for a man like you who does not care for the limelight. And if I am a little more bossy, a little less delicate and ladylike around you, it is because I feel that I can show you my true self. It's why I came here today. I wanted to be honest with you.'

'Honest! Bah, humbug!' Scrooge exclaimed, but the momentum of his rage was gone. The ghosts were calmer now, flitting back and forth at the edge of his field of vision. Christina watched particularly closely, as if she were at a play.

Mrs Tassell, too, sensed a change in the mood, and she began to speak.

'It began as a hobby, while my husband, Hubert, was away. I confess I have always been interested in crime stories, in what the evil men do and why. In a way I think I find it a comfort – to understand a thing is to become less afraid of it. Then I began writing penny blood stories for myself. Just as an amusement, understand, not for publication. Ladies are not meant to do such things, and I did not want dear Hubert to be upset. He was considerably older than I, you remember, and had some old-fashioned ideas about propriety.'

'Old-fashioned!' Scrooge spluttered, but the widow held up a gloved hand and he fell silent.

'Then, during one of his long wine-buying trips to the continent, I was unfortunate enough to witness a street robbery in a marketplace and as an experiment, I wrote up a description of the experience and published it as a broadside. It sold reasonably well, despite not being a murder, and so I began to publish my fiction. That did well too and . . . things began to expand. I became adept at following crime stories, made contacts in the criminal underworld. Some of them almost respect me. *Almost.* One must never take the trust of a rogue for granted.'

A smile played about the widow's lips and Scrooge recognised something in her – it was the same expression he had himself when he was closing a particularly tricky deal or writing profits down in his ledger. The pleasure of a job well done. This wasn't just a case of a nosy widow seeking amusement to fill her days. This job was her passion.

'When poor Christina was found dead, the first thing I did was to try and find out more about her, about who she was. I found out that she was a Parley, which immediately made me suspect she had become embroiled in some gang-related feud, but everyone I spoke to was insistent that she was a hard-working young woman, somewhat preoccupied with helping her former workhouse inmates and looking forward to spending Christmas with her brother. But there was, I was told, a sweetheart. An unsuitable man she was meeting in secret. Unfortunately all too often a woman is killed by the man she believes loves her, and I thought that might be the case here.

'I managed to trace a witness who said she had been seen arguing with a man the day before. I must admit I did not think of your dear Bob Cratchit when I wrote it. When a crime like this happens we have to work fast, to get our stories onto the street first. I did not stop to think who would have a white comforter like that. And who would connect your loyal Bob with a murder?

'Since his arrest I have done everything I can to prove his innocence. I promised Mrs Cratchit, and I promise you too. I will move heaven and earth to see him freed.'

Scrooge noticed that as the widow spoke Christina's spirit had become calmer. She had drifted away from Bailey and the tree, and hovered near Mrs Tassell, making her support clear. The widow shivered and drew her fur tippet more tightly around her shoulders.

Scrooge turned away, walked towards the window to give himself time to think. Outside, the mist had cleared and he could see Amos Buddle lounging against a railing eating a crust of bread and waiting for him to come out. Scrooge felt the last smoky remains of his fury dissipate. He turned back to the widow. She was not forgiven, not in any sense, but they had a common cause now. He drew up a chair of his own and sat next to her.

'And what of the second murder?'

Her brow creased. 'What second murder?'

'Dr Alastair Bailey. Another partner in my Christmas card venture. Chemist. Nephew of Scabble. *Close friend* of Christina Parley.'

He had the satisfaction of seeing the widow surprised.

'*He* is the lover? Oh, stop looking shocked, Scrooge, I am fully capable of saying the word "lover". And he is dead?'

Scrooge turned and glanced over at the Christmas tree, where the young man still wove his way back and forth, leaving a trail of vapour as he passed through the branches. Bailey's face was still contorted with horror but there was something oddly scientific about the way he was testing his new physical structure. A wave of sadness passed over Scrooge. He had not liked the man, but Bailey had been so young, so full of ideas and energy – and now he was but a ghost.

Unaware of his distraction, Mrs Tassell was still talking. 'There *was* a body found last night, a police contact told me. But he said it was not connected to the Parley murder. The man was found in an alley, beaten and stripped of his belongings, whereas Miss Parley died with all her valuables in her possession. They believe it to be a street robbery gone wrong.'

'It was Dr Bailey. His throat was also cut, was it not?'

Her eyes narrowed. 'How do you know all this?'

Scrooge batted the question away with a wave of his hand. 'I have my own sources. Perhaps the police are unaware of his – ah – association with Miss Parley.'

Mrs Tassell sank down onto a chair. 'Oh, that poor man.'

Scrooge knew what she was thinking. If the police had not arrested Bob Cratchit they might have caught the real killer by now and Bailey would still be alive. He felt a flutter of fear that the widow would break down into feminine tears, but she pressed a handkerchief to the corner of her eyes, gave a businesslike sniff, then drew out her notebook and pencil.

'We must ensure this killer is stopped,' she said. 'Tell me what you know.'

Scrooge told her everything he had discovered over the last few days – his visits to Dr Bailey and Edgar Parley, his conversation with Jenny at the workhouse and even his suspicions about Aldous Scabble. Everything except the ghosts.

Mrs Tassell wrote furiously.

'So we know the razor blade was not the one Bob Cratchit bought,' she said, underlining something. 'And that the murder weapon was planted in his drawer.'

'But why frame him? My clerk has no enemies.'

'Shh!' Mrs Tassell held her hand up. 'We are talking about what we *do* know, not what we don't.

Scrooge lowered his voice, in the hope that the ghosts would not hear him.

'Miss Parley was a thief, too.' He told the widow about the watch chain.

'But we only have Scabble's word that the chain was stolen,' she said.

Scrooge opened his mouth to say that Mr Scabble was a respectable businessman and would not lie, but it sounded ludicrous even to him.

'But what of her generous donations to the poor?' he said instead. 'And where else would she come by that money if not by theft?'

He became conscious of Christina watching him. The sensation felt like a living thing, crawling down his spine. He needed to tread carefully.

Mrs Tassell nodded thoughtfully. 'I agree with you, she was a thief. But she was a thief with a purpose. I spoke to a close friend of hers who said she had given hundreds of pounds to the poor. When she learned I was one of the organisers of the Feast, she told me that Christina had donated quite a large sum to our own endeavours. I can find no record of it, but the friend said she was at great pains to conceal her generosity.'

Scrooge could not stop his jaw from gaping. Hundreds of pounds? Where did a young person like that get so much money? And if she was wealthy, why would she walk around town wearing Mrs Cratchit's cast-off dress?

'Did she steal it from Scabble, like the watch chain?' he wondered. Scrooge tensed as Christina's ghost drew closer, afraid that he had provoked her. But then, to his surprise, she shook her head.

He felt a jolt of excitement. For the first time the ghost was communicating with him, beyond the primal lashing out of fear and anger. He looked at her again and could see she shared his excitement. *She is relieved that I am finally listening.*

'No, it wasn't that,' he said. 'Where *did* the money come from then?'

Mrs Tassell, thinking the question was for her, began to answer with some wild theory or other and at that moment he wished her at Jericho. Christina was trying to speak too, her white, cracked lips were moving – she was waving her hand, contorting her mouth into a strange, ghastly grin displaying a row of teeth stained with blood. Scrooge fought not to shudder.

Just then there was a muffled cough from the hallway outside. Scrooge sprang to his feet, wrenched the door open. And there was Tiny Tim, face red from a coughing fit, crouched in the doorway, clearly eavesdropping.

'I am shocked at you, Tim!' Scrooge gasped and then, because the coughing did not stop, 'Please, go back to bed! Miss Belinda, do not allow him to come down here when he's still feverish.'

'This is your fault, not mine,' Belinda snapped. 'You see what you do to him? He's still trying to work for you, even though he's sick.' Then suddenly, as if realising she had crossed a line, she trailed off and added, 'sir'.

Tim drew himself up to his full height – which was still not very much. He was weak and shaking but his jaw was set.

'You don't think I can help you, but I can.' He broke off and coughed again, and when he continued, he was fighting for breath. 'I found Edgar's flash house and I found Midding Mansion when even the police didn't. She was getting threatening letters too, just like the ones you spoke about!'

'He's delirious,' Belinda said, whirling on Scrooge. 'This is your doing! Giving him ideas he can work when he's unwell! He should be at home, where we can look after him!'

But Tim reached into his pocket and held out a piece of paper. Belinda snatched at it, urging her brother to calm down and deal with this when he had rested, but Scrooge caught it first, and unfurled it.

STAY AWAY FROM BOB CRATCHIT OR I WILL MAKE YOU PAY

There was the same brown ink, the same disguised scrawl as the letters which had arrived on his doorstep.

'I'm strong enough to do it, Mr Scrooge. I'm strong enough to help you.' Tim was trembling now, his skin sheened with sweat. 'I have to do it to save Father, and to save you from those ghosts!'

18

LUCRETIA TASSELL STEELED HERSELF AS SHE ENTERED LADY CRICK'S receiving room. Her head was still whirling from the conversation with Scrooge in his parlour. The old man had behaved very oddly indeed – staring into space, failing to respond when she had questioned him. And then poor delirious Tiny Tim had burst in with his talk of ghosts and poison-pen letters.

Ah yes, the letter writer. She had her own theory about that, but it would have to wait. She and Scrooge had agreed that their next move was to discover more information about this new victim, and that she was best placed to do so.

The word of Dr Bailey's death must have reached Miss Frome by now, but it had not yet become news, opening a narrow window of propriety which allowed her to call upon the lady without seeming like a prurient gossip seeker. Which, of course, she was.

Miss Frome's mother had died some years ago and it had fallen upon her aunt to present her into society, so it was to Lady Crick's house that Lucretia hurried.

There was no sign that a large party had been held in the house the evening before. The garlands of holly and ivy looked fresh, festive and new.

She drew herself up to her full height and set her features into the expression of a dignified widow paying a morning call. Lucretia found Lady Crick seated by the fire, her back ramrod-straight, hands resting on the hilt of her walking stick as if it were a sword – as strong and determined as ever. Lucretia smiled. She might not share the Lady's views, but she couldn't help but admire her style.

To her disappointment, Miss Frome was not in evidence. In fact, none of Lady Crick's retinue attended her today. There was usually an oppressed-looking companion or a blank-eyed house-maid lingering in her wake.

'Is Miss Frome not at home this morning?' she asked inno-cently after the usual pleasantries. 'Were the exertions of last night too much for her?'

'I think you know why Miss Frome is unable to receive visi-tors.' Lady Crick's tone was hard, flat.

'Oh no, has something happened?'

'You know very well something has happened, or else you would not be here.'

Lucretia felt a heavy thud of panic in her breast, which beat even harder as the Lady spoke.

'I know exactly who and what you are, Mrs Tassell. I know *everything* about you.'

Lucretia chilled. She did not like the emphasis on the word 'everything'.

'Lady Crick, I—'

'Silence,' the Lady snapped. 'We do not have time for your pretences. You heard what had happened to poor Alastair and have come here immediately to find out more for your revolting little rag. If you were so desperate for money that you would become a common gutter journalist, you should have turned to me for help.'

'It's not the money,' Mrs Tassell began but then stopped. There was no point explaining herself. Unlike Scrooge, Lady Crick would judge. Lady Crick would ruin her. And then what would happen to her beloved charity work?

'I have no intention of disclosing your sordid secret at this juncture.' The Lady had obviously read her mind. 'I intend to use your particular set of skills to my advantage. I need you to protect Miss Frome's reputation. At some point the gutter press will discover the connection between Alastair and that disreputable creature whose death you have been writing about. The scandal could severely damage Miss Frome's nerves. I need you to ensure that does not happen.'

Lady Crick was far too proper to add the phrase 'or else' but Lucretia understood her perfectly. The Lady had her on a hook and would never let her go.

She pressed her lips together, her mind already accepting the situation, figuring out the dozens of different ways she could turn this to her advantage.

'Very well,' she said briskly, taking out her notebook. 'And in exchange, you must tell me a thing or two about poor Dr Bailey. After all, Lady Crick, you know *everything*, don't you?'

Never a patient man at the best of times, Scrooge was finding waiting impossible. After uttering his pronouncement about ghosts, Tim had sunk down upon the battered chaise longue in the parlour and, despite his agitation, fallen into a deep and restful sleep. Scrooge had carried him back up to his study, the boy's weight birdlike in his arms, and allowed Miss Belinda to take over and make him comfortable. She was a rude child, but had been looking after her little brother for most of her life and applied liniment to his chest in an efficient, expert manner that impressed Scrooge despite himself.

'The fever will break after this sleep,' she pronounced confidently. 'Time was, a fever like this would have us all praying with fear, but that was before. When he didn't have enough food or medicine.'

Scrooge burned with guilt under her hard look.

'He'll be tired when he wakes,' she continued. 'No silly questions. No work.'

Sure enough, when Tim woke his eyes were clearer, brighter. He drank deeply from the glass of water Belinda offered and looked shamefaced at his master.

'Sorry, sir,' he said weakly.

'Good lord, why?'

Tim shrugged. 'Cluttering up your study? Eavesdropping? Running around the bad part of town? Falling behind with my work?'

Scrooge did not resist the wave of guilt that crashed over him. The boy feared him still, even after all this time. He did not speak, words could not mend this, but sat down beside Tim's makeshift bed, drew out his handkerchief and folded it in quarters, mopping the boy's head. The tips of his fingers brushed Tim's hair. He could feel the rise and fall of his breathing, slowing down now as his fear began to ebb away.

'There, there, child. Don't fret so.'

As he felt Tim relax, a warmth came over him. So this was what it felt like to love someone. It was not all pain and loss and worry – it had power too. The ability to calm someone with simple words and gestures. It felt beautiful.

Belinda looked at him curiously, but Scrooge ignored her.

'My boy, I don't think you understand,' he continued. 'I am not angry. I was never angry with you. Only at myself for not realising how exhausted you had become.'

They stayed like that for a while, the man and his apprentice, while Belinda fussed and fetched. It wasn't until she went out to get herbs for a steam inhalation that Tim finally spoke.

'I can't see them anymore. Your ghosts.'

Scrooge looked up. Christina had been at peace since Mrs Tassell's departure and was hovering next to Tim, her spectral brows furrowed with concern. Bailey had vanished, in the way that Christina had frequently done at first. He toyed with the idea of denying their existence to Tim. It would be easy to put the whole thing down to delirium, but it seemed cruel to make the boy doubt himself. Not after his outburst before.

'One of them is still here,' he said quietly. 'Perhaps the fever helped you see them before.'

Tim tried to sit up, gripped Scrooge's sleeve.

'It's her, isn't it? The pretty lady from the graveyard. Can she tell you what happened? Can she free Father?'

'They cannot speak. But I am learning to listen to them in other ways.'

Christina nodded and stepped forward, holding out her bloodied, blackened hand. Scrooge suppressed a shudder, but he stood to face her. There was intelligence in her eyes, he could see it now. And a lively, wry sense of humour much like Bob Cratchit's. For the first time since he had learned of their friendship, he understood it.

'Miss Parley, you can understand me, you can reason. Am I right in thinking you did not see your attacker? That you cannot simply name him?'

She inclined her head.

'But there are people who wished you ill? People you had stolen from?'

A nod, and again she waved her hands and grinned in that strange and grisly way.

After spending the past day wondering if Bailey had murdered Christina through some kind of corrupted love – either for Christina or for Miss Frome – Scrooge felt as if he was on firmer ground. Of course the killing was financially motivated. Everything boiled down to money in the end. And there was nothing he did not know about money.

'She gave my father a bundle of five-pound notes,' Tim piped up. 'The police didn't find it because I kept it hidden. It's in the map drawer in your office. That's not all. Father let her move into one of your vacant properties, on Midding Street. Please don't be angry, I know he would not have done it unless she was truly in need.'

Curiously, Scrooge found he was not angry at all, just hungry for more facts, more clues to get him closer to finding the culprit. Follow the money. It was a rule he'd stuck to all his life, and it would serve him well now.

'If only I could understand her,' he said.

'Sir, could I suggest something?' The boy had his hand up, as if he were at school. 'Perhaps you could get a piece of paper and write yes and no on it, then she could point to the answer?'

Scrooge chuckled at the simplicity of it, astonished that he had not thought of this himself. He felt another rush of pride at the intelligence, the resourcefulness of the boy and ruffled his hair. Then he ripped a page from the back of his ledger, wrote a large YES on the left side, and a NO on the right.

'My dear Miss Parley,' he said, sitting back down by Tim's makeshift bed. 'Let us talk.'

THE GHOST

I cannot identify the moment I realised that Ebenezer Scrooge was not my murderer. The discovery came slowly, like link after link in a chain, beginning with the way he retraced my steps through life, visiting the workhouse, talking to Bob, to Edgar, to Alastair. But as I watch him stroke that little boy's hair with such tenderness I let go of the last shreds of my suspicion. He is no killer. I look at him now and I see a cynical old man, crabbed and cranky and obsessed with money, but one who is trying to be better. Just like I tried.

And he still does not know what I did to him.

And so I play his game, pointing at the paper with my finger.

'Did you meet someone else after you argued with Bob Cratchit?'

YES.

'Who was it? No, dammit, that will not work. Was it Scabble?'

NO.

'But you had his watch chain?'

YES.

'*Why?*'

A fresh outburst of frustration from both of us.

The truth is that my memories of that day are clouded. Every time I try to recall it I am pulled back to that sudden, brutal pain in my throat, the sickening battle to keep blood in my body and air in my lungs. I feel a rush of shame; it is a sign that I am less than I was when I died. How long until I fade away entirely? Fear surges and I find I am on the ceiling, and then bouncing off the wall, weaving in and out of the Christmas tree branches. I cannot control myself, and all I want to do is scream but no sound comes out of this wretched mouth of mine.

I fight for control, make an infuriated gesture, pointing to my temples, mouthing the words 'I don't remember.'

The old man throws up his hands in frustration and jumps up, striding across the room. Stares out of the window. And then his shoulders sag, and he lets out a sigh. When he turns around, his expression is gentler, kinder even.

'Lord knows, I saw my own grave once and it sent me damn near out of my senses,' he says. 'You, madam, have been killed by an unseen attacker and seen your beloved slaughtered. That is more than any human spirit can bear, living or dead. I will find out who did this to you, and I will ensure they pay.'

For the first time since my eyes opened into this new world, I feel a quiver of hope.

19

SCROOGE'S OFFICE WAS COLD AND THERE WAS A MUSTY SMELL about it. For the first time since he and Marley opened its doors it had been largely unattended for more than twenty-four hours. Even when old Marley had died, it had been shut for less time. A half-day, Scrooge seemed to recall, out of respect. Marley would probably have given him less.

His chilly hands scrabbled for the box of matches on Bob's desk, and he lit his lamp, which threw a pool of eerie light around the dingy room.

'Good lord, it is even less salubrious in here than usual.' Mrs Tassell wrinkled her nose as she stepped across the threshold, one gloved finger running over the dust on the windowsill.

'I did not ask you to come, madam.'

'Two pairs of eyes are better than one.'

In truth, though, they had left the house because they did not wish to excite Tiny Tim further. When the widow had returned from Lady Crick's the little boy had been agog to hear the news, jumping up and down in his seat, and Scrooge had found himself agreeing with Belinda when she said that he was becoming too agitated and must rest.

He and Mrs Tassell had made up this spurious errand – to go to the office and inspect the letter from Christina and the five-pound notes – simply so they could speak freely about the case without drawing him in further.

Initially they had tried to leave via the front door, but Amos had positioned himself there, leaning against a nearby cart, tossing his walking cane from one hand to the other while he waited for Scrooge to emerge. He had no desire to accept the man's 'help' for the second day running, so they had crept out the back way, through an old cellar hatch. Quite the adventure, the widow had said.

Now seated in the office, with the beginnings of a fire in the grate, they traded information. He told her everything Tim had revealed, working in what little knowledge he had gleaned from the ghost.

Lady Crick, it seemed, had been surprisingly honest with Mrs Tassell – the woman clearly had cunning ways of getting information out of people. She had confirmed that the police were not currently connecting Bailey's death with Christina Parley's – although she was unsure if this was down to corruption or incompetence. The broadside journalists Mrs Tassell had spoken to had also not made the connection, accepting the explanation that it was a street robbery.

'Well, you must tell them,' he said. 'I know Lady Crick will not like it, but if it helps expose the truth . . .'

Mrs Tassell looked uncomfortable for a moment and then changed the subject.

'What I did learn, though, was that Dr Bailey was planning to use some kind of scientific method of tracking down the killer,' she said. 'Something to do with the unique patterns on our fingers. He had borrowed the murder weapon and the razorblade case from the police and was planning to perform some kind of experiment.'

So that was why Bailey had had the case on his workbench. What had he said? *We leave little imprints of ourselves on everything we touch.* Scrooge shivered – if only he had listened.

'We are clearly dealing with someone dangerous and desperate,' Mrs Tassell said. 'Someone prepared to kill anyone who gets close to discovering them.'

There was a moment of silence as both of them considered the fact that this was precisely what they were trying to do. But then she took a deep breath and continued.

The last few hours of Alastair Bailey's life had chiefly been spent dashing around London haranguing people – first he had tracked down Scabble to Merrypaw's printworks and caused a scene there, then he had descended upon Lady Crick. He had, bizarrely, seized hold of her teacup and put it in his pocket although she had not understood why.

'I believe he was hoping to compare Lady Crick's finger patterns to the one on the razorblade case.'

Scrooge laughed aloud. 'That's absurd!'

'It is,' agreed Mrs Tassell. 'If Lady Crick wanted to kill someone, she would never stoop to doing it herself.'

After leaving Lady Crick's, Bailey had not returned to the Scabble household to dine and change for the fundraising party and had been found in the early hours of the morning by a terrified knocker-up, going about her business of rousing people for work.

The widow stood, going over to the chest of drawers in the corner.

'Is this the map drawer of which Tim spoke?' the widow asked.

Scrooge nodded, looking distractedly around the room. From the moment he had arrived in the office a thousand tiny tasks had crowded in his mind. Unpaid money to chase, letters to be written, items to be filed neatly away. They were almost as intrusive as the ghosts. Christina hovered by his desk, stable and calm now. Bailey lay curled in the corner, sobbing silently, looking up occasionally to beg Scrooge for something – he wasn't sure what. Every now and then Christina would go over and stretch her hand out to comfort him, but the gesture only seemed to increase his distress.

He walked over to his own desk and flipped open his ledger, looking once again at his donations to the Feast. He remembered the widow's words the other day, when she had called him their most generous benefactor.

'Mrs Tassell, how much money have I donated to the Feast in total?'

'Do you not know?' she sounded justifiably surprised.

'Humour me.'

'I really could not tell you off the top of my head,' she said. 'But your generosity has been astounding. You are truly an example to us all.'

Scrooge's lip curled into a smile. Now it made sense, how Mrs Tassell had always sought him out, buttered him up, treated him like they were intimate friends. She was after his money for her fund, milking him for all he was worth. He had to admire the woman's business acumen.

'I hate to step down from your heroic pedestal,' Scrooge said, 'but I really have not given as much as you think. The money you received came from elsewhere. I think . . . no, I am sure, it came from Christina Parley.' He looked at the spectre and murmured: 'Didn't it?'

Christina nodded.

He continued cautiously, 'You . . . I mean *she* gave Bob her charity donations and he passed them along to the Feast fund through Scrooge & Marley.'

'But where would she get such sums from?' Mrs Tassell asked, coming through with the package of notes in her hand. 'Just look at all this!'

'Let me see,' he said, snatching the notes up. And there it was, the familiar heft of banknotes in his hand. His miser's fingers itched to count them. He lit the oil lamp, lengthening the taper so it burned a little brighter – always worth spending a little extra when the inspection of money was at hand. He placed the stack on his desk and counted, moistening his finger before touching each one.

Five . . . ten . . . fifteen . . . twenty . . . He had just got up to forty pounds when he sensed something was awry. He paused, laying the notes out in front of him. They looked fine. Perfect, in fact, but there was still something not quite right about them.

Scrooge had spent hours – possibly years – of his life touching money, feeling it, caressing it. He knew that there was something wrong with these notes, even though he could not put his finger on what.

'These are forgeries!' he exclaimed. Mrs Tassell looked up and started towards him, but he wasn't paying attention to her. His mind was too busy putting together the clues. The black ink on the ghost's fingers which was mixed with blood. Her artistic talent. Christina Parley had made these notes. Not by herself, that much was obvious, one would need far greater resources to create such fine quality forgeries, but still.

As the realisation settled, angry heat flared through him. This was what Bob had been hiding, the reason he had not been honest with Scrooge, even after his arrest. He had been using Scrooge & Marley to distribute forged bank notes to the poor.

His fist closed around the notes, screwing them up tight.

'Did Bob know?' He kept his voice low and tight, but Mrs Tassell still looked up at him, curious.

Christina shook her head. And through his fury came realisation.

'He found out. That is why you fought on the day you died,' he murmured.

A nod.

'Mr Scrooge, what is wrong with you?' There was a note of unease in Mrs Tassell's voice, but Scrooge's fury and fear had taken over now. Forgery was a hanging offence. His hand flew unconsciously to his neck. He could hang for this. He and Bob both. He kept his glare fixed on Christina's tissue-paper face.

'You look so innocent,' he snarled. 'Bob said you were pure and virtuous, Jenny said you were a saint, the broadsides write column inches about your virtue and yet you did this to me! I, who had never done you any harm! And Bob, your closest friend! How could you?'

'Mr Scrooge!' Mrs Tassell's voice was afraid. She had seized his arm and was shaking it. He knew that she would think him mad now, but he did not care.

The ghost flickered in front of him and held up her hand. That's when he noticed it for the first time – the chain that had formed around her waist, coiled around her body. It was not as big, nor as heavy as Marley's, but it was there. Had it always been there? Had he just failed to see it because he didn't want to see *her*? The chain clinked softly, and Scrooge realised that was the sound he had been hearing over the past week. Not the clink-clink of his own future burden, but the sound of Christina's snapping into place.

But there was no shame in her eyes, no apology. She held up the chain with pride. Her face said: *I did what I had to. I am not sorry.*

THE GHOST

He cannot hear me but still, *I* speak to him.

'*You think you know everything about money. You've seen and touched so much of it that you can tell a forgery within seconds. You do not know what life is like without money. You have never found a farthing on the pavement and been flooded with gratitude that you will not starve that day after all. You have never gone through winter with frostbite on your toes because your stockings have fallen apart. You have never had to choose between feeding your fire and feeding your belly. Money controlled you for most of your life, but money has controlled me from the moment I was born. And I was expected to accept it, that this was my place in the world, to starve along with many other beautiful, bright, intelligent people because that was where God had placed us. But I did not accept that. I used the tools I had been given, the talents that God Himself gave me, to help those in need. It was not just your paltry Feast for the Poor I funded. I paid for children to go to school. I bought food and supplies for women who could not work during their pregnancy. There is so much*

242

poverty, so much suffering that my actions did not scratch the surface, but I did something. Who among your business friends, your respectable upstanding gentlemen, can say that they did the same? That they placed money directly in the hands of those who needed it? And if I have to bear this chain in my afterlife, so be it. It is my burden to bear, so that others could live a better life.'

As I speak I feel my form break free of the memory of what I once looked like. I grow and grow, filling the room. I open my mouth and, although my throat has been cut and there is no air in my lungs and I don't even have lungs at all, I scream.

The lights in the room go out.

20

JEM ARRIVED JUST AS BELINDA WAS BECOMING UNBEARABLY annoying. Earlier that day she had inserted herself between Tim and Mr Scrooge at every opportunity, berating his master for being a cold, heartless employer when really all Tim wanted was to talk more to Mr Scrooge about his ghosts. Then, when Mrs Tassell had returned to discuss her findings, Belinda had hounded them both out of the room saying that they needn't bother Tim with this nonsense, and he needed to rest.

Scrooge, who already seemed to have a healthy and entirely justified fear of Belinda, did so without protest. Mrs Tassell, however, gave her a curious, hard stare before she left the room.

The frustrating thing was that Tim was not ill – not truly, like he had been in the past. His fever was simply something which happened to him sometimes when he was tired and had over-exerted himself. All he needed to recover was somewhere warm to sleep it off and something to eat and drink when he awoke, and now he felt fine. Absolutely fine. Even the cough had receded, but it had left in its wake an unpleasant croaky voice which made him sound as though he were about to breathe his last.

When there was a knock at the door, Tim took advantage of Belinda's absence and slipped into his coat and shoes, ready to flee at the first opportunity. And he was glad he did, for it was Jem who appeared at Scrooge's study door and Tim would have hated to greet his friend from under a blanket.

'Don't excite him,' Belinda warned darkly as Jem crossed the threshold. To Tim's delight, he was holding an apple. Tim was not sure where it had come from – it could even have been stolen from a fruiterer's stall, rascal that his new friend was. Tim's mouth watered at the sight of the rare, sweet, crispy treat. Belinda eyed the gift jealously.

'Heard you were sick,' Jem said.

'Oh, that? I'm fine.'

'He's not.'

'Shut up, Belinda.'

'I'm just saying you should be abed,' Belinda insisted. Tim protested that Belinda was not his mother and the whole conversation would have deteriorated into a tongue-poking, apple-throwing argument if Jem hadn't sat down next to Belinda and told her what a pretty ribbon she had in her hair, and that he would not bother Tim any more than he ought.

'But a child can die of boredom as easy as an inflammation of the lung,' Jem said. 'Trust me, I shine the shoes of the medical men over at the London Infirmary so I am practically a doctor myself.'

It was very hard to be angry with Jem when he was in such a silly mood, and Belinda soon sat beside him and even offered

245

him a crust of bread with a bit of Tim's expensive restorative pork jelly.

'Mr Scrooge knows all,' Tim said, when she was away fetching it. 'I told him everything – about the money, the secret hideout.'

'Was he angry?'

'He was more angry with Mrs Tassell. She's the one who's been writing all the broadsides about Father – well, some of them at least.'

'Mrs T!' Jem said admiringly, leaning back in his chair. 'Well, that explains the disguise, the skulking around with criminals – oh, and her coming home from the court and pressing your ma with all those questions. And the nosiness, although I think that's just her. So, it was all her fault then!'

Tim was aware he should be cross with Mrs Tassell. Her stories had got Father into trouble and he knew Mother would not approve of a lady writing penny bloods. But he sensed good in her, and desperately hoped that she would be able to help.

Just then Belinda returned and drew up a chair to sit close to Jem, fixing a beady, protective eye on him.

'Can't you leave me alone?' Tim asked irritably. He knew his mother would tell him off for being a disrespectful brother but really, he could not help it. She had been nothing but an impediment since she got here.

'It's my job to look after you,' she snapped back. He felt a stab of resentment. It had always been Belinda's job when Mother was busy, and she used it to lord over him, as if being his nurse put her in charge of him somehow, and he was tired of it.

'I'd rather you went home and helped Mother,' Tim said. 'I'm fine here with Mr Scrooge.'

Belinda snorted. 'As if I would leave you here with that crusty old scab!'

'Belinda, that's not fair! Since last Christmas Mr Scrooge has been nothing but kindness—'

'He doesn't deserve you, Tim. All my life I've watched Father run around after him, bowing and scraping, taking the most horrible treatment you can imagine. And then what – we're supposed to believe he has become a good man overnight? I see no sign of it. He still sits behind his desk counting his pennies and ordering Father around. And when they took Father away did he use some of that money to get Father out of prison? No, he did not. And now Father is ill and rotting in jail and it's all his fault. And who's to say it wasn't him who killed her? She was sneaking around with Father, doing something to do with Scrooge & Marley, so she probably deserved it . . .'

'Wait, you saw her with Mr Cratchit?' Jem said.

And then Tim felt a rush of clarity.

'It was you, wasn't it? You wrote those anonymous letters Mr Scrooge was talking about!'

'Of course not!' Belinda's denial was so quick, so dripping with fake outrage and shock, that Tim immediately knew it to be true.

Tim stood on trembling legs, blazing with rage at his sister.

'Don't lie! Lying is a sin! I know you make acorn ink – Father was helping you just last week. I bet that's the brown stuff they found on Pa's sleeve! It's not a bloodstain at all, it's your ink!'

Belinda crumbled, weeping and begging him not to be a beastly brother.

Tim spat out a retort, all the frustration of the last few days flaring up in him, as if Belinda was responsible for everything – his father's arrest, his own illness – but Jem lay a hand on his sleeve.

'Easy on her, Tim,' he said. 'You're so angry you're missing the point. Listen to what she has to say.'

Belinda sank down onto her own chair, staring shamefacedly down at her hands. 'I was running an errand, fetching supplies for Martha, when I saw them together about a month ago. They were walking along with their arms linked like a couple. She was looking up at him with such an adoring expression . . . it made me sick.'

'How could you have thought that about Father!'

Belinda looked ashamed. 'I didn't know what to think. But after that I followed her around a bit, thinking I could warn her off somehow. I only did it to protect the family.'

Tim opened his mouth to deliver a fresh round of scorn to his sister, but then Jem spoke.

'Wait, so you know where she was living when she wasn't at Midding Mansion?'

'Of course I do.'

Jem leaped to his feet. 'Then what are we waiting for? Let's go there and see what we can find out!'

21

LUCRETIA TASSELL DEPOSITED SCROOGE AT HER HOUSE, UNLEASHING him upon the Feast's accounts so he could calculate how much money Bob and Christina had siphoned through his company and into the funds. His eyes lit with a kind of feverish delight as he ran one crooked finger down the columns, counting under his breath. It was the happiest she had seen him in days. In turn, she played to her own strengths and toured the streets, laying false information about Bailey's death as instructed by Lady Crick, and gathering true information about counterfeiting operations in the city.

The lying made her palms itch, it felt almost like there was dirt trapped under her immaculate fingernails, a stain that she could not scrub away.

I will make it right somehow, she promised herself.

Her investigations had, however, produced a lead. A colleague had told her that the curate of St Gideon's had landed himself in trouble for passing forged notes earlier in the year, and it seemed like too much of a coincidence to pass up, so she made her way once again to the churchyard.

Many feet had worn a smooth path through the gravestones to Butch Parley's grave and the notorious bloodstain. Surely it could have been washed away by now – but then if it drew people to the churchyard, and to the church collecting box, why would anyone bother? People killed for money, Scrooge was right about that, but she was only just beginning to grasp just how closely money and murder were entwined. She thought of the small nest egg of profits she had made from her broadside sales to date, and shook her head. She was not in a position to judge.

She found the curate of St Gideon's pottering in the vestibule – he immediately remembered the wealthy and dark-complexioned widow who had asked all those curious questions and made him feel terribly important.

'I come to you because as a man of God, you see people's goodness and their flaws better than anyone,' she said. 'I have heard a disturbing rumour that Miss Parley was involved in the crime of forgery.'

The curate paled slightly but endeavoured to cover it up with another chin-expanding smile.

'Why, madam, you should not trouble yourself with such a thing. Miss Parley was a lost soul who never had a chance to find redemption in this life.'

Being told not to trouble herself always irritated Lucretia. When a man said that, he actually meant 'do not become distressed because I don't want to deal with your distress'. Sometimes, when people said that, she became distressed on purpose just to annoy them. This time, however, she bit her lip and continued.

'Well, who among us has not sinned? She may not have been perfect, but her efforts made a large contribution to a Christmas Feast for the Poor, which I myself am organising.'

The curate did not ask how a poor young woman could have helped with the feast, which indicated that he knew. Lucretia fixed him with a knowing gaze.

'You do not need to be coy with me, sir. I just wish to know a little bit more about where that money was coming from. And I understand you already have expertise in that area.'

'I don't do that sort of thing anymore. I nearly lost my living – nearly found myself on the gallows! All because I was weak, because I gambled.'

'I think Christina did lose her life because of this,' she said quietly. 'Her employers found out that she was stealing from them and took action accordingly. I also know that the man in the white comforter was not the last person to see her alive. That there was a gentleman afterwards.'

The curate's gaze sank even lower, drooping with shame.

'Was he a young man, with strawberry-blond hair and side whiskers?'

'I cannot say.'

'That man is dead now,' Lucretia said. 'Perhaps if you had spoken out, perhaps if you had not accepted money from his uncle to keep his name out of this, it might not have happened. And now another man, a man you know to be innocent, is to stand trial for murder.'

The curate turned away, and at first she expected him to take his leave, but then she saw he was looking at the altar. A sob escaped him, and he sank to his knees.

'I swore that I would be your servant.' A sob choked his voice and Lucretia realised he was talking to God rather than her. 'Lord, I knew you would test me but to test me in this way . . .'

Lucretia rose to her feet, and laid a hand on the man's shoulder. He started back, as though he had not experienced physical contact for some time.

'She asked me to help her launder her stolen money, but I couldn't. My uncle will string me up himself if I get into trouble again. I don't know where the notes came from, but I know they're not from Wantage. He's the main coiner and counter-feiter in this part of town but Christina would not work with him. They must have come from somewhere else.'

'And where would I find this Wantage?'

'Madam, I have no idea, and I would advise that you do not go looking.'

22

'YOU ARE NOT GOING IN THERE,' BELINDA SAID, BETWEEN GRITTED teeth. 'Mother put me in charge, and I forbid it.'

Tim's irritation with his sister was spilling over. Not only had she believed the worst of Father and of Mr Scrooge, but she had refused to tell them where Christina had lived and worked unless they allowed her to come too. And now the three of them were crouched behind a large crate outside Felix Merrypaw's printworks.

It made sense that she worked there. She was an artist – Tim had seen as much from the picture of Father Christmas on the Midding Mansion wall. And he had seen several artists at work when he had been to that nice Mr Merrypaw's.

Nice Mr Merrypaw – Tim had always felt a little wary of him, and what he'd seen and heard at the fundraising party had only confirmed that he wasn't as jolly and kind as he pretended to be.

Jem, meanwhile, had wandered off to one side, was peering in the window of a nearby shop selling second-hand watches, trinkets and jewellery. He felt for something in his pocket, then looked at the others.

'You two keep arguing, I'm just going in here for a minute.'

Belinda was so busy berating Tim, she didn't even notice Jem leave.

'Tiny Tim Cratchit, you are not even listening to me!' Belinda shook him. 'I absolutely forbid it. You just had a fever and you're weak enough as it is!'

'I'm not weak, Belinda!' Tim snapped. 'Actually, I'm getting stronger. The first time I walked here with Mr Scrooge I kept having to stop and rest, and this time I didn't! I know I get sick, and I know I still need to rest more than you, but stop treating me like I'm going to die!'

Belinda went to speak, but instead a sob came out. She hated crying and dashed the tears impatiently away. 'Fine! You do what you like! You don't know what it's like to watch you make yourself ill, never knowing if this is going to be the fever that gets you!'

It was true, Belinda had spent her whole childhood looking out for him, nursing him, rubbing liniment on his skinny chest and he knew he should be grateful. But nevertheless, he knew his own body a thousand times better than she did.

'I promise you I'm not taking stupid risks. I'm strong again. And we have to do this for Father, don't you see?'

A few minutes later, Jem emerged from the shop, the irate shopkeeper shouting after him.

'Don't you come in here with your stolen goods, you young ruffian!'

Jem turned, aiming a rude gesture at the shopkeeper with one hand and pushing something white into his pocket with the other. 'How dare you! I'm an honest businessman!' he shouted and then ran away to join Tim behind the crate.

Both Cratchit children looked at him.

'What? I didn't steal nothing. I found it, it's . . . what's the word pirates use? Legitimate salvage.'

Belinda started to lecture Jem on the path to hell, and a memory floated to the top of Tim's mind – the thing he'd seen Jem pick up in the churchyard.

'What did you really find near Butch Parley's grave, Jem? It wasn't a sixpence, was it?'

Jem flushed. 'No, it's some sort of carving. It's proper good quality ivory, one of the toffs who visited the crime scene must have dropped it. I'm sorry, it was just such a good find, and my mum's been sick. If I can sell it, it'll help pay for a doctor.'

'You don't have to explain,' Tim said. 'Shall we just start spying on Merrypaw instead?'

'I still think we should just go to the police,' Belinda said.

'Oh yes, I'm sure the police will listen to us,' Jem put on his fake upper class accent. 'Fine respectable urchins such as we are!'

Tim nodded agreement. The police could not help here.

'Come on, help us,' Jem said, turning on his considerable charm. 'You'd make a great lookout, Belinda. Can you whistle? A proper loud one, I mean.'

'Of course not! I'm a young lady!'

'She can whistle,' said Tim.

'Good. Let out a big one, three blasts, if you see any danger coming. And if we don't come out by the time the clock strikes five, run and fetch Mr Scrooge. Can you do that?'

Belinda nodded.

Right now, the printing house was a hive of activity, with workers coming and going, bringing in paper, taking out freshly printed Christmas cards and broadsides with the very latest updates on the Christina Parley murder. Merrypaw had not even mentioned to Mr Scrooge that he knew her. He had let his printing presses produce broadside after broadside about her death without saying a thing. He had to be hiding something.

As usual, the front door to the printworks was open, and it was easy for Jem and Tim to pass into the noisy, chaotic hall on the pretence of being errand boys.

'We don't really need a lookout, do we?' Tim whispered.

'No, but if you'd told her to go home, she never would have done it,' Jem said. 'Besides, she feels guilty about what she did. This will make her feel better. Now what do we . . . Cor! Look at that bloody great machine!'

'Shh! Try to look like you've seen all this before,' Tim said. He grabbed a slip of paper from a nearby pile of scrap and folded it. 'If we look like we're carrying messages nobody will question us.'

'But what are we looking for?'

Tim paused, suddenly realising that Jem was looking to *him* for ideas. It was a new experience, and Tim had no idea what to do with it. He tried to think: they were looking for something that proved Christina had worked here and that Mr Merrypaw was up to no good somehow.

'Let's start in his office at the top of those stairs,' he said. 'It's where he keeps all his papers but also, it's really nice and warm in there, and there's food.'

Climbing the stairs to Merrypaw's office was easy, but the problem was that Merrypaw himself was standing at his desk, poring over some printed pages. The two boys were trapped, crouching at the top of the stairs just under the office window.

'We need to get him out of there.'

Tim's brain turned over and over, running through different ideas until . . . 'Jem, can you read?'

'Yeah. Got all my letters, A to Z.'

'Then I think I know what to do.'

A few moments later, a knock at Merrypaw's office door revealed an angelic-looking Tiny Tim, staring up at him with his full innocent-boy gaze.

'Why, it's Scrooge's little crippled office boy! How delightful!'

Tim's jaw tightened at the hated word, but he knew he must not react. He must keep his innocent cherub face firmly in place.

'If you please, sir,' he piped up, 'Mr Scrooge has sent me to collect some of the Christmas cards to send to his family and business associates.'

Merrypaw rubbed his hands together. 'Excellent! I knew the old boy would come around! Come with me to the stockroom

– now, was it the robin design he was interested in, or the angel? Or was it – ha ha – the more personal one?'

Closing his office door behind him, oblivious to Jem crouched behind it, Merrypaw led Tim down the stairs, talking at his captive audience without looking back. Tim himself could not bear to look over his shoulder and only had to trust that Jem would do as instructed. *He keeps his papers in the drawers behind him*, he had told his friend. *Look for anything which might lead us to Christina.*

The stockroom was on the far side of the printing press, and despite his nerves, Tim could not help but watch with fascination as the workers moved the machinery, printing page after page rapidly, their fingers almost a blur as they moved the paper in and out.

'You think this is clever, my boy, but you should see the new technology which is around the corner! Soon we will be able to flood the streets with thousands of broadsides or Christmas cards at a moment's notice!'

They moved past an area which Scrooge had told him was for the workers to rest, and into a narrow corridor, where Merrypaw opened a door to a shelf-lined room. They had arrived at the stockroom already. Tim's heart pounded – this was all happening too quickly. Jem hadn't had enough time.

Tim hesitated, lingering in the corridor, trying to think about how to distract the man for longer, and just then the door opposite opened. A worker slipped through, being careful not to open the door too wide and if Tim had not been so small and close to the ground, he would never have spotted the strange machine inside. It looked similar to the printer in the main section of the warehouse, but it was smaller, and there were only one or two workers using it.

These successful men liked to be asked questions about their pet subjects, Tim knew. Mr Scrooge could expound on the principles of economics for hours if Tim asked him the right questions. And right now he needed to buy Jem more time.

'Is that the new technology in there?' Tim asked in his best cherub voice.

Mr Merrypaw spun around, the cards still in his hand, and locked his gaze on Tim. His usually russet cheeks had gone quite white.

'What do you mean, boy?'

Tim's heart began to thud even more. He knew he had made a wrong step, but couldn't see how to pull things back.

'What did you just see?'

'N-nothing, just someone coming out of that room there. I thought I saw another printing machine but I m-must have been wrong.'

Mr Merrypaw's expression did not change, but he flushed red again. 'Ah, my boy, that is not the technology of which I spoke, simply an old, outmoded machine we use during very busy times. No, there are the printing devices being developed in the United States which will change the way we work for ever. Would you believe it, they print from giant rolls of paper bigger than you!'

Tim allowed himself to breathe and felt Mr Merrypaw's hand on his shoulder, heavy and possibly a little controlling. 'Let me explain the principle to you, young lad. If you decide clerking is not your path in life, perhaps there's a place for you here among the typesetters . . .'

Tim could see it now, the way the man took hold of the conversation and directed it as he chose, away from something he didn't want to talk about. And he had not wanted to talk about what was in that room.

Mr Merrypaw walked Tim to the front gate of the printworks, placing the bundle of Christmas cards into his hand. 'Give these to your master with my compliments. Tell him the first ten are free to trusted investors but I shall have to start charging him after that,' he chuckled. 'It is a joke! But I would love to see his face when you tell him! Also, please do invite him to my workers' Christmas party tomorrow. I would love to see Ebenezer Scrooge in all his festive glory!'

Tim bowed his head, fighting not to glance up at the office to see if Jem had managed to slip in and out. Instead, he bade Mr Merrypaw a polite farewell and made off down the street, ducking behind the crate as soon as the gentleman was out of sight.

Belinda threw her arms around him, pulling him so tight she knocked the air from his lungs. Then she pinched his arm. Hard.

'Never do that again!' she said. 'I nearly died from worry waiting for you. It wasn't until you got inside that I worked out there was no way you could hear someone whistling from all the way out here! Next time don't take me for an idiot. Take me in with you.'

Tim smiled. She had said *next time*.

They both watched the front gate nervously until the nearby church clock struck five.

'He's not coming out, is he?' Belinda said quietly.

'He will,' Tim murmured. 'He has to.' For if he didn't that would mean Tim had led him into danger . . .

They waited until the darkness began to close in on them. A group of workers came out to collect the crate and shouted at them to go away, and there was no sign of Jem.

Time passed, and more and more workers came out through the front gates, laughing and joking, jostling each other and talking about the Christmas Eve feast to come tomorrow. How much they would eat, how much they would drink, whether that pretty colourist Sally would be there.

'Where did you get that bloody hat, Silas?' one ink-stained printmaker said to another as they left the building, drawing their scarves tightly around them for it was coming on to snow.

'Hah! Found it on the floor by the big man's office! It was all stuffed up with newspaper, so whoever dropped it, it didn't fit them anyway. What do you reckon, does it suit me?'

Tim began to tremble, panic rising in his belly. Because the hat the worker was wearing – the shabby, battered topper – was Jem's.

23

ALTHOUGH CHRISTMAS WAS JUST AROUND THE CORNER, THE whey-faced girl who kept the stall outside Edgar's flash house had not troubled to hang holly sprigs among her wares. She eyed Scrooge warily as he approached, but when she saw Mrs Tassell at his side, her expression softened.

'Good afternoon, Elspeth,' the widow said. 'How's your eye?'

'Still crusty, missus, but not as painful, thank you for asking.'

Scrooge was disconcerted by how easily and confidently Mrs Tassell trod these trash-strewn back alleys, and how many people she seemed to recognise.

It had been her idea to come here, to the darkest part of town, after the sun had gone down. 'We need to find this Wantage fellow, and it's likely Edgar Parley will know where he is.'

Scrooge had thought it unwise, but did not want her to go alone. Now, on the threshold, he hesitated.

'Are you sure we are not walking straight into the forger's den?' he asked, keeping his voice low so Elspeth could not hear.

The widow shook her head dismissively.

'Edgar does house-breaking, pickpocketing and street robbery. Forgery isn't in his line. Besides, you've already said you don't think he killed his sister.'

'It's a relief to know you listen to me,' Scrooge retorted.

'Sometimes – but only sometimes – you say something quite useful.'

There was a jolly atmosphere inside. The fiddler who had been playing refined tunes in Edgar's chamber on his last visit was performing an up-tempo version of 'We Wish You a Merry Christmas', and some of the assembled criminals were dancing and singing. But as they entered, Parley's door slammed open.

'Quiet!' he shouted. 'We'll have no Christmas nonsense here.'

The fiddler dropped his bow, the dancers froze. Parley looked as if he were about to say something else, when he caught sight of his two visitors.

'I suppose this is your doing, merry Mr Scrooge?'

Scrooge and Mrs Tassell took a seat in Edgar's chamber, the widow with her notebook and pencil on her lap giving the encounter the strange air of a business meeting. Christina was there too, hovering behind her brother, stroking his hair with her bloody, black-tipped fingers, as though he were a little boy again. There it was once more, that smell of flowers and death.

But there was something different about her, something calmer and stronger – less weighed down by the chain that still snaked its way around her waist and shoulders. The links were gleaming, as if she had polished them somehow.

'It's cold again,' Edgar said. 'Amos, throw some more coal on, would you?'

It was then that Scrooge saw the big henchman, who rose and obediently fetched the coal scuttle, scowling at them.

'Amos is not happy with you and neither am I,' Parley said. 'I offered you my best man to help, and you crept away without him.'

'Perhaps your man deserted his post?'

'Not Amos. He's loyal. My belief is you deliberately shook him off to keep me in the dark, and I am not pleased.'

Just then Scrooge caught sight of something pinned to the wall by the fireplace. He sighed. It was one of *those* Christmas cards. Edgar saw him look, and smirked.

'They captured your likeness pretty well, didn't they? You know I'm not one for Christmas decorations, but it does make me chuckle to see your skinny legs running about town!'

Scrooge knew he was going to have this conversation a lot over the Christmas season but would rather not have it with London's most notorious criminal.

It occurred to him then that people would laugh whatever he did, but their laughter would become more cruel and more persistent if he showed them it made him uncomfortable. If they were going to laugh, he might as well laugh along with them. After all, the picture *was* funny.

He chuckled too and, unlike his smiles, it felt natural, like something inside him being released. Edgar laughed in response,

Mrs Tassell let out an uncharacteristic giggle and Amos's mouth twitched into something resembling amusement. The atmosphere shifted, even Christina seemed to sense it. Parley was still a villain through and through, a scorpion who might strike at any moment, but this was not that moment.

'I hope that you are bringing me results,' he said.

'Of a sort,' Mrs Tassell said, taking out one of the five-pound notes and sliding it across the table.

Parley peered at the note.

'Tina's work?' He lifted it to the light, inspecting the fine detail of the lettering. 'She's good. She was always good.'

A flicker of a smile from the ghost.

'She told me she didn't want to do that anymore, Parley continued, still staring at the note. 'She went into the bloody workhouse to avoid doing this. What would make her start up in the trade again?'

'She did it for the poor,' Scrooge said quietly. 'It is my belief she was making these notes so she could steal some of them and donate the proceeds to the needy. We believe her employer discovered the theft and took revenge.'

Edgar's face hardened. He lifted the glass bulb on his oil lamp and held the note to the flame. The paper caught easily, burned closer and closer to his fingers.

'You find out who did this, and I will kill them myself.'

Scrooge suppressed a shudder, but Mrs Tassell kept her composure. The only sign that she was nervous was a tightened grip on her little silver pencil.

'Do you know who she was working for?' she asked. 'The name Wantage has been mentioned to me.'

Parley shook his head. 'Wouldn't have been him. She hated his guts.'

'He might know if there is a new player on the board, though,' Mrs Tassell said. 'Perhaps we ought to speak to this Mr Wantage.'

Edgar laughed. 'You interrogating Wantage! Now that I'd pay to see – the man's a snake. But you two are too entertaining to be killed. Take Amos with you – he'll show you where to go and keep you alive. And no dodging him this time.'

Just as they got up to leave, a memory popped into Scrooge's head, something Mrs Tassell had said earlier.

'You told me last time we spoke that you had no love for Christmas, and that you had not spoken to Christina in many years. And yet, I have also been told that she was planning to spend Christmas with you. Was our informant mistaken?'

Parley gave a sorrowful half smile.

'I told you, she wrote me a note and I burned it.' He paused, shook his head. 'I might have changed my mind and gone. But now she is dead, and I will never celebrate Christmas again.'

'I am sorry to hear that,' Scrooge said quietly. 'I never met Christina Parley before she died, but something tells me she would find that very sad.'

Scrooge and Mrs Tassell did not speak as they followed Amos through the streets. Christmas in this part of town was a very different affair. Already people were spilling out onto the cobbles, drinking. This, then, was the other side of Christmas, the chaos, the revelry, the upending of rules and the downing of as much gin as a man or woman could bear.

Above one of the local taverns someone had hung a kissing bough with mistletoe. A grubby, tired-looking woman stood beneath it, giving kisses.

'Look away, madam,' Scrooge said. Mrs Tassell scoffed.

'When I see a woman suffering, being exploited, being kept in poverty, I will never look away,' she snapped.

She marched over to the woman, rummaging in her purse for a coin.

'Oho! Look who's after a kiss!' a nearby man cried, waving his glass at Mrs Tassell, who shot him a furious look.

'Kiss her! Kiss her!' the assembled drinkers chanted. They drew nearer to Mrs Tassell, crowding around her. Panic clawed Scrooge's belly. He spoke up to protest, but the chanting was too loud, and the men got closer and closer to Mrs Tassell, reaching out, tugging at her shawl, touching her hair.

'Aaargh!' One of them reeled back in pain, clutching his cheek and spitting curses. Scrooge saw the glint of a jewelled hat pin in Mrs Tassell's hand, but the men had seen it too, wrenched it away. Her veiled hat toppled from her head and Scrooge saw a flash of fear. The redoubtable widow was afraid.

Scrooge roared at them to desist, ran forward with no plan, no idea how to stop them. But Amos was there first.

It happened so fast that Scrooge could barely recall the details afterwards, only that suddenly all the men were flying, falling back into the gutter. Amos brought the broken handle of his walking cane down on the head of one man, kicking at another who came too close. He worked in silence, he worked efficiently, and the other men did not stand a chance.

'It's Amos Buddle! Run!' a man shouted, and all of a sudden they were gone. Mrs Tassell sat on the floor, her skirts pooled around her, breathing hard, scared. The woman under the kissing bough stooped and helped her to her feet.

'You needn't have done that. I was all right you know,' the woman said irritably.

'You didn't look all right,' the widow said. Her hands were shaking as she brushed icy detritus from her skirts and retrieved her hat. She bestowed the bent hatpin on the woman and smiled upon Amos. 'Thank you for your assistance, Mr Buddle.'

'The Gentleman said keep you alive,' was his reply, but there was a quiet satisfaction in his tone. Perhaps it was useful to have him around after all.

They moved quickly through the streets after that. Mrs Tassell walked beside Scrooge, her fists clenched, biting her lip. Scrooge, ashamed that he had not known how to intervene, stayed silent.

'I know I have probably proved your point,' the widow said eventually. 'That I am an interfering do-gooder out of my depth, but I assure you I am not. I have been in tighter spots before, and I am well able to hold my own.'

Scrooge opened his mouth to reply, but the widow held up her hand.

'And do not speak to me about not interfering when I see a woman in need. I will do it again, a thousand times over.'

'You cannot hope to repair every wrong you see in the world,' Scrooge said.

'Of course not, but if I do not try, what kind of creature am I?'

268

Their silent guide ushered them down a back alley that was so narrow Scrooge's shoulders brushed against the damp, oozing bricks. Under his feet the ground was soft with detritus – straw, discarded objects and worse. They would never have found the opening if it had not been for Amos. It was not a door so much as a human-sized hole in a wall, an urban cavern with a ragged curtain hung just inside it. Amos drew the curtain aside and shouted a greeting into the darkness. A thin, wheezy voice answered.

'Amos Buddle, as I live and breathe, what business of Edgar's brings you here?'

The man who spoke was old. Truly aged, rather than merely grey-haired and crabby like Scrooge. And his life had not been easy. His grimy visage was a mass of wrinkles, his beard white and matted, mouth saggy, pink and ornamented with a single tooth. But the eyes, buried deep within the putrescent flesh of his face, were alert, focused on the two out-of-place people at Amos's side.

'What you bring outsiders here for?'

'Gentleman sent them,' was Amos's reply.

'Fucking Edgar,' Wantage said, but his tone was mild and his glance stole towards Mrs Tassell, as if his intention had been to shock or discomfort her. The widow did not react. He studied her for a moment, then with a thoughtful 'hmm' he beckoned them in with a filthy, skeletal finger. Scrooge held his breath as he passed inside. The man's lair – because it could not be called a home – stank of smoke and sweat and grease. A bench ran along one side, lit by smoking oil lamps and littered with tools. A few coins – genuine or forged – were scattered on the surface, alongside curls of metal and a magnifying glass which had been polished to a shine – easily the cleanest thing in the room. There was a flicker of movement in the furthest corner; Scrooge caught sight of a pink rat's tail and a pair of clawed hind feet, before the creature burrowed into a pile of discarded blankets.

'Mr Wantage,' Mrs Tassell said briskly, visibly fighting the urge to hold her hand to her mouth. 'We are not here to disrupt your trade. We only want you to look at this.'

Scrooge handed him the five-pound note.

'Is this one of yours?' he asked.

Wantage turned and spat onto the floor, which Scrooge took for a no.

'Whose work is it, then? Who is making these?'

'Quality,' Wantage said, moistening his lips with the tip of his yellowed tongue. 'People with more money and connections than your humble servant here. People who have no respect for the way things are done.'

'Could Christina Parley have made this?'

'I fucking know she did,' Wantage said, bestowing a gummy smile upon them. 'She had a rare and special talent – and she wasted it.' He held the note up to the lamplight. 'Look at the detail on that! How could you even tell it was a shifty note? Nah, I found out what she was doing back in the spring when she started trying to get my own people to launder the money for her.'

'Launder it?' Scrooge did not understand the term.

'Yeah, break 'em up, put 'em into circulation, like. Look the first thing you do after you've made your counterfeits is pass them on. The Quality folk, they must have their own way of doing this but Christina, she got greedy, she was skimming some of the notes they made and trying to use my circle of launderers to pass them on!'

Scrooge felt a creeping sense of unease. He knew business. If Christina's employers, the so-called Quality, had stolen Wantage's trade and then Christina attempted to use his associates to distribute her own notes, then Wantage would have taken measures to stop this happening. Could he have killed Christina?

He began to edge towards the doorway, glad for once of Amos's looming presence.

Wantage caught sight of him and laughed, a wheezing, humourless sound.

'I didn't kill her. Just sent some of my lads round to discuss things with her. She soon stopped her poaching. Found another outlet for her money.'

Scrooge pressed his lips together into a tight line. That would be Scrooge & Marley.

Mrs Tassell made an impatient sound and waved her hand dismissively. 'Yes, yes, I understand that, but do you know who they are, the Quality?'

'Not a clue – otherwise there'd have been a nasty fire at their place by now. These bastards don't play fair. Whoever they've got working for them, nobody's talking. When my boys had their little chat with Tina they couldn't beat it out of her. Whoever it is has got money to burn, no respect for us stalwarts of the trade, and their workers locked up so tight so they can't speak.' Wantage shook his head in reluctant admiration. 'Must have the lot of them chained in a dungeon to keep everything so tightly guarded. I'm a good master by comparison – my brats might take the odd flogging if they're cheeky or light-fingered but at least I've always given them Christmas off.'

They left Wantage and his stinking mire of a den, and Amos guided them out of the maze of backstreets. After that, they were unable to dismiss him and he followed them, like a grey shadow of death. Like the Spirit of Christmas Yet to Come. The ghosts of Christina and Bailey followed behind. They did not seem to take note of Amos, and Scrooge wondered if it was because he did not appear fully human. Without Edgar's instructions, he might not exist at all.

Unable to talk freely before Amos's hulking presence, Scrooge began to think about what he had learned. Christina Parley was a sinner, a criminal who had created counterfeit money and passed it off to innocent people . . . but she was a philanthropist who had done what she could to help the needy. She had been raised at the heart of a criminal family, but she loved Christmas and all it symbolised. He surveyed her now, a chill presence, like an extra-thick wisp of fog. She had done good things; she had done bad things. He had tried to put her in a box marked good or evil from the moment he had first started to investigate her death. Could it be that the real Christina was far more complex than this simple binary? All he knew was that Christina had been a remarkable young woman and her killer had committed a great evil.

'Farthing for your thoughts?' Mrs Tassell asked.

'Doesn't the saying usually require a penny?'

'I thought you would appreciate the cost saving,' she replied. 'Well, it looks like you were right: money truly is at the root of all evil. Christina was stealing from her masters, and they must have discovered the crime and turned on her. Do you believe Edgar Parley when he says he does not know who her employers are?'

Scrooge nodded. 'If he knew who they were, they'd be dead by now.'

They both glanced back at Amos, following closely behind.

'We should talk about this later. I wish nothing more than to bring the killer to justice, but Her Majesty's justice, not Edgar Parley's.'

And so, as they walked, Scrooge made a mental list of everything he had discovered so far. Christina's connection with the Scabble household, her affair with Bailey. Christina had been closely linked with two of his business partners and . . .

Oh.

He kept his head down, kept walking but Mrs Tassell could clearly read the change in his expression.

'What is it?'

Scrooge stole a glance at Amos and bit his lip with the effort of not talking. 'Nothing.'

But his heart was beating faster, his head thrumming with ideas. The counterfeiters were some kind of quality. Not common criminals who lurked in flash houses but wealthy folk with resources behind them . . . Or was it just one wealthy someone? A man who was already acquainted with Christina's sweetheart. Someone who knew how to turn everything into a business opportunity and had loyal workers who would not speak out . . . What if the workers were kept quiet with kindness rather than beatings?

He now knew exactly who Christina had been working for.

273

24

LUCRETIA TASSELL HAD TO TROT TO KEEP UP WITH SCROOGE AS he stalked through the streets, and by the time they reached his front door she had passed through irritation and arrived at worried. Once the door was safely closed on Amos, Scrooge leaned back against the wall and let out an almost animalistic growl.

'Merrypaw.'

Lucretia stared at him. There almost seemed to be an aura about him, a flickering mist as he paced back and forth in the hallway. He did not look like a crabby miser now, or a credulous fool filled with Christmas spirit. He was all righteous wrath, drive and purpose. But was he right, could the jolly, friendly man of business be mixed up in this?

'Pray explain,' she said.

'He was Christina's employer, I am sure of it. He has the printing presses, the loyal staff. And while he appears a friendly fellow, I now know he is ruthless in his pursuit of profit. He said it himself when I first met him – *Everything is a business opportunity, even Christmas.* Christina Parley met a gentleman before she died. I thought it might be Dr Bailey or Mr Scabble, but what if it was Merrypaw? And . . .' His eyes took on a fervent, unnerving gleam. 'Yes! Now I understand why she was grinning at me like that and waving her hand. Merry. . . paw! And of course – I saw her for the first time in Merrypaw's office!'

'Scrooge, *stop!*' Lucretia said in exasperation. 'You're not making any sense. Saw who in his office?'

Scrooge flushed. 'Nobody. Never mind that. But we have our man, I know it! Now I just have to give him a piece of my mind.'

Lucretia gave a groan of frustration. 'You cannot just march down to his place of business and accuse him. We have nothing if we don't have proof. Your word is good on 'Change but in a court of law we need concrete evidence.'

'Then we must find it,' he said. 'What do you suggest?'

This. This was why she liked Scrooge. Most other men of business she knew would rather pursue their own ludicrous plan to the point of catastrophic failure than demean themselves by asking a woman what she thought. Scrooge was different, not because he was a perfect gentleman or because it was polite to encourage the ladies with their little endeavours – far from it – but because he was wily and a pragmatist. He used the tools he had to hand and that included her.

'We must create a link between Merrypaw and Christina,' she said. 'One which does not implicate Bob Cratchit or Scrooge & Marley as I am assuming you would prefer to avoid the gallows yourself. If Merrypaw finds out what Christina was doing with Bob, he could hold that over you.'

Scrooge bit back a curse. 'Naturally, he would do that. *I* would do that – or at least I would have done. It is excellent business.'

'Then we must both make sure this does not happen. Perhaps you could enquire more into Mr Merrypaw's reputation. I assume you already gathered information like this before signing the contract?'

Scrooge looked a little ashamed. 'I did make enquiries, yes, but such was my enthusiasm for the endeavour I did not dig as deeply as I ordinarily would.'

Lucretia politely held back her laugh.

'I do have some paperwork I could look at, and perhaps I can speak more closely with Mr Scabble . . .' he began.

'I shall leave you to it,' Mrs Tassell said. 'But I would like to speak to the children before I leave. I need to have a private word with Miss Belinda.'

Scrooge raised his eyebrows at that, and it was clear that he had not observed Belinda's shifty behaviour, her ill-disguised dislike of him, the way she had tried to snatch that poison-pen note from her brother's hands. She hoped there was a way to defuse the situation without shaming the girl.

Just then Mrs Miller appeared, looking distracted, with a bundle of pine fronds in her arms.

'Oh, sir, I'm glad to see you back! The children went out earlier but then they came back, and they look worried. They won't tell me, but I think something happened to them. Something bad.'

The children were here now, rushing down the stairs. Belinda's blonde curls were in disarray, and she was crying.

'He's lost, Mr Scrooge! He's lost and it's all because of me! I'm so sorry!'

'It's Jem, sir!' Tim was close behind her, leaning heavily on the banister to speed his descent. 'He went into Mr Merrypaw's warehouse with me, but he didn't come out!'

彡

They took a cab to the printworks. Scrooge stared out of the window, tense and distracted as Tim filled them in on the tucked-away room he had discovered at the rear of the building, the smaller printing press he had glimpsed inside. Just the sort of equipment one might use to print forged notes.

'Perhaps Jem just ran off,' Belinda suggested. 'How much do you trust him, really? After all, he was trying to sell some stolen property earlier.'

'Leave it, Belinda,' Tim snapped. 'That wasn't stolen. It was something he picked up in the churchyard when we went to see the bloodstain. Some kind of carving, he said.'

'In the churchyard?' Mrs Tassell said. 'Why, that could have been an important clue! Why did he not give it to the police?'

'I think it was valuable, ma'am. And his mother is very sick.'

Mrs Tassell nodded with understanding, and Scrooge felt ashamed for not knowing about Jem's mother. He was a good lad, with more than his fair share of intelligence, alongside a staggering level of cheek. But although Scrooge pretended to disapprove of his sense of humour, Jem often made him laugh. Jem had a spark about him, a determination to do well for himself. It was not always easy, Scrooge knew, for Londoners of African descent to make their way in the city. The way he was treated daily could have discouraged him, but Jem faced it with breathtaking confidence and bravado.

277

And the last words I said to him were 'get out'.

Guilt closed its grip around his heart again. He had been angry, wildly protective of young Tiny Tim, but that had been no excuse. He had shouted at Jem because he had foolishly believed he had a right to, because Jem was just a child and owed him money. How was he ever to become a better man when his own petty nature kept tripping him up?

When Tim fell silent, Mrs Tassell asked, 'What took you three to Merrypaw's anyway? You said you thought Christina was living and working there, but why?'

There was a heavy silence. The children looked at each other and finally Belinda spoke.

'I saw her with Father, before. And I followed her. I was the one who sent her those notes. And I was writing to you too, Mr Scrooge. I'm sorry. I thought you didn't care for Father or Tim, and when that poor woman died and you said nothing to help Father I was convinced you had something to hide. But I was wrong. I know now.'

Scrooge had every right to be angry, to shout and rant. But how could he, when he had spoken those last words to Jem?

'I do care about your father,' Scrooge said, nodding. 'But I have not always shown it, and I should have spoken for him in court. So I was wrong too.'

When they arrived at Merrypaw's gate, the building was in darkness. The gas lamp which usually burned above the door had been extinguished. Scrooge pounded on the door with the handle of his walking stick.

'Merrypaw! Come out!' His voice was a desperate croak.

He ripped off his gloves and hammered at it again, until his fists hurt. The ghost of Alastair Bailey watched him, head cocked to one side as though Scrooge was a matter for scientific study, and Scrooge noticed the beginnings of a chain forming, cuffed around his wrist. Christina passed anxiously back and forth through the solid wood but gave no indication about what she saw on the other side.

'Merrypaw! Open up, I say!' Pressing his ear against the door, he thought he could hear something, the clank and whir of machinery inside. But he couldn't be sure.

'What's going on here?' A rough, assertive voice in the darkness. Scrooge looked around into the shadowed figure of Constable Baldock.

'Ah, Mr Scrooge,' Baldock said, adjusting his tone slightly to reflect Scrooge's social standing. 'May I help you?'

The four of them spoke at once, different versions of events competing to be heard. Baldock stepped back, holding his hands up in frustration.

'I'm sorry, Mr Merrypaw has done *what*? Do you have proof of that?'

'Not yet.' Mrs Tassell pressed her lips together, frustrated. 'The one thing we can tell you is that a boy went in there and has not come out.'

'And he was trespassing.'

'He was carrying a message for me,' lied Scrooge. 'And he did not return.'

Baldock continued to look sceptical, to offer any number of possible explanations. Perhaps Merrypaw had given him a tip and he'd gone off to spend it. Perhaps he had been distracted by the play showing at the gaff on the corner. Or a pretty girl, maybe.

'I cannot help you tonight,' Baldock said. 'But I will pop around in the morning, before I finish my shift, to enquire after the lad. Now, please go home.'

The adults turned to walk away, but Tim and Belinda lingered, their hands pressed against the gate as if they were trying to will it open. Baldock crouched down to the children.

'I know you are worried, but leave the investigating to the professionals. You're children, and tomorrow is Christmas Eve. Enjoy it! What's your favourite part of the day? Mine is telling spooky ghost stories by the fire.'

25

THE MORNING OF CHRISTMAS EVE. THE AIR FELT DIFFERENT, even the very light felt different as Scrooge dragged his chilly legs out from beneath his bedcovers. The sky was a dull greyish-white colour, as if the Almighty had thrown a grubby sheet over the skies of London. More snow was on the way.

But despite the dullness of the morning light, there was a palpable excitement in the air. On the street below, one man hurried past, lifting his hat to a woman walking the other way and wishing her a Merry Christmas with such joy in his voice that it hurt Scrooge's heart. He had looked forward to this day all year, he had fantasised about it his chance to enjoy the build-up to Christmas, to join in with the carollers, drop a coin in every collecting tin he saw, to gather around the fire at his nephew Fred's house and send Bob Cratchit home with a fat bonus and even a Christmas gift. This was not the day he had expected, the day he had hoped for.

For at the end of his bed stood a third phantom. A third death, and this one heavier on Scrooge's heart than all the others.

In life, Scrooge had never seen Jem afraid. Now he watched it, over and over again, as the boy's ghost started, turned in surprise, dropped something and collapsed forward, his hand to his throat.

Jem began to weep, silently, then the image flickered and began again.

'Oh, Jem,' Scrooge croaked. His throat was sore from weeping. He had not been able to stop since Jem appeared at his bedside in the early hours bringing with him that cold, that smell of death.

He had looked forward to Christmas Eve as a day of second chances, the day he could shuffle off the problems of the world and be merry, just like everyone else. But now he could not imagine smiling again.

'Forgive me,' Scrooge cried, but even those words curdled in his mouth. What point was forgiveness when Jem was gone for ever?

On one side of him stood Christina Parley. On the other, the ghost of Alastair Bailey, still tortured with grief. Scrooge could see the manacle at his wrist more clearly now and wondered what sins had forged themselves into metal to torment the scientist. Scrooge shuddered at the thought of how heavy his own sins would be in comparison.

He had not caught the killer, and now a strong, courageous child was dead.

'Please,' he turned to Christina Parley, 'please comfort him if you can. He looks so frightened. I don't think he can hear me yet; he is in a state of panic. Please do for him what I could not do for you. And I will see to it that the animal who did this is brought to justice.'

Christina gave a curt nod, her eyes brimming with a fury that Scrooge shared. The killing must stop.

Outside, the clock chimed nine – Scrooge had overslept. He dressed and went downstairs, rejecting his breakfast, ignoring Mrs Miller's cheerful cry of 'A merry Christmas Eve to you, sir!'

The Christmas market was already in full swing and was full of women smiling as they bustled along, weighed down by parcels and attending to their ever-expanding to-do lists. Children laughed as they wove between the stalls playing, goggling at the gigantic sailboat in the toy shop window. Men cried out the compliments of the season to each other with a cheery smile and wave.

As he passed, all fell silent at the sight of him, just as they had done in years past.

'There goes old Scrooge with a face like thunder,' one stall-holder said.

'I knew he'd go back to his old ways.'

'Leopards don't change their spots, and rich men don't neither.'

Scrooge knew he should be afraid; this was exactly the kind of behaviour the spirits had warned him against. But to be merry in the face of such horror was impossible. Scrooge did not know if he could ever be merry again and if the Spirit of Christmas Yet to Come returned and dragged him to his early grave, it felt like a fitting end for him.

Jem. So brimming with mischief and promise. Working hard, polishing the shoes of rich men for a pittance. Running through the streets playing tag with his friends. Leading Tiny Tim goodness knows where on goodness knows what adventures. Since they had begun spending time together the smaller boy had brimmed with confidence, had developed an independent spirit that Scrooge had not seen before.

'Scrooge.' A voice at his side. It was Mrs Tassell. He strode on. He could not speak. If he spoke, he would break down.

'Scrooge, I know what happened to Tim's friend.' Her voice was heavy with sadness too. 'A police source told me this morning. They found him in an alleyway two streets away from Merrypaw's printworks. It is profoundly wrong. We must see to it that this never happens again.'

'Then will you come with me to Merrypaw's?'

'I will,' she said. 'But I counsel discretion. Today is the day he treats his workers to a Christmas feast. Come to the party bearing gifts, smile at him, put him at his ease and then we must search for clues while he is not looking. We must find evidence that links him to these crimes, now more than ever.'

The printworks looked different, with boughs of holly hung over the door and a brazier burning outside roasting chestnuts. A knot of cheerful workers gathered around it, warming their hands, talking and laughing.

Scrooge and Mrs Tassell had bought two large baskets of mince pies and other sweetmeats, and Scrooge fought to keep a smile in place. It was grimmer, more terrifying than any of his smiles had been before. Jem was clinging to him for comfort, making his arm so cold it was as if it had been plunged into ice water. It was so childlike, so different to the swaggering, confident Jem he knew, that his chest ached again.

'I cannot do it,' he murmured to the widow. 'I cannot be pleasant to that man.'

'And yet we must,' Mrs Tassell said, the revulsion showing in her voice too. 'This is for Jem.'

'For Jem.'

They linked arms. Her touch reassured him as they stepped forward, and the Christmas merriment swallowed them whole.

There were no sounds of work today, no mechanical clanking or businesslike shouts from one worker to the next to bring more paper or stand clear of the press. There was instead a great hubbub of laughter and chat. The staircase outside Merrypaw's office had been turned into a minstrel's gallery – one worker played a drum, another squeezed an accordion, and still more sang, creating a raucous version of 'We Wish You a Merry Christmas'.

The festive drinking must have started first thing, as the smell of beer and gin and meat in the process of being roasted mingled with the inky, greasy, metallic smell which usually filled the air at the printworks. A Merry Christmas sign had been draped over the inactive printing press, and extra tables had been added to Mr Merrypaw's famous resting area. There was feasting, there were card games, there was much laughter and there at the centre of it was Felix Merrypaw, his cheeks every bit as cherry red, his eyes as twinkling as they had ever been and his waistcoat embroidered with . . . were those Christmas puddings? He seemed to be over-seeing a rowdy game, which involved putting one's bare hands into a bowl of liquor which had been set on fire.

'Ah, Mr Scrooge! Mrs Tassell! Welcome both! May I offer you the compliments of the season!' His smile was joyful, it seemed so genuine.

Scrooge's grip on his basket tightened so hard, the willow began to creak.

'Care to join the boys here in a game of snapdragon, Scrooge? You simply have to pluck the raisins from the flames and then eat them. I admit it is not for me, but the young people seem to love it!'

Scrooge could not do it. He could not open his mouth and speak pleasantries to this man. It had been easier to talk to Edgar Parley.

Mrs Tassell, sensing Scrooge's rising ire, stepped forward. 'Delighted to see you, Mr Merrypaw! And a Merry Christmas to you!'

Scrooge felt a glass of something warm and spiced being thrust into his hand and heard muffled pleasantries, but his head was full of a rushing sound, of rage, of grief, of impotent anger. Christina, a woman who had done many things wrong but had been an innocent in her own way. Bailey, an ebullient genius with a bright future ahead of him. And Jem, a boy with more enterprise and ingenuity than any captain of industry he had ever met. Gone, because of this man.

Once again, Mrs Tassell slipped her hand through his arm to encourage restraint. Scrooge smiled. He lifted his glass. He drank a bitter mouthful so that he did not have to speak, and splinters of cinnamon stuck in his teeth.

'I'm glad to see you have come around, old boy!' Merrypaw said. 'Of course poor Scabble is unable to attend, it is not proper when he is mourning his nephew, but he sends his regards. We could not have achieved this without your help – your Christmas card was the best-selling one of all. More popular than Cupid, you are, Mr Scrooge! I have already received advanced orders for next year; we are about to become very rich men indeed. And all because we have the wisdom to see Christmas for what it truly is: the commercial opportunity of a lifetime!'

Mrs Tassell's grip on Scrooge's elbow tightened. Jem, seeming to recognise his surroundings, flickered, dropped his mysterious object again. It looked like some kind of white carving. Jem's expression filled with pain and fear once more, then blinked out of sight. Bailey and Christina fizzed and crackled dangerously at his side, though. They sensed it too – the furious desire for vengeance fighting to control Scrooge's mind. It was their presence which held him back more than anything. He would not allow them to hurt Merrypaw. He had the unaccountably strong feeling that if he allowed them to take direct action, to kill this monster of a man, their chains would become even heavier. No, he would bring him to earthly justice.

'What a wonderful thing you are doing here, Mr Merrypaw,' Mrs Tassell said, smoothly diverting attention away from Scrooge.

'And of course we look forward to welcoming the poor at the Feast tomorrow!' Merrypaw said. 'I trust these three long trestle tables will suffice? And there is a small kitchen in one of our back rooms which should be more than adequate for the reheating of pies and such.'

'May I inspect it, sir?' Mrs Tassell asked. 'It is most unusual, I hear, for a place of work to have a kitchen like this.'

Merrypaw inclined his head to Scrooge, urging him to sample the fresh meat pies, and walked off with Mrs Tassell, spouting his hypocrisies about the fair treatment of workers.

When Merrypaw was out of sight he met Christina Parley's eye.

'Show me,' he said.

Christina inclined her head and glided softly towards a dingy corner at the back of the printing hall, down a cramped corridor to a narrow door reinforced with metal studs. To his surprise it was unlocked. Perhaps the Christmas celebrations had led to a lapse in security.

The room was unoccupied – even Merrypaw's most secret employees were permitted to go to the party. Like the main printing room it smelled of oil and metal and Dr Bailey's ink. It had a high ceiling, and the dull, snow-heavy light crept through a high barred window. The room was dominated by a smaller version of the printing press outside, this one specifically designed to produce one thing and one thing only: banknotes. On a table to one side was a pile of freshly made notes, awaiting the application of the forged teller's signature which would make them appear valid.

Christina indicated a drawer, and when Scrooge opened it, he found the counterfeit plates themselves, perfectly engraved counterparts to the five-pound notes locked in his drawer at the office.

Just then he saw the small bed in the far corner of the room, a nest of grubby blankets. On the wall behind it someone had drawn an intricate, graceful pattern – were they waves? Or leaves? Or flowers? Did it matter what they were at all? It was clearly Christina's work.

'You slept here.'

She nodded.

'And you made money for this man.'

Another nod.

'So that you could help the poor of the city?'

An expression flickered across her face, and Scrooge understood. It was more complicated than that. Her intention had been to help the poor, but there was also the exhilaration of creating something. The challenge of it, the satisfaction of seeing those notes roll off the printing press, the feel of them in her hands. He understood. There is no pure good or pure evil, there are just humans, subject to their own needs and desires, doing the best they can not to be *too* bad.

'Ah, Mr Scrooge – spying I see?' Merrypaw's voice was still as friendly, as merry as it had ever been. But now Scrooge found its insincerity chilling.

The businessman stood in the doorway, blocking Scrooge's exit, his expression one of faint disappointment. Scrooge was relieved – there was no more need for politeness.

'Christina Parley worked here. And she stole from you, and so you killed her.'

Merrypaw's merry expression became one of shock. 'Indeed, Miss Parley did work here. Forgive me for not saying so earlier but our friend Mr Scabble is very careful about his reputation. I am not one for gossip, but before Bailey arrived Scabble was involved with her himself. He found the whole thing terribly embarrassing. It was Bailey himself who recommended her to me, just to get her away from his uncle's clutches. He was very sweet on her.

'But to say that I killed her! That talented, bright spark! Oh no, no, no!'

'Not even when you discovered she was stealing from you?'

Just for a fraction of a moment, Merrypaw's eyebrows flickered up in surprise. The muscles around his mouth tightened just a little. 'I had no idea that she was stealing from me. Well, I suppose once a Parley . . .'

Scrooge felt that violin-string tension from the ghost at his side and held his arm out as if to restrain her. She held still, but thrummed with energy and rage.

'What of Bailey?' Scrooge asked.

'Another talent lost.' Merrypaw shook his head, looking genuinely sorrowful. 'Wait – you think I killed him too? Why would I do such a thing, when we could have made so much money together? He did not even write down his formulations, they are lost now.'

'To protect your secret! Bailey had a scientific method of identifying the killer—'

'Oh, you mean his finger pattern idea? He told me about that. I must say it is unlikely he could have found the true culprit that way, he would have needed samples of every suspect's finger patterns! I gave him mine freely knowing my complete innocence. This is absurd, sir. I knew you for an eccentric, Mr Scrooge, but I did not take you for a madman.'

Scrooge's ghosts began to whirl around him, echoing his growing frustration. He should be afraid for himself, for Merrypaw, but he was starting not to care.

'What of Jem?' Scrooge spat out the words. 'What did you do with him?'

'Who on earth is Jem?' Merrypaw's brow creased. 'You cannot mean that urchin I found scurrying around here yesterday? Dark hair, dark skin, cheeky mouth? Why, I did nothing beyond give him a clip around the ear and have one of my men escort him to Clack Street Workhouse. The urchin gave him the slip and I have no idea where he went after that.'

Scrooge studied the man. The genial crinkles around his eyes, his plump fingers curled complacently around a brandy glass. But his business head took hold, supressing his anger. Morality aside, it made commercial sense to eliminate Christina if she had stolen from him. But Merrypaw was right – killing Bailey was illogical. Another thought occurred to him too: why on earth would Merrypaw have framed Bob Cratchit? He had got this all so spectacularly wrong.

'Would your men have done it, without your express permission?' It was a faint hope, clutching at straws.

Merrypaw laughed. 'Why on earth would they commit a capital offence when I have not asked them to? They would not make a move without me.'

Another thought appeared in Scrooge's mind – as perfect and fully formed as a spirit on Christmas Eve. *He talks about killing as if it is a necessary part of his business. And now I have discovered his secret, will he kill me?*

Visceral panic spread through him. Merrypaw was blocking his escape. The party was loud and exuberant; nobody would hear him cry out. And if they did – would they really speak out against the employer who treated them so well?

Just then, two more men entered the room. Both large, burly and muscled from carrying heavy stacks of paper. One of them was restraining Mrs Tassell, her jaw set and brows furrowed with outrage, her arm twisted unpleasantly behind her back. The other pointed a small but serviceable pistol at her.

'Oh dear, dear, dear!' Merrypaw said. 'Why on earth would you bring a respectable widow in here? And with firearms too!'

'Found her in your office, going through your drawers,' the taller of the two men said.

'I was merely looking for a pen,' Mrs Tassell protested. 'And then your bully boys burst in and seized me.'

'She was looking in the Special Drawer, sir,' the second henchman confirmed. 'She had forced it with a knife. We didn't make a mistake.'

Merrypaw rolled his eyes. 'And so you saw fit instead to bring her here, to the very heart of our operation? Possibly not your most sensible choice, Will.'

Will looked chastened, but his master was already studying his two prisoners, his jaw agape. 'You two are in some kind of partnership! Well, Scrooge, you old scallywag, I never would have thought it of you!'

'It's not like that!' protested Mrs Tassell, with a vehemence that Scrooge found a little hurtful.

Merrypaw wandered over to the table which bore the stacks of notes, and sank into a nearby chair.

'It might surprise you to hear that I am not a person who commits murder lightly.' Merrypaw sighed. 'I am a businessman, not a thug and I would prefer to come to some kind of arrangement with you both. But Mr Scrooge looks as if he is about to combust, and Mrs Tassell, you could also do with calming down. George and Will, would you be so good as to lock them both in the store cupboard and give them a chance to think about their situation? Perhaps violence will not be necessary.'

'You would not dare, sir,' Scrooge cried out. 'Christina Parley was an orphan with few friends – I am a respectable businessman, and the lady is an upstanding member of the community!'

Merrypaw shook his head. 'The state of street crime these days is quite shocking. There are people out there who would cosh you over the head for a ha'penny! I'd hate for that to happen to you on your way home on Christmas Eve.'

Mrs Tassell struggled and tugged against Will's grasp. She opened her mouth to scream and the man laid a huge, inky hand over her mouth, stifling her cries just as George seized a rough hold of Scrooge's shoulders and shoved him forward, pushing the gun into the small of his back. He felt helpless, overpowered. If they went into that store cupboard they might never come out . . .

'Please, spirits of the departed, help us!' Scrooge cried.

The two toughs gave a bemused chuckle at this, and George took the opportunity to put a knee in the crook of Scrooge's leg, causing him to stumble forward. For one desperate moment Scrooge thought they were alone, that the ghosts had disappeared again to wherever it was that the afterlife took them . . . But then he felt a surge of cold envelop him, and the heavy weight of George's hands drop away from his shoulders. He spun, just in time to see Will also collapse to the floor.

Merrypaw jumped up from his chair in shock, gaping at his fallen henchmen. He backed away from them, pressing up against the table of banknotes. Only Scrooge could see Christina approach him, could understand the press of cold that Merrypaw felt.

'Scrooge, what's happening?' Mrs Tassell's voice was heavy with fear.

Christina reached out and caressed Merrypaw's cheek. Merrypaw shuddered, and when she pushed her hand into his chest he gave a gurgle, a gasp, before consciousness left him and he slumped back over the table. Still, the ghost pressed on – leeching, *feeding* with more determination than she had with the other men. Merrypaw's countenance was cherry red no more; a greyish tinge swept across it. And still the ghost remained, her hand inside his ribcage, closed around his heart.

'Stop!' Scrooge called out. 'It wasn't him! He did not kill you, Christina Parley.'

He did not complete the sentence out loud but added internally: *and I now have absolutely no idea who did.*

26

Scrooge's heartbeat did not calm down until they were in a cab, safely away from Merrypaw's printworks. He and Mrs Tassell went straight to the police station to report his counterfeiting activities – it was not only the correct thing to do as upstanding citizens, but the only thing they could do to defend themselves, should Merrypaw decide to come after them.

The officers had been in a jubilant mood – a Christmas cup had already been passed around – but the sergeant was just sober enough to be shocked by their statement.

'See that something is done about this,' Scrooge said. 'I have ways of making your life very uncomfortable if you don't.' It was not what a good man would say, but sometimes one simply had to get the job done.

In a corner they found a tired-looking Baldock, his jacket removed and a drink in his hand, indicating that he was off duty.

'How is Bob Cratchit?' Scrooge asked anxiously.

'Sleeping. His fever has broken, but he is still weak,' the officer said. 'If it was down to me I'd let him go home for Christmas, he's hardly the kind of man to run away, but my superiors won't have any of it.'

'I shall be sending his daughter in with more blankets and good food. I know that you are an honest officer and shall not insult you by offering you money, but I trust that she will be admitted.'

Mrs Tassell hailed a cab and once they were both in the carriage, she finally asked him what had happened in the printworks.

He hesitated. He was surprised to realise that he cared what she thought of him. Not because of his reputation, or his standing in the community, but simply because he respected her opinion. The thought of seeming mad to her, of losing her respect, made something in his chest seize up.

'I cannot say,' Scrooge said. 'The three gentlemen must have been overtaken by some kind of fever.'

She looked at him askance, raising one sculptural eyebrow.

'You know, I was not born in this country. I am from a part of the world which considers all possibilities, not just scientific, rationally proven ones.'

It was Scrooge's turn to raise an eyebrow. He had heard the rumours that she was not native to these shores, but in the past Mrs Tassell had always maintained she grew up just south of Rochester, the daughter of a respectable pastor. He thought for a moment of confiding in her, but her revelation only proved to him that she was a woman who had many secrets, who could not be trusted. Plus, she delighted in mocking him, and perhaps this was another way of her doing so.

'I cannot explain what happened, madam, only that we were most fortunate that it did.'

At this moment Christina was the merest wisp of cold smoke, clinging to the outside of the carriage. He could sense her more than he could see her, but he gave her a smile and whispered, 'Thank you.'

Mrs Tassell leaned back against the stained leather seat and sighed.

'We are stuck, aren't we? Three people are dead, and we still cannot say who killed them.'

Scrooge wondered then if he should share his suspicions about Mr Scabble. If Merrypaw was telling the truth then he too had been involved with Christina. He had also bribed witnesses to lie. But yet again Scrooge came up against the impossible question. Why would Aldous Scabble go to the trouble of framing Bob Cratchit? Especially when doing so would disrupt business at Scrooge & Marley, imperilling their business venture.

'We should have done more digging in Christina's life.' Mrs Tassell sighed. 'The roots of a crime are always in the past. I wish sometimes that we had the power to travel there, to tread the roads she trod. And to warn her.'

Scrooge shook his head. His journey to Christmas past last year had helped him trace the origins of his own downfall, but he had not been able to forewarn himself. You cannot change the past, the spirit had been clear about that, you can only observe it.

All this talk of time forced Scrooge to check his watch – and start with surprise. The day had run away from him. It was now afternoon, darkness was coming on and he had done nothing festive, nothing Christmassy except nearly choke on a glass of mulled wine at Merrypaw's party. Would that be good enough for the spirits? Or would they return tonight, to teach him an altogether harsher lesson?

His one chance to redeem the day was Fred's Christmas Eve gathering – and he was late for that already.

'I must go to my nephew's,' he said. 'I promised to spend Christmas Eve with them, and I must not let them down.'

A short while later, the cab dropped him off at Fred's. He waved goodbye to the widow, who was already fretting about finding yet another location for the Benevolent Feast, and rapped upon the shiny, wreath-embellished door. The divine Petunia answered it with a smile.

'Uncle, welcome! You are just in time, we are about to start the music!'

Fred's house was warm and merry. It was far smaller than Lady Crick's, and the garlands of holly and ivy draped around the room were less elegant but somehow more sincere for it. Over the fireplace stood a beautiful arrangement of holly with bright red berries surrounding Scrooge's own Christmas card – yet again he was forced to look upon those little pink legs charging along the street as the merry figure threw gold to the crowd.

The room was full to bursting with smiling people and Scrooge recognised many of them from last year. There were Petunia's sisters, Rose and Lily. The latter was wearing a brand-new engagement ring and sat close to Fred's friend, Topper.

There was such liveliness, such happiness in that room. Scrooge longed to feel it, but then he thought of Jem and the warmth slid from his body.

'Why, if it isn't the miser reformed!' Topper greeted him. 'Well met, Mr Scrooge, well met! I must say that your Christmas card has been a regular hit with my family. I'll be sending one every year from now on.'

Scrooge held his smile well, but the spectre of Dr Bailey stood directly behind Topper and the two of them were so similar in manner, so full of cheer and ebullience, that he could not make the smile carry to his eyes. *I must be merry*, he repeated to himself. *I must show Fred, and the spirits, that I am a good man now.*

Rose sat at the piano and played a rousing chorus of 'God Rest Ye Merry Gentlemen' while the rest of the party sang along.

'Come!' Petunia smiled as she ushered him towards a spare seat. 'Make space! Let Uncle Scrooge sit down, and do stop ribbing him, Topper. This is his first Christmas Eve with us, and we want him to enjoy it!'

Scrooge endeavoured to join in, knowing that his voice was more like the creaking of a crypt door, and that his heart was broken.

Next to the fireplace, trembling and cowering once more through the last moments of his life, was Jem.

Behind Fred's chair he could make out the form of Christina Parley watching the proceedings with an expression of true sadness. *She always did love Christmas*, Edgar had said. Now she would never spend another one on this earth.

How could he make merry in the teeth of such horror? He felt a growing sensation that if he did not catch this killer then Bob Cratchit would find himself on the gallows, and the true culprit would be free to murder again and again.

The Christmas carol ended, with Topper getting the words wrong and Lily throwing a napkin at him and howling with laughter.

'This is all fine and well,' Fred pronounced, but now it's time for another of our Christmas Eve traditions, one which I am sure Uncle Scrooge has not experienced before.'

'Ooh, you mean the ghost story!' Rose enthused, jiggling about with excitement on the piano stool. 'I love this part! Who will go first tonight?'

'I have a tale which is guaranteed to send a shiver down the spines of all present,' Topper bragged, leaning expansively back in his chair with an air of satisfaction.

'We'll have to see about that!' Fred laughed.

Scrooge stared at them all as if some kind of madness had overcome them.

'What is this? Ghost stories, at Christmas?'

'It is the perfect time to tell them,' Petunia said, laying a hand upon his arm. 'When we are safe in our homes, surrounded by those we love, it's exciting to contemplate the frightening world beyond!'

Something broke in Scrooge. He stood, gazing at the flushed, bright, happy faces around him and the horrific shadows between them, their throats doused in blood.

'Ghosts are not entertainment,' he snapped.

'Come now, Uncle . . .' Fred began, rising from his chair. 'It's just a bit of fun! I have a story about a haunted mill which will have your hair standing on end! Pray, sit with us and listen!'

'No!' the word ripped out of Scrooge's mouth. He could take no more. He could barely bring himself to smile during the merriment, but to be asked to listen to a ghost story, while all around him stood the spectres of people who had died because of him, *his* failure to find the murderer. He could not do it, he could not pretend.

He felt a flutter of fear. *If I cannot find joy in my heart at Christmas after losing so much, does that make me a miser again? Would that bring the unforgiving spirits back to my door?*

Would it? he asked himself and then, as an idea grew in his head . . . *could it?*

With a rush of certainty, he knew what he had to do. The thought of it terrified him to the core, but it was the only way.

He tried not to hold the idea – that terrible, chilling idea – in his head for too long. He was not sure how much the spirits could sense his thoughts, his mind. He would have to show them by his actions exactly how he felt. He turned, looking at the beautiful arrangement of holly on Petunia's mantel. Fear and desperation raged in him, and he dashed it to the ground. The Christmas card went tumbling with it too, down into the fire where it caught light, the paper curling, the caricatured figure of Scrooge slowly eaten away by a black line of soot.

The assembled guests gasped in shock. Petunia let out a small sob which tore at his heart, but he would not let it. He could not.

'I've said it before and I'll say it again,' he said, surveying the horrified expressions that surrounded him. 'Christmas is nothing but humbug!'

27

'IT CANNOT BE.' TIM'S MOTHER'S VOICE WAS FAINT, AND FOR A moment he feared the worst, that something had happened to Father. But to his relief she was just talking to Mr Pinching, the poulterer.

'I'm afraid there's no mistake, Mrs Cratchit.' The man sounded embarrassed. 'Mr Scrooge was very clear in his message to me. He will no longer pay for the turkey he reserved for you. I am sorry for your distress, ma'am. We do have a goose left over. It is a little on the small side, but should just about feed you all.'

Mother crumpled at the knees, Belinda rushing forward to help her to a chair. Since Father's arrest she had been strong and determined that they would celebrate Christmas just as they always did. Even that morning, after she had broken the news about Jem, she had insisted on going about the Christmas Eve chores as usual – her smile brittle as she worked. She had not shown a moment's doubt.

Until the turkey man came.

Tim stepped forward, feeling strangely grown-up as he spoke. 'It is a mistake, sir – I know it is. Please keep the turkey for us and I will speak to Mr Scrooge.'

The angelic look worked again, the man could not say no, but Tim was shaking as he closed the door.

Belinda looked at him, ashen. 'But I thought . . . you said he was good now.'

'It's a mistake,' he said again.

Mother had that pinched expression he had seen in the depths of his illness, when she was trying very hard not to cry in front of him.

'Pray, Tim, visit Mr Scrooge, and try to find out what has happened.' Tim and Belinda looked at each other in surprise. His mother was asking Tim for help, to do something she knew only he could do, and despite his recent illness. This either meant she was distracted with fear about Father or . . . could it be that she trusted him?

'Yes, go. Do the face at him,' Belinda added. 'You know the one I mean. He'll change his mind for you. I'll walk you there, it's starting to snow.'

Tim agreed, but he did not want his sister with him, saying provoking things which might upset his master. So he slipped out while she was distracted, grabbing Father's comforter for extra warmth.

The first few flakes of snow whirled around him, settling in his hair, the folds of his comforter, his little shoulders weighed down with responsibility. He had to save his family Christmas – and save Mr Scrooge.

You can do it. The voice in his head sounded very much like Jem. He had not let himself cry for his poor lost friend. Not in front of his family. But he knew that Scrooge would understand. Once this business with the turkey was cleared up, they could sit down together and talk about the wonderful rascal.

As he rounded the corner of Scrooge's street, he heard a crash and a cry of distress. It sounded like Mrs Miller. That beautiful Christmas tree had been thrown out onto the street, pine needles and decorations scattered everywhere and the housekeeper stood next to it, staring up at her master's door.

'Mr Scrooge! Sir! Stop!' Mrs Miller cried.

And then he heard a roar of rage and bitterness echo around the row of quiet buildings.

'This tree is humbug, a waste of good resources! Better to season the wood and burn it!'

The door slammed and Mrs Miller sank down onto her knees, slumped over the Christmas tree, weeping onto the wreckage of her hard work in the reflected light from Scrooge's hallway window.

'Mrs Miller?' Tim's voice wavered as he spoke. She looked up, drew out a handkerchief and blew her nose, hard.

'Don't go near him, he has gone quite mad!' she said, sniffing. 'He was always a cantankerous old bastar— . . . I mean man . . . but now he has taken leave of his senses.'

The door opened. A bough of holly flew out of it, narrowly missing both of them. Tim started to cry out to his master, but the door slammed shut again.

'I don't know what happened!' Mrs Miller wailed. 'He came home from Mr Fred's house like this, all humbuggy and full of bitterness. I . . . I'm frightened, Tim Cratchit.'

Tim stood and climbed the steps to Scrooge's front door, passing the discarded holly wreath, snowflakes settling on its prickles. He had to stretch to reach the door knocker but just about managed it.

'Is that you, Tiny Tim?' Scrooge's voice was muffled but close, as if he was waiting on the other side of the door. His tone was crabby and cantankerous, the voice Scrooge usually affected when Father was behind with his work but somehow harsher. Fear crawled in Tim's stomach.

'Please, sir, could you let me in?'

'Go away, boy,' Scrooge snapped.

'But . . . please, sir! There's been some confusion with the turkey and . . .' Tim began to cry. 'And Jem's dead, sir. I miss him so much.'

There was a hesitation from inside. Tim thought he heard a whimper, a dry sob. The door opened a crack and Scrooge's pointed nose poked out. The dim light from the lamp at the end of the street cut harsh lines in his grey, unforgiving countenance. But there was a flicker of something else in his eyes – sadness, loss and guilt. It lasted only a moment, and then his mouth twisted into a frown.

'I have no need of you today, boy. Go home.'

'But sir, it's Christmas Eve!'

Scrooge's answer was a roar of rage. 'Christmas! What nonsense! Christmas is a day like any other, a day for work, a day to make money. And you, boy, are wasting my time!'

Tim staggered back, gazing up in disbelief as the old man slammed the door.

'You see?' Mrs Miller said, shaking her head in disbelief. 'That kind Mrs Tassell came by earlier and he said something similar to her only his language was much more shocking. He's torn down all the decorations and sent a message to Mr Fred to say that tomorrow's festivities have been cancelled. He's cracked, I tell you. I'm off to my sister's and hope she's got a spare bed for the night! As soon as Christmas is done I'll be looking for a new place. You should do the same. The man's past redemption.'

She looked at the tree lying discarded on the cobbles, surrounded by scattered ribbons and twists of hand-made trimmings. A crumpled paper angel was still clinging lopsidedly to the top branch. 'It was so beautiful, wasn't it, Tim? The prettiest tree I ever saw.'

But Tim was staring at the closed door, his mind whirling. This did not read right, the story did not make sense. He thought back to a year ago, when he sat perched on Ebenezer Scrooge's knee and he had whispered his tale of ghosts and chains, of spirits and redemptions.

First came the Spirit of Christmas Past – it showed me scenes of great festivity from my youth, so that I could weep at what I had lost. Then came the Spirit of Christmas Present, who showed me household after household all around the world keeping Christmas with great merriment and joy so I could see what I was missing. Already I was filled with regret, but then came the Spirit of Christmas Yet to Come. It showed me my future, and yours too . . .

What Scrooge told him then had frightened Tiny Tim to his core. A future where Scrooge lay unlamented in a neglected grave and Tim himself had suffered and died. 'Because of me,' Scrooge had said, fighting back tears. 'In that future you died because of my selfishness.' Seeing Tim's shock, Scrooge had tried to take back his words, telling him it was just a silly ghost story, but it was too late. From then on, in his young mind their two fates were tangled together like roots and branches. Like hawthorn and mistletoe.

It was his vision of me which turned him good.

If he stays good, we both live.

And if he turns bad again, we both die.

Tim had sat there, curled warm and safe on Mr Scrooge's lap and promised he would never let it happen, never let Mr Scrooge lose his way.

He had failed.

Mrs Miller put her hand on his shoulder. 'Shall I walk you back home, lad?'

He shook his head and as she left, he continued to stare at the closed door as if it bore all the answers. His mind travelled back again to that Christmas night, the sound of the old man's voice, the spiced scent of smoking bishop on his breath, the warmth of the fire on Tim's knees.

'Why did these spirits come for you, Mr Scrooge?' he had asked.

'Why, I was a terrible, terrible man. I cursed the name of Christmas, shut myself off from goodwill and festive spirit. I showed myself as a miser in need of reform.'

'And then they came?'

'And they will come again, no doubt, to finish the job if I fall away from the straight and narrow.'

'You must be very afraid,' Tim had said.

Scrooge gave him a smile, but Tim felt his body shudder. 'Perhaps fear is what I need to keep me in line, to tread the path of goodness.' Tim had not been brought up to question his elders, but those words sounded wrong to him. Men didn't miraculously become good out of pure fear. There had been a goodness in Scrooge already, the spirits had just given him a reason to let it grow.

But his master had been terrified of those spirits. And now he was doing everything he could to lure them back. He must have a reason.

The snow was coming down fast now, covering the discarded tree, erasing Mrs Miller's outraged, stomped footprints. He looked up at the darkened house, then stood, brushing the snow from his knees and set off to get help.

28

THE GHOSTS OF CHRISTINA, BAILEY AND JEM DID NOT KNOW Scrooge as well as Tiny Tim Cratchit. They watched him go from room to room tearing down every decoration, quelling every fire, every lamp. Now he sat hunched and alone at his bedroom fireside, a blanket over his shoulders, staring into the distance.

Christina flitted around him like an angry fly, her lips moving as she silently threw every possible insult at him. Alastair Bailey crumpled in the corner and bled miserably, until the liquid covered him and began to ooze across the floor. Poor Jem went back into a loop, re-enacting his death over and over. The start of surprise, the dropping of something smallish and white out of his hand, a four-legged animal maybe, before crumpling forward once more.

'Either freeze me into unconsciousness, or leave me alone,' Scrooge snapped at them.

The ghosts drew back, shocked, Alastair Bailey flickered into nothing. He felt a tiny flame of satisfaction at that. His former crotchety self might have been a risk to his immortal soul but by God it was fun sometimes, delivering put-downs, giving people a piece of his mind whether they wanted it or not.

That was good. He had a feeling the spirits could sense when he took genuine pleasure in being unpleasant. Earlier, he had shouted curses at Mrs Tassell with a kind of glee.

Tim, though. That had been harder. He could still picture the boy's grieving face shrinking back in the moonlight, the horror and hurt he had been unable to hide. Scrooge had intended to go further, to tell Tim that he was a poor worker and that he should not bother to come back after Christmas, but he had not been able to do it.

He could only hope that he had done enough damage.

In the distance, the church clock struck half past midnight. The candle guttered and died. Scrooge remained in the near-darkness, shivering in the cold, silent night. What if it didn't work? Or what if it did work, but the spirits would not do as he requested? It was a foolish man who trusted such ancient and wily creatures.

'Oh, Scrooge, you're in trouble now!' Marley's voice, which last year had caused such terror, made Scrooge want to weep with relief. The ghost emerged from the fireplace, the embers lighting Marley's cadaverous features with ghastly glee.

Scrooge moistened his lips with his tongue. 'How so, old friend?'

Marley gestured around the room, indicating the bare, unfestive walls, the empty fireplace, the disconsolate ghosts hovering by the doorway.

'They gave you everything, they gave you a chance at redemption and you have thrown it back in their faces – those of them that *have* faces. Last year was but a warning compared to what the spirits will do to you this year!'

At once Scrooge sat upright, flooded with hope.

'Then . . . they will come? They will understand why I had to do this?'

Marley's image flickered a little, in the way he had seen Christina and Alastair do when they first arrived. It meant uncertainty, it meant the ghost of Jacob Marley was not an all-seeing eye, not a fount of all wisdom after all. *As if he ever was, even in life*, Scrooge thought wryly to himself. He would never be afraid of ghosts again because when all was said and done, ghosts were just people. And he knew people, in all their greed and wickedness and surprising flashes of kindness.

Marley peered closer at him, his head to one side.

'Wait.' His translucent eyes narrowed. The canny old rogue was working it out. 'Oho, that's your game is it, old boy? You want to lure them back here. This is your idea of an invitation! It's a dangerous game you're playing, Ebenezer Scrooge!'

Scrooge's stomach was swirling with dread. 'I know it.'

'You know that a second visitation will bind you even more closely to the spirit world? There will be more ghosts, and more, especially in the deep midwinter.'

'That will be my cross to bear.' He bowed his head.

'And you know, too, that the Spirit of Christmas Yet to Come may still punish you for having the temerity to summon it?'

Scrooge knotted his hands tight on his lap to hide their trembling. He had looked into the gaping black hole under the spirit's cowl. He knew it was capable of so much darkness. And yet there was no other way.

311

'So they are coming?' Scrooge asked.

Marley inclined his head. 'They are.'

'Then sit.' Scrooge indicated the chair opposite. 'Wait with me. Those other ghosts are no company at all.'

They talked, then, catching up on old gossip. Scrooge told Marley about his Christmas card venture with Scabble, and together they weighed up whether the money he would make was worth the personal humiliation. They talked of the put-downs they had delivered to upstarts and business rivals over the years, and rejoiced that a particular competitor had passed away earlier that winter, exposing three mistresses and a string of gambling debts. Their laughter was dry and cynical and with every word Scrooge felt like less of a good person, but Marley made the process more bearable. Marley had died eight long years ago on this very night. Thinking back, that could have been when Scrooge's dislike of Christmas had hardened into hatred. The funeral parlour had been closed for the festivities and so Scrooge had sat by his friend's side in solitary vigil, listening to the peal of the bells and the distant voices of wassailers going from door to door with their damned songs and begging bowls. All were joyous, warm and bright, but Marley was gone.

'I have missed you, you scabrous old devil,' he told him. 'Why did you have to take your leave of this earth so soon?'

Marley gave a crack of laughter, his hand rested for a moment on his cheek, as if the ghost of his fatal tooth infection still remained. 'What was it you said at the time – too tight-fisted to go to the dentist? If only that were so! No, Scrooge, the laudanum drops I was taking for the pain – someone tainted them with poison.'

Scrooge shot up straight in his seat, the heat of anger rising in his body. 'What? Murder! Who would do such a thing?'

Marley peered at him curiously. 'I always thought it might be you.'

'Never! Marley, you were my friend!'

'But you would have made more money without me taking my half – and in fact you *did* go on to make more money. I watched you, remember?'

Horror clawed at Scrooge. All these years his closest friend – his only friend – had believed him capable of cold-blooded murder for financial gain. 'Never think that of me, Marley. I was a selfish old blaggard but never a killer. I mourned you by God, I missed you! And let me tell you now, I will not rest until your murderer is caught!'

Marley stretched out in his chair, like a gentleman of leisure after one brandy too many. 'There really is no need to put yourself out, old fellow.'

'No!' Scrooge sprang to his feet, trembling and furious. 'This gross injustice shall not stand! Why, whoever would have wished you ill?'

Marley gave his old partner a look as if to say *half of London and more besides*, then began to laugh. Scrooge laughed too, but the sense of injustice had not gone away. Eight years he had lived without his friend and now to find he had been murdered was too much to bear. He was about to question Marley, to ask who visited him in his last days, who might have had access to the laudanum bottle, but Marley sat up all of a sudden, fearful.

'It's coming! The first spirit, it's here!'

He rose and backed hastily towards Scrooge's window which, as it had done last year, stretched and deformed to let him out. Without a word of goodbye, his friend sailed across the rooftops, his chain trailing behind him and as he departed the ghost of Alastair Bailey flung himself against the wall, as if desperate to follow in his wake.

On its first visit, the Spirit of Christmas Past had pulled his bed curtain aside as he sat there in his nightgown, terrifying him to the core. This time Scrooge rose to meet it like a man, his slippered feet planted firmly on the ground.

'EBENEZER SCROOOOOOGE!' The spirit passed through Scrooge's bedroom wall, all fire and fury. Last year it had worn a burning flame on its head, this year its entire upper body was alight. Its long silver hair streamed out around its head, the strands twisting and burning. Its eyes were twin golden sparks, its childlike face was warped with fury.

Scrooge's bravado evaporated in the firelight, his breath caught in his throat, his legs gave way and he sank back onto his chair.

'You extinguished me last year!' it roared. 'You, who could not bear what I had to show you, who were too afraid to look upon the sins of your past *dared* to put out my light and banish me! And now you betray the spirit of Christmas again!'

Scrooge slid off the chair, down onto his knees, grovelling as if it was the most natural, easiest thing to do. As if he had never been an excellent man of business, respected upon the Royal Exchange.

'Forgive me! Have mercy upon this pathetic sinner! I am truly grateful for what you did last year.'

The furious spirit took a step back, the flames on its body subsiding a little, a frown creasing its alabaster brow.

'I have changed, or at least I am trying to. I give you my word that I intend to keep Christmas with all my heart this year. And even if you don't believe me I beg you to help me all the same, not for my sake, but for my humble clerk, Bob Cratchit. You know him, any spirit of Christmas would. He is a jolly fellow, and good – a kind husband and the very best of fathers. And if I do not find the evidence to clear his name he will be hanged for a murder he didn't commit, and all the while a monstrous killer walks free.'

The spirit peered at him curiously. Its flame had returned to normal size but was fizzing with a kind of blue light which seemed to reflect its confusion.

And then Christina Parley appeared at his side, fixing her steady gaze upon the spirit. She nodded, as if to say that Scrooge spoke the truth. That she wanted to help.

Scrooge held out the crook of his arm to the ghost, and she took it. Her grip was frigid and as firm as if she were real.

'Let us do this together, then,' Scrooge said. 'Spirit, we implore you to show us Christmas past.'

29

SCROOGE HAD FORGOTTEN HOW WONDERFUL IT FELT, THE sensation of flying through the snow-blasted sky with all of London at his feet. Last year he had not dared look down, but this year he did, and the sight of the snowflakes tumbling down onto the neat white rooftops below made him pleasantly dizzy.

'Remember,' the spirit said. 'I am the ghost of your past, and can show you only your own Christmases, and those of the people you have loved.'

Scrooge thought, fleetingly, of his lost love, Belle. Seeing her last year had been so painful he had indeed put out the spirit's flame without permission. He was thankful he would not have to see her again. But who else had he loved? He loved Fred in his way, and Jacob Marley as much as one could feel that way about such a cantankerous old soul. And, of course, who could not love Tiny Tim? But there was one other. Scrooge would never have called it love, but it was nonetheless, and he was also the only living person who linked him with Christina Parley.

'Show me Bob Cratchit,' he said.

Laughter. Merriment. A lively tune and voices raised in song. It was an echo of Merrypaw's party earlier in the day, but instead of a vast printworks, the setting was an office. Scrooge recognised it as Spindle & Syme, a company of excellent repute which had once kept offices quite near to his own, before Scrooge and Marley had driven them out of business. There was old Fitzroy Spindle, sitting enthroned, his chair up on a table. He had a glass of negus in one hand and a piece of cake in the other, as he surveyed his kingdom. Mr Syme, a less sociable type but very good with numbers, lingered in the corner looking deeply uncomfortable.

And there – his heart leaped. There was Bob. He looked so young, his cheeks flushed with the warmth of the room, and a merry smile on his lips. This had been his first job. Scrooge had recruited him after putting his previous employers out of business. Bob's first child had been on the way, and he'd been so desperate for work he had accepted fifteen shillings a week. Sharp needles of guilt prickled Scrooge at the memory.

'This must have been sixteen years ago,' he murmured.

He noticed that Christina had been able to follow them, though there was no sign of Bailey or Jem. She stood at his side, watching closely as Bob made his way through the crowd towards Spindle, with another figure in tow. Christina put her hand to her mouth in surprise – it was her brother. In a room full of sensibly dressed clerks, the thief stood out. He was young, still in his late teens, but had clearly begun his habit of dressing in other gentlemen's clothes. His hat was a fine-quality high-crown beaver, and his nascent whiskers, while small, were elegantly groomed. Instinctively Scrooge looked around for Amos, Parley's shadow, and found him hovering by the door, his expression blank. Scrooge and his ghostly companions drew closer, until they were able to hear what Bob was saying.

'Sir!' Bob addressed Spindle. 'This is the man of whom I told you! He's quick-witted, loyal, a real hard worker.'

Spindle leaned forward, his chair creaking ominously. He lifted his pince-nez glasses to inspect Bob's friend.

'Ah! Well, if you work half as hard as Cratchit here you would be an asset to the company! Tell me, boy, what's your name?'

'Parley, sir.'

Spindle leaned even further. Another creak. Cupped his hand around his ear.

'What's that? Speak up!'

'Parley, Edgar Parley.'

Spindle's manner changed immediately. 'Butch Parley's boy? Bob, what were you thinking, bringing Butch Parley's boy to me?'

'He's different,' Bob said. 'He wants to better himself and—'

'I do,' Edgar said. There was a tremor in his voice as he spoke, a sincerity. He truly meant it. If Spindle gave this boy a chance his path would change. 'I don't want a life in the gutter. I want to better myself. I want to be a gentleman, see?'

Spindle's jaw dropped as if he couldn't believe what he was hearing. Then he threw back his head and laughed until his cheeks went red, until he was short of breath, until some of the other revellers stopped what they were doing and stared.

'You?' Spindle took out a handkerchief and wiped tears of mirth from his eyes. 'Edgar Parley, a gentleman? You have bad blood, boy, and nothing will ever change that. And as for you, Bob Cratchit, I did not know you associated with such criminals. Perhaps you are not as trustworthy as I thought.'

'Oh, fuck this,' Parley said. 'Why did I even come here? Come on, Bob, we know when we're not wanted.'

Bob, pale and panicked, stood frozen on the spot. Parley spat in disgust, and rounded on his heels, walking away. By now the band had stopped playing, the chattering voices had fallen silent. All the revellers were watching the scene.

'You can keep your petty little job,' Edgar said. 'I'll be a finer gentleman than you one day, Mr Spindle, you'll see!'

Over by the door, Amos's mouth twitched with a smile. At last Bob rushed after his friend, flustered and angry. 'Why would you speak that way to my employer? You got me in trouble, and it only makes him think he's right about you . . .'

Edgar leaned towards his former friend, sneering. 'You just want to make me small, like you. With your tiny little house, your nicey-nicey new wife, your eighteen shillings a week and time off for Christmas. Christmas! Pah! It's a sop to keep you wage slaves in line.'

'Well, at least I'm not a—'

'A what?' His voice was dangerous. 'What am I, Bob Cratchit?'

Bob was trembling, but he stood his ground. 'You're so clever, you could do so much good, Edgar, if you just put your mind to it.'

Edgar turned slowly on his heels and left. Bob made to follow him, but Amos blocked his path.

'Stay away from him,' Amos growled. 'He's too good for the likes of you.'

There was a curious look of triumph in the man's eyes as he turned away to follow his master.

At his side, Christina shook her gory head in sadness.

This, then, was how the friends had parted ways for ever.

'Have you seen enough?' The spirit's voice was strangely hollow, its flame shrunk as if the lack of Christmas spirit in the room had weakened it somehow.

Scrooge nodded and Christina put out her hand, rested her gaze meaningfully on the spirit.

'She wants to show you something,' it said.

'You can understand her?'

'She does not speak, but I know her feelings.'

And then they were in an altogether different time, standing in a street which Scrooge knew very well, for it was his own. Christmas bells were chiming, and the streets were filling up with men and women clad in more recent fashions, smiling happily. Then he saw the nimble figure of Jem, dashing past and calling out to his friends. An ache of loss clutched at his insides and for a moment it seemed Jem had noticed them, was about to come over. But then a window above opened, scattering new-fallen snow onto the street below and Scrooge witnessed his earlier self calling out to Jem, grinning, the bobble of his nightcap swinging comically around.

'What's today, my fine fellow?'

'Today!' Jem's voice was heavy with disbelief that someone could not know what day it was. 'Why, CHRISTMAS DAY!'

Looking up at his former self, present-day Scrooge found he was smiling, a true and pure smile rather than one of his frightening ones. He could still recall the joy, the relief of finding himself alive and with a second chance on this most wonderful of mornings, even if the sight of Jem's lively face added a thread of sadness to the memory.

Jem was back in a jiffy, struggling under the weight of the enormous turkey and last-year's Scrooge danced out of his front door in his best frock coat, his nightcap still on his head at a jaunty angle. He sent a half-crown flipping through the air, and Jem caught it with one skilful hand.

'You see!' Scrooge said in a tone of triumph. 'That damned Christmas card artist got it wrong. I was not in my nightgown, I just forgot to take my nightcap off!'

He felt a chill at his elbow. Christina was touching his arm, pointing. His former self was approaching a figure hunched in one of the doorways – a thin, pale mite huddled in a threadbare blanket, a straggle of dark hair fallen over her eyes. Scrooge remembered that moment.

The young woman had looked at him and said, 'What a change in you, old man! Why, just yesterday I saw you through your window, I heard you say Christmas was humbug.'

Suffused with happiness, he had answered: 'Last night I saw something which changed my mind for ever! Let me be an example to all – even the worst sort of man can change!'

Present-day Scrooge looked at the waif's delicate features, the very particular way she had of looking at him, and recognition snapped into place. It was Christina Parley.

He turned to her ghost, opening his mouth to ask her more, but the Spirit of Christmas Past spoke first. 'My time with you runs out, Ebenezer Scrooge, but know this: you cannot call upon us in this way again. My siblings may not be as forgiving as I.'

30

LUCRETIA TASSELL HAD NEVER BEEN SO INSULTED IN HER LIFE. At the time she had been furious, treating Scrooge to some language a lady should definitely not know and striding off into the coming snowstorm, letting her skirts whirl around her, her veil whip in the wind.

It was only after her righteous indignation had subsided that it occurred to her there was something strange about the way he had done it, almost as though he were reading from a script. 'Interfering harpy', 'do-gooding busybody'. The insults were so uncreative, so mealy-mouthed. This was not like Ebenezer Scrooge at all.

She dined on a supper of cold meats – of her servants only Mary-Ann remained – and after dinner put the problem of Scrooge aside for a while, for she had a far more pressing problem. With any luck Merrypaw's printworks would be swarming with police looking for evidence, but that left the Feast for the Poor without a home again. There was a very real danger that they would end up at Clack Street Workhouse after all.

Still, as she drafted urgent notes to her fellow charitable ladies, her mind kept wandering back to the mystery. She and Scrooge, and Tiny Tim of course, had amassed so many clues, but the picture was still no clearer.

Merrypaw was not the killer. The man was a liar and a counterfeiter, but she believed him in that. Her pencil flew over the page sketching out all that they knew. The watch chain, which had been Scabble's; Bailey and Christina's tragic love affair; the planting of the razor blade to frame Bob. And then there was the hideaway Tim had found on Midding Street. She would go there as soon as she could and search the place for clues the boy might have missed.

Scrooge had said that Christina and Bailey had been killed for money, that money was the root of all this, but Lucretia wasn't so sure. People killed for financial gain all the time and Christina as a lone woman with a large quantity of forged money was a natural target, but she also created strong feelings in everyone she had known – fierce loyalty, respect, love and perhaps also hatred.

Just then, the library door opened, and Mary-Ann entered, accompanied by a shivering Tiny Tim.

'Poor little mite, look at him, he's so cold!' Mary-Ann said. 'I will fetch him a blanket and some nice fresh gingerbread at once.'

Lucretia gave Tim a look. 'Have you been manipulating my maid? Shame upon you, Tim Cratchit! Now come closer to the fire and make yourself warm. I imagine you're here because your master has taken leave of his senses.'

'I don't know where else to go,' he said. 'He cancelled our turkey, and I promised Mother I'd change his mind but he was . . . horrible.'

He looked away for a moment, took a breath and when he turned back to her he looked different – determined and intelligent beyond his years.

'Madam, could you tell me what happened today?'

As Tim ate his gingerbread she told him about the trip to the printworks, admitting they were no nearer to finding the culprit than they had been before. To her surprise Tim merely nodded.

'Then I was right,' he said. 'Mr Scrooge is trying to bargain with the spirits to show him the truth.'

The tale the boy told her was as fine a Christmas ghost story as she had ever heard, full of twists and turns and fantastical events. It was ludicrous, of course, but no more absurd than the tales she had grown up with, some of the things she had seen. It would explain why, when they were in need, Scrooge had cried out to something or someone that only he could perceive, as well as what had happened to Merrypaw and his henchmen . . .

'You don't believe me, do you, ma'am? But I swear it's true. I'm scared,' Tim said. 'I don't want him to die. I don't want *me* to die . . .'

'The spirits don't work like that,' she said kindly. 'From what you say, the whole purpose of their visit was to set Scrooge on the path of goodness. If he fails, they would not seek to punish you!'

She had no idea if she was right. Spirits, as far as she knew, could be capricious, but the boy was all goodness, surely they would never harm him?

325

She gathered him into her arms and he began to weep for his father, for Mr Scrooge and for his poor lost friend. She had not known Jem well, but he had been a fine fellow, and—

'Tim,' she asked. 'Did you ever find out what it was that Jem found in the churchyard? The thing he wanted to sell?'

'No.' The boy's voice was sleepy. 'When he picked it up I saw something pale-coloured and too big to be a sixpence, but I didn't want to say anything when he'd been so kind to me. I saw it again as he was coming out of the second-hand shop. It looked like a carving of some sort, and it was white, but I couldn't see what it was.'

She closed her eyes, let her mind make connections. *Something small, carved and white. Something precious enough to sell. Something which, if recognised, could be incriminating.*

As her mind whirred, Tim's grip on her shawl loosened a little and he leaned into her as the elegant ormolu clock on her mantel chimed nine times.

'Come,' she said. 'It's Christmas Eve, and past your bedtime. Do not fret about the turkey. I will speak to the poulterer myself in the morning. You need to be at home with your family.'

The two of them started out on foot into the darkness. Lucretia cursed herself a little for giving her driver the night off as the air was filled with fat, heavy snowflakes, building a carpet of snow on the cobbles and there was not a cab in sight. It was beautiful, though. Revellers, insulated from the cold by copious amounts of ale, ran around them, throwing snowballs at each other like children, trying to knock each other's hats off. Christmas spirit was everywhere.

Tim kept his head down, digging his crutch into the piling snow and announcing proudly that he would lead the way.

To distract him from the cold, she quizzed him again on every single detail of Midding Mansion, the decorations, the three sad stockings, the discarded note from Belinda in the hearth.

'There were other notes too,' Tim said. 'I think Miss Parley had been trying to write a letter asking someone to help her.'

Lucretia felt a small burst of sadness. 'She was writing to her brother, trying to get him to spend Christmas with her. He burned the note she sent him, but I think he regretted it. I think, if Christina had lived, Parley might have changed his mind.'

Tim shook his head. 'The letters weren't to Edgar Parley. They were to someone else, some nickname I didn't recognise.'

Lucretia pondered who Christina might have been writing to – Bailey perhaps? And then Tim took an unexpected turning.

'Tim, it is late. We do not have time for diversions. I must take you home.'

'But I want to show you the mansion,' he said. 'And it's not far now. Please come, ma'am.'

Lucretia knew that she should get Tim back to his family as soon as possible, but curiosity nagged at her. It was not far, there was no harm in looking, and perhaps they could find a cab to take them the rest of the way home. Besides, she was starting to suspect that the key to all three murders lay in Christina's festive hideaway.

As they passed the rowdy tavern at the end of Midding Street patrons were singing 'Hark the Herald Angels Sing'.

Tim bit back a sob. 'It's Father's favourite,' he said. 'He knows all the verses and sings it every year. He should be at home now, not lying in some horrible prison.'

Lucretia laid a gloved hand on his. 'We'll get him home,' she promised.

Tim looked up at her curiously. 'You're not lying,' he said.

'Of course not,' Lucretia said. 'I would not lie to you about something like this. I won't give up until I've proved his innocence.'

The door to the building gave way easily into the darkened hallway. It was warm inside, a relief after the driving snow. The residents had clearly stockpiled their fuel supplies to make this Christmas a cosy one and there was still the sound of merriment behind some of the doors. Lucretia gathered in her skirts and trod carefully up the narrow, creaking staircase.

It did not take long to look around Midding Mansion, with its charcoal-scrawled walls, the stockings, the mismatched but neatly lined up cups and plates. She stooped and unfurled the letters Tim had left near the hearth, but the name on the page meant nothing to her. She thought she knew Christina Parley, but there could be a whole section of her life which remained hidden. She wondered how Scrooge's outlandish plan would play out. She believed Tim's story, but that did not mean the spirits would appear on request and show him Christina's past. No, they still needed to do some solid detective work.

Outside, the snow was worse than before, a wall of white. The streets were empty now as most people had rushed back to their homes, although the sound of Christmas carols still drifted up from the pub on the corner. She bit her lip in frustration. She couldn't take Tim back out in this.

'We will wait for half an hour,' she said. 'See if the snowstorm passes.'

Tim nodded drowsily and sank down onto the narrow bed in the corner, laying his head on the pillow. Using shreds of broadside and kindling, Lucretia set about making a fire, a task she had not done herself for years, then sank into the chair Christina had positioned by the hearth. The one she had probably set aside for her brother. Gazing into the flames, Lucretia turned the problem around and around in her head until exhaustion took over and she, too, fell asleep.

31

SCROOGE AND CHRISTINA WERE STANDING IN A LARGE HIGH-ceilinged room, the dining hall of a country squire's mansion with wood-panelled walls and rich paintings and hangings. But the carpet had been rolled back to accommodate a large trestle table. On each side sat men and women in plain dress, laughing and talking. Children scampered around, crawling under the table between their parents' legs, playing hide-and-seek and skidding along the polished floor in their stockinged feet. Like the adults, the children were in their Sunday best, but did not look rich or well-dressed enough to justify their surroundings. None of them seemed to notice either the reformed miser or his deceased companion. But standing on the trestle table itself, holding a tankard which looked like it was overflowing with beer, was the Spirit of Christmas Present.

He – and unlike Christmas Past he was undoubtedly male – looked a little different to the spirit Scrooge had met the year before. The Spirits of Christmas Present were born anew each year – there had been more than eighteen hundred of them. They lived for a brief season, which was probably what made them so determined to live life to the full. Last year's spirit had been bare-chested but this one wore his green fur-trimmed robe belted firmly over his belly which, although Scrooge would never point it out, was somewhat rounder than last year's incarnation and when he laughed it shook, for all the world like a bowl full of jelly. His beard and hair were a little whiter than his predecessor, but his smile was just as broad and friendly. He also carried the same horn of plenty, which sprinkled droplets of goodwill upon all around him.

'Welcome my fine visitors!' His voice was loud, jolly, echoing through his barrel chest. To Scrooge he also sounded a little drunk. 'And so this is Mr Scrooge! I may be a new-born spirit but I have still heard much about you. You were planning a feast every bit as merry as this one, were you not? But then you changed your mind.'

Scrooge stammered his explanation, but it was evidently too complex for the spirit to understand, and he waved his hand dismissively and grabbed a nearby tankard, drinking deeply.

'I live but a short while, and I live in the moment. Here the squire is laying on a feast and for his workers!' His brow furrowed beneath its crown of holly and ivy – Scrooge noticed that this year it was festooned with ribbons too – and his very own Christmas card, poking out from behind the spirit's ear. 'There are precious few of these feasts now: squires are forgetting their duties and peasants are leaving their land to work in cities where there are jobs with machines – and no squires. The rich buy trinkets and pretty pictures and gorge themselves with their families. The poor pick upon whatever scraps are left. My two wards are growing in power.'

He lifted his robe, and just like last year Scrooge saw the two twisted children nestled there, Ignorance and Want. Ignorance's countenance was sharp and filled with suspicion and Want clung to the spirit's leg, digging her clawed nails into his flesh. As before, Scrooge was overcome with a combination of horror and sympathy. The two crooked creatures were vile, but they were man's creation; they could not help being this way.

Christina knelt down and held her hand out to them both. She seemed to understand instinctively who and what they were.

'This is what I saw,' he told her, in answer to the question that she had asked him on Christmas morning almost one year ago. 'This is what changes a man.'

It was a relief to share this journey with someone, even if that person was a silent, bleeding corpse.

He tore his gaze away from the children and addressed their spirit guardian. 'This young woman with me, she was planning a celebration. I need to see it.'

The spirit shook his head. 'But this celebration never happened! I cannot show what will not come to pass, there is no spirit of Christmas that never was!'

'But you can show us anything which happens this festive season?' Scrooge asked. He had thought a lot about this, how the spirit last year had shown him families celebrating on Christmas morning, carousers celebrating Twelfth Night even though his journey had taken place on Christmas Eve. He wasn't sure how the spirit achieved this. He didn't want to think about it too much.

The spirit nodded. 'I have never tested my powers, I am but a few weeks old, but yes. From the lighting of the first Advent candles to midnight on Twelfth Night is when I rule.'

Scrooge felt a bolt of triumph – this was what he needed. But before he could speak, Christina reached out and touched the Spirit's robe. The spirit looked up and gasped in surprise, and suddenly the world blurred around the three of them. Scrooge suffered a sensation of falling, more dizzying and disorientating than he had ever felt before.

Until he landed with a bump, in the churchyard near Marley's grave.

THE GHOST

I AM USED TO THE WHIRLING, THE FALLING, BUT MY COMPANIONS ARE not, and they flail and scream. The miser, the spirit, the strange, unnerving children hurtle onto a cobbled street near St Gideon's churchyard. Where I ended. Where this began.

I am meeting Bob at the churchyard gate. He is shivering in his white comforter, but he smiles when he sees me. That silly grin of his.

'You're wearing the dress! It suits you.'

'I'm sorry to ask it of you, of your wife,' I say. I smooth down the fabric, worn soft by Elizabeth Cratchit's diligent laundering and careful ironing. It's clean, marred only by an old stain on the sleeve. I feel ashamed. Every day I sift banknotes, hand-finishing them and inspecting them for the tiniest flaws. Thousands of pounds of counterfeit money have passed through my hands, enough to buy myself silk if I choose. But I do not want to take any of it for myself, only to help the needy. On Christmas Eve, when everyone is busy at the party, I will leave Merrypaw's for good. And I don't want to take anything of his, even the clothing he provided.

Bob waves my concern away with a generous hand. 'It was all the prompt I needed to buy new cloth for Elizabeth for Christmas.'

'Are you able to come? To the mansion on Christmas Day?' I ask.

'I'll be there. What about Edgar?'

I nod, even though I am still not sure. But he has to come. This crazy idea is our last chance – his last chance.

The idea had wormed its way into my head from the moment that penny-pinching old miser slipped a coin into my desperate hand last year. I had never seen such a complete, such a sincere transformation. Something had happened that awakened the Christmas spirit in him, unlocked his youthful innocence. That's what I am going to do for Edgar. Midding Mansion is my recreation of Midden Mansion, and I will remake the Christmases of our past and show him that he can be good again.

I will give him the Ebenezer treatment. I will Scrooge him.

'Do you think it'll work?' Bob asks.

'I think so. If I can take him away from that world, from Amos and all his criminal cronies who lap up his talk of being a gentleman, I might just reach him.'

Bob clutches at my hand, and through our gloves I can feel it trembling. I squeeze it tight.

'We will get him back,' I say. 'We have to, or he will end his life on the gallows, and then who knows what torment he will suffer after that?'

It is as if I always knew about the chains.

Bob starts to bid farewell, something about needing to get back to Scrooge & Marley, but he has forgotten something. His final bundle of five-pound notes.

'Wait,' I call, holding out the package.

'No, Tina, I can't. I should never have started this. I was foolish not to realise where this money comes from. Now I've figured it out, I can't take it.'

'This is the last one, I promise,' I tell Bob. 'I can't expect Edgar to start a new life if I am a criminal too.' Bob shakes his head stubbornly, turns to leave and we begin to argue. My own guilt flares up and makes me defensive. I tell him he won't get caught, that my money is flawless and that I'm taking something bad, something criminal, and making it into a force for good. Bob shakes his head again, calls me naive, rends at his hair in frustration.

'Don't you see? You could get me fired! I could end up in prison, or worse! This could ruin me, Christina, and Mr Scrooge too.'

I shove the money into his hands and make to run away. He catches me by the shoulders, just as he used to do when he was young.

And suddenly a wave of shame washes over me. I am no different to my brother, flouting the law and not caring whether anyone gets hurt in the process. My intentions may have been pure, but my actions are every bit as selfish as Edgar's. My eyes fill with tears, I tear away from his grasp, dropping the bundle of notes and flee into the churchyard before my old friend can hear my sobs, leaving him there with the bundle on the street in front of him.

He does not follow me inside, and I am thankful. I sink down next to Father's grave. He was a bad man, a terrifying father, but for some reason being here comforts me and after a moment my heartbeat calms.

I become aware that this is just a vision of the past, like all the others I've experienced since I died. Scrooge and the Christmas spirit are watching. The spirit gazes at me with compassion, but Scrooge is looking sadly back towards where his loyal Bob had been. Perhaps he is feeling ashamed he ever doubted him.

It is a dull day, but it becomes a little darker as a man's shadow looms over me.

'I knew I'd find you here.' It is Alastair. Of course, just like before. I remember this now – he is laughing, brimming with excitement and possibly intoxication.

'I told Uncle. I finally did. I told him to send word to Miss Frome immediately. My engagement is over! We can go to our country cottage!'

In the background I hear Mr Scrooge comment, 'Oh, naive boy!' and I couldn't agree more. But Alastair can't hear Scrooge and won't listen to me. He waves something shiny at me – it is Scabble's watch chain.

'Look what I got! For your poverty fund! Who's the coward now, then? Steal from the rich and give to the poor. That's what we do from now on!'

Another wave of self-disgust hits me. I don't want that horrible old man's treasure.

'Please,' I say to Alastair. 'Just go.'

I feel another link attach itself to my own ghostly chain. The sound rings in my ears, filling my mind, telling me I have sinned.

But then I remember what I said to Scrooge earlier, even though he could not hear me. I can bear this weight. In life I did not shy away from hard work or breaking the rules to make things better. And in death, I am still strong. In a world full of wrongdoers, full of evil, I did what I needed to do to make things better for the poor, for those who could not help themselves.

'I am not ashamed.'

As I say this, the world around me freezes. Alastair stands as still as the weeping angel next to him. He cannot see me now as I rise up above the churchyard, the links sliding around my body. 'I AM NOT ASHAMED!' I roar it this time, and the words ring out into eternity. I close my hand around my chain and pull. It comes away as if it were made of daisies.

It turns out we make our own prisons in life, and beyond.

As I rise up, I see Ebenezer Scrooge rushing across the icy grass towards a tree that stands not four feet away from Alastair's frozen form. There is someone there. I did not see it before, but there is a human figure, a slice of darkness against the grim, textured bark of the yew. Poised and dangerous.

Amos Buddle lies in wait, watching. And there is murder in his heart.

32

JUST AS SCROOGE REACHED THE YEW TREE, THE AIR AROUND HIM
changed, the grass under his feet became solid boards and Scrooge
and Christina found themselves in a public house full of carousing
men laughing and wishing each other a merry Christmas. The
spirit had brought them back to the early hours of Christmas
morning, to a scene of celebration once again.

The spirit's holly, ribbon and Christmas card crown had slipped
to one side and his brow was sheened with sweat. He grabbed a
gin bottle with his free hand and drained it dry in moments.

'I was not made for that,' he said. 'I am the spirit which builds
a wall between mankind and reality. I am the torch which keeps
the darkness at bay for a few brief days every Christmastime.
I sprinkle joy – it is not for me to know such evil. And that man
in the churchyard had something evil in his mind.'

Was it evil, Scrooge thought, or was it a deviant kind of love?
Amos had lived his life in Edgar's shadow, his entire identity

shaped by being at his side. Together they ruled the criminals in this part of London and were even becoming, in their own curious way, gentlemen. If Christina had appealed to Edgar, had persuaded him to step away from it all, Amos would have lost everything – not just his standing in the underworld but the friend who gave his life meaning.

The spirit turned away and climbed onto a nearby table. Some revellers were singing 'Hark the Herald Angels Sing' and he sang along in a harmony that only they could hear. But Christina stayed, swaying slightly with shock as she began to understand why she had died.

Scrooge reached out as if to take her hand.

'Dear lady,' he said. 'You were not killed for money after all, but for love.'

'Amos.' Christina spoke. She truly spoke.

The wound at her throat still gushed blood, the ghastly slash moved and glistened with each word, but in the lamplight of the public house she looked stronger, more solid and the chains which weighed her down were gone now. She had found her voice, just as Marley had predicted.

A surge of pure joy shot through Scrooge. He was astounded by how happy he was to hear her voice, this woman who had endangered his business in life and tormented him after her death. This immoral, uncouth, brazen, brave, resourceful and intelligent woman. Not innocent, not guilty. Just human.

In his imagination her voice had been lilting and innocent, befitting of her elfin features, of her status as a young and beauteous victim. But she had been raised on the streets of London and in the depths of the workhouse and there was a smartness, a cockney cheek about her. A smile touched her lips as she said, 'Pleased to meet you too, you old goat.'

'So it was Amos Buddle.'

'It was him. He didn't want me back in Edgar's life. He didn't want Edgar turning away from their life of crime, and he knew I could persuade him, especially if Bob helped me.'

'Of course, framing poor Bob would cut off the last of Edgar's childhood friends,' Scrooge added. Then he thought of Alastair Bailey, and a tight, sickening feeling compressed his belly. 'When I sent Amos to interview Scabble's servants, he learned of Bailey's finger pattern idea.'

'But why would he feel threatened by that?' Christina asked. 'Alastair told me about this method, it would not work unless he had a sample from Amos to compare it to.'

Really, Scrooge thought, the young woman was exceptionally intelligent, and he felt another blaze of hatred for Amos Buddle. Then a memory clicked into place.

'That's who the "mooncalf swell" was! Your brother mentioned a swell — some kind of gentleman I infer — interfering with the investigation. Bailey must have visited Parley's lair on the same day I did,' Scrooge exclaimed. 'He probably collected samples from both of them! Stealing from thieves — it's no wonder your brother thought him touched in the head.'

But why kill Jem? Scrooge thought back to his first visions of the poor boy's spirit. There had been an item he had dropped, over and over again. It looked like a carving of an animal.

'Tell me, Miss Parley,' he asked. 'Amos's sword stick — was there some kind of carving on top?'

'An ivory elephant,' she said.

That elephant had not been there when he had met Amos at the police station. It must have broken off in the churchyard when he struck Christina, and fallen into the weeds. A bit of ivory like that would have seemed like a treasure to a boy like Jem. When he and Mrs Tassell had climbed out of the coal cellar to dodge Amos, he must have followed the children instead and seen what Jem had been hoarding . . .

Scrooge had to go, he had to get the police immediately. Force them to arrest Amos, bribe them if need be, before anyone else died. Scrooge turned to the door, pushing out through the hot, stinking revellers into the chill air outside.

He stepped out to a cold, furious blizzard. Snowflakes whipped into his eyes, blurring his vision; a drift was forming on the pub threshold and the street lay under a fresh white blanket. In the distance a church clock chimed the hour: one o'clock.

He started off through the blizzard, thinking to head to the police station, Christina at his side. But by the time he had gone halfway down the street he realised that although his slippered feet seemed to sink into the snow, they were not getting cold or wet, not leaving tracks.

'I'm still in the spirit's vision,' Scrooge said. 'I'm invisible, like you.'

Christina began to answer, but her words fell away as she looked up at a first-floor window lit with a flickering lamp.

'Oh,' she said. 'We are here, at Midding Mansion.'

Impulsively she ran across the narrow street, flickered and passed through the door. Scrooge followed, realising that he too could pass through the solid wood, a most disconcerting feeling.

He remembered this property now – it had been a fine building at the time, but he made a mental note to fix the front door and that the stairway needed a lick of paint.

'This would have been my Christmas haven,' Christina said as they climbed the narrow stairs. 'A place to hide for a few weeks, until Merrypaw stopped looking for me. So I could think, decide on my future. Bob said he'd pay you back somehow.'

Scrooge waved his hand. 'It is not important. I am glad Bob could help you.' And he meant it.

The room was warmer than he had anticipated, with a fire low in the grate, and on the chair beside it sat the widow Tassell fast asleep, a sheaf of papers resting under her hand. Tiny Tim was curled up on the truckle bed in the corner.

They must have come here looking for more clues and become trapped by the storm. Scrooge peered closer at the papers Mrs Tassell held, a series of scrawled and scribbled-out letters addressed to *Dear Scrag*.

Christina gave a short, dry laugh. 'When Edgar did not reply, I decided to appeal to Amos,' she said. 'Scrag was our old name for him. Perhaps the letter I finally sent was what persuaded him to kill me.'

Scrooge, overcome with sadness, went over to look out of the window. It was then that he saw two figures making their way up the street, heads down, pushing into the wind. At first he took them for gentlemen, by the sweep of their quality coats, but then he recognised the familiar bulk of the man behind.

It was Edgar and Amos. And they were heading for this building. Panic surged. *If Amos saw Mrs Tassell with these letters . . . He had killed Jem for much less.*

'Wake up!' Scrooge cried. He tried to grab the widow by the tops of her arms and shake her. His hands passed through her just as easily as he'd passed through the door.

'They cannot hear you or feel you.' The Spirit materialised at his side, radiating heat and alcohol fumes. 'You are still but a part of my vision.'

'Then release me! Let me talk to them! My friend, and my dear, dear wonderful boy – they're in danger!'

'I am sorry, Scrooge, you know how this works. My time with you is done, and another spirit awaits you now. I wish you luck, for it has plans for you, Ebenezer Scrooge.'

Scrooge launched himself forward, attempting to grab the spirit's robe and travel with him, but he fell forward. He was no longer in Midding Mansion, but had stumbled into a cold, dark place which was soft underfoot. He slipped and fell, his hands making contact with what felt like woodland floor, the ground uneven, stony and slippery with frost. He looked around for Christina, but she had vanished, taking her luminescence with her.

'Spirit, come back!' he called. 'Please! My friends are in danger, they need help!'

He struggled to see, to find something to focus on in the darkness. And suddenly it seemed that a deeper, darker level of black was pulling itself together, like a bitter cloud of shadow. The shadows became a shape, and the shape became a shroud.

Scrooge drew his legs up in front of him, curled up and trembling like a child. The Spirit of Christmas Yet to Come was ready for him.

33

THE SOUNDS UPON THE STAIRS WOKE TIM, AND FOR A MOMENT he thought he was curled up in his own bed at home, waiting for fairies to fill his Christmas stocking. But then he heard a loud, slurring male voice.

'I just wanted to come here,' it said. 'I just wanted to see!'

'There's nothing here for you.' Another voice, gruffer, harder. 'Forget her. She just wanted to change you, make you soft. She couldn't see what you wanted to do.'

Suddenly Mrs Tassell was awake, bolt upright.

'It is Edgar and Amos,' she hissed. 'Hide!'

Tim reacted quickly. In the corner which served as a kitchen there was a low cupboard with a curtain instead of a door. He flung himself inside, pulling the curtain closed after him. Mrs Tassell had fewer options. She positioned herself behind the door, just moments before it opened.

'Oh!' A man walked into the room. Peering around the curtain he saw him, tall and confident, with well-groomed side whiskers. This must be Edgar, and even from his hiding place Tim could smell him – he stank like a pub. The Gentleman rushed straight to the chimney piece, running his fingers over the sketched mural. 'Oh, my poor Christina! Still drawing Father Christmas to look like Pa. And the stockings – one for her, one for me, one for Bob! And of course: that razor Bob had, it must have been a gift for me! Oh, the Christmas we could have had . . .' His voice trailed off and Tim felt a lurch of fear. Parley had seen Mrs Tassell. Immediately, his tone changed, becoming darker, sneering.

'Oho, what do we have here? The merry widow!' From his hiding place, he saw Edgar yank Mrs Tassell away from the wall.

'There is no need to be so rough, Mr Parley,' she said, casting an eye at Tim, her expression urging him to stay quiet.

'I don't know why you're here,' Parley slurred. 'You should be ashamed of yourself. You and that penny-pincher have done such a bad job of finding out who killed my sister.'

Amos laughed. 'Told you they wouldn't do it,' he said. 'Pair of fools.'

'We are nearly there!' through her fear, Mrs Tassell sounded insulted. 'We have discovered a cache of letters here addressed to someone called Scrag. We've discovered that the other two victims were killed to silence them. Alastair Bailey was going to track the killer down using the latest science and Jem – why, Jem had found some small piece of ivory the killer had left in the churchyard and . . .'

Her voice trailed off. Edgar was staring at her, his eyes narrowed. When he spoke, it was in the kind of voice Tim had never heard before. Cold. Dangerous.

'Scrag, you say? And a bit of ivory? What kind of ivory?'

The widow hesitated, and Edgar shook her. 'I said what kind?'

Tim leaned forward – he could see the widow standing by the stockings on the mantel, and Edgar holding her roughly by the shoulders.

'A carving—' the widow began to say, but her words ended in a piercing scream as Amos moved forward and with one fluid motion, struck her on the back of the head with the handle of his walking stick.

The broken ivory handle of his walking stick.

In an instant, Tim understood that Jem's lucky find had snapped off Amos's cane – and Edgar knew it too. He stared at his closest friend, face blank with horror. Tim knew from his eavesdropping that Parley had threatened to kill his sister's murderer but he just stood there, his arms limp at his side.

'I don't understand, Amos,' Parley murmured. 'You were my brother, you were *her* brother. How could you?'

'She wanted to control you!' Amos snarled. 'She wanted to make you weak. Her and Cratchit. I did what I had to do to keep you on the path. You and me, the Gentlemen. The kings. We'll be rich; we'll be feared by all. She would never understand that.'

Tim waited for the Gentleman to react, to attack his friend, but he still seemed frozen with shock as Amos advanced on the widow. He pulled away the main body of the walking stick to reveal the gleaming sword-stick concealed inside.

347

To Tim's surprise the blade was short – it had been deliberately broken to less than six inches long. But the edge remained wicked sharp. Amos stood over Mrs Tassell.

'It never was a razor,' he said. 'This is the only weapon I need.'

Do something, Tim told himself. He dragged himself from the cupboard, his fingers closing around the handle of a large pan. It was heavy, but his shoulder was strong.

He threw it, and it rebounded off the back of Amos's head – not hard enough to knock him down, but enough to draw his attention away from Mrs Tassell. He whirled to confront Tim.

'Boy!' he roared.

Tim hefted his crutch and fled, throwing himself through the door and tumbling down the staircase, his bones rattling. He tried to struggle to his feet, but Amos was there, looming over him, his huge hands reaching down.

'I don't need no razor for you,' he said. 'Your tiny neck will snap like a twig.'

Tiny Tim. Poor, weak little boy. He had heard it all his life. And it was true, death had come for him more than once. But he had survived. Every. Single. Time. That wasn't weakness, that was strength.

With a hot flare of determination, he tightened the grip on his crutch, suddenly remembering what he had intended to do to those boys, but hadn't. Good people turn the other cheek, he had thought at the time, but sometimes good people had to fight, and if it meant carrying a chain in the next life like old Marley, then so be it. He pivoted his body and stabbed the pointed end upwards, as hard as he could. The point went into Amos's upper thigh and the hulking man grunted with pain. Slick dark blood began to soak through his trousers, and he staggered back against the wall, panting and cursing. Tim tried to get up, but his legs were weak, his lungs bursting from the effort of running away, his hands throbbing with pain from falling down the stairs. All he could do was writhe and wriggle, try to push himself towards one of the other doors in the hope that help lay on the other side.

A scream ripped out of him as Amos pulled himself upright again, and began to advance. With a supreme effort Tim pulled himself to his feet. He would not let this man break him. Amos smiled, revealing a row of yellowed teeth, and lunged, throwing Tim back against a wall like a cat playing with a mouse.

The shock of it sent Tim's head ringing. Instinctively he balled up, as he had done with countless playground bullies over the years. He braced himself for the end.

And then there was a sharp oof and a crunch and then nothing more. He looked up into the grim smile of Constable Baldock, cudgel still held aloft. And next to him, wild-eyed and panting, his white hair straggly and his face as pale as if he had seen Death himself, was Ebenezer Scrooge.

34

THE NEWS SPREAD THROUGH THE STREETS OF LONDON LIKE snowflakes in a blizzard, blowing down alleys, into corners, through windows and under doors.

'He's cracked. Old Ebenezer Scrooge has finally lost it.'

'Dashing around in public shouting about Christmas.'

'Blimey, not in his nightclothes again!'

'Probably. Yes, definitely. My brother's grocer's daughter saw it.'

'Free grub at his place though! Meat pies and turkey and pudding!'

'Oh, well then – see you there!'

And so they came, pushing through the snowdrifts in their warmest clothes. They filled the large parlour at Scrooge's house to capacity – the paupers, the servants, the shopkeepers, the gentry. Fred, Petunia and her sisters, and Cratchits all. Scrooge had sent them a heartfelt apology and Tim had done a lot of begging. Mrs Miller arrived back from her sister's in time to defend her kitchen against the onslaught of ladies and servants, but after some jostling and misunderstanding they set to work together, roasting and baking. Plates were found or donated, those who could brought their own cups and the public house around the corner supplied the rest.

There was feasting, there was singing, there were children running and sliding on the polished wooden floor. The Christmas tree had been set back in place and repaired. The candles were even lit for a short time, before Mrs Miller panicked about fire and blew them all out again.

In the midst of it all, old Mr Scrooge busied himself, running back and forth straightening garlands, fetching items for the ladies, throwing snowballs with the children outside, joining in with the carols around the tree. Those late to the gathering were disappointed to see that he was not in his nightgown as advertised, but there was something about the old man, a festive joy that was infectious. One guest was heard to ask where he got his energy from, and Scrooge laughed and said, 'I am just happy to be alive!'

As the celebrations went on, new rumours began to snake around the room. Felix Merrypaw, a jolly and generous type, had been arrested for running a counterfeiting operation. And Amos Buddle had been arrested for the murder of Christina Parley and two others – which meant that poor Bob Cratchit had been exonerated.

'I always knew he was innocent!'

'Such a quiet man, never said boo to a goose, he could never be a killer!'

They did not speak of Amos; they were still too afraid. And when, as the day began to dim, Edgar Parley slid into the room, the lively chatter trailed off.

'I hear all are welcome here,' he said quietly. There was something shamefaced and broken about the Gentleman as he sat himself in the corner of the room. The old man himself put a cup of smoking bishop in his hands. What they said to each other went unheard, but it looked like a condolence. That was when everyone remembered that the poor man's sister had died, that his best friend had been the murderer and it might be best to leave him alone with his cup for a while.

A half-hour later, another figure appeared, leaning heavily on his wife's arm.

'Why, Bob, welcome and Merry Christmas!' The old man's tone started out joyful, but then he came over all sombre and quiet. One fellow in the crowd muttered that the old goat would probably dismiss Cratchit for bringing scandal on the company. But instead, Ebenezer Scrooge said he was sorry.

'I want the world to know that Bob Cratchit is a good man who would never do anyone harm,' he announced. 'And that I never doubted him, not for one moment. I should have spoken up. I should have said it sooner – it was my own foolish fear and weakness which stopped me. I will understand if you no longer wish to be my clerk, but know that you have all the time you need to recover on full pay, and when you return, you have a job for life at Scrooge & Marley.'

Bob Cratchit looked mighty confused at this, before laughing that infectious laugh of his and saying that of course he would not even consider leaving and could someone please bring him a brandy and a chair to sit in for he was mightily tired, but his heart was full of Christmas cheer.

There was much toasting after that. The oldest Cratchit child, Peter, leaped onto his chair and raised a glass to the best father, the best clerk and the best friend a person could have. And to his brave little brother Tim, who had helped the police see their mistake. Tim made the sweetest little bow that had all the mothers in the room cooing over him, but those in the know kept their attention on Bob, as he glanced over to where Edgar Parley had been sitting – only to find that the Gentleman had slipped quietly away.

Then that bossy widow lady, Mrs Tassell, lost all sense of delicacy and climbed upon a chair, holding her glass aloft.

'I would like to say a few words,' she said in a tone that reminded everyone there of the strictest schoolteacher of their youth. Silence fell.

'For many months now, we have been planning this Christmas feast. Many people have given money, many more of you here today have volunteered your labour, your furniture and crockery to create this merry gathering. But we owe our greatest debt to one man. When we lost our venue for a second time, he was the one who volunteered to open his own home to visitors, and to invite everyone, rich or poor, to share in the celebrations. It was he who, despite an . . . eventful . . . night, managed to find enough tables and enough supplies to feed us all. So I would like to thank Mr Ebenezer Scrooge.'

There was a roar of applause, and some jostling at Scrooge to get up out of his chair, which he did with a show of some reluctance. Something seemed to be troubling him.

'Thank you, Mrs Tassell,' he said, He had turned pink with a mixture of mulled wine and embarrassment. 'I am sure many of you recognise me from my picture postcard. I apologise for my state of dress today. I know that some of you were hoping to glimpse me in my nightgown.'

A few charitable titters ran around the room.

'I did play a role in organising this illustrious event, and it was my privilege to open my doors to you all today, but it would never have happened without the eminently determined Mrs Tassell and her group of ladies, who truly made this merry gathering a success.' And then a strange look crossed his face. For all the world, one onlooker said, as if he was seeing a ghost. 'Christmas is a time to make merry, but it is also a time to remember those who are no longer with us. Such as my departed partner Jacob Marley, whom many of you may remember and none of you liked. And poor Jem who you did know and who everyone liked. And Alastair Bailey, whose scientific genius created the bright colours you see on those Christmas cards. And one more: a young woman with a generous heart who was taken from us far too soon. She did not lead a blameless life – indeed who among us has? – but she was determined, above all, to improve the situation for the poor and destitute in this city. She would do anything to achieve her aim, even imperil her own soul. And so I would like to announce that all my share of the money made from the sale of the Christmas cards will be set aside to begin a new charitable fund, the Christina Parley Foundation.'

As he spoke, a strange glimmer filled the room, as if every candle on the tree had been lit once again, and everyone experienced a kind of warmth spreading over their skin. It felt like the comfort and relief of returning home to a warm fire and a loving family. Scrooge had a faraway look, staring at a spot close to the ceiling.

The widow Tassell laid a hand on his arm, all concern. He looked down at her and smiled, a truly serene smile as if he had seen something wonderful happen.

'She is gone,' he said quietly. 'Christina Parley is at rest.'

35

THE FIRE CRACKLED COMPANIONABLY AS SCROOGE SIPPED ON his brandy. Tim lay curled up beside him slumbering under a blanket. Mrs Cratchit had found him there as the family prepared to depart. She had seemed reluctant to leave him. She trusted Scrooge even less since the cancellation of the turkey, but it had seemed a crime to move him, and Bob, smiling in his new coat, said his employer would take excellent care of the boy. Surprisingly, Belinda had agreed.

On the chair opposite, Mrs Tassell sat slumped in exhaustion. He had never seen the widow slumped before, and it was disconcerting, but he felt very much the same. He had not slept in more than twenty-four hours, and although the merriment of the day had carried him through, the last shreds of his energy were falling away. He just needed to stay awake a little longer, to finish telling his story to her.

On the far side of the room sat the ghost of Jem, also listening avidly. Alastair Bailey had disappeared shortly after Christina,

following her into a dazzling light, his own chain draped negli-
gently over his shoulder and trailing after him like a winter
scarf. But Jem had remained and was becoming less frightened
and more Jem-like by the hour. Now he sat cross-legged on the
floor, tossing a spectral ivory elephant from hand to hand. The
police had discovered the real elephant carving hidden in Amos's
mattress, and in the morning they would take it to the shopkeeper Jem had tried to deal with. With luck he would identify it,
linking Amos to both Jem's and Christina's deaths. Perhaps then
poor Jem would move on.

Aware of Scrooge's scrutiny the young scamp looked up and
poked out his tongue. It struck Scrooge that Jem might choose not
to move on at all – he seemed to enjoy being a ghost. Children
always knew how to make a game of any situation, even the afterlife.

Mrs Tassell listened to his outlandish tale with surprising calm,
nodding politely.

'And so do you believe me, madam?'

'Every word. Mankind is foolish to disbelieve such things as
ghosts and spirits and arrogant to think that we can explain the
mysteries of the world with just the logic of our own minds. I am
just glad the final spirit released you in time for you to fetch the
constable and save us. But please tell me, what did it say?'

Scrooge sighed as for a moment he remembered the chill press
of the chain around his neck, the death, devastation and evil
which lay in his future. But he had seen good things too, flashes
of hope and happiness and a glimpse of what he craved most in
the world – the chance to be part of it. If only he kept to the
straight path. And if only, like Christina, he accepted that the
chain was his burden to bear.

'That particular spirit doesn't speak, it just shows you what you need to see,' he said, suppressing a shudder. 'Last year it showed me my destruction, this year it showed me a path through. I will see ghosts now every midwinter for the rest of my life. If I help them, if I find justice for them and their families, I could lighten my burden in the next world.' He sighed, took another sip and let the brandy burn its way down his throat. 'And so it is. I will never be free.'

Mrs Tassell sat up straighter, leaning forward. 'We will help you, the boy and I. You don't have to do this alone.'

Scrooge's body filled with a comforting warmth at these words. Moisture trickled into the corners of his eyes and for a moment he was too overcome to speak. In the corner, Jem creased up in silent laughter at the old man's emotion, but Scrooge just smiled.

A strange new feeling settled over him. Exhaustion, contentment. And a certainty that although life was full of terrible loss and injustice, there would always be these times when he was gathered safe and full-bellied by the fire. And that there would always be these people, gathered safe and full-bellied with him.

It was the feeling of Christmas.

ACKNOWLEDGEMENTS

THE FIRST THANK YOU IS THE BIGGEST: CHARLES DICKENS. A hundred and eighty-two years ago you created a set of characters who are still so real and beloved that they will be entwined with Christmas for ever. Scrooge, Tim and the others were such a joy to write, and it was a pleasure to dip back into *A Christmas Carol* finding new meaning in every line, and between them too. I apologise for any deviations from the text, but I have tried to keep the spirit of your Christmas story alive in this. Whatever ghostly realm you're in, I hope you approve.

And in the land of the living, thank you to all at Bonnier for letting me be the Christmas Death Fairy again, including Emily Langford for the spooky, Scroogey cover design, Clare Kelly for her amazing publicity support and especially Kelly Smith, who fell in love with this idea as much as I did. Thanks to my agent, Lina Langlee, for her all-round brilliance. Then there's my ever-expanding network of writing friends who once again showed me that writing is not a solitary pursuit. To the UKYA group, thanks for the severed hands. The growing Bournemouth Writing Festival gang are wonderfully supportive and thanks to SCM for providing encouragement in its own unique way. To all the reading communities out there especially the Good Housekeeping Book Room. I couldn't fit it in the book, so here it is especially for you: *I let out the breath I didn't realise I was holding*. Special mention to fellow criminal masterminds Flic Everett and Catherine Cooper, and to my family: thanks a bunch, you lovely lot. Finally, thank you Jenny Redman for taking me seriously when, age fifteen, I showed you my first tragic attempts at historical fiction. Every kid needs That Teacher, the one who makes you believe you can be something, and that's what you did for me.